A Sister's Test

SISTERS *of* HOLMES COUNTY

A Sister's Test

WANDA & BRUNSTETTER

BARBOUR
PUBLISHING

© 2008 by Wanda E. Brunstetter

Print ISBN 978-1-63609-710-7

Adobe Digital Edition (.epub) 978-1-63609-711-4

All Scripture quotations are taken from the King James Version of the Bible.

All German-Dutch words are taken from the *Revised Pennsylvania German Dictionary* found in Lancaster County, Pennsylvania.

For more information about Wanda E. Brunstetter, please access the author's website at the following internet address: www.wandabrunstetter.com

Published by Barbour Publishing, Inc., 1810 Barbour Drive, Uhrichsville, OH 44683, www.barbourbooks.com

Our mission is to inspire the world with the life-changing message of the Bible.

ecpa Member of the Evangelical Christian Publishers Association

Printed in the United States of America.

Dedication

To my sister, Joy, who is also my friend.

But he knoweth the way that I take:
when he hath tried me, I shall come forth as gold.
JOB 23:10

Chapter 1

R uth, watch out! Get out of the way!"
Ruth Hostettler halted. A hammer slid down the roof of her sister's new house. *"Ach!"* She jumped back as it bounced off the sheets of plywood, just missing her head.

Martin Gingerich scrambled down the ladder and rushed to her side. "Are you okay, Ruth?"

Ruth nodded as she looked up at his strong, handsome face. She saw tenderness there, and something more. Did she dare believe he might be falling in love with her?

Her heart pounded like a blacksmith's anvil as Martin pulled her to his side.

"You need to stay away from the work site. It's too dangerous." His hazel-colored eyes were wide with obvious concern.

"I—I was coming to see if the workers wanted something to drink."

Martin wiped the rivulets of sweat running down his forehead; then he bent to pick up the hammer lying in the dirt near Ruth's feet. "I think we could all use a break." He leaned his head back and stared at the roof. "Luke most of all, since he's the one who lost his grip on that hammer."

Ruth's gaze followed Martin's. Luke Friesen sat near the edge of the roof, shaking his head. "Are you all right, Ruth?"

"I'm okay. Just a bit shook up."

"I thought I had a good grip, but that hammer slipped right out of my hand."

"You need to be more careful!" Martin's harsh tone took Ruth by surprise. Usually he was very soft-spoken.

"*Jah*, well, she shouldn't have been standing where she was. The work site's no place for a woman." Luke grunted. "Hand me that hammer, would ya, Martin?"

"Why don't you come down and take a break? Then you can get the hammer yourself."

"Guess I will."

As Luke descended the ladder, Martin smiled at Ruth, lifted his straw hat, and brushed back his coffee-colored hair. "Would you like me to go with you to get something to drink for the workers?"

"That would be nice." Ruth appreciated Martin's kindness. In all the time she and Luke had courted, Luke had never offered to help with anything. For that matter, he'd never shown much concern for her welfare, not even when her family's home had been broken into and other acts of vandalism had taken place. Instead, Luke had admitted to Ruth that he owned a truck he kept hidden in the woods and made her promise not to tell anyone. On several occasions, he'd acted as if he might be hiding something. Ruth was sure she'd done the right thing by breaking up with him. Having Martin as a suitor made her happier than she'd ever been during her courtship with Luke.

"I'm glad you weren't hit by Luke's hammer," Martin said as they started for the house. "It's bad enough that your sister and her husband lost their home in that horrible fire a few weeks ago. The last thing we need is for anyone to get hurt today."

Ruth nodded. "We were all relieved that nobody was hurt in the fire. I know Grace and Cleon appreciate all this help building their new home. This is the second Saturday in a row that they've had a large crew working on it."

"That's what friends and family are for."

Martin's dimpled smile made Ruth feel tongue-tied and tingly. She hadn't felt like that when she and Luke were together. More than anything, she'd felt irritated the last few months they'd been courting.

"Sure is a good turnout today," Martin said.

"Jah. The house is almost done, and it will be good for Grace and Cleon to have their own place again."

"I heard your *daed* say that the fire chief found a cigarette lighter on the ground outside their old house. He thinks the fire might have been intentional."

Ruth nodded, wondering if she should tell Martin that Grace thought the English reporter she used to date might have started the fire before he left the area. She decided it would be best not to say anything since they had no proof it was Gary Walker. Besides, Dad had his own suspicions about who might have set the fire.

When they reached the home of Ruth's parents, she turned to Martin. "If you'd like to have a seat on the porch, I'll run inside and see if Mom's fixed anything to drink yet."

"Okay."

Martin took a seat on the porch swing, and Ruth hurried into the house.

She found her mother, Judith, and two sisters in the kitchen, along with a few other Amish women and their nearest English neighbor.

Mom smiled at Ruth and pushed a wisp of dark brown hair back into her bun. "Are the men ready to take a break?"

"Jah. I came in to get them something to drink."

"There's iced tea and lemonade in the refrigerator." Grace motioned toward the stove. "We've got some coffee heating too." Her blue eyes twinkled like sparkling water.

"You'll need help carrying the beverages out," Ruth's younger sister, Martha, put in.

"Martin's waiting on the porch to help me with that."

"Martin Gingerich?" Sadie Esh asked.

Ruth nodded, and her cheeks turned warm.

"That fellow's really sweet on my sister, and I think she's equally sweet on him." Martha grinned at Ruth, and the skin around her blue eyes crinkled. "Look how red in the face she's getting."

Ruth shrugged. She couldn't deny her interest in Martin, but she wasn't about to admit it either.

"Leave your sister alone," Mom said, shaking her finger at Martha. "When you find a fellow you like more than your dogs, you'll turn red in the face whenever his name's mentioned too."

"How are things going with the new house?" Grace asked.

"Everything was fine until I nearly got hit in the head," Ruth said as she removed a jug of iced tea from the refrigerator.

Mom gasped. "Oh Ruth, are you all right?"

"I'm fine. It just shook me up a bit."

"How'd it happen?" their English neighbor Donna Larson questioned.

"A hammer tumbled off the roof. It could have hit me if Martin hadn't shouted a warning."

"Was it Martin's hammer?" Cleon's mother, Irene, asked.

"No, it belonged to Luke."

Mom pursed her lips. "Luke Friesen's here today?"

Ruth set the jug of iced tea on the counter and turned to face her mother. "He and his boss both came to help."

"Your daed's not going to like that. He doesn't trust Luke, and if he thought for one minute—"

"Ach, Mom, surely you don't think Luke would intentionally let his hammer fall." Martha's face had turned as red as a pickled beet. "I think Dad's still angry because Luke's not working for him anymore."

"Luke was fired, and you know it."

"That was only because he didn't see eye to eye with Dad on everything."

Mom squinted at Martha. "Luke came to work late on several occasions, and he thought he knew more than your daed about things. And don't forget about those sunglasses of Luke's that were found near my clothesline after it had been cut."

Martha stared down at the table. "That doesn't prove he cut the line."

"Toby says Luke's been acting strange for several months," Sadie put in. "He thinks Luke hasn't been right in the head since he started running with some rowdy English fellows."

Ruth was glad Luke's mother hadn't come today. It wouldn't be good for her to hear such talk about her son. In fact, she didn't think they should be having this conversation, especially not in front of Donna Larson.

Martha shot Sadie an exasperated look. "You can tell your boyfriend that *he's* done some strange things too. Does that make *him* a suspect?"

Sadie opened her mouth as if to comment, but Cleon's mother spoke first. "It's not our place to judge Luke or anyone else. It might be good if we change the subject."

"I agree." Ruth headed back to the refrigerator for a pitcher of lemonade. "I'm taking this outside. If some of you would like to bring out the coffee and cookies, I'm sure the men would appreciate it."

———————————◆◆◆———————————

As Martin waited on the porch swing for Ruth, he thought about her near mishap with the hammer and thanked God that she hadn't been hurt. He'd had an interest in Ruth for a long time—ever since they were children. Even back then, he thought she was beautiful, with her dark brown hair and matching eyes, not to mention her gentle, sweet spirit. During their teen years, when they'd first started attending singings and other young people's functions, he'd been too shy to ask if he could give her a ride home in his buggy. Then Luke Friesen began courting Ruth, and Martin figured his chances were nil. Now that Luke was out of the picture, Martin hoped he might be able to win Ruth's heart.

"What's the matter, Martin? Did you get tired of crawling around on the roof?" Abe Wengerd asked as he clomped up the steps to the back porch.

Martin motioned to the house. "I came here to help Ruth get something to drink for the workers."

Abe glanced around, then tipped his head in Martin's direction. "Don't see any sign of Ruth. Looks to me like you're taking a break."

Martin chuckled. "Guess I am at that. But just until Ruth returns from the kitchen."

"How come you didn't go in with her?"

"Figured I'd only be in the way." Martin's cheeks warmed. "Besides, she asked me to wait out here."

"Reminds me of the way my Alma used to be." Abe reached under his straw hat and pulled his fingers through the ends of his unruly reddish-brown hair. "That woman could get me to do most anything." A shadow crossed his face as he stared down at his boots. "Sure do miss her."

Martin couldn't imagine what it must be like for Abe, losing his wife after she was struck by a lightning bolt. Now the poor fellow had six children to raise on his own. Martin wondered whether Abe would marry again—and if so, whether it would be for love or so his children could have a mother.

"Did you come up to the house for a particular reason or just to see if I was loafing off?" Martin asked.

Abe leaned against the porch railing. "From what I've seen of your work habits at the harness shop, I'm convinced you're not the kind to loaf around." He nodded toward the back door. "In answer to your question, I was heading in to use the facilities."

"What's wrong with the portable outhouses that were put up for the workers to use?" Roman Hostettler asked as he stepped onto the porch. "Are they too smelly for your sensitive nose?" He snickered and bumped Abe's arm with his elbow.

Abe nudged him right back. "They were both in use. I figured you wouldn't mind if I used the one inside."

"Don't mind at all." Roman pushed the screen door open. "Go right on in."

When Abe disappeared into the house, Roman flopped into one of the wicker chairs that sat near the swing and fanned his damp face with the brim of his hat. "Sure has turned into a warm day, jah?"

Martin nodded. "That's why Ruth went into the house to get something cold to drink. As soon as she comes back, we'll take it to the workers."

"It's nice of you to want to help," Roman said with a sly-looking smile. His brown eyes twinkled, as though he knew Martin's secret.

Martin's ears burned with embarrassment. Did Ruth's dad know how much he cared for his daughter? Would Roman approve of his courting Ruth? He was tempted to ask but decided to bring up another subject instead. "Did you see that hammer fly off the roof a while ago?"

"Sure didn't. Did anyone get hurt?"

"No, but the hammer almost hit Ruth."

Roman's dark bushy eyebrows drew together. "How'd it happen?"

"It was Luke's hammer. He said it slipped out of his hand."

"Humph! As much training as that fellow's had using a hammer, he shouldn't be losing his grip. That was just plain careless." Roman's eyes narrowed as he glanced at the place behind his house where the section of property he'd given Cleon lay. "I never invited Luke to this work frolic. If I'd had my way, he wouldn't have come."

"Who invited him?"

"Cleon. He invited Luke and his English boss, John Peterson. Guess he wanted all able-bodied carpenters to help so we could get the job done quicker."

"Even so, if he knew you didn't want Luke invited—"

"Since it's Cleon and Grace's house, I didn't think I had the right to say who could help and who couldn't." The scowl on Roman's face was enough to curdle fresh goat's milk. "Now that I know one of my daughters could have been injured because of Luke's carelessness, I have a right to say what's on my mind." He stood and pivoted toward the porch steps.

"Where are you going?"

"To send Luke Friesen home!"

Chapter 2

As Ruth neared the back door with a jug of iced tea in one hand and a pitcher of lemonade in the other, she almost collided with Abe Wengerd, who had just entered the house.

"Ach, sorry. I didn't know anyone was there." His face had turned nearly as red as his hair.

"No harm was done." Ruth took a step back, being careful not to spill the beverages. "How are your *kinner* doing? I assume they're home with your sister today?"

Abe nodded. "They're getting along okay with Sue, but they still miss their *mamm*. That's especially true with Esta. She seems to be taking Alma's death harder than the others." He smiled, but it appeared to be forced. "I appreciate the kindness you showed Esta on the day of Alma's funeral."

As Ruth thought about that sorrowful day, she remembered her promise to buy Esta one of Martha's puppies. "Esta seemed interested in having one of my sister's *hundlin*. Would that be all right with you?"

Abe's forehead wrinkled. "I can't afford to buy any pedigree dogs right now."

"Oh no. I was planning to buy the dog for Esta."

The lines in his forehead deepened. "Why would you do that?"

"I thought having a puppy to care for would be good for Esta. It might help her deal with losing her mamm better if she had a dog to take her mind off her grief."

Abe compressed his lips, mulling the offer over. Finally, he nodded. "Jah, okay, but she'll have to be responsible for the *hundli*. My older kinner already have critters to care for, so they won't have time to babysit hers."

"I'll make that clear to Esta when I bring the puppy over." Ruth smiled. "Would tomorrow be a good time, since it's an off-Sunday from church?"

Abe nodded. "That'll be fine."

"I'll be over sometime before noon." Ruth moved toward the door again. "I'd better get these cold drinks out to the men."

Abe held the door, and Ruth stepped outside. Martin was sitting on the porch swing, and her heart skipped a beat when he smiled at her.

"What took you so long?" he asked.

"I was on my way out when Abe Wengerd came into the house. I asked if it would be okay with him if I brought one of my sister's puppies over to his house tomorrow. I'm buying it for Esta."

"That's real nice of you." Martin stood and reached for the jug of iced tea. "Let me carry that for you."

"Danki."

As they walked up the driveway leading to Cleon and Grace's new house, Martin commented on the unseasonably warm spring weather they were having.

Ruth nodded. "I hope it's not a sign that summer will be hot and dry."

"Never know what the weather will bring."

As they neared the house, he stopped and turned to face her. "Say, I was wondering. . ."

She tipped her head. "What were you wondering?"

"Would you mind me going with you when you take the puppy to Esta? It would give us a chance to spend some time together."

"That sounds like fun."

"Maybe afterward, we can drive over to the pond near Abe's place and see if the fish are jumping."

"I'd like that," she said as they began walking again.

When they reached the work site, the crisp scent of wood being sawed mingled with the acidic aroma of sweaty bodies, and Ruth knew the men were in need of a break. She set the jug of lemonade on a piece of plywood that had been placed over some sawhorses, and Martin did the same with the iced tea.

"Guess I'll have a glass of lemonade and then get back to work," he said.

"Aren't you going to take a break with the other men?"

"I took my break while I was waiting for you on the porch." Martin gave her a heart-melting smile and headed toward the house.

Martha and Sadie showed up with a tray of cookies and a pot of coffee. Ruth motioned Martha to one side. "Can I speak to you a minute?"

"Jah, sure. What's up?"

"I'd like to buy one of Heidi's hundlin."

Martha's eyebrows lifted. "I never thought you'd want to buy one of my puppies."

"The puppy's not for me; it's for Esta Wengerd. I thought it might help her deal with her mamm's death a little better."

"Then I should just give her a pup."

Ruth shook her head. "You're trying to build up your business so you can buy more dogs for breeding. I insist on paying for the puppy."

"You're a good sister and a good friend to little Esta." Martha gave Ruth a hug. "When did you plan to take the puppy to her?"

"Since tomorrow's an off-Sunday, I thought I'd head over to the Wengerds' sometime after breakfast."

Martha smiled. "Sounds good to me. I'll have the puppy ready for you then."

"Guess I'll go back to our place now and see what Mom has for me to do."

"Sadie and I will serve the men their snacks, then we'll come back to the house to help get lunch ready to serve."

When Ruth returned to the house, she found Grace and Mom sitting at the table, drinking lemonade. "I figured you'd be making sandwiches by now," she said.

Mom smiled. "They're already made, and since the rest of the women have gone outside to either check on their kinner or see how things are going with the house, Grace and I decided to take a break."

"Guess I will too, then." Ruth pulled out a chair and sat down. "I'll be taking one of Martha's puppies over to Esta Wengerd tomorrow, so I hope you haven't made any plans that will include me."

Mom shook her head. "Your daed and I thought we would visit my sister, Clara, but there's no need for you to go along."

"If you're goin' to see Esta, can I go, too?"

Ruth turned at the sound of Anna's voice. She hadn't realized her six-year-old niece had come into the room. The child's vivid blue eyes were wide with expectation, while a wisp of dark-colored hair peeked out of her *kapp* and curled around her ear. Not since before the fire had Ruth seen Grace's daughter looking so enthused. There was no way she could say no to Anna's request. "If it's all right with your mamm, you can ride along," she told the child.

Anna hurried to her mother's side. "Can I go with Aunt Ruth to see Esta?"

Grace nodded and gave her daughter a hug. "It's fine with me."

Ruth thought about Martin's offer to drive her over to Abe's place and wondered how he would feel about Anna tagging along. It meant they wouldn't get to spend time alone, but she hoped he would understand.

———————◆•◆———————

Martin had just started up the ladder on the back side of the house when he heard angry-sounding voices nearby. He glanced to the left and spotted Ruth's dad talking to Luke.

"Your carelessness could have caused serious injury to my daughter." Roman squeezed his fingers around his straw hat so tightly that his knuckles turned white.

"It was an accident; the hammer slipped out of my hand." Luke looked over at Martin. "You were there when it happened. Tell Roman I didn't drop the hammer on purpose."

Martin swallowed hard, not sure how to respond. Even though it had appeared to be an accident, he wasn't sure it was. Fact was, he didn't trust Luke Friesen and had been relieved when Ruth broke up with him.

"Speak up," Luke said, moving closer to Martin. "Tell the man how the hammer slipped out of my hand and slid down the roof."

"It did that, all right," Martin said with a nod. "And if you'll recall, I told you that you needed to be more careful."

"What he needs to do is stay away from my daughter." Roman planted his hands on his hips and stared hard at Luke. "I don't trust you. Haven't since we found your sunglasses on the ground under my wife's clothesline that *somebody* cut."

"Well, it wasn't me." Luke's eyes darkened to the color of the night sky.

Roman continued to glare at Luke. The tension between them blazed like a hot fire. "Why'd you come here today?"

"To help rebuild Cleon and Grace's house, same as all the others who came."

"Everywhere you go, trouble seems to follow. I'd appreciate it if you'd go home." Roman's eyebrows furrowed. "Better yet, go on back to John Peterson's woodworking shop and do some work there. He's still your employer, isn't he?"

Luke kicked at a dirt clod with the toe of his boot. "John and I both took the day off so we could help here."

"I appreciate John showing up, but you can spend your day off doing something else, because you're not welcome in this place!"

Luke grabbed his work pouch from the patch of grass where he'd laid it and stalked off.

Roman looked over at Martin and slowly shook his head. "I don't trust that fellow."

Martin glanced across the yard. When he saw Luke heading toward his buggy, he made a promise to himself. *Whenever Luke's around Ruth, I'm going to keep a close watch on things.*

Chapter 3

As Martin headed down the road toward the Hostettlers' place the following day, a wave of excitement coursed through his body. He could hardly wait to see Ruth again, and he looked forward to the time he would spend with her on the drive to Abe's place. If he had his way, he would ask Ruth to marry him today. He figured he'd better not rush things though. He had to be sure she cared as much for him as he did for her. He needed to know that her folks approved of him as well.

When Martin pulled into the Hostettlers' yard a short time later, he was surprised to see Grace's daughter, Anna, sitting on the porch steps beside Ruth.

After securing his horse to the hitching rail near the barn, Martin sprinted across the yard and stepped onto the porch. *"Guder mariye,"* he said, smiling at Ruth.

"Good morning."

"Are you ready to go?"

"I am, and I hope you don't mind, but I said it was okay if Anna went with us today." Ruth slipped her arm around Anna's shoulders. "Esta's a good friend of Anna's, so she'd like to be there when we deliver the puppy."

Even though Martin was disappointed that he wouldn't have Ruth to himself, he understood why Anna would like to go along. "We can make the drive to the pond some other time," he said.

"I'm sure we can." Ruth reached for Anna's hand. "Shall we go out to the kennels and see if Martha's got that hundli ready for us?"

Anna nodded and clambered to her feet. "I hope Esta lets me help her name it."

Martin seemed awfully quiet on the way over to Abe's, and Ruth wondered if he was unhappy about her bringing Anna along. Of course, the reason he hadn't said much could be because Anna had been talking nonstop ever since they'd left home. The little girl had turned into a regular chatterbox.

"I hope Esta likes the hundli," Anna said from her seat behind Ruth. "She's lost her mamm and needs this little fellow to comfort her."

"I'm sure she'll like it fine," Ruth replied.

Martin smiled at Ruth. "Anna's caught on to the *Deitsch* pretty well, hasn't she?"

"She had a little trouble fitting in and learning our Pennsylvania Dutch language when she first came to live with my sister," Ruth whispered, "but she's finally adjusted and is looking forward to her mamm having a *boppli* soon."

Anna tapped Ruth on the shoulder. "What do you think of the name Winkie for Esta's puppy?"

"Why would you want to call him that?" Ruth asked the child.

" 'Cause he likes to wink. If you watch him real close, you'll see his one eye wink when I pet him behind the ear." She stroked the pup behind its ear, and one eye closed, then opened again.

Ruth laughed. "That's some *schmaert* dog we're giving Esta."

"*Schmaert* means smart, right?"

"Jah."

"Sounds like you're pretty schmaert too," Martin called over his shoulder. "Danki."

Ruth turned to look at Anna. With the little reddish-brown-and-white sheltie nestled in her arms, the little girl looked quite content. "Are you sure you wouldn't like another dog, Anna?" she asked. "I could have given you one for your birthday two weeks ago."

Anna shook her head. "I don't need one of my own 'cause I'll have a baby sister to play with soon. Besides, I can play with Esta's puppy whenever I visit her."

"Okay." Ruth hoped Anna wouldn't be too disappointed if she ended up with a baby brother. The child had already faced so many disappointments. Even on her sixth birthday, she had suffered the disappointment of not having much of a celebration. Cleon had spent most of the day cleaning up the mess that had been left after their home had been burned. Mom had invited Grace's family for supper that evening, but Cleon and Dad had returned to work on the cleanup right after they'd eaten their meal. Of course, Anna had received some gifts, but Ruth had seen the dejected look on her niece's face and knew she felt let down because there hadn't been a real party to celebrate her special day.

Ruth glanced back at Anna again and was pleased to see the dreamy look on the little girl's face. Apparently her disappointing birthday had been forgotten, for her concentration seemed to be on the puppy she held.

When they arrived at Abe's place, Ruth spotted three of his children—Owen, age four; Willis, age six; and Josh, age ten—playing in the yard. None of them wore jackets, despite the chilly wind and dark clouds hovering overhead. Ruth was sure if their mother were still alive, they wouldn't have been playing outside on a day like this without jackets. She was tempted to mention the chilly weather to the children but decided it wasn't her place to do so. Abe's sister, Sue, had left her parents' home in Illinois and moved into Abe's house to care for his children soon after Alma died. It was Sue's responsibility to look after Abe's kinner now.

Eight-year-old Esta darted out of the barn as soon as Martin pulled the horse up to the hitching rail. Her older brother Gideon, who was twelve, stepped out from the door behind her.

"Where's your daed?" Martin asked as he hopped down from the buggy and went around to help Ruth and Anna out.

"He's in the house takin' a nap." Gideon's forehead wrinkled. "He's been sleepin' a lot since Mama died."

Esta nodded. "That's right. As soon as Papa's done eating supper every night, he goes right to bed."

"Your daed works hard in his harness shop," Martin said in his boss's defense.

"It ain't the harness shop that's got him feelin' so tired," Gideon mumbled. "He misses Mama, same as we do."

"Only we don't sleep so much," Esta said as she sidled up to the buggy and stood on her tiptoes. "Papa said you were bringin' me a hundli. You got him in there?"

"Of course we do," Anna replied. "Winkie's right here." She handed the puppy to Esta.

Esta stared at the pup. "Winkie? Where'd you get that funny name?"

"I chose it 'cause he likes to wink."

Gideon snorted. "Jah, right. Like any dog knows how to wink."

"This one does," Anna said with a nod.

"It's true," Ruth put in. "I saw the puppy wink."

Gideon shook his head. "People wink; dogs don't."

"Uh-huh." Anna stepped closer to Esta and reached out to stroke the puppy behind its right ear. Winkie closed one eye, opened it, and closed it again.

"I told you he could wink. That's why his name should be Winkie," Anna said.

"I like that name." Esta looked up at Ruth with a dubious expression. "Are you sure he's mine?"

"Absolutely. But you must promise to take good care of him."

Esta's head bobbed up and down. "I'll feed him and make sure he gets plenty of exercise too."

Ruth bent down and gave Esta a hug. "I'm sure you will."

"Winkie's a dumb name," Gideon mumbled as he shuffled back to the barn.

Esta's lower lip protruded. "I don't know why my *bruder* has to be so mean."

Martin patted Esta on the head. "Maybe he's jealous because you've got a new puppy and he doesn't."

"That's just plain silly," Esta said with a shake of her head. "Gideon's got a goat and a whole lot of other barn animals to care for. He's a mean old *schtinker*."

"Does Gideon smell bad?" Anna asked.

Esta grunted. "Sometimes, after he's been workin' in the barn."

Ruth chuckled. "I think Esta was calling her brother a stinker because he wasn't acting nice about the name you chose for the puppy."

Anna nudged Esta. "Are you gonna keep the name *Winkie* for him?"

"Don't see why not. He can wink real good, so I think it's a fittin' name." Esta motioned to her brothers playing in the yard. "Let's show the others my new puppy."

The girls scampered across the lawn.

"She seems real happy to have the hundli, doesn't she?" Martin asked as he and Ruth followed the girls.

"Jah. It's good to see her smiling again."

"It was nice of you to buy the dog from your sister."

"I could almost feel that little girl's pain the day her mother was buried." Ruth stopped and turned to face him. "I wanted to do something to give her a sense of joy again."

"You did that, all right." Martin nodded toward Josh, Willis, and Owen, who had gathered around Esta, begging to hold the puppy. "I think you'll make a fine mamm someday, Ruth."

"I hope so."

"What's going on here?" Abe called as he stepped out of the house and headed for the group on the lawn. "All that hollering woke me from my nap."

"We're lookin' at the hundli Ruth brought over for Esta," Josh announced. "Come see how cute he is, Papa."

Abe left the porch and joined them. "It's a nice one, all right," he said with a yawn.

"Where's Aunt Sue and baby Molly?" Esta questioned. "I want them to see my new puppy too."

Abe grimaced. "Molly woke up fussy from her nap, so Sue's trying to get her calmed down."

Ruth was tempted to ask if she could be of assistance but figured Abe might not appreciate her butting into his family's business.

"It's not fair that Esta gets a puppy and we don't," Willis complained to his dad.

Abe patted the boy's head. "There are plenty of animals around our place for you to play with."

"I'll share Winkie with everyone." Esta held the pup out to her brother. "You can play with him whenever you want."

Abe quirked an eyebrow. "Winkie, is it?"

"I gave him the name," Anna explained. "It's because he winks whenever I do this." She stroked the pup behind its ear, and just like before, the puppy winked.

Everyone laughed. Ruth was glad she'd given the dog to Esta. Despite all of the horrible things that happened in people's lives, it was good to still have some things to laugh about.

Chapter 4

W ould you be interested in seeing the harness shop while you're here?" Martin asked Ruth as they sat with Abe on his back porch, watching the children frolic in the yard with the puppy.

"Oh jah," she said with an eager nod. "I think that would be quite interesting."

Abe grunted. "Don't see what's so interesting about a bunch of leather harnesses, straps, and buckles, but if you'd like to see my shop, I'd be happy to show you around."

"Will the kinner be all right?" Ruth questioned.

"Sure," Abe said with a nod. "Sue's in the house if they need anything, and we'll be within hollering distance."

"Let's head out to the shop, then, and give Ruth the grand tour." Martin reached for Ruth's hand as she rose to her feet, and their gazes met. He looked pleased at her interest in his work.

When they stepped into Abe's harness shop, Ruth's nose twitched at the distinctive odor of raw leather and pungent dye. It seemed strange that she'd never visited here before. But whenever Dad had come to see Abe during Ruth's childhood, she'd either been in school or been doing chores at home. Now she kept busy with her job at the bakeshop and never had a need to visit the harness shop on her own.

"This is quite impressive," Ruth said as she gazed around the room, awed by all of the equipment and supplies. She pointed to a tall machine on one side of the room. "What's that over there?"

"It's a riveter. We use it to punch silver rivets into leather straps." Martin glanced over at Abe and shrugged. "Guess I should let you do the telling since this is your shop."

"No problem," Abe said. "You go ahead and show Ruth around. I'll take a seat at my desk and relax awhile."

After the comment from Gideon about Abe sleeping so much since Alma died, Ruth wondered if Abe had lost his zest for working. Could he be putting the workload on Martin's shoulders while he sat around feeling sorry for himself?

Ruth mentally scolded herself. She had no right to judge the man. She hadn't walked in his shoes, and it wasn't fair to speculate on how Abe ran his business or how he was coping with Alma's death. Besides, he had come to the work frolic the other day and worked hard to rebuild Grace and Cleon's house.

"Here are all the buckles, snaps, rings, and rivets we use." Martin pointed to a group of open-faced boxes lining one wall.

"I don't know how you keep track of everything," Ruth said, letting her gaze travel from the boxes to the harnesses and bridles looped from ceiling hooks overhead, to the scraps lying on the cement floor, looking like thin spaghetti noodles.

"We know where everything is." Martin moved to stand between two oversized sewing machines. "This is what we use to stitch leather straps together. They're run by an air compressor."

"It's all so impressive. I like what I see."

A wide grin spread over Martin's face. "So do I."

Ruth felt the heat of a blush cover her cheeks. Did Martin mean he liked looking at her, or was he referring to the harness shop? She didn't dare ask.

"How did you learn the trade of harness making?" Ruth asked, turning to face Abe.

He leaned back in his chair with his fingers locked together behind his head. "Learned it from my daed, and he used to say he learned it from making mistakes."

"Your daed must have taught you well," Martin said, "because you've got a lot of customers who are always telling me what a good job you've done for them." He grinned. "You're teaching me real well too."

"That's because you're a good learner, and you've always been cooperative." Abe looked back at Ruth. "Not like Luke Friesen, who gave your daed nothing but trouble when he was working as his apprentice."

Ruth wasn't in the mood to talk about Luke, and she wished Abe hadn't brought him up.

"Come over here and take a look at all the tools we work with," Martin said, steering Ruth across the room. She figured he knew talking about her ex-boyfriend made her feel uncomfortable.

Ruth followed Martin around the room as he explained how they cleaned and repaired old harnesses and made new ones. She reached out to touch a strap that lay on one of the workbenches. "This feels so soft and oily."

"It's recently been dipped in neat's-foot oil," Martin explained.

Ruth glanced over at Abe and noticed that his eyes were closed. She figured the poor man must be either very tired or bored with playing chaperone for them. Or maybe he was trying to shut out the world as he suffered the loss of his wife in silence.

Martin stepped closer to Ruth and whispered, "Would you be interested in going to the pond with me next Saturday for some fishing and a picnic?"

"Just the two of us?"

He nodded. "Since we couldn't go there today, on account of bringing Anna along, I thought maybe next Saturday would work better. You don't have to work at the bakeshop, do you?"

"I have that day off. What about you? Won't you be working here at the harness shop?"

"Nope. Abe's only got the shop open one Saturday a month now, and that won't be this Saturday."

Ruth hesitated before giving Martin her answer. The last time she'd gone to the pond with a man, it had been Luke. He'd acted odd and secretive that day, despite his kidding around. Of course, now she knew that was because Luke had a truck hidden in the woods not far from the pond and didn't want anyone to know about it.

"Maybe you'd rather we make it a double date," Martin said. "We could ask your friend Sadie and her boyfriend, Toby, to join us."

"That's a good idea," Ruth was quick to say. "Sadie's been after me to go someplace with her, and that would be a nice way for us to spend the day."

Martin tipped his head. "For who—you and Sadie or you and me?"

"Both."

His face relaxed into a smile. "Do you want to speak to Sadie about it, or should I talk to Toby?"

"Sadie and I are both scheduled to work at the bakeshop on Monday, so I'll ask her then. But if you happen to see Toby between now and then, feel free to mention it to him as well."

———————◆◆◆———————

Abe released a sigh as he sat at his desk, resting his eyes and listening to Martin and Ruth's conversation. The joy of being young and in love. He could still remember how excited he felt when he and Alma first started courting. He couldn't wait to be with her. Whenever they went somewhere together, he didn't want to take her home. Even after they'd been married a few years and had started their family, he'd continued to enjoy her company and looked forward to their time alone after the kinner were in bed.

Abe thought about his sister, whose boyfriend, Melvin Zook, lived in Illinois. He knew it had been hard for Sue to leave Melvin and her family to come care for his kinner. He also knew that should Sue and Melvin decide to marry, he would lose his housekeeper.

"Then what'll I do?" he mumbled.

"Were you speaking to me, Abe?"

Abe's eyes snapped open, and he squinted. Martin stood a few feet from his desk, and Ruth was right beside him. "Uh. . .no. I was just thinkin' out loud, is all."

Martin nodded. "I do that sometimes too."

Abe grunted. "Been doin' it a lot more since Alma died."

"I'm sorry for your loss." Ruth's pained expression revealed the depth of her compassion.

Abe swallowed hard. "You know what happened the first time I brought Alma out here to show her around?"

"What happened?" Martin asked.

"She ran around the room touching everything in sight, saying how much she liked the place. Alma was full of love and life, and I sure do miss her. Even though my kinner and Sue are around, I feel lonely without Alma."

"Of course you do. It's only natural that you and your children would miss her," Ruth said, touching Abe's shoulder. "My grandma Hostettler used to say that when we're lonely, we should reach out to family and friends and allow them to reach out to us in return."

Abe sniffed. "Esta's got her puppy now, but I wish there was something that could help my oldest boy cope with his mother's passing. Gideon hasn't shed a tear since Alma died. Yet I know he's grieving. He's been acting moody and kind of sassy lately."

"Would you like me to speak with him?" Ruth asked. "Maybe I can help in some way."

"I appreciate the offer," Abe replied, "but I believe in time the boy will come around."

"I think we'd better go," Martin said before Ruth could respond. "We don't want to get Anna back to her folks too late, or they might start to worry."

"Oh, okay." Ruth glanced over her shoulder as Martin led her toward the door. "Danki for letting me see your shop, Abe. It's very interesting in here."

"Jah, sure. I'm glad you like it."

———————◦•◦———————

Grace entered her new living room and seated herself in the rocking chair near the fireplace. She leaned her head against the cushion and placed both hands on her stomach.

"You feeling all right?" Cleon asked as he took a seat on the sofa across from her.

"I'm fine," she said with a nod. "I just felt the boppli kick."

"He's an active one, isn't he?"

"Jah, but it could be a girl, you know."

He shrugged. "I guess Anna would like a baby sister."

"What about you? Will you be disappointed if the babe is a girl?"

"I'll be fine with whatever God chooses to give us," he said.

"Me too." Grace smiled. "I was pleased to see how Anna perked up when she found out Ruth was taking the puppy over to Esta. I'm glad Ruth didn't mind taking Anna with her."

"I'm not sure Martin was so pleased about Anna tagging along, though."

"What makes you say that?"

"I've got a hunch Martin wanted to be alone with your sister today."

"Then he should have said so."

"Probably didn't want to hurt Ruth's or Anna's feelings."

"Anna would have been disappointed, but I'm sure she'd have gotten over it." Grace stopped rocking and stood.

"Where are you going?"

"I've got a cramp in my leg, so I need to walk around a bit."

Cleon was immediately at her side. "Want me to rub it for you?"

Grace appreciated her husband's concern, but sometimes he could be a bit overprotective. "If it doesn't relax soon, I might take you up on that offer," she said with a smile.

Despite the uncomfortable knot in her calf, Grace felt peace and joy in her heart. It was hard to believe that just a few weeks ago things had been strained between her and Cleon. Then the day their house had burned, Cleon had apologized for his part in their marital problems, and she'd done the same. Grace had never felt closer to him, and with each passing day, their relationship seemed to grow stronger. *Let it always be so,* she silently prayed. *Let peace and joy reign in this house.*

Chapter 5

When Martin pulled his buggy into a grassy area near the pond, Sadie and Toby were already there. He and Ruth hadn't planned to meet them until noon. According to his pocket watch, it was just a little past eleven thirty. So much for spending time alone with his girlfriend.

Ruth looked over at Martin and smiled. "Looks like they beat us here."

"Jah." Martin halted the horse, climbed down, and secured the animal to the nearest tree. He hurried back to the buggy to help Ruth down, but by the time he got there, she had climbed out on her own.

"Hey, you two," Sadie hollered with a wave. "Looks like we've got the perfect day for a picnic."

Ruth lifted her face toward the sun. "Jah, it's a beautiful spring day. Much better than the low-hanging clouds and gusty winds we had earlier in the week."

"Let's hope the fish are biting today." Toby thumped Martin's shoulder. "I'd like to catch a couple of big ones. How about you?"

"That'd be fine with me." Martin scooted around to the back of his buggy and withdrew his fishing pole.

"No fishing until we've had our lunch," Sadie said with a shake of her head. "If you fellows put your lines in the water now, we'll never get to eat, and I'm hungry."

"Aren't you the bossy one today?" Toby tweaked Sadie's freckled nose. "Sadie Esh, my bossy little *aldi*."

She pushed his hand away, and her blue eyes flashed indignantly. "I may be your girlfriend, but I'm not bossy."

"Are so." Toby whipped off his straw hat, revealing a thick crop of reddish-blond hair, and plunked the hat on Sadie's head.

"Hey, you're crushing my kapp!" Sadie lifted Toby's hat and sent it sailing through the air.

Ruth looked over at Martin and rolled her eyes skyward. "Shall I get the picnic food?"

"Might as well," he replied with a nod.

Ruth and Martin spread a quilt on the ground and retrieved their ice chest from the buggy while Sadie and Toby did the same.

Once everyone was seated on the quilt, all heads bowed for silent prayer. Afterward Ruth and Sadie passed out golden brown chicken, macaroni salad, coleslaw, carrot sticks, dill pickles, and lemonade.

"Everything looks good," Toby said, smacking his lips. He reached for a drumstick and took a bite. "Jah, it's *appeditlich*."

"If you think the chicken's delicious, wait until you taste some of Ruth's strawberry-rhubarb pie," Martin said. "I had some at her house last Sunday when I brought her home from Abe Wengerd's place."

"What were you doing at Abe's?" Toby asked, looking at Ruth.

"We took one of Martha's little shelties over to Esta, hoping it might help her deal with the grief of losing her mother," she replied.

"It was nice of Martha to give away one of her pups," Toby said as he reached for another piece of chicken.

Sadie swatted his hand. "You haven't finished the first piece you took, and already you're taking another?"

"Actually, giving Esta a puppy was Ruth's idea," Martin said. "Ruth even paid for the hundli."

Toby set the chicken leg down and licked his fingers. "Is that a fact?"

"Sure is." Martin smiled at Ruth. "My aldi's real kindhearted and generous."

Ruth blushed a crimson red, and he figured he'd probably embarrassed her. At least she hadn't denied being his girlfriend.

"You're right about Ruth being kindhearted," Sadie said, touching Ruth's arm. "My good friend is the nicest person I know."

The color in Ruth's cheeks deepened. "I'm not perfect, you know."

Sadie shook her head. "Never said you were. Just meant you're a good friend, and a nice one at that."

———————◆◆◆———————

Ruth finished her lunch in quiet as she mulled over what Martin and Sadie had said about her. She did care about others who were hurting, which was why she'd been concerned for Esta Wengerd. She'd always tried to be an obedient daughter, a helpful sister, and a trustworthy friend. But at times, Ruth felt as if she were being tested—always trying to do what was right, yet struggling with feelings of discontent. Her feelings of frustration over the break-ins at their home and Dad's shop were examples of how imperfect she was. Then there was the anger she'd felt toward Luke when he had refused to be honest with her.

"You're awfully quiet," Martin said, nudging Ruth. "Are you bored with being here?"

"Not at all. I was just thinking."

"I've been thinking too." Toby grabbed Sadie's hand and pulled her to her feet. "I've been thinking it might be a good idea to take a walk in the woods and work off some of the food I ate so I don't fall asleep while I fish." He glanced down at Ruth and Martin. "You two want to join us?"

Ruth looked over at Martin to get his opinion and was pleased when he said, "I'd rather stay here and enjoy the sunshine."

Ruth nodded. "Me too."

"Suit yourself," Toby said as he and Sadie hurried away.

Martin leaned close to Ruth, and she could feel his warm breath caress her cheek. "I enjoy being with you," he murmured.

She swallowed a couple of times, hoping she could speak without stammering. "I enjoy being with you too."

He reached for her hand, and they remained on the quilt, visiting and watching the ducks float on the pond until Toby and Sadie finally returned.

"You'll never guess what we found in the woods," Toby said as they plunked down on the quilt.

"A big black bear?" Martin asked in a teasing tone.

Toby snorted. "Jah, right. We found a big black pickup truck covered with a layer of dust. But no one was in sight." He squinted at Ruth. "Sadie says she's seen it before, and so have you."

Ruth nodded slowly. "Jah, that's true. We spotted it there one day when we were taking a walk."

"Do you know who it belongs to?" Toby questioned.

Ruth merely shrugged in reply. "It's not important. Let's talk about something else, okay?"

"No way!" Toby got right in her face. "If you know who owns that truck, then tell us. *Raus mit*—out with it!"

Ruth curled her fingers into the palms of her hands, remembering the day Luke had told her about the truck he'd hidden in the woods so his folks wouldn't know. She had promised she wouldn't tell anyone, and until now, she'd never been tempted.

"I'll bet it belongs to one of those rowdy English fellows who have been seen pulling some pranks in our area." Toby grunted. "I heard that a couple of 'em were caught throwing dirt clods at some buggies going down the road near Sugarcreek the other day."

Ruth gave a nonchalant shrug.

"I say we drop this subject," Sadie said, squeezing Toby's arm.

Toby turned his hands palms up and grunted. "Whatever."

"Why don't you and I do some fishing while the women visit?" Martin poked Toby's arm. "That's what we'd planned to do in the first place, right?"

Toby nodded and rose to his feet.

Martin glanced over at Ruth and smiled, then headed for the buggy to get his fishing pole.

Sadie nudged Ruth with her elbow. "I've been thinking about that truck in the woods."

"What about it?"

"You sure acted funny when Toby mentioned it. Do you know who owns the truck?"

"Do we have to talk about this? Can't we just enjoy our day?"

"Does that mean you know who owns the truck and just won't say?"

Ruth clenched her teeth. "I do know, but it's not for me to say."

"How come?"

"Because the person who owns the truck asked me not to say anything."

"You can tell me. I won't tell anyone else, I promise."

"Sure is a beautiful day. Just listen to the birds twittering in the trees overhead."

Sadie sighed. "All right, then, don't tell me who owns the truck."

Ruth leaned back on the quilt and closed her eyes. "Ah, that warm sun feels so good on my face."

"Remember last spring, when the two of us were here with our boyfriends?"

Apparently Sadie had given up on learning who owned the truck, and Ruth was glad. Sadie was her friend, but she was also being courted by Toby, who tended to be a blabbermouth. If Ruth told Sadie that the truck belonged to Luke, and Sadie repeated it to Toby, the word would soon get out to everyone in their community, including Luke's parents. If Dad was right about Luke, and he *was* trying to get even with Ruth for breaking up with him, he might think up even more malicious things to do in retaliation.

"Did you hear what I said about last spring?"

"Jah, I heard, and I do remember coming here."

"Only you were being courted by Luke instead of Martin." Sadie nudged Ruth's arm, and Ruth's eyes popped open. "I think Martin's a better match for you than Luke."

"Martin and I have been getting along pretty well," Ruth admitted. "The only thing is. . .*sis mer bang.*"

"You're afraid?"

"Jah."

"Why are you afraid?"

Ruth swallowed hard, refusing to give in to her swirling emotions. "Whenever things are going well, it seems as if they suddenly turn bad."

"Are you talking about the way things went with you and Luke?"

"That and all the things that have happened at our place over the last year."

"The break-ins and vandalism, you mean?"

"Jah, and also the fire at Cleon and Grace's house. Just when we thought things had settled down, something else happened to test our faith. It makes me afraid of being happy for fear something will go wrong and spoil it."

"Guess there will always be things in life that test our faith," Sadie said. "But we can't let it keep us from falling in love or finding joy in things."

Ruth smiled. "When did you get so schmaert, anyway?"

"I've always been smart; you've just been too busy to notice." Sadie motioned to the fellows. "Sure is nice to see how well they get along, isn't it?"

Ruth nodded. "Toby seems to have a better relationship with Martin than he does with Luke."

"You're right. For some time now, I've noticed tension between Toby and Luke, but I've never figured out the reason for it."

"Guess there doesn't have to be a reason," Ruth said. "Some folks just get along better with certain people than they do others."

"Maybe so, but it's like there's some kind of competition going on between Toby and Luke. Almost seems as if Toby wants to make Luke look bad."

"Why would he do that?"

Sadie shrugged. "Beats me, but the other day I heard Toby speaking with his daed about Luke. He said he knows that Luke's been running around with some rowdy English fellows."

"What'd the bishop say about that?"

"Said he was aware that Luke had been keeping company with some Englishers, but there wasn't much he could do about it since Luke's still going through his *rumschpringe*."

Ruth sighed. "I had hoped he would get that out of his system, settle down, and join the church while we were courting, but he seems bent on kicking up his heels."

Sadie patted Ruth's arm. "You're better off without him."

Ruth nodded. "I know."

"That lunch Ruth and Sadie fixed sure was tasty," Toby said as he baited his hook with a plump worm. "Made me almost wish I was married."

Martin cast his line into the water and took a seat near the edge of the pond. "Why aren't you, then?"

"I'm not quite ready to settle down."

"But you've joined the church."

"That's true."

"And you've got an aldi you seem to like."

"Uh-huh. Sadie and me have been courting a little over a year."

"Then what's the problem? Why don't you ask her to marry you?"

Toby shrugged.

"Are you in *lieb*?"

"In love with Sadie?"

Martin's gaze went to the sky. Sometimes Toby seemed so dense about things. "Of course I meant Sadie. She's the only one you're courting, right?"

"Jah, but I'm not sure what I feel for her is love." Toby dropped his line into the water and sat back on his heels. "I like her a lot, and we get along pretty well, but—"

"Are you afraid of marriage?"

"Why would I be afraid?"

"Don't know. Just asking, is all."

"I ain't afraid of nothin'."

Martin chuckled. "Jah, right."

As Martin fished, he found himself thinking of Ruth and wondering about her response to the pickup Toby and Sadie had found in the woods. Whose secret was Ruth keeping, and why? He was tempted to press her about it but didn't want to do anything that might drive a wedge between them. Maybe after they'd been courting longer, he would feel free to ask about the truck. If she was honest about it, she could be trusted and might be the right woman for him. If not, he didn't know what he would do.

Chapter 6

"Are you sure you want to move these?" asked Cleon's brother Ivan as he and Cleon lifted one of the bee boxes onto the back of an open wagon early Monday morning.

Cleon nodded. "I think it will be better if I have the boxes closer to home. That way I won't have to leave so often in order to check on the bees and extract the honey."

"Guess that makes sense." Ivan wiped the sweat from his brow and squinted his dark eyes. "Sure hope no one will try to burn out your bees again."

"Me too. At least with these new boxes out behind our house, I can keep a closer watch on things." Cleon grimaced. "First my bee boxes were burned and then my house. Makes no sense why someone would want to do such hateful things."

"I heard that the firemen found a cigarette lighter outside your home the day of the fire," Ivan said as they headed over to get the next bee box.

"Jah, that's right."

"You know anyone who smokes?"

Cleon shrugged. "None of my Amish friends."

Ivan's forehead wrinkled. "I've heard rumors that Luke Friesen smokes."

"Where'd you hear that?"

"Toby King mentioned that Luke's been hanging around a bunch of English fellows who smoke and that he's smelled smoke on Luke's clothes a time or two."

"That doesn't prove he's a smoker. Could be that Luke just smells like smoke because he's been with others who do."

"Maybe so."

"As far as who's responsible for the fires that were started. . .it could be the same person who broke into the Hostettlers' place, took some of Roman's tools from his woodworking shop, and did several other acts of vandalism."

Ivan's eyes narrowed. "You think Luke could have done all those things?"

"I hope not. Grace thinks it was Gary Walker, that reporter who hung around the area for a time taking pictures and asking a bunch of nosy questions." The brothers set the bee box on the wagon.

"Why would the reporter want to do anything to hurt the Hostettlers, or you?" Ivan asked.

Cleon pulled his fingers through the back of his hair and frowned. "You know the story. Gary Walker used to date Grace when she left home to try out the English world. After she broke up with him, he said he would get even with her someday."

"But the reporter left Holmes County to do some other stories. So if he's the one who did the attacks, then they're not likely to happen again."

Cleon nodded, but his mind raced on. What if the reporter wasn't responsible for any of the crimes? He hated to think it could be Luke or anyone else they knew. The one thing he did know was that he planned to keep a close eye on Grace and the rest of her family. That was the real reason he'd decided to move the bee boxes from his folks' property.

"Say, Ivan, I was wondering. . ."

"What's that?"

"Would you be willing to make some of my honey deliveries when you're not helping Pop in the fields?"

"You don't plan to make your own deliveries anymore?"

"I will when I can, but with me working for Grace's daed and tending my bees, I don't have as much time for making deliveries."

Ivan nodded. "I'll help whenever I can."

"I appreciate that, and I'll pay you something for your time." Cleon clasped his brother's shoulder. "Could you start this afternoon?"

"Making deliveries, you mean?"

"Jah. There are a couple of shops in Charm that sell my honey. The last time I was there, they were getting down on their supply."

"I can't do it today," Ivan said with a shake of his blond head. "I promised Pop I'd help him clear that back field."

"What about Willard and Delbert?"

"They'll be helping too. The ground's really rocky there, and it's gonna take all four of us to get the job done."

Cleon grunted. "Guess I'll have to deliver the honey myself. Maybe I'll take Grace and Anna along. It's been a while since they've been to Charm."

⸻

Grace stood at her bedroom window, watching Cleon and his brother unload the bee boxes they'd brought to the field behind their new home. She was glad he'd decided to move the boxes so he wouldn't be gone so much.

She pressed her hand against her lower back to ease out some of the kinks and moved away from the window, knowing it was time to wake Anna and get breakfast on the table before Cleon came inside.

A short time later, Grace, Cleon, and Anna gathered around the kitchen table. "Too bad Ivan couldn't join us for breakfast," Grace said after their silent prayer. "He would have been more than welcome."

"I'm sure he would have stayed if he hadn't had to get home and help our daed and *brieder* clear a new field. We'll invite him some other time." Cleon gave his dark brown beard a quick tug, then looked over at Anna and smiled. "How would you and your mamm like to go with me to Charm this morning to deliver some honey to Grandma's Homestead Restaurant and a couple of other places?"

Anna's eyes brightened. "Could we eat at the restaurant?"

Grace chuckled and pointed to the child's plate, still full of fluffy french toast and sticky syrup. "You're eating right now, silly girl."

Anna shrugged her slim shoulders. "Figured we could eat lunch at the restaurant."

"Sorry," Cleon said, "but I've got to get the deliveries made right after breakfast. Then I'll need to hurry back home and go to work in your grandpa's woodworking shop."

Anna's lower lip protruded. "Seems like you're always workin', Papa."

"That's what daeds do when they've got a family to support." Cleon reached for the bottle of syrup. "The good news is I won't be gone so much now that my bee boxes have been moved closer to our home. Ivan's agreed to make some of my honey deliveries, which means I can spend more time with you and your mamm."

Anna grinned and forked a hunk of french toast into her mouth.

Grace looked over at Cleon, and he winked at her. Despite the fact that Anna was the daughter of Wade Davis, an Englisher who had died when Anna was a baby, Cleon had accepted her as his own child, and Grace felt grateful. During the time when her family had been under attack, she'd looked toward the future with dread. Now she anticipated the new baby who would be coming soon and hoped they would have many happy days ahead.

"I was talking with Irene Schrock the other day, and she mentioned that her daughter slipped on the stairs and broke her arm a few days ago," Ruth's mother said as Ruth helped her and Martha clear the breakfast dishes from the table.

"Does that mean Carolyn won't be able to help Irene with the dinners they do for tourists?" Ruth asked.

Mom nodded. "Not for several weeks. Carolyn won't be able to do much with only one hand."

"I could go there and help," Ruth offered.

"What about your job at the bakeshop?" Mom asked.

"I'm usually off by early afternoon, so that shouldn't get in the way of my helping Irene. I could help on my days off too."

Mom shook her head. "I don't know. . .seems like a lot of work to me, especially since you already have a job."

"Guess I could help," Martha said. "Of course, Ruth's better at cooking than I am."

"I'm sure you would do fine." Mom patted Martha's back.

Martha shrugged. "I'd better let Ruth do it."

"I think I'll drop by the Schrocks' on my way to work and speak with Irene about helping." Ruth smiled. "Since Abe Wengerd's place is on the way, I might stop and see how Esta's doing with her puppy."

Mom nodded. "That's a good idea. We need to check on Abe and his kinner often."

———————•◦•———————

Martin reached for a piece of leather that hung on a hook above him and spotted Ruth outside the window, talking with Esta. When Ruth bent down and gave the little girl a hug, he thought about how well she got along with Abe's children. No doubt she would make a good mother someday, and he hoped the children she had would be his.

"What's so interesting?"

Martin whirled around at the sound of Abe's resonant voice. "Huh?"

"Out the window. You've been holding that piece of leather and staring out the window for several minutes."

Martin's face heated up, and he dropped the hunk of leather to the workbench. "I. . .uh. . .just noticed Ruth Hostettler's here. She's in the yard, talking to Esta."

Abe moved over to the window and nudged Martin's arm. "You're in love with her, jah?"

Martin couldn't deny it, yet he didn't want to admit it either. "Would you mind answering a personal question?" he asked.

"What do you want to know?"

"I was wondering when you first knew you were in love with Alma and how long you waited until you asked her to marry you."

Abe chuckled. "I can't imagine why you'd want to know that."

Martin glanced out the window again. He hoped Ruth would drop by the harness shop and say hello.

Abe tapped Martin on the back. "Are you gonna stand there all day staring out the window, or did you want to hear the answer to your question about when I fell in love with Alma?"

Martin pulled his gaze back to Abe. "I do want to hear it."

Abe motioned to a couple of wooden stools. "Have a seat, and I'll tell you about it."

Martin listened as Abe told the story of how he'd taken an interest in Alma soon after she and her folks had moved to Ohio from Pennsylvania. "When Alma turned sixteen and started attending some of the young people's functions, I asked if I could court her. Soon after our first date, I knew I was in love. Two years later, I asked if I could marry her," Abe said, dropping his gaze to the floor.

Martin figured talking about Alma must have conjured up some nostalgic feelings. He wished he hadn't brought up the subject of Abe and Alma's courtship. "Sorry if I've upset you."

"I miss my wife, but it's good for me to talk about her." Abe touched his chest. "Keeps her memory alive in here."

Martin nodded solemnly. If he were married to Ruth and lost her the way Abe had lost Alma, he didn't know how he could go on living. No wonder Abe slept so much when he wasn't working. It was probably the only way he could deal with his grief.

"Want my advice, Martin?" Abe asked as he stood.

"Jah, sure."

"If you're in love with Ruth, don't let her get away. Don't waste a single moment you have together."

Martin's forehead wrinkled. "Are you saying I shouldn't wait to ask her to marry me?"

"That's got to be your decision. But if it were me, I wouldn't wait too long." Abe lifted his shoulders in a brief shrug. "One never knows what the future holds. One never knows how much time they have left on this earth."

"You're right, Abe. Danki for the good advice. I'll be thinking on what you said."

A few seconds later, the shop door opened, and Ruth stuck her head inside. "I'm on my way to work, so I can't stay," she said, smiling at Martin. "But I wanted to say hello."

"Glad you did. It's always nice to see you." Martin moved toward the door. "I had a good time with you at the pond last Saturday," he whispered.

She nodded. "I enjoyed myself too."

"Maybe we can do it again sometime soon."

"That'd be nice." She glanced toward her horse and buggy, parked outside the harness shop. "Guess I'd better go."

Martin fought the urge to hug her; he knew it wouldn't be appropriate. Especially with Abe right behind him, no doubt watching and listening to their conversation. "See you soon, Ruth," he said. "Have a good day."

As Martin returned to his workbench, Abe shot him a knowing look.

Martin grabbed a hunk of leather and set right to work. Every time he saw Ruth, he fell deeper in love with her. How long would he have to wait until he felt free to ask her to marry him?

———◆◆◆———

As Ruth headed down the road toward the Schrocks' place, the pleasant scent of wildflowers growing in the woods wafted through the open buggy flap, and she drew in a deep, satisfying breath. She was glad she had been able to stop by the harness shop to see Martin.

Ruth's thoughts turned to Esta. She'd been pleased to see how well the child was doing. From what she could tell, the puppy had adjusted to its new home. As time allowed, she hoped to continue her visits to the Wengerds' to check on Abe's children.

Ruth was about to turn into the Schrocks' place when a black truck whizzed past, causing the horse to whinny and veer to the right. She hadn't been able to get a good look at the driver, but she thought he was wearing a baseball cap and sunglasses.

"Sure wish folks wouldn't drive so fast," she muttered.

A few minutes later, she spotted a horse and buggy up ahead. It didn't take her long to realize it was Martha's rig. Ruth followed as the horse and buggy turned to the right and headed up the Schrocks' driveway past the sign reading SCHROCKS' HOME COOKING.

"How'd your visit with Esta go?" Martha asked as she stepped up to Ruth moments later.

"It went fine." Ruth squinted. "What are you doing here? I thought you weren't coming to speak with Irene."

44

"Changed my mind. Since my dog business isn't doing too well yet, I figured I could use some extra money."

"I doubt Irene will need us both."

"Then I guess she'll have to choose between us."

Ruth frowned. She didn't think it would be fair to put Irene in that position, and Martha should have realized it too. "Never mind. You can have the job."

Martha shook her head. "I won't work for Irene if you want to. I just figured since you already have a job—"

"You're right. I don't need two jobs. I'd much rather spend my free time with Martin—and of course little Esta, who still needs extra encouragement."

"Speaking of which, is the pup doing okay?"

"Seems to be."

"I'm glad." Martha motioned to the Schrocks' house. "Guess I'd better go see what Irene has to say about me helping her."

Ruth gave Martha a hug. "See you this evening."

"Jah. Have a good day." Ruth climbed back in her buggy, feeling good about things. Martha would be earning some extra money, Esta was getting along well with Winkie, and Martin was definitely showing interest. This was the beginning of a very good day.

Chapter 7

One early summer morning, Grace entered the barn to look for Martha. She drew in a deep breath, enjoying the pleasant, prickly aroma of fresh hay as she leaned against one of the wooden beams. She felt the baby kick and placed one hand against her bulging stomach. "I wonder if you're a *buwe* or a *maedel*."

"Are you talking to yourself or me?"

Grace turned and saw Martha heading toward her. "I was talking to my boppli, wondering if it's a boy or a girl."

Martha grinned. "I think Anna's hoping for a maedel."

"Jah, and speaking of Anna, I was wondering if you could watch her so Mom and I can go to town to get some material for baby things."

"What time will you be back?"

"Soon after lunch, I expect."

Martha nodded. "That should be okay, since I don't have to be at Irene's until three o'clock."

"I'd forgotten about your new job. Would you prefer that we take Anna with us?"

"I'm sure you'll be back in plenty of time. Besides, I enjoy spending time with Anna. It'll be better than being out here alone, fretting over my failing business."

"Things aren't going so well with your plans to raise dogs, are they?"

Martha shook her head and handed Grace a breeders magazine. "I was reading this and spotted an ad about trading dogs to strengthen the breeding lines. I might consider doing such a thing if I had some extra dogs to trade."

"I'm sorry Flo still isn't pregnant."

"I may allow Heidi to get pregnant again soon," Martha confided, "since she did so well with her first batch of puppies."

"She did okay giving birth, but things went a bit sour after that."

"You mean with the one puppy dying?"

"Jah."

"That was too bad, especially since you had just said Anna could have the pup."

"Hopefully nothing like that will happen again," Grace said firmly.

"I'm sure everything will work out."

Grace touched Martha's arm. "I'd better head back to the house. As soon as Mom's ready to leave for town, I'll send Anna to the barn."

Martha held up the magazine in her hand. "Thought I'd sit on a bale of straw and thumb through the rest of this. Then I need to get busy and clean out the kennels. Maybe Anna can help."

Grace started for the door but turned back. "We'll probably stop by the bakeshop and see Ruth while we're in town. Is there anything special you'd like me to bring home as a thank-you for watching Anna?"

Martha shook her head. "No payment's needed. But if you're stopping at the bakeshop, I wouldn't turn down a couple of lemon-filled doughnuts."

Grace chuckled. "Consider it done."

Martha had just started cleaning Heidi's cage when Anna darted into the barn. "Mama said I get to spend the morning helping you!"

Martha smiled. "It's a good thing too, because there's lots of work to be done. I'm in need of a big helper like you."

"What do you want me to do?"

"All the cages need to be hosed out."

Anna's forehead wrinkled. "That's a dirty, smelly job, and Mama wouldn't like it if I got wet."

"How about if I do the hosing? When I'm done, you can put clean straw in the dogs' beds."

"Okay."

Martha motioned to a bale of straw. "If you'd like to have a seat over there, we can visit while I work."

"I hope Heidi has some more puppies soon. I liked playing with 'em," Anna said as she flopped onto the straw.

"You can play with Esta's puppy whenever you go over to the Wengerds'."

Crack! The window shattered, and a small canister crashed to the floor. Anna screamed, and a terrible odor permeated the barn.

Martha's eyes began to water. She grabbed Anna's hand and ushered her quickly out the door.

"How come the window broke? And what was that awful smell?" Anna asked, rubbing her eyes.

Martha glanced around the yard. No one was in sight. "I think it was a homemade stink bomb. We'd better let Cleon and your grandpa know about this right away."

Cleon had just begun to sand a new chair when the door to Roman's shop flew open. Martha and Anna rushed into the room.

"I think the attacks are beginning again! Someone just threw a stink bomb through one of the barn windows!" Martha panted.

Roman looked up from the hunk of wood he'd been sanding. "Are you sure about that?"

"Of course I'm sure. I heard the window break and saw the cylinder hit the floor, and Anna and I definitely smelled the putrid stench."

Anna nodded vigorously. "It smelled like rotten eggs, and it made my eyes water."

Cleon dropped the sandpaper he'd been using and rushed across the room. "Are you all right?"

"She's fine. It just took us by surprise," Martha replied before Anna could respond.

"Did you see anyone?" Roman asked, moving over to Martha.

Martha shook her head.

"It was probably some prankster. I heard some English kids have been fooling around the area again, doing all sorts of goofy things."

"I don't know. I think maybe. . ." Martha's voice trailed off when she noticed Anna's wide-eyed expression. "I'd better go back to the barn and get things aired out."

"I'll take care of that," Roman said before he rushed out the door.

Cleon picked Anna up and seated her in the chair behind Roman's desk. "Why don't you draw awhile?" He handed Anna a tablet and pencil, then moved toward the door and motioned Martha to follow.

"I think it would be best if we didn't say anything to Grace about this," he whispered. "With her expecting our first boppli this fall, I don't want her getting upset or worrying that this could be another attack on her family."

"I won't mention it, but Anna might blab."

"I'll have a talk with her," Cleon said with a nod.

Martha's fingers curled around the doorknob. "Guess I'd better go talk to my daed and make sure he doesn't say anything either."

Ruth had just finished waiting on an English woman when Mom and Grace showed up at the bakeshop, chattering about the baby things they had bought that morning.

"Anna's excited about being the baby's big sister," Grace said as she stepped up to the bakery counter, wearing a smile that stretched ear to ear. "I think she's hoping for a maedel."

"Not Cleon, though," Mom put in. "He told your daed that he'd like it to be a buwe."

Grace stroked her stomach. "It doesn't matter to me whether it's a boy or a girl. I just want it to be born healthy."

"We're all praying for that," Mom agreed.

Ruth smiled despite the pang of jealousy she fought. She wished she was starting a family. If Luke hadn't been so undependable and secretive, she might be planning a fall wedding right now. Instead, she was in the early stages of courtship with Martin, and it could be another year or two before he proposed, if at all.

"Do you have any lemon-filled doughnuts?" Grace asked, breaking into Ruth's thoughts. "I promised to bring some home for Martha."

Ruth pointed to the section in the bakery case where the doughnuts were kept. "Still have half a dozen lemon ones left."

"I'll take them all," Grace said with a wink in Mom's direction. "That way there'll be enough for our menfolk to have some."

Mom chuckled. "Better give the doughnuts to the men before Martha gets her hands on the tasty treats, or there might not be any left."

Ruth reached into the case and removed the last of the lemon-filled doughnuts, placed them inside a small cardboard box, and handed it to Mom. She'd just put the money into the cash register when the bell above the door jangled and a red-haired English man stepped into the room.

"Hello, ladies," Gary Walker said, stepping between Grace and Mom. "Have you come for some sweets to make you sweeter?"

Mom blinked a couple of times, and Grace grabbed the side of the counter, as if needing it for support. "Wh–what are you doing here?" she rasped. "I thought you had left Holmes County for good."

He wiggled his eyebrows. "I did go to Pennsylvania for a while, Gracie, but I decided with all the interesting people here, I needed to come back and do a few more stories."

Grace's face turned paler than goat's milk as she swayed unsteadily. Ruth feared her sister might pass out, so she skirted around the counter and slipped one arm around Grace's waist. "There's a stool in the back room. Would you like to sit awhile?"

Grace shook her head and moved toward the door. "I'll be fine. I just need some fresh air."

Mom scurried to the door and was about to open it, but Gary beat her to it. "May I help you outside to your buggy?" he asked, looking at Grace.

"I can make it on my own," she mumbled.

Gary looked her up and down. His gaze came to rest on her stomach. "Well, well," he said with a smirk. "When's the blessed event?"

Grace hurried out the door behind Mom.

Gary lifted his shoulders in an exaggerated shrug as he turned to look at Ruth. "That sister of yours sure is testy."

Ruth clenched her fingers into tight balls and moved back to the bakery counter. "May I help you with something?"

He sauntered over to the counter and glanced at the baked goods, then looked back at her. "Nothing looks quite as good as the one selling these sweet treats. How'd you like to have supper with me after you get off work?"

Gary's piercing gaze sent shivers up Ruth's back, and she shook her head.

"Ah, come on, Ruthie. I just want to get to know you a little better." Gary leaned across the counter, and the spicy scent of his aftershave caused Ruth to pull back, feeling like a turtle being poked with a sharp stick.

"You're sure jumpy," he said with a smirk. "I don't bite, you know."

Ruth's face heated up. "If you don't want anything, then—"

"Oh, I want something, all right, but it's not one of these," he said, motioning to the pastries.

Ruth swallowed against the bitter taste of bile rising in her throat. This man frightened her. No wonder Grace got so upset whenever Gary came around. She clasped her hands tightly behind her back to keep them from shaking.

Just then, Jake Clemons stepped out of the back room, where he and his wife did the baking. "Is there a problem here, Ruth?"

Before Ruth could reply, Gary looked at Jake and shook his head. "Nope. No problem at all. I just came in to get something for my sweet tooth." He pointed to a layer of maple bars. "I'll take two of those."

Ruth released a sigh and quickly filled the man's order. When Gary left the store, she turned to Jake with a grateful smile. "Thanks for coming to my rescue. That man makes me nervous."

Jake skimmed his fingers along his temples and into his receding blond hair. "If he ever bothers you again, please let me know."

"I will."

When Jake returned to the other room, Ruth leaned on the counter and closed her eyes. *Dear Lord, please don't let Gary Walker stay in town.*

Chapter 8

Hesh ow's it going in here?" Martha asked her father when she stepped into the barn and found him holding a spray can in one hand.

"I sprayed some of your mamm's room deodorizer around and opened all the windows. I think the smell will be gone before she and Grace get back from town." Dad's eyebrows pulled together in a frown. "I think it's best if they don't know about this. No point in causing them to worry for nothing."

"I'm in agreement with that, but I don't think this is nothing." Martha motioned to the shattered window across the room. "Someone deliberately threw that stink bomb into the barn. If it's the same person who did the other things to us, then we have every reason to be worried."

Dad set the can of deodorizer on a shelf. "Regardless of who's responsible for this, I don't want the rest of the family getting all upset. Especially not your mamm. She's been through enough these past several months."

"I don't think the attacks affected Mom nearly as much as they did Grace," Martha said. "With her being in a family way, it wouldn't be good for her to have more stress added."

Dad nodded solemnly. "Unfortunately, most of Grace's upsets have been of her own doing."

Martha didn't argue. She had a hunch Dad hadn't completely forgiven Grace for leaving home when she was a teenager or for keeping her previous marriage and the birth of her daughter, Anna, a secret for so long.

"How's that new job you've got with Irene Schrock working out?" Dad asked, redirecting their conversation.

"It's okay." Martha nodded toward the back of the barn, where the inside section of her dog kennels had been built. "With summer being here, more tour buses are scheduling dinners at the Schrocks'. Even though Carolyn's able to help again, Irene asked if I would continue to work for her. So once I get enough money saved up, I'm going to buy a few more dogs. Maybe a couple of poodles this time."

Dad grunted. "Poodles are too prissy to suit me. Besides, they yap too much."

"Maybe I should get a pair of hunting dogs. From what I've read in the breeders magazine, they seem to have more puppies than some of the smaller breeds."

"Now that makes good sense." Dad removed his straw hat and slapped the brim of it against his knee, sending sawdust blowing off his pants in every direction. "Why don't you get some German shorthaired pointers? Then Cleon and I can do some pheasant hunting this fall."

"Since when have you ever gone hunting?"

"Went all the time when I was a boy. Might be nice to try it again."

"I'd like to go hunting sometime," Martha said.

"Hunting's for men, not girls."

"I'm not a girl, Dad. I turned nineteen a few months ago, remember?"

He grunted. "That may be so, but you've never shot a gun. It wouldn't be safe for you to hunt."

Martha's defenses rose. Even though she'd never shot a gun, she didn't think it would be too hard to learn. She couldn't help but wonder if Dad was disappointed because he'd never had a son. Maybe that was why Dad and Cleon got along so well.

"If Cleon doesn't want to hunt, I could see if Abe would like to go," Dad continued. "Might do Abe some good to get out in the fields and away from his harness shop awhile."

"Ruth mentioned that Abe's been sleeping a lot. Do you think it's to avoid thinking about his loss?"

Dad nodded. "Everyone deals with grief in their own way, but it's my job as Abe's friend to help him." He took a seat on a bale of straw, and Martha did the same.

"That's what friends are for," she agreed. "To encourage each other and help during times of need."

Dad pulled a piece of straw from the bale he was sitting on and slipped it between his teeth. "Between your job at Irene's and raising your dogs, I guess you'll be plenty busy all summer."

"Jah."

"Doesn't leave much time for socializing."

Martha merely shrugged in reply.

"A woman your age ought to be courting by now." He eyed her curiously. "Have you got your sights set on any particular fellow?"

Martha cringed. She did have an interest in someone, but she didn't dare say so. Dad would have a conniption if he knew she'd come to care for Luke Friesen. Especially since he thought Luke might be the one responsible for the attacks against them.

Dad nudged Martha's arm. "Is there someone you're interested in?"

"I'm too busy with other things to be worried about having a boyfriend," she said, carefully choosing her words.

"Guess there's still time for you to find the right man."

"Jah."

When Martha heard the rumble of buggy wheels outside, she stood. "Do you suppose that's Mom and Grace back from town? If so, they didn't stay very long. I figured they wouldn't be back until this afternoon."

"Only one way to find out," Dad said, rising to his feet. "Let's go have a look-see."

As Grace climbed out of the buggy, her legs shook so hard she could barely stand. All the way home, she couldn't stop thinking about Gary showing up in town. When he'd left a few months ago, she had hoped they'd seen the last of him. Her plans to treat Mom to lunch at the Farmstead

Restaurant had been forgotten when Gary came into the bakeshop. All she'd wanted to do was go home.

"I didn't think you'd be back so early," Martha said as she and Dad stepped out of the barn. "Figured you'd have lunch after you finished shopping."

"We ran into that reporter fellow at the bakeshop." Mom took hold of Grace's arm. "After that, Grace didn't feel like eating."

Dad's lips compressed into a thin line. "What's that guy doing back in town? I thought he'd left Holmes County for good."

"He said he's decided to do a few more stories on the Amish in our area." Grace's voice trembled as she spoke. It was all she could do to keep from crying. She'd been especially emotional lately and figured it had to do with her changing hormones. The distress she was dealing with right now, however, had nothing to do with her pregnancy. She was worried that Gary had come back to the area to fulfill his promise to get even with her for breaking up with him after they'd dated awhile during her rumschpringe years. Grace's life was just getting back to normal, and she didn't think she could deal with more attacks on her family.

Dad looked at Martha, and they exchanged worried glances. "Maybe you should get Anna so Grace can go home and rest," he said.

Martha nodded. "That's a good idea."

"Where is Anna?" Grace asked. "Is she in the barn?"

"She's at the woodworking shop with Cleon," Dad said.

"What's she doing there? I've told her not to bother Cleon when he's working."

Dad rocked back and forth on his heels. "She. . .uh. . .came out there with Martha to talk to us."

Grace frowned as she turned to face her sister. "I thought you were going to keep Anna entertained in the barn, not haul her out to the shop to bother the men."

"I didn't *haul* her out there. We went there because—" Martha stopped speaking and glanced over at Dad.

"What's going on, Roman?" Mom asked. "You and Martha are acting so *missdrauisch*. Is there something you're not telling us?"

"We're not acting suspicious," he was quick to say. "It's just that—well, we had a little incident in the barn a while ago, and I didn't want to worry you."

"What kind of incident?"

"Someone threw a stink bomb through one of the barn windows, and Martha brought Anna out to the shop to tell us about it."

Mom hurried into the barn, and the rest of them followed.

Mom's nose twitched. "I do smell something funny in here."

"I thought I had the barn aired out pretty good, but I guess the putrid odor will linger awhile." Dad motioned across the room. "I'll have the window fixed before the day's out."

Grace's stomach clenched as she gripped her mother's hand. "This was Gary's work. I'm sure of it."

Dad shook his head. "*Sell kann ich mir gaar net eibilde.*"

"What do you mean you can't conceive of that? Gary's back in Holmes County. He promised to get even with me someday, and I'm sure he's the one who did all those horrible things to us before he left for Pennsylvania." Grace's knees nearly buckled, and she leaned against a wooden beam for support. "I think Gary may have come here and thrown the stink bomb into the barn before he went to town. I–I'm afraid if he's not stopped, he'll continue to do more things."

"You're worried for nothing, Grace. I'm guessing that stink bomb was thrown by some prankster," Dad said.

"You said that before, when the attacks first began. But things only got worse." Grace drew in a deep breath to settle her nerves. "Anna or I could have been killed when our house was set on fire. I don't think that was done by any prankster."

"She's right, Roman," Mom put in. "Whoever did most of those things to our property was out for more than a good time."

Dad stared at the ground, and a muscle in the side of his cheek quivered. "Cleon and I will keep an eye on things; I can promise you that."

Grace shrugged and headed out of the barn. "I need to get Anna and put her down for a nap."

"I'll do that," Martha said. "Mom, if you'd like to walk Grace up to her house, I'll be there with Anna real soon."

Mom nodded, and they started up the driveway toward Grace and Cleon's new home, Mom leading Grace by the arm.

———————◆•◆———————

Martin hurried down the sidewalk toward the bakeshop. He'd come to Berlin to pick up some supplies for the harness shop, and since Abe had told him to take all the time he needed, he figured he may as well stop at the bakeshop and say hello to Ruth. He might even pick up a few doughnuts and take them to Abe.

When he stepped into the bakeshop, the pleasant aroma of freshly baked pastries flooded his senses and made his stomach rumble. He was pleased to see that no customers were there at the moment, but then he spotted Ruth sitting behind the counter with her head resting in the palms of her hands.

"Ruth, what's wrong?" he asked, rushing over to the counter. "Do you have a *koppweh?*"

Ruth lifted her head, and his heart clenched when he saw the weary look on her face.

"I don't have a headache, but I have had a rough morning," Ruth said, rising to her feet.

"What happened?"

"That reporter, Gary Walker, is back in town. He came into the bakeshop a while ago, while Grace and Mom were here."

Martin pursed his lips. "Grace used to date that fellow, right?"

Ruth nodded. "She thinks he's the one responsible for all those acts of vandalism that were done at our place."

"What do you think?"

"I—I'm not sure, but I do know that Gary is a troublesome fellow."

"Did he do or say anything to bother you?"

Her gaze dropped to the floor. "Well—"

"What did he say?"

"He just gave me a hard time, but Jake put a stop to it."

"What exactly did the reporter say to you?"

Ruth's face flushed the color of ripe cherries. "He wanted me to have supper with him after I got off work today."

Martin's spine went rigid, and he clenched and unclenched his fingers. He had enough to be concerned about, worrying whether Luke was still interested in Ruth. He didn't need some fancy-talking Englisher chasing after her.

"I wouldn't have gone with Gary, even if Jake hadn't come into the room," Ruth was quick to say. "So you needn't look so concerned."

"How long ago did the reporter leave the bakeshop?"

"Twenty minutes or so."

"Maybe he's still in town." Martin turned toward the door.

"Where are you going?"

"To see if I can find him."

"What for?"

Martin stopped walking and turned to face her. "I think it might be good if I had a talk with him—asked him to stop bothering you."

Ruth dashed around the counter. "Oh no! Please don't do that."

"Why not?"

"I don't trust the man. If Gary is the one who did those attacks, then he could be dangerous."

"I'm not afraid."

"Well I am." Ruth clutched his arm, and tears glistened in her eyes. "Please don't go looking for him."

"All right, I won't. But if he ever bothers you again, I want to know about it."

Chapter 9

Cleon couldn't believe his eyes. Sometime during the night, Roman's shop, house, and barn had been covered with long strips of toilet paper.

He spotted Roman standing outside his shop, shaking his head and muttering, "I don't have time for this. Don't have time at all."

"I wonder if the same person who threw the stink bomb through the barn window did all this," Cleon said, motioning to the tangle of toilet paper draped over the shop.

Roman grunted. "I don't know, but I think whoever did it must be a smoker."

"How do you know?"

Roman reached into his shirt pocket and withdrew a pack of cigarettes. "Found these on the ground near our back porch. I'm thinking that whoever hung toilet paper all over our buildings must have dropped his cigarettes." Roman frowned deeply. "I told the women yesterday that I thought the stink bomb was the result of a prankster. But Grace thinks it might have been done by Gary Walker, that reporter who likes to write articles about our people." He grunted. "Want to know what I really think?"

Cleon nodded.

"I believe Luke may have done this, as well as thrown the stink bomb yesterday."

"What makes you think that?"

"I've smelled smoke on his clothes a time or two, and since he doesn't care for me—"

"But he could have smoke on his clothes just from hanging around other folks who smoke," Cleon interrupted.

Roman made a sweeping gesture toward the mess above them. "Either way, he still could have been involved in this."

"If you're convinced Luke's the one who did this, then maybe you should talk to him or his folks about it."

"I've thought about that, but I'm not sure if I should."

"Why not?"

"If I speak with Luke, it might give him some sort of satisfaction to know he's got me riled. And if I talk to his folks, it might upset them too much." Roman reached up and snatched a strand of toilet paper from the roof. "Guess I'd better get this disaster cleaned up before we begin work for the day. Judith was pretty distressed when she woke up and saw the mess. I don't want it hanging around all day to remind her of what happened."

"If you have something you need to get done in the shop, I can take care of getting the toilet paper down," Cleon offered.

Roman shook his head. "Nothing pressing. If we clean this up together, we'll get to work that much quicker."

"Sounds good to me." Cleon shielded his eyes from the glare of the sun and stared in the direction of his home. "Grace was quite disturbed last night about the stink bomb episode, not to mention seeing that reporter again. I think it would be good if we get this cleaned up before she has a chance to see it."

———————◆◆◆———————

Grace held Anna's hand as they headed down the driveway toward her folks' house. She hadn't slept well. Had Gary really come back to Holmes County to write more stories, or did he have evil on his mind? Were the attacks some sort of test to see how much her family could endure? *Maybe a good talk with Mom over a cup of tea might make me feel better.*

She gritted her teeth and tried to focus on something positive—the cloudless sky overhead, the emerald grass beneath her feet, the bounty of multihued flowers in bloom, a warbling bluebird calling to its mate. The babe in her womb kicked just then, and she smiled. She had good things to think about, and as the Bible reminded in Philippians 4:8, she would try to think on those things.

"Can we go see Esta today?" Anna asked, giving Grace's hand a tug. "I wanna see how Winkie's doing."

"Maybe after lunch."

As they neared her folks' place, Grace noticed a strip of toilet paper hanging from a branch in the maple tree. Her gaze traveled around the yard. Had Mom and Dad been the victims of a TP party? If so, it seemed odd that there was just one strip of toilet paper hanging from the tree. "That's sure *fremm*," she murmured.

"What's strange, Mama?" Anna asked as she tromped up the back steps.

"It's nothing for you to worry about."

When they entered the house, Grace found her mother sitting at the kitchen table with her Bible open and a cup of tea in her hand.

"Wie geht's?" Mom asked as Grace took a seat at the table and Anna dropped to the floor beside a milky white kitten.

"I'm feeling a little better than yesterday." Grace reached for the teapot sitting in the center of the table and poured herself some tea.

"You looked so pale and shaken when we returned from Berlin yesterday. I was worried about you."

Grace glanced over at her daughter, who sat cross-legged on the floor with the kitten in her lap. "Anna, why don't you take the kitten out to the porch and play with her there."

"Why can't I stay here?"

"Outside's a better place for the kitten."

Anna clambered to her feet and headed out the door.

Mom pushed a jar of honey in Grace's direction. "With the boppli coming soon, you need to get plenty of rest and remain calm."

Grace added a spoonful of honey to her tea. "It's hard to relax knowing Gary is back and might have been the one who threw the stink bomb into Dad's barn."

Mom nodded. "Did you see the mess we woke up to?"

"What mess was that?"

"Someone strung toilet paper all over the house, barn, and your daed's woodworking shop."

"I saw a piece of toilet paper hanging from a branch in the maple tree, but that was all."

"The men cleaned it up before they went to work this morning."

Grace shivered and leaned back in the chair, her thoughts racing.

"Are you cold? Would you like one of my shawls to drape around your shoulders?" Mom asked with a look of concern.

Grace shook her head. "I'm not shivering because I'm cold. I'm afraid Gary might have come back to continue harassing our family. The stink bomb and TP mess could be just the beginning."

"I hope not." Mom lowered her voice, even though Anna was no longer in the room. "Your daed mentioned that Luke dropped a hammer during the work frolic on your new house and that it almost hit Ruth. Did you hear about that?"

Grace shook her head, then pushed her chair aside and stood.

"Where are you going?"

"I think I should make another trip to Berlin to see if I can find Gary. If he's hanging around town, I'm going to have a talk with him."

"Ach, Grace, I don't think that's a good idea. And I don't think Cleon would like you going into town alone—especially if he knew what you had in mind."

"I won't go alone. If you're able to watch Anna, I'll see if Martha's willing to ride along."

"I guess I could watch Anna, but—"

"Where is that little sister of mine?"

"Out in the barn as usual."

"I'll go see if she's free." Grace rushed out the door before Mom had a chance to respond.

———◆●◆———

Since there was a lull between customers, Ruth decided it was a good time to clean the outside glass of the bakery case, where fingerprints from customers were always a problem. She enjoyed her job at the bakeshop but looked forward to the day when she became a wife and mother. Cooking, cleaning, and wiping children's runny noses would be more rewarding than waiting on impatient customers all day.

Ruth squirted liquid cleaner on the front of the glass and began wiping it with a clean rag, but her thoughts were on Martin and his gentle, caring ways. She was quickly falling in love with him and hoped the feeling was mutual. *Will Martin ask me to marry him someday? I'd say yes if he did.*

She smiled, picturing Martin's deep dimples and the genuine smile he so often gave her. *If we were to marry, I wonder if our kinner would have his cute little dimples.*

The telephone rang, and Ruth's musings were halted. Someone probably wanted to place a bakery order.

A few minutes later, she hung up the phone and had just slid a tray of maple bars into the bakery case when she heard a man clear his throat. She looked up and saw Gary Walker standing on the other side of the counter, staring at her with a look so intense it made her toes curl inside her shoes. "Y–you're back," she stammered.

"Sure am," he said with a twisted grin.

She gestured to the baked goods inside the case. "Do you want more maple bars?"

"No, but I wouldn't mind a strong cup of coffee."

"We don't serve coffee here, just baked goods."

He raked his fingers through the back of his thick auburn hair. "How about you and me having a cup of coffee somewhere? Maybe we could go to that restaurant on the other side of town where your sister used to work."

She shook her head. "I can't leave the bakeshop. My boss wouldn't like it if I left the front counter unattended."

Gary placed both hands against the display case and leaned toward her. *So much for cleaning the glass.*

"You do get breaks, don't you?" he asked.

She nodded and leaned away from the disgusting odor of cigarette smoke that made her want to sneeze. She hadn't noticed a smoky smell on him before. Maybe his spicy aftershave had covered it up.

"Tell me when your break is, and we'll meet wherever you like."

Ruth's mouth felt so dry she had to swallow several times in order to speak. "Wh–why would you want to meet me for coffee?"

"I'd like to talk to you about some things, and it would be easier to do it away from here."

She looked over her shoulder, hoping Jake would come into the room, but she figured he probably couldn't hear the conversation over the noisy mixer running in the back room.

"I don't believe we have anything to talk about," she said through tight lips.

He leaned so close she could feel his sultry breath blowing against her face. "You'd be surprised how much we might have to talk about."

Ruth closed the sliding door on her side of the bakery case. "If you'll excuse me, I have work to do."

Gary chuckled. "From what I can tell, I'm your only customer right now. Don't you think I deserve your undivided attention?"

Ruth gripped the edge of the counter so hard her fingers turned numb. "If you didn't come here to buy anything, then I'd appreciate it if you'd leave."

"I'll take a maple bar."

"Just one?"

"Yep." He thumped his stomach. "Don't want to get fat, or pretty women like you may not find me attractive."

Ruth clenched her teeth, placed a maple bar on a square of waxed paper, and handed it to him. "That will be fifty cents."

He paid her, then bit into the maple bar and smacked his lips. "This tastes almost as sweet as your big sister's lips." He gave her a flirty wink. "How about you? Have you ever been kissed by an English man?"

Ruth heard the echo of her heartbeat in her head.

An English couple entered the bakeshop. Gary grunted and stepped aside as they approached the counter.

"May I help you?" Ruth asked.

The man nodded. "We'd like a dozen chocolate doughnuts and an angel food cake."

As Ruth reached into the bakery case to remove the items, she looked up and saw Gary heading for the door. "I'll come back when you're not so busy," he called over his shoulder.

Ruth cringed. The last thing she wanted was to see that man again!

Chapter 10

When Martha pulled her buggy up to the hitching rail near the back of the bakeshop, she pointed to Gary Walker as he came around the corner of the building. "There he is. Are you sure you want to speak with him, sister?"

Grace nodded despite her sweaty hands and rapidly beating heart.

"I'll park the buggy and go with you."

"I think it would be better if I speak with Gary alone. Why don't you wait for me inside the bakeshop?"

Martha's forehead wrinkled. "I don't think—"

"I'll be fine."

Martha shrugged and stepped down from the buggy.

As her sister headed for the bakeshop, Grace hurried toward Gary, who was almost to his car.

He whirled around to face her. "You following me, Gracie?"

When she opened her mouth to reply, the only thing that came out was a little squeak.

"I wouldn't think a married woman who's expecting a baby would be running down the street chasing after other men."

"I'm not. I mean, I just wanted to ask you a question."

He leaned on the hood of his car and folded his arms. "About what?"

"I was wondering how long you plan to stay in Holmes County."

"As long as it takes."

"For what?"

"For me to write the stories I'm after." He leveled her a penetrating look that sent shivers up her spine. "Are you feeling the need to check up on me, Gracie?"

She swallowed hard, unsure of how to respond.

"I didn't come back to Holmes County to make your life miserable, if that's what you're worried about."

The urge to ask if he had toilet-papered their buildings and thrown the stink bomb into the barn was strong, but Grace figured he might take satisfaction in knowing she was afraid. "I would think you could find other things to write about than the Holmes County Amish," she said as a horse and buggy rumbled by and turned into the cheese store parking lot across the street.

Gary leaned away from his car and moved closer to her. "None quite as interesting as you."

Before she could comment, he snickered and said, "I think your sister who works at the bakeshop is pretty interesting too."

Grace's fingers pressed into her palms until the nails dug into her flesh. "Stay away from Ruth."

"If I don't?"

"I'll tell the sheriff what I think you're up to."

Gary snorted and slapped his knee. "It's a free country, Gracie. I have every right to visit the bakeshop whenever I get the urge for something sweet. Besides, it's not like the sheriff's going to arrest me for buying a few doughnuts."

"The sheriff's aware of the break-ins and vandalism that went on at our place several months ago. He told my dad that he plans to keep an eye on things."

"I told you before that I had nothing to do with any of those occurrences." Gary flung open the car door. "Now if you'll excuse me, I've got work to do."

"That man makes me so angry," Grace fumed as Gary pulled away from the curb. "I'm sure he's the one responsible for those attacks, and he's probably trying to make it look like it's someone else."

"I can't believe you let Grace speak to that reporter by herself," Ruth said after Martha came into the shop and told her what Grace had decided to do.

"I tried to talk her out of it, but she wouldn't listen." Martha groaned. "You know how stubborn our big sister can be when she makes up her mind about something."

"Jah, I know." Ruth skirted around the front counter and hurried over to the window near the door. She craned her neck to see up the street but saw no sign of Grace or Gary.

"Do you want me to go after her?" Martha asked.

"She probably wouldn't like it. Besides, I'm sure Gary wouldn't do anything foolish right here in town." Ruth moved back to the bakery case, and Martha followed.

When Grace stepped into the bakeshop a few minutes later, her face looked pale, and she shuffled across the room as if she had no strength in her legs.

Ruth rushed into the back room and grabbed a stool. "You'd better sit down."

Grace nodded and did as she was told. "I held up pretty well while I was talking to Gary, but after he left, my knees felt so shaky I thought I might not make it here."

"What did the man have to say?" Martha asked.

"I asked how long he plans to stay in Holmes County, and he said as long as it takes to get the stories he wants. Then he mentioned Ruth, and I threatened to notify the sheriff if he doesn't stay away from her."

Ruth's heart slammed into her chest. "I hope Gary doesn't think I'm interested in him, because I'm surely not."

Martha looked over at Grace. "Did you ask if he knew about the stink bomb or the toilet-papering?"

Grace shook her head. "I didn't want him to know what I suspect. I think it gives him pleasure to know I'm scared."

"You shouldn't have spoken to him alone." Martha pursed her lips. "You should have let me go with you."

Grace stared at her hands clasped tightly in her lap.

"The stink bomb and the toilet paper mess could have been pranks like Dad mentioned," Ruth said. "I'll bet if we asked some of our neighbors, we'd find out that their places were toilet-papered too."

Martha touched Grace's shoulder. "I think we should go. You look all done in and need to get home, where you can rest."

Grace nodded and slipped off the stool.

As Ruth's sisters headed out the door, she offered up a prayer. *Lord, please be with my family—especially Grace.*

Cleon had just finished staining the legs of a table when Judith and Anna entered the woodworking shop.

"We brought you some lunch," Judith said, holding out two metal lunch boxes.

Roman moved away from the desk where he'd been doing paperwork and greeted her with a smile. "We appreciate that."

Cleon straightened and set his staining rag aside. "Where's Grace? She usually brings my meal if I don't go home for lunch."

"Mama went to town," Anna said.

Cleon's brows knit together as he looked over at Judith.

"She was upset when she found out about the toilet-papering. So she decided to go to Berlin, hoping she might see Gary Walker there."

"What?" Cleon's voice echoed in his ears. "She went to town alone—to speak with that man?"

Judith shook her head. "She's not alone. Martha went with her."

"As if that's supposed to make me feel better. Doesn't my wife ever think things through? Must she always make decisions without asking my opinion or getting my approval?"

Judith glanced down at Anna, whose eyes were huge as saucers; then she looked back at Cleon and shook her head. "I think this discussion can wait, don't you?"

After seeing the frightened look on Anna's face, Cleon realized he had let his emotions get the better of him. He knelt on the floor in front of the child. "I'm sorry for yelling. I'm just worried about your mamm."

"Did Mama do somethin' wrong?" Anna's chin quivered as she stared up at Cleon.

"She didn't do anything wrong. I just wish she'd told me where she was going."

"Maybe you should go after her," Roman suggested as he tapped Cleon on the shoulder. "Just to be sure everything's okay."

Cleon stood. "You wouldn't mind? I know you have a lot of work going."

"Nothing I have to do here is as important as the safety of my girls. I know you won't get much work done if you stay here stewing over things."

"Danki. I'll have Grace and Martha back soon," Cleon called over his shoulder as he hurried out of the shop.

"I guess we'd better go too," Judith said. She steered Anna toward the door.

Judith and Anna had no more than left the shop when Bishop King showed up. "Wie geht's?" Roman asked.

"I'm doing all right. How about you?"

Roman blew out his breath in a huff that lifted the hair off his forehead. "There have been a couple of attacks here lately. At first I thought they were just pranks, but now I'm not so sure."

"What kind of attacks?" the bishop asked as he moved closer to Roman's desk.

"Someone tossed a stink bomb through one of the barn windows the other day. Then this morning we found toilet paper all over the house, barn, and my shop."

Bishop King compressed his lips. "Any idea who's to blame?"

"I can't be sure, but I found a half-empty pack of cigarettes lying next to the barn, and I've got a hunch whose it is."

"Who would that be?"

"Luke. I told you once before that I thought Luke might be upset with me for firing him. I wouldn't be a bit surprised if he's trying to get even."

"What makes you think the cigarettes are Luke's?"

Roman's eyes narrowed. "I smelled smoke on Luke a time or two when he was working for me."

The bishop raked his fingers through the ends of his beard. "Now that I think of it, not long ago, my son Toby made mention of smelling smoke on Luke."

"Remember the time Judith's clothesline was cut?"

"Jah."

"She found a pair of sunglasses on the ground not far from the line, and they turned out to be Luke's."

"Did he admit to cutting the line?"

"No, but—"

"Would you like me to speak with Luke?"

"Can you do it without letting him know I told you what I suspect?"

Bishop King nodded. "I'll feel him out—maybe tell him what's been going on here and see what kind of reaction I get."

"Sounds good. You'll let me know what he has to say?"

"Jah, sure." The bishop shifted from one foot to the other. "I'm a bit concerned about your attitude though, Roman."

"What do you mean?"

"Seems to me as if you're jumping to conclusions—judging Luke with no real evidence. Don't you think you should give him the benefit of the doubt?"

"I just think he's the one with the most likely reason to want to get even with me. If that's the case, it could be why he won't get baptized and join the church."

"The fact that Luke hasn't left the faith and gone English gives me hope that eventually he'll settle down and do what's expected of him. More than likely that will happen when he finds the right woman and decides to get married."

"Maybe so. I'd still appreciate you talking to him though."

"No problem." The bishop glanced around the room. "So do you have that set of dressers I ordered last month ready for me yet?"

"Sure do. We can load them into your buggy right now."

———————◆◆————————

Cleon had just begun hitching a horse to his rig when another horse trotted up the driveway, pulling a buggy. He realized right away that it was one of Roman's mares, so he hurried over to the barn and waited by the hitching rail until the horse came to a stop. "Are you okay?" he called to Grace through the open buggy flap.

She nodded, although he noticed that she looked exhausted.

Martha climbed down from the driver's side, and Cleon helped Grace out of the buggy. "Why'd you run off like that without telling me where you were going?"

"Because I was afraid you would say no." Grace spoke so softly he could barely hear the words.

"You're right, I would have. You're in no condition to go traipsing around after someone you *think* might be responsible for the things that have been done here these past two days."

"I needed to speak with Gary and see how long he plans to stay in Holmes County." She drew in a ragged breath. "It's not just what's been done here recently either. There were other attacks that took place when he was here before."

"So what did you find out?"

"Gary said he's come back to the area to write more stories and that he'll be here until they're done."

Cleon took hold of Grace's arm and looked over at Martha, who stood near the buggy with a concerned look on her face. "Would you let your folks know that you and Grace are home?"

Martha nodded. "Jah, sure."

"Oh, and would you see if Judith can keep Anna for the rest of the day? My *fraa* looks exhausted and needs to go to bed."

"Your wife will be just fine once she's had something to eat and has rested awhile, so there's no need for Mom to keep Anna," Grace argued.

Cleon slipped his arm around her waist. "I can't go back to work in your daed's shop unless I know you're resting."

71

Grace finally nodded, and Cleon felt relief. He might not be able to do anything about the vandalism that had been done at his in-laws' place, but he could take care of his wife.

Chapter 11

When Martha directed her buggy up Abe Wengerd's driveway, she spotted Martin walking toward the harness shop. She needed to be at Irene's by three o'clock but had decided to stop on her way and see how Esta was getting along with Winkie.

Martha halted the horse near Abe's barn and climbed out of the buggy. She was greeted by Esta, who had been in the yard playing with the puppy.

"Wie geht's?" Martha asked.

"I'm doin' good," Esta replied. "Just givin' Winkie some exercise."

Martha smiled. "Winkie's a cute name."

Esta nodded. "Anna chose it 'cause the pup likes to wink one eye."

"Jah, she told me."

"How come Anna didn't come with you? I like it when she comes over to play."

"I didn't invite her because I can't stay very long."

"Why not?"

"I'm on my way to work, and I'll need to leave soon." Martha bent down and stroked the puppy's ears. "I'm glad Winkie has a good home."

Esta nodded and scooped the little sheltie into her arms. "I'm takin' good care of him."

"I'm sure you are." Martha squeezed Esta's shoulder. "I'll try to bring Anna along the next time I come over."

"Okay."

As Martha started for her buggy, she spotted Luke coming out of Abe's harness shop, and her heart missed a beat. She wished she didn't feel so giddy every time she saw Luke. She was sure he had no interest in her. If Dad knew she had a crush on Luke, he wouldn't approve.

"Hello, Luke," she said as he approached. "How are you?"

"Fair to middlin'," he replied with a shrug. "And you?"

"Doing okay." She was tempted to mention the acts of vandalism earlier in the week but thought better of it, in case Luke was the one responsible. She hoped he wasn't. Even if Luke was angry because Dad had fired him, Martha couldn't imagine Luke being behind any of the things that had been done to her family. Dad had asked around the day after they'd discovered all of the toilet paper on their buildings, but none of their neighbors had been bothered. That made Martha wonder if more attacks would be forthcoming.

"How's the dog business going?" Luke asked, pulling her thoughts aside.

"Not so well. The female beagle I bought still isn't pregnant, but I'll be breeding Heidi and Fritz again when the time is right."

"Maybe you should sell off the beagles and buy some other breed of dog."

"I've thought of that, and I might put an ad in *The Budget* soon."

"Or you could try the *Bargain Hunter*," he suggested. "Might have better luck there."

"That's a good idea. Maybe I'll run an ad in both papers."

Luke moved away from the building. "Guess I'd better go. Just came by to check on a bridle Abe's making for my daed. Now I've got a delivery to make for John."

"How are things going with you working for him?" she asked.

"Compared to your daed, John's real easy to work for." He averted his gaze. "Guess I shouldn't be saying this, but working for your daed every day was like going to the dentist to get a root canal."

Martha bristled. As much as she liked Luke, she didn't care for him saying things against her dad. "From what I hear, you weren't so easy to work with either."

Luke shook his head. "Your daed didn't like that I had my own ideas about how things should be done. He blamed me for Steven Bates's cabinets falling off the wagon, and it wasn't even my fault."

"It doesn't matter who did what or who said what. My daed let you go and you should accept that."

His eyes narrowed. "Who says I'm not?"

"You wouldn't try to get even with Dad, would you?"

"No way. I'd never do that, no matter how much he might irritate me."

A sense of relief flooded Martha's soul. "I didn't think you would try to get even, but we've had a few more incidents at our place this week, so—"

"What's been done?"

"A stink bomb was thrown into our barn, and then our house, barn, and Dad's shop got toilet-papered."

Luke frowned. "Sounds like some pranksters to me. I heard there was some toilet-papering done at one of the schoolhouses near Berlin the other day."

"Dad thought it might be pranksters at first, but then he mentioned that he thought it could have been—"

"Me?"

She nodded.

"Puh! I've got better things to do than make stink bombs and spread TP all over the place." Luke started walking toward his buggy.

Martha was more certain than ever that Luke wasn't the one responsible for any of the attacks. The only question unanswered—who *was* responsible?

———————

As Martin headed down the road in his buggy, his stomach twisted as though it were tied in knots. He'd come to a decision about his relationship with Ruth, and this evening he planned to talk to her about it.

When he arrived at the Hostettlers', he spotted Ruth sitting in the glider under the maple tree in the backyard, reading a book. He halted the buggy, secured his horse to the hitching rail, and sprinted across the lawn.

"I'm surprised to see you," Ruth said as he approached her. "I didn't know you'd be coming by this evening."

He licked his lips, and the knot in his stomach tightened. "I thought I would surprise you."

"You did that, all right." She set the book aside and patted the cushion beside her. "Would you like to join me?"

Martin took a seat. "I. . .uh. . .need to talk to you about something." He removed his straw hat and twisted the edge of the brim.

"Are you all right? You seem kind of *naerfich*."

"I am feeling a bit nervous."

"How come?"

"Well. . .I. . ." He scooted a bit closer. "I know we haven't been courting very long, but I've come to care about you."

"I care about you too."

"Enough to be honest with me?"

"Of course."

He drummed his fingers along the armrest of the glider. "Remember that day at the pond when you said you knew about the truck Toby and Sadie found in the woods?"

She nodded.

"You acted like you knew who owned the truck, but you didn't seem to want to talk about it."

She stared at her lap, and her chin trembled slightly. "I. . .uh. . .do know who owns the truck, but I promised I wouldn't tell anyone."

"Does it belong to someone I know?"

"Jah."

He reached for her hand. "If we're going to have a close relationship, then I don't think we should keep secrets from each other, do you?"

She slowly shook her head.

"I'd like to know who owns that truck."

Ruth's forehead creased. "If I tell, will you promise not to repeat it to anyone?"

"Jah, if you don't want me to."

"The truck belongs to Luke."

"Luke Friesen?"

"Jah. He keeps it hidden there so his folks won't know."

Martin groaned. "I knew Luke was still going through rumschpringe, but I had no idea he owned a truck. Doesn't it seem strange that he would keep it hidden—especially since many Amish young people openly own cars?"

Ruth nodded. "The fact that he kept secrets from me and wouldn't settle down and join the church was the reason I broke up with him."

Martin brushed his thumb back and forth across the top of her hand. "I can't say that I'm glad Luke's not settled down, but I am glad you broke up with him." He swallowed a couple of times. "I. . .uh. . .have another question I'd like to ask you."

"What's that?"

"Will you be my wife?"

Her mouth hung slightly open. "You—you want to marry me?"

He nodded. "I love you, Ruth. I know it's sudden, but I feel a strong need to make you my wife as soon as possible."

A blush of pink cascaded over her cheeks.

"It's not just a physical need," he was quick to say. "It's a sense of urgency I can't explain."

"I—I don't understand."

"I have a feeling that if we don't get married soon, we might never marry."

"Is it because you're worried about the attacks against my family? Are you afraid something will happen to me?"

He nodded. "Could we be married this fall—maybe early October?"

She lifted her gaze to meet his. "Most couples have a longer courtship than that."

"I know." He squeezed her fingers. "Will you at least give some consideration to my proposal?"

"I don't need to consider the proposal, Martin." A smile spread across Ruth's face as a flicker of light danced in her dark eyes. "I'd be honored to marry you."

"Really?"

She nodded. "Shall we go inside and discuss this with my folks? I want to be sure we have their approval."

"Maybe it would be better if you talked to them alone. In case they don't approve of you marrying me."

"I don't see why they wouldn't approve."

"Jah, okay."

When Ruth and Martin stepped into the kitchen, Ruth spotted her parents sitting at the table, each reading a section of the newspaper. Her throat felt so swollen she wasn't sure she could speak. What if they didn't approve of her marrying Martin? What if Mom and Dad wanted them to wait until they'd been courting longer?

Martin squeezed Ruth's hand, and the warmth of his fingers gave her the confidence she needed. "Mom, Dad. Martin and I have something we'd like to tell you."

"What's that?" Mom asked, glancing up from her paper. She smiled at Martin. "It's good to see you."

"Good to see you too," he replied.

Dad merely grunted as he kept reading the paper.

Ruth shifted uneasily. "Martin has asked me to marry him."

"What?" Mom and Dad said in unison.

Dad dropped his paper to the table, and Mom reached to steady the glass of iced tea sitting before her.

"I've asked Ruth to be my wife." Martin gave Ruth's fingers another squeeze. "She said she's willing—that is, if you approve."

Dad squinted as he leveled Martin with a most serious look. "I have no objections to you courting my daughter, but I think it's too soon for you to be thinking about marriage."

Ruth opened her mouth to comment, but Martin spoke first. "I love Ruth, and I'd like us to be married as soon as possible."

Dad held up his hand. "What's the rush?"

Martin moved closer to the table. "I—I feel a sense of urgency to marry her."

"He's worried something will happen to me," Ruth quickly explained.

Mom's eyebrows furrowed as she looked at Martin. "Why would you think that?"

"All the things that have happened in our community lately have made me realize life is fragile, and one never knows when they'll lose someone they love."

"Are you thinking about Abe losing Alma?" Dad asked.

Martin nodded. "That's part of it. I'm also concerned about all the attacks on your family. If Ruth and I were married, she would be in my care."

A muscle in Dad's cheek twitched rhythmically. "Are you saying I haven't cared well for my fraa and *dechder*?"

Martin's face flamed. "I'm not saying that at all. I'm sure you're doing a fine job caring for your wife and daughters."

"I do my best," Dad mumbled.

Mom reached over and patted his arm. "Of course you do, Roman."

Ruth cleared her throat. "Do you have any objections to Martin and me being married in October?"

"I think it would be better if you waited until November," Mom said. "That will give us time to get some celery planted, make your wedding dress, and get everything done before the wedding."

"It will give you more time for courting too," Dad put in.

Ruth looked at Martin and was relieved when he nodded and said, "November it'll have to be, then."

She smiled and bent to hug her mother. "Where's Martha? I want to share our good news with her."

"Out in the barn with those dogs of hers," Dad said with a scowl. "Where else would she be?"

Ruth kissed her father's forehead. "Danki, Dad." Then she grabbed Martin's hand, and they rushed out the door.

Chapter 12

On a Friday morning two weeks later, Ruth stepped out of the house to hitch a horse to her buggy and discovered a message in bold black letters written on the side of their barn. It read You'll Pay!

"Oh no," she gasped as a shiver zipped up her spine. "Who could have done this? Why would they do such a thing?"

Ruth rushed around the corner of the house, knowing her father was probably heading to his shop by now. That's when she saw her mother's garden. All of the plants had been destroyed.

"Ach! My celery!" she screamed.

Dad rushed toward her then, his eyes wild. "What's all the yelling about?"

"Look over there!" Ruth's hand shook as she pointed to her mother's garden. "Someone's ruined all our plants, and—and they wrote a threatening message on the side of the barn."

Dad's eyebrows furrowed. "What message?"

"You mean you haven't seen it yet?"

He shook his head.

"Come see for yourself." Ruth led the way to the barn and halted in front of the message. "Who could have written such a thing, and what would someone think we need to pay for?"

"Not *we*," he said with a shake of his head. "It's me that's being targeted; I'm sure of it."

"But why? What have you done that would make someone want to ruin our garden and paint a hateful message on the barn?"

Dad moaned as he bent to pick up an empty can of spray paint. "Several people might be carrying a grudge against me—Steven Bates, Luke, and that land developer who wanted to buy our property."

"But the land developer left our area some time ago, Dad."

He nodded. "That's true."

"You don't think it could be the English reporter who used to date Grace, do you? Maybe it's her he's trying to get even with, not you."

Dad shook his head. "If the attacker wanted to make Grace pay, then the attacks would have been against just her, not the rest of the family."

"But if it's someone wanting to get even with you, then wouldn't he have done things to hurt just you?"

"Anything that hurts my family hurts me," Dad said as he hurled the empty can into a box full of trash near the barn door.

"The more things that happen, the more scared I become." Ruth gulped in some air. "I just wonder how much longer this will go on."

"I don't know. Our bishop came by the shop yesterday morning and said he'd spoken to Luke."

"What did Luke have to say?"

Dad shrugged. "Guess he told the bishop that he thinks I've got it in for him and that he's not responsible for any of the attacks against us."

"Do you believe him?"

"No, and I've been thinking about talking to Luke myself, but I don't want to rile him. He might be capable of doing even worse things if he gets mad enough."

"I can understand that he might have been upset with you for firing him, but that was some time ago. Why would he be doing spiteful things to us now?"

"Maybe he heard about your betrothal to Martin and feels jealous because you're marrying him."

"Oh Dad, I don't think so. If Luke had wanted to marry me, he wouldn't have kept secrets during our courtship. I think he was relieved when I broke up with him."

"Maybe so, but he wasn't relieved when I fired him."

"Are you talking about Luke?" Martha asked, stepping up to them.

Dad nodded and pointed to the garden. "Look what was done to your mamm's vegetable plants."

Martha's eyebrows lifted high on her forehead. "What in all the world would cause someone to do such a thing, and who could have done it?"

"The same one who did that." Ruth pointed to the writing on the side of the barn. "*Somebody's* trying to make *someone* in this family pay for *something.*"

Martha clasped her father's arm. "You've got to phone the sheriff. We can't allow this kind of thing to continue. Sooner or later someone's going to get hurt."

Mom stepped into the yard just then. "What's going on? I figured Ruth would be on her way to work by now. And you too, Roman. What are you all doing out here on the lawn?"

"Look," the three of them said in unison as they pointed to the garden. Mom let out a yelp and lifted her hands. *"Ich kann sell net geh!"*

"There isn't much you can do except tolerate it." Dad slipped his arm around Mom's waist. "What's done is done. We just need to hold steady and keep trusting God to protect us and our property."

"How can we trust God when things keep happening and we never know when or why?" Ruth questioned.

Before Dad could reply, Cleon showed up. "What's going on? Why are you all standing out here in the yard?"

"Someone left a message on our barn, and they—they killed my garden," Mom said in a shaky voice. "Somebody's out to get us, and I'm very much afraid."

"That's what they want—to make us afraid." Dad's lips compressed into a thin line. "We can't give in. We must hold steady."

Cleon frowned. "When Grace hears of this, she's going to be awfully upset. Probably more convinced than ever that the reporter is behind it."

"Grace might be right," Ruth agreed. "That reporter seems real sneaky to me."

"I think it's safe to say that whoever's been doing this must be someone close by, as they seem to know our family's comings and goings," Cleon said. "I wouldn't be surprised if they're not keeping a watch on the place."

"As I've said before, I'm not convinced the reporter's doing it," Dad said with a grunt. "I still think it could be Luke."

"I don't believe Luke's the one responsible," Martha protested.

"We won't solve anything by standing around playing guessing games." Dad nodded at Cleon. "We've got work in the shop that needs to be done."

"What about the garden?" Ruth wailed.

"I'll see about getting another spot plowed and spaded as soon as I'm done for the day," Dad said. "Then you and your mamm can begin planting tomorrow morning."

Cleon leaned close to Mom. "Would you go to my house and speak with Grace? I don't want her coming out here and seeing what's happened without some warning."

She nodded. "Jah, sure. I'll do that now." Mom headed up the driveway toward Cleon and Grace's house, and the men turned toward the woodworking shop.

Martha paced in front of her mother's garden, anger bubbling in her soul. "Something needs to be done about this."

Ruth knelt on the grass and let her head fall forward into her outstretched hands. "I have a terrible feeling that I'll never marry Martin—that something will prevent our wedding from taking place."

Martha dropped down beside Ruth and gave her a hug. "Maybe I should go out to the shop and talk to Dad again—try to convince him to phone the sheriff."

"Sheriff Osborn knows about some of the other things that have happened here, and what good has that done?"

"He said he'd keep an eye on things."

"True. But he can't be watching our place all the time."

"Even so, I think Dad should let the sheriff know about these recent happenings." Martha rose to her feet and was about to walk away when Sheriff Osborn's car pulled into the driveway. It stopped beside her father's shop, and the sheriff got out of the car and went inside.

"Now that's a surprise," Ruth said. "I wonder what he's doing here."

"I'm going to see what the sheriff has to say." Martha sprinted toward the shop, leaving Ruth sitting on the grass by herself.

"Got a call from one of your neighbors," Martha heard the sheriff say when she stepped into the shop a few minutes later. "They said someone had written something threatening on the side of your barn."

"Don't tell me. Ray Larson called. He was probably checking things over with those binoculars of his. After that first round of attacks against us several months ago, Ray's wife said she would ask him to keep an eye on things." Dad folded his arms and grunted. "I never thought that was necessary though."

Sheriff Osborn shrugged. "The caller didn't identify himself. Just mentioned seeing the writing on your barn."

"There was more done than that," Martha announced as she closed the door behind her. "Somebody put weed killer on my mother's vegetable garden, and now everything's ruined."

Dad shot Martha a look of irritation. "What are you doing out here, girl?"

"I saw the sheriff's car pull in, and I wanted to see if he knew anything about what's been going on here lately."

Sheriff Osborn tipped his head in Dad's direction. "Has something happened besides the message on the barn and the garden being ruined?"

Dad waved a hand. "It wasn't much. Just a stink bomb thrown into the barn, and some toilet paper draped all over our buildings."

"Sounds like whoever bothered you before might be at it again." The sheriff pulled a notebook and pen out of his shirt pocket and began writing. "When did you say these other things happened?"

"A couple weeks ago," Dad answered.

"Did you see anyone lurking around the place before or after the incidents?"

"Nope."

"Just Ray Larson." Cleon spoke up from across the room, where he'd been quietly working on a set of cabinets. "I spotted him walking up and down our fence line the day before the stink bomb happened. His binoculars were hanging around his neck." He shrugged. "I figured he was out looking for some unusual birds."

"How come you never mentioned this before?" A muscle in Dad's cheek twitched.

Cleon shrugged again. "Didn't seem important at the time. It just came to mind now, when the sheriff asked if we'd seen anyone hanging around the place."

Martha stepped between the sheriff and her father. "There's no way Ray Larson could be responsible for any of the things that have been done to us."

"How do you know?" the sheriff asked, turning to face her.

"I just do. Ray and Donna are good neighbors. They often drive us places we can't go with the horse and buggy, and they bought one of Heidi's pups."

The sheriff arched one eyebrow and stared at Martha as if she'd taken leave of her senses. "I hardly think buying a puppy is reason enough to remove the Larsons' name from our list of suspects."

Martha's eyes widened. "You have a list?"

The sheriff nodded. "The last time your father and I spoke, he mentioned a few people he thought might have a grudge against him."

"You never told us you'd given the sheriff a list of names," Martha said, turning to face her father.

"I talked to him about it once when he stopped by my shop to see if there had been any more attacks." Dad gave his earlobe a quick pull. "Saw no need to mention it."

Martha turned back to the sheriff. "Did Dad tell you about Gary Walker?"

"Who?"

"He's that reporter who's been hanging around Holmes County doing stories about the Amish," Cleon explained. "He used to date my wife when she was going through her running-around years."

Sheriff Osborn nodded. "Ah, I remember now. He's the one who wrote that article some time ago that included a picture of Grace and told about some of the acts of vandalism that had been done at your place."

"That's right," Dad said. "We were afraid the article might make things worse by giving someone the idea that they could get away with doing such a thing." He grunted. "And maybe it has, because things sure have gotten worse since that article came out."

"Might be good for me to speak to this reporter." The sheriff scribbled something else on his tablet. "Find out what he knows and feel him out."

"I doubt he's going to admit anything," Martha said. "I was with Grace one day when she confronted him, and he was real arrogant and denied knowing anything about our problems."

"He might be willing to talk to me." Sheriff Osborn looked over at Dad. "Were any clues left after these recent attacks? Something that might point to the one responsible?"

"Just a pack of cigarettes I found on the ground after the toilet-papering was done," Dad said. "I suspect the culprit's a smoker."

"Do you still have the cigarettes?"

Dad shook his head. "Threw them out that same day, just like I did with the empty spray can I found on the ground near our barn this morning. Martha could get that for you."

"If there are any more attacks and you find any clues, I don't want you to touch them—and certainly don't throw them away." The sheriff frowned. "I might be able to check for fingerprints." He started for the door but whirled back around. "Let me know if you see or hear anything suspicious."

Dad nodded, and Martha hurried out the door after the sheriff. After she showed him where the can of spray paint was, she said, "You will let us know what Gary Walker has to say after you speak to him, I hope."

The sheriff nodded. "If there's anything worth repeating, your dad will be the first to know."

Chapter 13

"Do I have to go to school, Mama?" Anna whined as she sat at the table, poking her scrambled eggs with the tip of her fork.

Grace nodded and took a sip of her tea. "This is your first day of school, and you should be happy about attending the first grade."

Anna's lower lip protruded. "What if I don't like my teacher? What if the work's too hard?"

"Clara Bontrager is a good teacher, and I'm sure you'll do fine. Your friend Esta will be there, and you know most of the other children, so you won't be alone."

Anna's forehead wrinkled. "I wonder if Esta will miss her puppy while she's in school. Winkie makes Esta laugh, you know. He helps her forget she lost her mamm."

"I'm glad about that. I'm also pleased that you and Esta have become such good friends." Grace gave Anna's shoulder a gentle squeeze. "Now hurry and finish your breakfast so I can take you to school."

"Can't I walk? The schoolhouse isn't far down the road."

Grace shook her head. "If you had older brothers or sisters to walk with you, I might allow it, but it's just you, and I want to be sure you get to school safely."

Anna shrugged her slim shoulders. "Jah, okay."

A short time later as Grace directed their horse and buggy down the driveway past her folks' place, she was shocked to see the writing on her father's barn. She halted the horse and climbed out of the buggy so she could get a better look at the words that had been painted in bold black letters.

Her heart pounded. "Gary's at it again," she fumed. "That man won't rest until he's made me pay for breaking up with him and marrying Wade."

Mom rushed up to her. "I hated for you to see this, and I was coming up to tell you about it," she said, motioning to the barn. "Your daed and Cleon won't have time to paint over it until they're done working for the day. They promised to dig a new garden plot for me too."

Grace's forehead wrinkled. "You already have a garden plot. Why would you need a new one?"

"Whoever painted those threatening words on the side of our barn also put weed killer on my garden." Mom slowly shook her head. "Everything's dead—including the new shoots of celery we planted for the creamed celery dish we were going to serve at Ruth's wedding."

Grace glanced at the buggy. She was grateful Anna hadn't gotten out. She didn't want her daughter to know what had happened. Anna was already nervous about her first day of school; she didn't need something else to worry about.

"I'm so sorry, Mom," Grace said, clasping her mother's hand. "If there was something I could do to make these horrible attacks stop, I surely would."

"There's nothing we can do but pray. Things will ease up. We just need to hold steady and trust God, like your daed has said many times."

Grace stared at the ugly words written on the barn until they blurred before her eyes. "I don't think things will ever ease up unless Gary Walker leaves town for good." Without waiting for Mom to comment, Grace climbed into the buggy, grabbed up the reins, and headed down the driveway.

As they traveled to the schoolhouse, all she could think about was the latest act of vandalism. By the time she pulled into the schoolhouse parking lot, she'd developed a headache.

"Oh, there's Esta," Anna said, clambering across the seat and hopping out of the buggy.

"Don't you want me to walk you inside?" Grace called after her.

Anna shook her head. "I'll walk with Esta."

The child scampered off, and Grace took up the reins. She didn't feel like going home and looking at the words on Dad's barn, so she decided to drive over to Abe Wengerd's place to see how he was getting along and maybe visit with Sue. Focusing on someone else's problems might help take her mind off her own.

———————◆◆◆———————

As Martin hauled a piece of leather over to a tub of black dye, his thoughts went to Ruth and how interested she had seemed the day he'd shown her the harness shop. She'd said she liked it here, and that was a good thing since they would be getting married in a few months. He would probably come home from work every night smelling like leather, neat's-foot oil, or pungent dye.

Martin remembered how nervous he had felt when he'd proposed to Ruth, and how relieved he'd felt when she said yes. He could hardly wait to make her his wife.

Martin's thoughts were halted when Abe's youngest boy, Owen, burst into the room, shouting, "Molly won't let me play with her wooden blocks!"

Abe stepped away from the oversized sewing machine where he'd been working and lifted the boy into his arms. "Molly's only two, son. She doesn't understand yet about sharing."

Owen's lower lip quivered. "I always have to share with her."

"I know." He patted the child's back. "Did you speak with Aunt Sue about it? Maybe she can convince Molly to share the blocks with you."

Owen shook his head. "Aunt Sue's busy bakin' bread."

"I'm sure Molly will take a nap after lunch." Abe placed Owen on the floor. "So while she's asleep, you can play with the blocks. How's that sound?"

"Okay." Owen hugged his father around the legs.

Abe opened the door and ushered the boy out. "You be good now."

Martin was impressed with Abe's patience. He could only hope he would be that patient when he and Ruth had children someday.

"Sorry about the interruption," Abe said, smiling at Martin. "Sometimes family business comes before work."

"No problem. It was nice to see the way you handled things with Owen. Sure hope I'll be as good a daed as you when Ruth and I have kinner."

Abe thumped Martin on the back. "I'm sure you'll do just fine."

"Guess I'd better get this hunk of leather dyed. Then I've got some straps that need cutting," Martin said, turning back to the tub of dye.

"I'd better get busy on those straps I was stitching too."

Except for the steady hum of the air compressor, the men worked in silence.

When the door to Abe's shop opened again, Martin was surprised to see Grace Schrock step into the room.

"Wie geht's?" Abe called, turning off his machine. "What can I do for you this morning?"

"I just came by to see how things are going here and to tell you about some vandalism done at our place during the night."

Martin's ears perked up. "Is Ruth okay?" He'd been consumed with worry ever since Ruth's family had come under attack.

Grace nodded. "No one was hurt, but someone wrote the words 'You'll pay' on the side of my daed's barn. They also put weed killer on Mom's garden—which means the celery that had been planted to be served at your wedding meal was ruined."

Martin sucked in his breath, and Abe released a groan.

"I was hoping there would be no more attacks at your folks' place," Abe said.

"So were we."

Martin could see by the expression on Grace's face that she was frightened. Well, he was scared too. Scared for everyone in the Hostettler family. Ruth most of all.

He turned to Abe. "Would it be okay if I take my lunch break a little early so I can go to town and speak with Ruth? I know she'll be upset about the celery."

"Jah, sure," Abe said with a nod. "You can head to Berlin right now if you like."

"You wouldn't mind?"

"Nope. We don't have much work today, so take all the time you need."

"Danki." Martin grabbed his straw hat off the wall peg and dashed out the door.

After Martin left the shop, Abe turned to Grace. "I'm sorry about the things that have been done to you folks. Nobody should have to live in fear."

"You and your family have been through a lot lately too," she said.

"It helps to know we have the prayers and assistance of others in our community."

She nodded.

"Maybe you'd like to go up to the house and say hello to Sue and my two little ones," Abe suggested. "Sue would probably enjoy a chat with someone closer to her age. She looked kind of frazzled this morning, and I think she's having a hard time keeping the house running smoothly and taking care of my six *raubels* kinner."

"Your children aren't so rowdy from what I can tell," Grace said. "In fact, they seem pretty well behaved compared to some I know."

"They did real well when Alma was alive, but since she's been gone, they've been kind of unruly and moody." He grimaced. "Never know what Gideon will say or do next. I'm a little concerned about how he'll do in school this year."

"We'll continue to pray for all of you." Grace smiled. "Guess I'll go see Sue now."

After Grace left the shop, Abe turned the air compressor on again and resumed work at the sewing machine. It was good to keep busy. It kept his mind off missing Alma. If he didn't keep busy, he might want to sleep, and that wasn't a good thing during working hours.

Abe had sewn only a couple of straps together when Ivan Schrock entered his shop.

"What can I do for you, Ivan?" he asked the young man.

Ivan shuffled his feet a few times. "Just dropped by to see if you might need any help."

"Help with what?"

"Here, in the harness shop."

"Have you had any experience with harness making?"

Ivan's face flooded with color. "No, but I'm sure I could learn."

"Don't you have a job working for your daed on his farm?"

"Did have until last night."

Abe tipped his head in question.

"Pop announced during supper that he was getting out of the farming business. Said there wasn't enough money in it anymore and that he's planning to sell off some of our land. Guess he got an offer to work at the lumber store in Charm. My brothers Delbert and Willard may work there too."

"I see." Abe drew in a quick breath. "The thing is, I've barely got enough work to keep me and Martin going right now, so I can't afford to hire another man."

Ivan's gaze dropped to the floor, and he made little circles in the dust with the toe of his boot. "Guess I'll have to look elsewhere for a job. I can't expect to live at home and not pull my share of the load. The only money I'm making is what Cleon gives me whenever I make a few honey deliveries for him. So unless something else turns up, I may end up applying at the lumber store too."

"Sorry I can't help," Abe said. "If things change and I get real busy, I'll let you know."

"I appreciate that." Ivan pulled the door open and stepped outside.

"Everyone has their troubles these days," Abe muttered as he returned to his work. "Some more than others, but each has his own."

"It's nice we're both working today," Sadie said to Ruth as they stood behind the bakery counter, slipping fresh pastries inside. "Don't get to see you much when we have different hours."

"We see each other every other Sunday during church," Ruth reminded her friend.

"That's true, but there's always so much going on before and after preaching that it's hard to visit."

Sadie placed a tray of banana muffins in the case. "Anything new at your place these days?"

"As a matter of fact, there is," Ruth replied. "This morning we woke up to find a threatening message painted on our barn."

Sadie squinted. "What kind of message?"

"It said 'You'll pay.'"

"That's *baremlich*!"

"I know it's terrible, and that's not all. Mom's garden is dead; someone sprayed weed killer all over the plants."

Sadie's eyes grew wide as she slowly shook her head. "What about the celery you planted for your wedding? Did that get ruined as well?"

Ruth nodded. "Every last plant is gone, and now we'll have to start over."

"Any idea who did it?"

Just then the door to the bakeshop opened, and Martin stepped in.

"I heard about what happened at your house this morning, and I wanted to see if you were okay," he said, rushing over to the counter.

"I'm fine. Just upset over losing our garden and all the celery we'd planted for the wedding."

"Grace dropped by the harness shop a while ago and told Abe and me what happened." Martin's eyebrows drew together. "She said someone had painted 'You'll pay' on the side of your daed's barn."

"Whoever did that has to be sick in the head," Sadie put in. "I hope the sheriff catches the crazy fellow and puts him in jail."

Martin turned to Sadie. "How do you know it's a man? Could be a woman who's been bothering Ruth's family."

Sadie snorted in an unladylike manner and wagged her finger. "No woman I know could think up all the horrible things that have been done to the Hostettlers."

"Whether it's a man or a woman doesn't really matter. What counts is keeping Ruth safe." Martin leaned across the counter. "Now do you see why I wanted us to get married right away? I want to be there to watch out for you every day."

"I'm okay," Ruth assured him. "No harm came to any of us—just our garden."

"Maybe not today, but what about next time?"

"Let's hope there is no next time," Sadie said.

Deep wrinkles formed in Martin's forehead. "I couldn't stand it if any-thing happened to you."

Ruth smiled. It was nice to know Martin was concerned about her. Luke never seemed to care so much. "God will watch over us," she said with a nod. "We just need to trust Him and try to not worry."

Chapter 14

"It's nice to have things back to normal again," Mom said to Ruth as the two of them hung out the wash one Monday morning in early fall.

Ruth nodded. "I'm glad they are, and I'm hoping it's because the sheriff's been keeping an eye on our place."

"Now we can keep our focus on getting ready for your wedding."

"I'm glad I have today off," Ruth said. "It gives me a chance to wash and dry the material I bought for my wedding dress."

Mom reached into the basket of clean clothes and withdrew a towel. "Have you and Martin decided where you'll live once you're married?" she asked, clipping the towel to the line.

"We'd talked about staying with his folks for a time, but Martin found a little house to rent near Abe's place. It's owned by the Larsons, and Martin plans to talk to them about renting it soon."

"It makes sense that he'd want to live near his job."

Ruth nodded. "And since we'll be living close to Abe's, I can stop in more often to see how Esta and the other kinner are doing."

"Speaking of kinner," Mom said, reaching into the basket for another towel, "Grace says Anna's adjusting well in school, and she seems to like her teacher."

"I figured she would. She's smart and gets along well with others." Ruth smiled. "Even though she's a couple years younger than Esta, they've become best friends. You should see how much fun the girls have playing with Winkie."

"That was a thoughtful thing you did when you gave Esta the puppy." Mom squeezed Ruth's shoulder. "You'll make a fine *mudder* someday."

"I hope so. I'm also hoping Martin and I will be blessed with kinner right away." Ruth clipped the piece of blue material that would soon be her wedding dress to the clothesline. "I love Martin, and I'm sure he'll make a good daed."

"I think you're probably right about that." Mom reached for the empty basket. "Now that our wash has been hung, I guess I'll head back inside and see about baking some bread." She smiled. "Oh, and speaking of bread, I just want to say that I think Martha's gotten pretty good at baking since she started working for Irene."

"She'll need baking skills if she's ever to marry."

"She's got to find herself a boyfriend first."

"I'm sure she will when the time is right. I hope it's someone as *wunderbaar* as Martin."

———◆◆◆———

"Are you getting nervous about your wedding day?" Abe asked as he cut a piece of leather and handed it to Martin to trim the edges.

"A bit."

"I thought so. You've been acting kind of jittery lately, and you haven't said more than two words since you came to work this morning."

"I've been trying to stay focused on the job at hand."

"More than likely you're thinking about that little woman we'll soon be calling Martin's Ruth."

Martin smiled. "I suppose I have been thinking about her some."

Abe bumped Martin's arm with his elbow. "Some?"

"Okay, more than some. I've been thinking about Ruth a lot these days." Martin sucked in his breath. "I hope I can always keep her safe."

"There are no guarantees of that."

Martin's heart went out to Abe. It had to be hard for him to come to work each morning and stay focused when his heart was full of sorrow and regrets. It couldn't be easy for him to go home every night and father his kids when all he wanted to do was retreat to his room and sleep away the pain.

Abe grabbed a hunk of leather that had been dyed cinnamon brown and snipped a curved shape with his scissors. "Guess we'd better quit gabbing and get back to work."

Martin nodded. "Harnesses sure don't get made themselves."

———————◆◗◆———————

"I'll go out and check the clothes drying on the line if you like," Martha said to Mom as they finished washing the dishes after lunch.

"That would be much appreciated. As soon as Ruth comes up from the cellar, she can help you."

Martha grabbed the wicker basket from the utility room and scurried out the back door. As she came around the side of the house, she screeched to a halt. "Someone's shredded the clothes!"

Mom rushed outside, with Ruth right behind her.

"Ach!" Ruth cried. "My material is ruined!"

Mom stood there shaking her head. "I don't understand why anyone would do something like this."

Martha headed for her father's woodworking shop.

"Where are you going?" Mom called after her.

"To tell Dad what's happened."

"He's not there. He had a dental appointment, remember?"

Martha started running. Dad might not be there, but Cleon would be.

———————◆◗◆———————

Ruth sat on the grass holding what was left of her wedding dress material and rocking back and forth. "Why, Mom? Why did this have to happen now when everything was going so well?"

Mom knelt beside Ruth and gently patted her back. "I don't know, dear one. I just don't know."

A few minutes later, Martha showed up with Cleon at her side.

"Martha said someone ruined the clothes you hung on the line this morning," he said, a look of concern etched on his face.

Ruth choked back a sob. "Every last one has been shredded."

"Look there." Cleon pointed to a set of footprints in the dirt that seemed to be headed in the direction of the Larsons' place. "Whoever did this must have gone that way."

"Surely the Larsons wouldn't be involved in something so terrible," Mom was quick to say. "They're our good friends and neighbors."

"Maybe it was Drew, that rowdy fourteen-year-old grandson of theirs who's been visiting them this week," Martha put in. "Think I'll go over and ask a few questions." She took off running before anyone could stop her.

"Want me to go after her?" Cleon asked, looking at Mom.

She shook her head. "She'll be all right. I'm sure neither the Larsons nor their grandson had anything to do with this."

"Let me help you clean up this mess." Cleon bent down to grab a couple of shredded towels.

"That's okay; you have work to do in the shop. Ruth and I can manage. Right, Ruth?"

Ruth nodded as she stood, but she couldn't seem to find her voice.

"It will be all right," Mom said, stroking Ruth's back. "We'll get more material tomorrow, and then we can start making your wedding dress as planned."

Tears welled in Ruth's eyes. "And then what, Mom? Do we make the dress, wash it, then hang it on the line again so someone can shred it in two?" She let her gaze travel around the yard. "Where was the sheriff when this was done to our clothes? Why wasn't he watching out for us the way he said he would?"

"Sheriff Osborn can't be everywhere," Mom reminded. "He's got other obligations and isn't able to keep an eye on our place all the time. Besides, this is the first attack we've had in many weeks. The sheriff probably figured things were fine and dandy around here since he hasn't heard anything to the contrary."

Ruth stared at her mother as she gulped in deep breaths; then she dashed across the yard and sprinted up the driveway to Grace's house.

———————— ◆•◆ ————————

Grace had just taken a loaf of bread from the oven when the back door swooshed open and Ruth rushed into the room, wide-eyed and waving a piece of blue material in her hands.

"He's at it again, Grace! Whoever attacked us before has shredded all the clothes on our line, including the material for my wedding dress!"

Grace hurried across the room. "Ach, I'm so sorry," she said, wrapping her arms around Ruth. "This had to be Gary's doing."

"But why?" Ruth sobbed. "Why would he want to ruin the material for my wedding dress?"

Grace shook her head. "It's me he wants to hurt, not you." She swallowed around the lump in her throat. "I'm sorry to say this, but he's hurting my family in the process."

Ruth leaned her head on Grace's shoulder. "How are we going to make it stop?"

"I don't know. I suppose we could talk to the sheriff."

Ruth's mouth dropped open. "Without Dad's permission?"

"If that's what it takes."

"But I thought Sheriff Osborn was supposed to be keeping an eye on our place. If so, it hasn't done much good."

"Maybe he's been too busy or decided to give up patrolling the area because things have quieted down. Since Anna's in school, I'm free to go with you to town. We can see Sheriff Osborn first, and then we'll head over to the fabric outlet and get more material for your wedding dress."

"Are you sure you feel up to it?" Ruth asked with a look of concern. "Maybe it would be better if you stayed home and rested. I can go by myself to see the sheriff."

Grace shook her head. "I'm fine, and I insist on going to town with you."

Ruth offered Grace a weak smile. "Danki. You're a good sister."

———————— ◆•◆ ————————

By the time Martha arrived at the Larsons' place, she was panting for air. She gave a couple of sharp raps on the front door and leaned against the porch railing, trying to catch her breath.

A few seconds later, Donna Larson opened the door. "What a nice surprise," she said, motioning Martha to come inside.

Martha stepped into the living room. "I hope I'm not interrupting anything, but I—"

"Not at all. Did you come to see how the little sheltie we bought from you is doing?"

"I. . .uh. . .yes, it would be nice to know how the dog's getting along."

"Real well. In fact, my grandson, Drew, is out in the barn feeding it right now."

"Speaking of Drew. . ." Martha cleared her throat a couple of times.

"What about him?"

"I was wondering where he's been all morning."

"Right here. He went to the barn to feed the dog and do a few chores." Donna motioned to the sofa. "Would you like to have a seat?"

Martha shook her head. "I can't stay long. I need to get back home and see how Mom is doing."

"Is something wrong with Judith? She's not sick, I hope."

"Not physically, but she was quite upset when she discovered that all the clean clothes she'd hung on the line had been shredded."

Donna's face blanched. "When did that happen?"

"Sometime this morning after Mom and Ruth hung some clothes out to dry. The material for Ruth's wedding dress was ruined."

"I'm sorry to hear that."

"We found footprints in the dirt that appeared to be heading in the direction of your place."

Donna's forehead creased as she pressed her lips tightly together. "I hope you don't think Drew had anything to do with the clothes being cut."

"Well, I—"

"Drew does tend to be a bit rowdy, but I know he would never do anything like that."

"Like what?" Ray asked as he stepped into the room from the kitchen.

Donna turned to face her husband. "Someone shredded the clothes on the Hostettlers' line this morning. Martha says there are footprints leading from their place to ours. She thinks Drew may have done it."

"I didn't say that—"

Ray's bushy brows puckered as he frowned. "Drew's been in the barn with me all morning, except for the short time he came into the house to pack his suitcase. He'll be going home in the morning," he added, looking at Martha.

"I see."

"I'm sorry about the clothes and all the other things that have been done at your place over the last several months." Ray tapped his foot and stared right at Martha. "I'm watching your place whenever I can, so my advice to you is to quit trying to play detective."

Martha recoiled, feeling like a glass of cold water had been dashed in her face. "Sorry to have troubled you." She turned and rushed out the door.

———————◆◆◆———————

"I think we should stop at the bakeshop before we go home," Ruth said to Grace as the two of them left the sheriff's office. "Sheriff Osborn didn't offer much help other than to say he's spoken with Gary Walker and that Gary claims he's innocent." She wrinkled her nose. "They don't allow smoking in the offices, but it sure smells like a lot of smokers work there. After a few minutes, I could barely breathe, much less think clearly enough to ask the right questions. Maybe a couple of doughnuts will make us feel better."

"The sheriff does seem to smoke a lot," Grace agreed. "Or at least, someone who works in his office does."

"So should we head to the bakeshop?"

"Don't you want to get the material for your wedding dress first?"

Ruth shook her head. "We can do that after we've had our doughnuts."

"Okay."

They hitched their horse to the rail behind the bakeshop and headed for the building.

Sadie greeted them with a smile. "I'm surprised to see you today, Ruth. I figured with this being your day off you'd be home sewing your wedding dress."

Ruth grunted. "I would be if the material I bought hadn't been torn to shreds."

Sadie frowned. "How'd that happen?"

"Someone shredded all the clothes Mom and I hung on the line this morning."

"Not *someone*," Grace put in. "It was Gary Walker; I'm sure of it."

"Gary Walker, the reporter?"

Ruth and Grace nodded at the same time.

"He was here earlier," Sadie said. "Came in to get a maple bar."

"How long ago was that?" Grace questioned.

"A few minutes after we opened."

Ruth was about to comment, but Sadie cut her off.

"He said he had one thing he needed to do, and then he'd be heading out of town and wasn't sure if or when he might be back again."

"That *one* thing was to destroy the clothes on Mom's line," Grace said with a groan.

Ruth touched Grace's arm. "I hope Gary is gone for good this time and never returns to Holmes County."

Grace released a gusty sigh. "I pray that's true."

Chapter 15

"What's got you looking so happy today?" Abe asked as Martin walked across the room carrying a large sheet of leather. "You've been wearing a silly grin on your face all morning."

Martin's smile widened. "Guess I'm excited about getting married. It won't be long now, just a few more weeks."

Abe's heart clenched when he thought of how happy he'd been as he'd looked forward to his own wedding day. He had never expected to lose Alma at such a young age, and the thought that he might be left to raise six kinner by himself had never even entered his mind.

"Have you found a place to live yet?" Abe asked, knowing he needed to think about something else.

Martin dropped the leather onto one of the workbenches and turned to face Abe. "Found a little house to rent that's not far from here. It's owned by Ray and Donna Larson, the English neighbors who often drive for Ruth's family."

"Didn't realize the Larsons owned any land except their own."

"Oh jah. They own a couple of places. From what I've heard, they tried to buy Roman's place some time ago too."

"I do recall Roman mentioning that, but I didn't realize they'd bought other pieces of property." Abe leaned against his desk. "The Larsons seem like pleasant enough folks, and I'm sure they'll make good landlords. Even so, it'll be nice when you and Ruth can have a place of your own."

Martin nodded. "I'd like to build a house like Cleon and Grace's place—one with plenty of space and lots of bedrooms for all the kinner we hope to have someday."

Abe grunted. "After what went on at my house last night, I'd gladly have given you a couple of my *beschwerlich* kinner."

Martin looked stunned. "I've never heard you refer to your kids as troublesome before. What happened last night?"

Abe gave his beard a quick yank. "Right before supper, Esta's puppy piddled all over the kitchen floor." He grimaced. "If I've told her once, I've told her a dozen times not to leave that critter in the house unattended."

"Doesn't your sister monitor things like that?"

"She's supposed to, but with six kinner to look after, not to mention cooking and cleaning, a lot goes on that Sue doesn't seem to know about or catch in time."

"I suppose it would."

"To give you another example of how things went last night, Molly spilled her milk on her plate of stew. Then she started howling and dumped the whole thing onto the floor." Abe shook his head. "Sue was so upset about having to clean the floor again, she broke into tears." Abe moved away from his desk and turned on the air compressor for one of the sewing machines. "I love my kinner, but they sure try my patience at times."

"I guess that's how it is with most parents, although I'm still looking forward to Ruth and me having children."

"And you should be." Abe nodded to the sewing machine. "Guess it's time we quit jawin' and get back to work."

As Ruth and her family sat around the supper table that night, she noticed deep grooves lining her father's forehead. Had Mom told him about the shredded clothes, or was something else troubling him?

"How'd your dental appointment go, Dad?" Ruth asked. "Did you have much pain with that root canal you were supposed to have done?"

Dad groaned. "Seems like all I do these days is go to the dentist. Dr. Wilson had me so numbed up, I couldn't feel a thing." He grimaced. "After the appointment, when I ran into Steven Bates, I felt pain."

"Pain from your tooth?" Martha asked.

Dad shook his head. "Pain because one of my used-to-be loyal customers won't speak to me anymore."

Mom reached over and patted Dad's arm. "Did you say hello to him?"

"I was going to, but he walked by like he didn't even see me." Dad wiped his mouth with a napkin and frowned. "Looked right at me when I came out of the dentist's office, and then he stuck his nose in the air and hurried into the building without so much as a word."

"Do you think he's still angry about those cabinets that fell off your delivery wagon a while ago?" Ruth asked.

Dad gave a quick nod.

"If you two don't mind cleaning up the kitchen without me this evening," Mom said as she pushed away from the table and picked up her dishes, "I think I'll go to bed."

"We don't mind," Ruth was quick to say. It was obvious by the dark circles under Mom's eyes that she was all done in. She probably didn't want to listen to Dad's complaints tonight either.

Dad's forehead furrowed as he stared at Mom. "Are you feeling *grank*?"

She shook her head. "I'm not sick—just tired. I've been fighting a headache most of the day too."

"Probably came about because of the clothesline incident," Martha said with a scowl.

Dad's eyebrows shot up. "What clothesline incident?"

Ruth looked up at her mother. "You didn't say anything to Dad about what happened?"

She shook her head.

Dad's face filled with concern. "What happened with the clothesline?"

"Someone shredded all the clothes we hung on the line."

Dad strode across the room to where Mom stood at the sink. "Someone shredded the clothes, and I'm just hearing of it now?"

"I didn't want to worry you, Roman." Mom placed her dishes in the sink. "Besides, I knew what your response would be."

"What's that supposed to mean?"

"I figured you'd probably say it was done by some pranksters. And I was sure you wouldn't bother the sheriff."

Ruth and Martha exchanged glances. When she and Grace had returned home from town, they'd told Martha they'd gone to see the sheriff. Then Martha had told them about her visit with the Larsons. If Dad found out about either incident, he wouldn't approve.

"No point in bothering Sheriff Osborn," Dad said with a look of disdain. "He knows about the other attacks, and what good has that done?" He made an arc with his arm. "Came around asking a bunch of nosy questions and saying he'd keep an eye on the place, yet here we go again with another attack."

Mom shuffled across the room. "I'm going to bed. Are you coming, Roman?"

He shook his head. "I'm not tired. Guess I'll go out to the barn awhile and think things through." He turned toward the table, where Ruth and Martha still sat. "If anything else happens, I want to be the first to know. Do you understand?"

They both nodded.

"Good." He tromped across the room and went out the back door.

———————————•◦•———————————

Martin felt a sense of excitement as he pulled into the Hostettlers' and tied his horse to the hitching rail. He was anxious to see Ruth and tell her that he'd put a deposit on the house they would be living in after they were married.

Taking the steps two at a time, he knocked on the door. A few seconds later, Martha answered. *"Gut'n owed,"* she said. "Won't you come in?"

"Good evening," Martin replied as he entered the house. "I came to see Ruth."

"I figured as much. She's in the kitchen." Martha stepped onto the porch. "Tell my sister I've gone out to the kennels to check on my dogs," she called over her shoulder.

Martin found Ruth sitting at the kitchen table with a cup in her hands. "Are you busy?" he asked.

She looked up and smiled. "Just having some tea. Would you like to join me?"

"Sounds good, if you've got some cookies to go with it."

"I think that can be arranged." Ruth set the cup down and scurried across the room. A few seconds later, she was back with a plate of cookies and a cup for him. "These are ginger cookies from the bakeshop, and they're really good, so help yourself."

"Danki."

"So what brings you by this evening?" she asked after taking a seat.

"Came to see you of course." He grabbed a cookie and bit into it. "Mmm. . .this is good."

She nodded. "Most everything from the bakeshop is pretty tasty."

"I'll bet the Clemonses are going to miss your help when you quit work after we're married. Speaking of which, I stopped over at the Larsons' this morning and gave them our first month's rent."

"So we're definitely taking the place?"

"Jah, if you're still okay with the idea of living there until I'm able to build our own house."

"I'd be willing to live anywhere with you." Ruth's tone was sincere, and the tender look she gave Martin made him wish he could marry her right then.

He took her hand. "Just a few more weeks, and we'll be husband and wife for the rest of our lives."

"If I can get my wedding dress done in time," she said, dropping her gaze to the table.

"I thought you were going to make it today."

"I was until the material got shredded."

"Huh?"

"Someone shredded all the clothes Mom and I hung on the line this morning—including the material for my wedding dress."

The rhythm of his heartbeat picked up. "Someone deliberately shredded your clothes?"

She nodded. "We found footprints leading from the clothesline into the field that separates our place from the Larsons'. We think whoever did it ran over there."

Martin's jaw clenched as he mulled things over. "If I'd known about this sooner, I would have mentioned it to the Larsons when I went by their place."

Ruth leaned forward with her elbows on the table. "Martha thought it might be Drew, the Larsons' grandson who's been visiting for the past couple of weeks. After we discovered the footprints, she headed over there to ask about it."

"What'd they say?"

"They assured her that Drew hadn't left their property all morning."

"Did Martha believe them?"

Ruth shrugged. "I guess so. She had no reason not to."

"Was Sheriff Osborn notified?"

"Grace and I went to town while Martha was at the Larsons', and we stopped to see the sheriff."

"What'd he say?"

"Just that he'd be keeping a closer eye on things and that we should let him know if anything else happens. Oh, and also that he's questioned Gary Walker and doesn't think he's had anything to do with the attacks."

"That's it? He didn't come out to look at the footprints or check around the place for evidence?"

She shook her head. "If you want my opinion, he hasn't taken anything that's been done to us seriously enough. But don't tell Dad I said so, because as you know, he doesn't want the sheriff involved any more than he already is."

Martin nodded. "So if it wasn't the Larsons' grandson who shredded the clothes, do you have any idea who might have done it?"

"Grace thinks Gary Walker, that reporter, did it. According to Sadie, Gary has left town now, so hopefully things will settle down again."

"Let's hope so," he said, giving her fingers a gentle squeeze. "I can't have my bride wearing shredded wedding clothes."

She offered him a feeble smile. Martin had a hunch that Ruth was a lot more upset than she was letting on. He leaned close to her ear and whispered, "Everything will be all right once we're married; you'll see."

"I'm worried about your mamm," Roman said as he entered the section of the barn where Martha kenneled her dogs and found her kneeling on the floor, brushing the female sheltie.

"You mean because she went to bed early this evening?" she asked, looking up from her job.

He nodded and took a seat on the wooden stool sitting in the corner of the room.

"It's been a trying day, and Mom said she had a headache. I'm sure she'll feel better by morning."

"Sure hope so." He drew in a deep breath and released it with a groan. "I'd really hoped these attacks would end, but it doesn't look like they will until someone is caught."

Martha put Heidi back in her cage and set the brush on the table where she kept her grooming supplies. "How's that ever going to happen, Dad?"

"I don't know." He gave his left earlobe a tug. "Were there any clues near the clothesline?"

She shook her head. "Nothing except for some footprints leading to the Larsons' property."

"The Larsons'?"

"Jah. I'd thought at first it could have been done by their grandson, Drew, but when I went over there to talk to them, I learned that Drew had been there all morning."

"Hmm. . . Sure wish I knew for sure who's been doing all these things."

"I hope you don't still suspect Luke."

"Well, his sunglasses were found on the ground after your mamm's clothesline was cut. And then his straw hat was found near the barn right after that brick was thrown through the kitchen window."

"Those incidents happened last year," she reminded him. "Besides, Luke admitted the items were his and said he had dropped them."

Roman folded his arms. "I didn't believe him then, and I've got my suspicions that the pack of cigarettes I found the day our place got toilet-papered might have belonged to Luke too."

"Maybe someone's trying to make it look like Luke's the one responsible. Have you thought of that possibility?"

He shrugged. "Guess anything's possible, but Luke more than any of the other suspects on our list has reason to get even with me."

"How do you know the one doing the attacks is trying to get even with you? Maybe it's as Grace says, and the reporter's trying to get even with her."

"I suppose it's possible, but—"

"I don't believe Luke would boldly commit acts of vandalism against his own people, even if he is angry with you."

"Bishop King thinks I'm being too harsh and judgmental where Luke's concerned."

Martha stared at the floor.

"Well," Roman said as he stepped down from the stool, "we won't solve anything by gabbing. I've got some horses that need to be fed."

"And I still need to brush Fritz," Martha said, reaching for the dog brush.

"Don't stay out here working with those dogs too late, you hear?"

"I won't, Dad."

As Roman headed for the horse stalls, he offered up a silent prayer. *Father in heaven, please keep my family safe.*

Chapter 16

"You don't look so well. Are you feeling all right?" Cleon asked Grace as they sat at the breakfast table the next morning.

She pushed her spoon around in her bowl. "I'm tired and not so hungry."

"Can I have your piece of toast?" Anna asked. "I'm very hungry this morning."

Grace handed her toast over to Anna. "Do you want more oatmeal, too?"

Anna shook her head. "I think I'll be full after I eat the toast."

Grace offered Anna a feeble smile as she reached for her cup of tea.

"Are you still upset about what happened yesterday?" Cleon asked.

"A little," she replied with a shrug. "But I think everything's going to be okay now that Gary has left town."

"We don't know if he's the one who. . ." Cleon's voice trailed off when he noticed Anna staring at him. "Let's talk about this later, okay?"

Grace nodded and pushed away from the table. "Right now I need to get lunches fixed for you and Anna so you can be off to work and I can take her to school."

"Would you like me to take her this morning?" he asked.

"I'd better do it since you have to open the woodworking shop."

"I'm sure your daed's done that already."

Grace shook her head. "While you were out checking on your bee boxes earlier, Dad stopped by the house and said he was taking Mom to see the chiropractor this morning. She complained of a headache yesterday, so he thinks her neck might be out of adjustment."

"Sorry to hear she's hurting." Cleon stood and moved over to the counter where Grace had begun making their lunches. "I could still drive Anna to school and then open the shop after I get back."

"There's no need for you to do that."

Cleon reached for his lunch box. "Guess I'll head to work, then. If you're feeling up to it, stop down during my lunch hour and we can talk some more."

She nodded. "I will."

Cleon gave Grace a kiss on the cheek and started for the door. His fingers had just touched the doorknob when Anna called out to him.

"Have a good day, Papa."

He turned and smiled at her. "You have a good day too, Anna."

By the time Grace returned from taking Anna to school, she'd noticed some pain in her lower back, so she decided to rest on the couch awhile.

She punched the pillow under her head a few times, trying to find a comfortable position, then finally dozed off.

Sometime later she awoke. Finding the sofa damp, she realized her water had broken. Her stomach cramped, and she groaned. "I think I'd better get to the birthing center as soon as I can."

Figuring her folks were probably back from town by now, Grace headed over to their place to see if Mom would walk down to the phone shed and call someone to give her a ride to the Doughty View Midwifery Center, where many Amish women from their community went to have their babies.

By the time Grace reached her folks' house, the pains had increased. They were still far enough apart that she figured they had plenty of time to get to the birthing center before the baby came.

She opened the back door and stuck her head inside. "Mom? Are you to home?"

No answer.

"Martha, are you here?"

No response.

Grace stepped into the kitchen and leaned against the counter as another contraction gripped her stomach. When it eased, she moved over to the table to take a seat and spotted a note lying there. It was from Martha, letting Mom know that she'd gone to work at Irene's.

"I'd better go down to the woodworking shop and let Cleon know what's happening," Grace murmured. "I don't think this boppli will wait until Mom gets home."

Cleon had just begun sanding a set of cabinets when Grace entered the shop, looking pale and shaken.

"What's wrong?" he asked, moving quickly to her side. "Has there been another attack?"

She shook her head. "I'm in labor."

Cleon's mouth fell open. "Are you sure?"

"My water broke, and I'm having some pretty hard contractions." Grace grasped the edge of his workbench. "Mom and Dad still aren't home, and Martha left a note on Mom's table saying she was going to your mamm's place to work. So I came here to see if you'd call someone to drive me to the birthing center."

Cleon nodded. He led Grace over to a chair behind her dad's desk. "Sit right here. I won't be long."

He made a dash for the door and ran all the way to the phone shed. His fingers trembled as he dialed the Larsons' number, and he felt relief when Donna answered on the second ring.

"Grace is in labor. We need a ride to the Doughty View Midwifery Center," he panted.

"Ray's gone for the day, but I'll be right over," Donna said.

"We'll be waiting for you at Roman's shop."

When Cleon returned to the shop, he found Grace slumped over the desk. "What's happened? Are you okay?"

She lifted her head. "Yes."

"I spoke with Donna, and she's on her way. We should be at the birthing center soon."

"I hope so, because the pains are coming quicker."

"Do you think I should call 911 and get an ambulance here?"

Grace shook her head. "I'm sure we have enough time to get there before the boppli's born."

"That had better be the case, because I've never delivered a baby before—just a couple of calves."

Grace gritted her teeth, and Cleon figured she was having another contraction. "I don't think you'll have to deliver this baby, so you needn't look so worried," she said.

A horn honked. "That must be Donna." Cleon helped Grace out the door and into Donna's car. "I'd better ride in the back with my wife," he told Donna.

She nodded. "No problem."

They'd only gone a short distance when Donna's car overheated and she had to pull onto the shoulder of the road. "I told Ray to check under the hood the last time he filled my car with gas," Donna mumbled. "I suspected there was a leak in the radiator, but he said he would check things out and take care of it if there was a problem."

Grace moaned and clutched the front of Cleon's shirt. "The pains are coming faster."

Cleon's mouth went dry. Was he going to have to deliver this baby?

———————◆◆◆———————

As Ruth headed down the road toward home, her thoughts went to Martin. In just a few weeks they would become husband and wife, and she could hardly wait. She planned to work on her wedding dress this evening, and things were coming together. Cleon's sister, Carolyn, would provide candles for the tables, and Martha and Sadie had agreed to be her attendants. Martin's brother, Dan, and the bishop's son, Toby, would be his attendants.

Ruth's thoughts were halted when she spotted Donna Larson's car stopped along the side of the road with the hood up and a curl of steam pouring out. Donna stood beside the car shaking her head.

Ruth guided her horse and buggy to the shoulder of the road, climbed down, and hurried over to Donna's car. "What's the problem? Did your car overheat?"

"Yes, and your sister's in the backseat, about to have her baby." Donna grimaced. "I left my cell phone at home, so I can't even call for help. I was hoping another car would come by, but you're the first person I've seen since the car overheated."

Ruth hurried around to the back of the car and jerked the door open. She was surprised to see Cleon there, red-faced, wide-eyed, and hunched over Grace. "Don't push, Grace. Not yet," he instructed.

Grace's face twisted in obvious pain. "It's coming, Cleon. The boppli is coming."

Ruth's knees nearly buckled as she struggled against a wave of dizziness. She couldn't just stand here like a ninny; she had to do something to help her sister. The only experience she'd had with birthing was watching one of their barn cats deliver her kittens, so she wasn't sure what to do.

Cleon didn't seem to notice Ruth as he continued to coach Grace. "Easy now. We're almost there. That's it. . . . I can see the head. . . . Okay now, push!"

Unable to watch, yet reluctant to look away, Ruth felt her eyes mist as she witnessed the miracle of birth. A few seconds later, she heard a lusty cry, and a newborn babe lay across her sister's stomach.

"It's a buwe!" Cleon cried. "We have ourselves a boy!"

Grace lay exhausted against the seat as she stroked her son's downy dark head. *"Gott is gut,"* she murmured. "Jah, God is good."

Chapter 17

As Grace settled herself against the cleaned sofa cushions, snuggling a tiny bundle of joy in her arms, she reflected on all that had transpired during the last twenty-four hours. She'd fully intended to have her baby at the Doughty View Midwifery Center. Instead, she'd ended up giving birth in the backseat of Donna Larson's car, with Cleon acting as midwife. After Ruth went to the nearest phone shed to call for help, Grace and the baby had been taken by ambulance to the hospital in Millersburg to be checked over. Then Ruth had gone home to tell her folks and Martin's family the news and to see that Anna was picked up from school. This morning, Cleon had called Ray Larson to pick them up at the hospital, and now Grace and the baby were home where they belonged.

"Come say hello to your little bruder," Grace said, motioning for Anna to take a seat beside her.

The child hovered near the sofa, wearing an expectant look on her face, but she finally sat down. "He's sure tiny and red in the face. What's his name?" she asked, leaning close to the baby.

"Don't put your face so near to his," Cleon said as he took a seat on the other side of Grace. "You've had a cold, and I don't want you giving it to the boppli."

Anna scrunched up her nose. "That was last week, Papa. I'm feelin' fine now."

"Even so, I'd prefer you not breathe any germs on the baby."

Grace pursed her lips. "Cleon, I don't think—"

He held up his hand. "She can look at the boppli without putting her face right up to his."

Grace figured Cleon was just being overprotective and would soon relax, so she decided it was best not to make an issue of it.

"What's his name?" Anna asked again, looking up at Grace.

"Daniel," Cleon said before Grace could respond. He reached over and touched the baby's dark head. "Daniel Jacob Schrock."

Anna's forehead wrinkled. "Is he gonna cry all the time? Esta said her little sister, Molly, cried so much when she was a boppli that Esta had to stuff cotton in her ears so she could sleep."

"Some babies do cry a lot, but hopefully Daniel won't cry much at night," Grace said.

"Can I hold him?"

"Yes."

"No!"

Cleon and Grace had spoken at the same time, and Anna appeared confused.

"He's too little for you to hold yet," Cleon said.

Again, Grace fought the urge to dispute what he'd said. She didn't want Anna to think she was usurping Cleon's authority. Except for Carl Davis, Anna's English grandfather, Cleon was the only father the child had ever known. They had developed a good relationship over the last several months, and Grace didn't want anything to spoil it.

Grace patted Anna's arm. "You can hold him when he's a little bigger, okay?"

Anna nodded, but her eyes were downcast. She sat a few seconds, then hopped off the couch.

"Where are you going?" Grace called.

"To my room to play with my faceless doll. At least she's not too little for me to hold."

Grace turned to Cleon and was about to comment on his behavior toward Anna when Ruth stepped into the room, followed by Martha, Mom, and Dad.

Anxious to see her nephew, Ruth rushed into the room ahead of her family. "What a sweet little bundle of joy," she exclaimed as she approached the sofa.

Grace smiled. "Danki. We think we'll keep him."

In a confused babble of voices, everyone asked Grace how she was doing, how much the baby weighed, and what name had been chosen for him.

"His name is Daniel Jacob," Cleon said. "He weighs eight pounds, four ounces, and Grace is doing fine."

"A nice, healthy size." Mom extended her hands. "May I hold my first grandson?"

Grace looked over at Cleon as if waiting for his approval. When he nodded, she handed the baby to Mom.

"It feels so good to hold him," Mom said as she took a seat in the rocking chair. "Makes me think of the days when you girls were *bopplin*." She smiled at Ruth. "Isn't he a fine-looking baby?"

"He certainly is," Ruth replied. "And when you get tired of holding him, it'll be my turn."

"I'll hold him after that." Martha turned to Dad. "Guess you'll have to go last."

He hunkered down next to the rocking chair. "Makes no never mind to me. Whenever I hold a boppli, they usually start crying."

Mom's gaze went to the ceiling. "You know that's not true, Roman. As I recall, our girls used to fall asleep as soon as you picked them up."

"Humph! That's not much better—saying I was so boring I put our girls to sleep."

"That's not what I meant, Roman."

"Where's Anna?" Ruth asked, changing the subject. "I figured she would be the first in line to hold her little bruder."

"Anna's upstairs in her room. She said she wanted to play with her faceless doll," Grace was quick to say.

"She's probably pretending she has her own boppli." Mom placed the baby over her shoulder and patted his back. "I remember when Martha was born, Grace and Ruth played with their dolls and pretended they were little *midder*."

Cleon reached for Grace's hand. "Are you getting tired? Would you like to go to our room and rest awhile?" he asked.

She shook her head. "I'm fine."

Ruth could see the weariness on her sister's face, and she felt concern. "Maybe it would be best if we went home and let Grace and the baby get settled in," she suggested. "The rest of us can hold the boppli tomorrow."

"You're right," Mom said as she handed the baby to Ruth. "You can put this little guy back in his mamm's arms, and we'll be on our way." She smiled. "I've got a big batch of stew simmering on the stove, so I'll have Martha bring some over for your supper."

"Danki, that'd be nice," Grace replied with a yawn. "It'll be a few days before I feel up to doing much cooking."

"We'll chip in to help wherever we're needed." Ruth stared down at baby Daniel, and a lump formed in her throat. Oh, how she longed to be a mother.

"Did you hear that Grace had her baby yesterday afternoon?" Martin asked Abe as he stepped into the harness shop and hung his hat on a wall peg near the door.

"Nope, I hadn't heard that. What'd she have?"

"A boy, and he was born in the backseat of Donna Larson's car." Martin moved over to the desk, where Abe sat making a list of supplies he needed. "Ruth came over to my folks' place last night and told us about it."

Abe's eyebrows lifted. "How'd that happen?"

"Donna was giving them a ride to the Doughty View Midwifery Center, and her car overheated. I guess Cleon was in the backseat with Grace when the boppli decided it couldn't wait to be born."

"Whew!" Abe let out a whistle. "I can't imagine what it must have been like for Cleon to deliver his own son. I'd have been a nervous wreck."

"Ruth was on her way home from work and spotted Donna's car. When she stopped to see if there was a problem, she discovered Grace in the backseat about to give birth." Martin leaned on Abe's desk and smiled. "I can't wait until Ruth and I are married and can start our own family."

"You might change your mind about that when you have to change dirty *windle* and are kept up all night with a colicky baby." Abe grunted. "Never liked either of those things, but then I—"

Abe's oldest son, Gideon, entered the shop. "Aw, Papa, do you have to work today?" he grumbled. "It's Saturday, and I was hopin' we could go fishing."

"Not today, son." Abe motioned to the stack of papers on his desk. "I've got supplies to order and bills that need to be paid."

Gideon kicked a scrap of leather lying on the floor and grunted. "If you're not workin', you're sleepin'. If you're not sleepin', you're workin'."

"I've got to make a living," Abe said. "Otherwise there'll be no food on our table."

Gideon shuffled out the door with his head down and shoulders slumped.

Abe looked up at Martin. "See what I mean? Being a daed isn't all sugar and cream. Fact is, there are times when it's more like vinegar and sauerkraut. 'Course, I wouldn't trade my kinner for anything. On their good days, they can be a real blessing."

Martin moved over to the cupboard where the dye was kept. One thing he knew: when he became a father, he would never be too busy to spend time with his kinner.

Chapter 18

I can't believe Ruth is getting married today," Grace said as she placed a dish of oatmeal in front of Cleon. "It seems like only yesterday that you and I were preparing for our wedding."

He smiled. "Are you sure you're feeling up to going? It's only been a few weeks since the boppli was born, and I know you're still pretty wrung out."

"I'll be fine," she said, taking a seat across from him. "There's no way I'm going to miss my sister's wedding."

Cleon nodded. "If you get tired or Daniel gets fussy, you can always come home and rest, since the wedding will be at your folks' place."

"That's true." Grace looked over at Anna, who sat in the chair beside her. "Are you excited about attending your aunt Ruth's wedding?"

Anna merely shrugged in reply.

"There'll be lots of good food served during the wedding meal."

"Will Esta be there?"

"I'm sure she will, and the rest of Abe's family too."

"Will Daniel be going?"

"Of course. We sure wouldn't leave him home by himself." Cleon frowned at Anna.

Anna reached for a piece of toast. "Can I take my doll along? Then I'll have a boppli to bring to the wedding too."

"That's fine with me." Grace pushed her chair away from the table. "Speaking of babies, I hear your little brother fussing in the other room, so I'd best tend to his needs."

"Want me to get him?" Cleon asked.

"I'd better do it. He's probably ready to eat by now." Grace smiled. "And then we'd better hurry or we'll be late to the wedding."

———————◆◆◆———————

As Ruth listened to Bishop King deliver the main wedding sermon, her hands turned sweaty, and her mouth felt so dry she could barely swallow. It seemed as if she'd waited her whole life for this moment. Becoming a wife and mother was what she had dreamed about ever since she was a girl. She glanced over at Martin, who sat across from her, and the rhythm of her heartbeat picked up when he smiled. Today was their day—a perfect day with clear blue skies and plenty of sunshine. Their families and friends were here to see them become husband and wife. There had been no more attacks on Ruth's family for the past several weeks, and despite the swirling sensation of excitement she felt in her stomach, her soul was filled with peace.

" 'Wives, submit yourselves unto your own husbands, as unto the Lord. For the husband is the head of the wife, even as Christ is the head of the church: and he is the saviour of the body,' " the bishop quoted from Ephesians 5:22–23.

He paused and said, "We have two people who have agreed to enter the state of matrimony—Martin Gingerich and Ruth Hostettler. If anyone here has any objection, he has this opportunity to make it known."

Ruth breathed a sigh of relief when everyone in the room remained quiet. Not that she thought anyone would really protest.

"Since there are obviously no objections, you may come forth in the name of the Lord," the bishop said.

Martin and Ruth left their seats and stood before him.

As Ruth stared into Martin's eyes and answered each of the bishop's questions, her heart swelled with joy and hope for the future—a future as Mrs. Martin Gingerich.

———◆◆◆———

After the wedding service, Martha took a seat at the table with the others from the wedding party and glanced across the room. Her breath caught in her throat when she spotted Luke sitting with a group of young men. He smiled and seemed to be joking around, so she was fairly certain he wasn't upset about Ruth marrying Martin. Funny thing, though, she hadn't seen him hanging around any other Amish women since he and Ruth broke up. She figured either Luke had decided he wasn't interested in courting right now, or he was seeing some English girl on the sly.

I don't suppose he'd be interested in anyone like me, she thought ruefully.

"You're awfully quiet." Sadie poked Martha's arm. "Are you upset because Ruth will be moving out of your house and settling into a new home with Martin?"

Martha frowned. "Of course not. I'm happy that both of my sisters have found good husbands."

"Martin and Ruth didn't have a very long courtship, did they?" Before Martha could comment, Sadie added, "Then there's me and Toby. He's been courting me over a year now, and still no proposal of marriage. I'm beginning to wonder if he'll ever ask me to marry him."

"Maybe he's having too much fun courting and doesn't feel ready to be tied down to marriage yet."

Sadie grunted. "Jah, well, if he doesn't make up his mind soon, I might just look for another fellow."

Martha blinked. "Do you have someone else in mind?"

Sadie shook her head. "There's no one I'd rather be with than Toby."

Martha glanced at Luke again. He wore his Dutch-bobbed hair a little longer than it should be, but she thought he looked appealing. The jaunty way he held his head whenever he spoke caused Martha's heart to race and made her wish she could be his girlfriend.

"How are things going with your business these days?" Sadie asked, changing the subject.

"Not so well." Martha sighed. "Flo still isn't pregnant, and neither is Heidi. As soon as I have enough money saved up from my job working for Cleon's mother, I hope to buy a couple more dogs."

"Have you considered offering boarding services?"

Martha nodded. "I have. In fact, I mentioned that idea to my daed not long ago, and he said he would think about it."

Sadie smiled. "Now that Ruth's married and won't be returning to the bakeshop, you might consider applying there if you need more money."

"Between my part-time job working for Irene and taking care of my dogs, I'm pretty busy these days. But I'll keep the bakeshop in mind."

"Don't wait too long to decide, because I'm sure the Clemonses will find a replacement for Ruth as soon as they can."

Martha shrugged. She caught sight of Luke and two other young men leaving their places at the table and heading out the door. She figured they were probably in need of some fresh air or wanted to visit without having to talk over the loud voices in the room. She was tempted to follow but knew that wouldn't be proper. Besides, she was one of Ruth's attendants, and her place was right here.

"Mama, is it all right if I spend the night at Esta's?" Anna asked as she tugged on Grace's dress sleeve.

"Jah, sure, that'll be fine," Cleon said before his wife could respond.

Grace turned in her chair and gave him an icy stare. "Don't I have anything to say about this?"

"I figured you'd be okay with the idea," Cleon said. "It'll be nice for us to have a quiet evening alone with Daniel."

Grace's eyes narrowed into tiny slits. Cleon knew she wasn't happy about what he'd said—but didn't she realize how important it was for them to have quality time with the baby without Anna being there asking questions and begging to hold her little brother?

"Is it all right if I go home with Esta?" Anna asked, giving Grace's sleeve another tug.

"Does Esta's daed know about this?" Grace questioned.

Anna nodded. "He said it's fine with him, and so did Esta's aunt Sue."

"All right, you may go." Grace squeezed her daughter's shoulder. "Grandma Schrock's holding baby Daniel right now, so I'm free to walk you home to get your nightgown and a change of clothes for tomorrow."

Cleon shook his head. "You look tired, Grace. I think we should go home now. You can pack Anna's things, and I'll bring her back over here so she's ready whenever Abe says it's time for his brood to go."

Grace didn't argue, and he felt relief. She did look done in.

Cleon pushed his chair aside and stood. "I'll get the boppli from my mamm, and we'll be on our way."

———————◆•◆———————

"Everything's going well today, wouldn't you say?" Martin asked Ruth as they sat at their special corner table eating a piece of wedding cake.

She smiled. "All our guests seem to be having a good time."

He thumped his stomach and grinned. "Can't remember the last time I ate this much food."

Ruth nodded. "There's so much chicken, mashed potatoes, dressing, gravy, salads, and vegetables, not to mention all the desserts and cakes. This morning I felt so nervous I could barely eat breakfast. But I've more than made up for it this afternoon."

Martin glanced across the room and spotted Abe sitting at a table with his boys. His shoulders were slumped, and he wore a forlorn expression, making Martin wonder if the man wasn't having a good time. Poor Abe still missed Alma and was probably thinking about their wedding day. It had to have been hard for him to come here today. Abe was not only Martin's boss, but a good friend. Martin was sure Abe had come to the wedding to let him know that he approved of his marriage.

Martin was about to excuse himself to speak with Abe when—*kaboom!*—an explosion sounded from outside, causing the windows to vibrate.

"Wh–what was that?" Ruth's eyes widened, and her mouth hung slightly open.

"I don't know, but I'm going to find out."

Martin, along with several other men, rushed outside. A quick glance around the yard revealed that one of the portable outhouses set up to accommodate the guests had been blown up.

"Talk about starting your marriage off with a bang." Toby slapped Martin's back. "Looks like some of our *yuchend* thought it would be fun to shake things up a bit."

Everyone laughed, and someone pointed to what was left of the outhouse. Martin was fairly certain it had been blown up by one of his youthful buddies as a prank. Well, he wasn't going to let it rile him. With a chuckle and a shrug, he headed back inside to carry on with the wedding meal. Someone else could clean up the mess.

Chapter 19

Ruth's heart hammered so hard she feared it might burst open. "What was it?" she asked when Martin returned to the house. "What caused that horrible noise?"

"It's nothing to worry about," he said, taking a seat beside her. "Someone blew up one of the outhouses."

"What?" Ruth touched his arm. "Oh Martin, have the attacks on my family begun again?"

"I don't think so. Some of the fellows were outside snickering, so I'm pretty sure they had something to do with the outhouse blowing up."

"How can you be so sure? I mean, with all the other things that have gone on—"

He smiled and took her hand. "It wasn't an attack—just some tomfoolery going on with some of the single fellows who wanted to be sure we remembered our special day."

"I'll always remember our wedding day." Ruth's voice was thick with emotion. "We sure didn't need some *verhuddelt* friends of yours blowing up an outhouse in order to make this day special."

"Someday when we're old and gray, we'll look back on our wedding day and laugh about what those mixed-up friends of mine did." Martin chuckled. "Just think what a fun time we'll have telling our kinner and *kinskinner* about it."

She nudged him in the ribs. "You might have fun telling that story, but I sure won't. I don't think it's one bit funny."

"I agree with Ruth," Martha said as she took her seat again. "What if someone had been using that outhouse when it blew up? They could have been seriously hurt."

"I wonder what Dad has to say about all this." Ruth glanced around the room, trying to locate her parents. "I don't see him or Mom anywhere."

"Mom's in the kitchen making sure everything's going okay," Martha said. "Dad's out on the porch, talking to Bishop King."

"I think they're discussing the outhouse incident," Toby put in as he joined the group at the table. "I told my daed that I'd seen Luke hanging around the outhouses when I went outside for some fresh air. Makes me wonder if he wasn't the one responsible for the explosion."

Martin's forehead wrinkled. "Why would Luke do something like that?"

"You don't know?" Toby asked.

He shook his head.

Toby motioned to Ruth. "You stole his girl. Maybe he's trying to get even."

Ruth shook her head. "Martin didn't *steal* me. I broke up with Luke before Martin asked if he could court me."

"Well, there you go. Luke's probably mad because you dumped him." Toby grunted. "That fellow's been acting strange for some time now. I wouldn't put anything past him."

Martha glared at Toby. "You have no proof that Luke blew up the outhouse or that he wants to get even with Ruth for breaking up with him." She breathed in deeply. "Besides, it's not your place to judge."

Toby squinted at her and dropped into a chair. "That may be true, but my daed's the bishop, and if he thinks Luke needs to be questioned, then he'll do it."

———◆◆◆———

"So what do you think about that outhouse being blown apart? Do you think it's another attack on our family?" Roman asked the bishop as they took seats in wicker chairs on the porch.

Bishop King folded his arms and stared out at the yard. "From what Toby said, it appeared to be a prank. Probably done by some of Martin's friends, hoping to make him remember this day."

"Humph!" Roman said with a huff. "I can think of better ways to help a friend remember his wedding than to scare all the guests half out of their wits."

The bishop pulled his fingers through the ends of his lengthy beard. "I remember on my wedding day, some of my friends took the wheels off my buggy and then set the rig on wooden blocks. I soon discovered that they'd also stuffed a bunch of straw inside." He chuckled. "Peggy and I were plucking straw out of our clothes for weeks after that."

Roman smiled despite his concerns over the outhouse incident. Maybe it had just been a prank. He certainly hoped that was all it was.

———◆◆———

As Abe headed down the road with some of his children and Anna in tow, he felt a sense of relief. He had decided to leave the Hostettlers' right after he'd finished eating the meal. It had been hard enough to sit through the wedding and watch Martin and Ruth say their vows, and he had no desire to stay all afternoon and into the evening as many other folks probably would do.

"Danki for letting Anna come home with us," Esta said as she snuggled against Abe's side. "We're gonna play with Winkie as soon as we get home. Right, Anna?"

Anna, who sat beside Esta, lifted the faceless doll in her lap. "I'd like to play with our dolls too."

"Okay," Esta said with an agreeable nod.

Abe smiled. It was good to see his daughter smiling again. Abe hoped Martin realized how fortunate he was to be getting such a fine woman for his wife. Ruth had a heart full of love; she'd shown that the day of Alma's funeral, when she'd comforted Esta, and then later when she'd given Esta the puppy.

Abe heard a grunt and glanced over his shoulder. Gideon sat in the backseat with his shoulders slumped and his head down. He hadn't said a word since they'd left the Hostettlers' place. Josh sat next to Gideon, leaning against the seat with his eyes closed. It was obvious that he'd fallen asleep. Abe's other three children had ridden in another buggy with Abe's sister, since there wasn't room for them all in one rig.

"Say, Gideon," Abe called over his shoulder, "how would you like to go fishing with me and Martin soon?"

No response.

"We've been talking about taking next Saturday off, since work's slowed up a bit. We'll do some fishing at the pond. What do you say?"

Gideon grunted.

"Would you like to go or not?"

"Maybe."

Abe smiled and shook the reins as the horse took them up a small hill. A day of fishing might do him and Gideon both some good.

Cleon took a seat on the sofa next to Grace and studied his son's precious face. The baby had just finished nursing and looked relaxed and sleepy.

"He's a good baby, jah?" Cleon looked over at Grace and smiled.

She nodded. "Anna was a good boppli too."

"I wouldn't know about that since I wasn't around to see her as a baby."

She flinched as if she'd been slapped. "As you know, I missed most of my daughter's babyhood."

"Then how do you know she was a good baby?"

"I was with Anna for her first six months. During that time, she hardly ever cried unless she was hungry or needed her windle changed."

Cleon stroked the baby's soft cheek with his thumb. "The Lord was good to give us this boppli to raise. Maybe it'll help make up for the years you lost when Anna's English grandparents took her away."

Grace shook her head. "I'm glad we have Daniel, but it doesn't bring back the years I missed with Anna."

"No, I don't suppose, but—" Cleon halted his words, realizing it would do no good to rehash the past. It couldn't be changed. They had a future to look forward to now. Reaching his arms toward the baby, he said, "How about I hold the little fellow for a while?"

She lifted the baby over her shoulder and patted him on the back. "He needs to burp first."

"Jah, okay."

The minutes ticked away on the battery-operated clock across the room.

"What's wrong with him? Why hasn't he let loose with a burp?" Cleon asked, feeling a sense of impatience.

"He will when he's ready."

Several more minutes went by, and finally Daniel released a loud burp.

Cleon held out his arms again, but then Daniel started hiccupping.

Grace continued to pat the little fellow's back, and Cleon's impatience grew stronger.

"Can't you do something to make him stop?"

She compressed her lips and glared at him. "I'm doing the best I can. Can't you learn to have more patience?"

"You don't have to be so snappish. I just want to hold my son."

"He's my son too, and right now he needs his mother." She continued to pat the baby's back, rubbing her fingers up and down his spine between each little thump.

"Want me to try?"

She shook her head.

"Maybe you're not firm enough with your touch."

With an exasperated sigh, Grace handed the baby to Cleon and stood.

"Where are you going?"

"Out to the kitchen to fix him a bottle of warm water. That always stopped Anna's hiccups."

Grace left the room, and Cleon continued with the pat-rub-pat-rub method she had begun, but Daniel's hiccups seemed to increase. By the time Grace returned to the living room, Cleon was ready to turn the baby over to her again.

She took a seat in the rocking chair, and Cleon placed the baby in her lap. After a few ounces of water, the hiccupping subsided.

Cleon was about to ask if he could hold Daniel again, but Grace spoke first.

"There's something I've been wanting to speak with you about, Cleon."

"What's that?"

"It's about Anna and the way things are between you."

His forehead wrinkled. "What's that supposed to mean?"

"Strained, like they were before when you were upset with me for not telling you about my past."

"I forgave you for that," Cleon said, feeling his defenses rise. "And I asked you and Anna to forgive me for the way I'd treated you both."

She nodded. "I know you did, and you were an attentive father to Anna until Daniel was born. Now you've started giving him all your attention and treating her like she doesn't matter."

"I haven't done that."

"Jah, you have. It's obvious to me that Anna's feeling your rejection, which might cause her to resent her little brother."

Cleon grunted. "I think you're making more out of this than there is."

"No, I'm not. I really believe that—"

He jumped up and started for the door.

"Where are you going?"

"I don't feel like arguing with you, Grace. I think I'll go over to your folks' and see if they need help with anything."

Cleon heard the rocking chair squeak and figured she had started rocking the baby, but he didn't turn around. So much for a quiet, pleasant evening with just the three of them.

Chapter 20

I'm so *uffgschafft*," Ruth said a couple of days later as she followed Martin into their little rental house.

Martin set the box he'd been carrying onto the kitchen counter and grinned. "I'm real excited too."

"I like it here." Her nose twitched. "Even if it does smell like *schtink-ich* paint."

"Jah," he agreed, "but it won't take long for the smelly odor to settle down."

"I'm looking forward to setting out my hope chest items, as well as all the wedding gifts we received."

He pulled her into his arms and kissed her tenderly. "You make me feel so happy. I'm thankful God brought us together."

Ruth nestled against his chest and sighed. "I hope He gives us many good years together."

He nuzzled her cheek with the tip of his nose. "Many good years and lots of kinner to love."

"Jah."

He pulled away slowly. "As nice as this feels, we have some work to do if we're going to make it over to my folks' for supper by six o'clock."

"Your mamm said she was planning to fix your favorite meal—stuffed cabbage rolls." She poked him playfully in the ribs. "And I wouldn't want to make you late for that."

He chuckled and gave her another hug.

"We won't get any work done that way."

He surveyed the small kitchen, and his face sobered. "Both of our families were a big help in getting our things moved over here yesterday, and then your daed brought us that load of wood for our stove last night. I think we ought to have them all over for a meal sometime after the first of the year."

"Since I'm no longer working at the bakeshop, I'll be home all day and will have time to cook up a storm." Ruth smiled. "I think it would be good if we had Abe and his family over soon too. It would be a nice break for Sue."

Martin drew her into his arms again. "You're such a thoughtful fraa. Have I told you how much I love you?"

"Only about a hundred times since our wedding."

He snickered. "But that was two days ago. I'm going to need to say it at least a hundred more times before this day is out."

"And I'll never tire of hearing it," she murmured.

"Are you busy, Dad?" Martha asked as she stepped into her father's wood-working shop. "I'd like to ask you a question."

He looked up from the cabinet he was sanding and smiled. "I've got work to do, but I'm never too busy for you."

She moved quickly across the room, stopping briefly to say hello to Cleon, who was staining a rocking chair.

"What would you like to ask me?" Dad gave the cabinet door a few good swipes with the sandpaper he held.

"It's about my dog business."

He chuckled. "Why am I not surprised?"

"Guess I do talk about my dogs quite a lot."

"That's okay. I know how important they are to you."

She showed him the newspaper in her hand. "I spotted an ad for a pair of cocker spaniels in the paper this morning. Now that I've made some money working for Cleon's mamm, I thought I might buy them. Just wondered what you thought of the idea."

Dad shrugged. "Guess it would be all right, but remember, your other dogs haven't made you any money."

She nodded. "I know, and I'm thinking of selling Flo or trading her at one of the dog auctions."

"Suit yourself. She's your dog."

Martha stared at the newspaper as she contemplated how to bring up her other idea.

"You got something else on your mind?"

"Jah."

"Then *raus mit*—out with it."

"I was wondering if you've thought about the idea of me boarding some dogs. That might give me a steady income."

His eyebrows drew together. "Boarding dogs would mean building more kennels, and that would be a lot of work."

"I know, but I'll help in whatever way I can."

"I'd be willing to build the extra kennels she'll need," Cleon put in.

Dad shook his head. "I can't ask you to do that. You've already got too much going, what with working for me, your beekeeping business, and helping Grace with those two young ones of yours."

"I could ask Martin about helping," Martha said.

"He's newly married and has a job working for Abe," Dad said.

"How about Luke? He's good with wood, and—"

"Absolutely not!" Dad's face turned red, and a muscle on the side of his cheek began to pulsate. "I don't want that troublesome fellow anywhere near you."

"But Dad—"

He waved the piece of sandpaper in front of her face. "Do not ask Luke Friesen for anything—you hear?"

She nodded as a lump formed in her throat. There'd been no proof that Luke was responsible for any of the things that had happened to them. In fact, everything had been quiet around their place for some time.

"I don't think you need to board any dogs right now," Dad said. "Maybe in a few months I'll reconsider. By then I might have the time to build some extra kennels."

Martha opened her mouth to say something more but decided against it. Instead, she whirled around and rushed out the door.

———————— ◆◆ ————————

"That was a great meal, Mom." Martin leaned back in his chair and thumped his stomach. "Danki for fixing my favorite dish."

Mom nodded and looked over at Ruth, who sat in the chair beside her. "If you want to keep my son happy, you'll need to fix stuffed cabbage rolls at least once a week."

"Or more," Martin said with a chuckle.

"I'll be happy to fix cabbage rolls anytime Martin wants, but I doubt I can make them as tasty as yours," Ruth said. "Do you have a special recipe, and if so, would you be willing to share it with me?"

"Jah, sure, only I don't have the recipe written down. It's right here." Mom tapped the side of her head and smiled.

Martin's dad nodded. "My wife's a good cook. Most everything she makes comes from memory."

"Maybe someday I'll have all of Martin's favorite recipes memorized." Ruth looked over at Martin and gave him one of her prettiest smiles.

Martin grinned, thumped his stomach again, and looked over at his mother. "So, Mom, what's for dessert?"

———————— ◆◆ ————————

As Martin and Ruth drove home in their buggy, her head lolled against the seat, and her eyes drifted shut.

"You sleepy?" he asked, reaching over to take her hand.

She yawned. "A little."

"It was a good supper we had, jah?"

"Uh-huh."

"Did you get that recipe for stuffed cabbage rolls written down?"

"It's right in here." Ruth tapped the black handbag lying in her lap.

"When do you plan to make them?"

Her eyes snapped open. "Martin Gingerich, your belly's still full of cabbage rolls and dutch apple pie, and you're already asking when there will be more?"

He snickered. "It's a good thing I've never had a problem with gaining too much weight."

She poked him gently in the ribs. "You might have a problem if you keep eating the way you did tonight."

"I doubt it. Ever since I was a boy, I've been able to eat whatever I want without gaining a bunch of weight."

"Well, there's a first time for everything."

He shrugged. "Would you still love me if I was chubby?"

"Jah."

"If my hair started falling out and I went completely bald, then would you love me?"

"Of course."

"How about if I jabbed myself with a knife while cutting a hunk of leather and got a nasty scar that made me look ugly. Would you love me then?"

Ruth pursed her lips. "You shouldn't even tease about such things. Just thinking about you getting hurt makes me feel grank."

He leaned closer and nuzzled her neck. "Sorry."

She pointed to the hill up ahead, and the buggy jostled. "You'd better keep your mind on your driving, or you might run off the road."

"All right, I'll be good." He gave her a quick wink. "For now, at least."

Ruth smiled as she relaxed against the seat and snuggled under the warm quilt tucked around her legs. This stretch of road was beautiful during the day—with plenty of trees on both sides, well-kept farms, and fields of fresh-cut hay along the way. During the night, however, she couldn't see much. But that was okay. She and Martin were together, and that was all that mattered.

Ruth's head drooped against Martin's shoulder. She was nearly asleep when he nudged her and said, "We're home."

She shivered and rubbed her hands briskly over her arms. "Guess I should have worn a coat instead of my shawl tonight. The quilt kept my legs warm, but not the upper half of my body. I can almost taste the cold."

"Never heard it put quite that way before." He smiled. "If the weather keeps getting colder, we'll soon have snow."

"Maybe you should forget about your plans to go fishing with Abe tomorrow," Ruth said. "I sure wouldn't want to fish in weather this chilly."

"Abe promised Gideon he could go, and I'm looking forward to it as well."

She shrugged. Truth was, she'd hoped she and Martin could spend his day off together—maybe get the house organized.

Martin hopped down from the buggy, then came around to Ruth's side and helped her down. "I'll get an armload of wood and bring it up to the house as soon as I put the horse away. It'll be good to have a nice warm fire this evening."

"Okay. See you inside." Ruth sprinted to the house, where she lit the gas lamps to dispel the darkness. It was almost as chilly inside as it was outside, so she grabbed a dahlia-patterned quilt from the sofa and wrapped it around her shoulders, then took a seat.

The gas lamps sputtered and hissed but brought her no warmth. "What we need is a fire," she murmured.

Martin entered the house a short time later, but his hands were empty.

"Where's the wood you said you would bring in?" she asked.

He shrugged, then shook his head. "It's gone."

"How can it be gone?"

"I don't know, but it is—every last piece."

Her forehead wrinkled. "Did you look all around?"

He nodded. "There was no wood in sight, but I did see some large tire marks near where the pile used to be. I think whoever took it might have been driving a truck."

Ruth's heart pounded. "Oh Martin, you don't suppose whoever took it is the same person who did all the horrible things at my folks' place, do you?"

Martin took a seat on the sofa beside her. "More than likely it's one of my friends—maybe the same ones who blew up the outhouse at our wedding." He touched her hand. "It'll probably be back by morning."

"Maybe we should go see Dad and tell him what's happened."

"What good would that do?"

"He's the one who gave us the wood. It's only right that he knows it was stolen."

Martin shook his head. "I don't think that's necessary."

"Why not?"

He squeezed her fingers. "I'm your husband now. It's my job to look out for you. Besides, your daed didn't seem to care much about the attacks that were done at his place. What makes you think he'll care that our wood was taken?"

Ruth's mouth dropped open. She'd never expected to hear her husband speak out against her father, and she told him so.

"I'm not speaking against him. I'm just stating facts."

Ruth folded her arms and stared straight ahead. "I think he does care about the attacks. He's just chosen to turn the other cheek and trust God to protect our family." She pursed her lips. "I think he has the right to know that the wood he gave us is gone."

"Maybe so, but it can wait until morning."

She shivered. "But I'm cold."

"Then let's go to bed and get warm under the quilts."

"You can go to bed if you want to," she said, rising to her feet.

"Where are you going?"

"I've got work to do in the kitchen."

"What kind of work?"

"We've still got boxes that need to be unloaded and put away."

"They'll be there in the morning, Ruth."

"I want to do them now."

"It's too cold in here to be milling about the kitchen. Let's turn off the gas lamps and head upstairs to bed."

Ruth was tempted to argue, but she didn't want the two of them to spend the night mad at each other. Besides, Martin was right—they could empty boxes in the morning. Maybe by then the wood would be back.

Chapter 21

When Ruth awoke the following morning, she was surprised to feel warm air drifting through their bedroom floor vent. She rolled over and discovered that Martin was gone. Apparently he'd gotten up and built a fire. Maybe the wood had been returned.

Ruth scrambled out of bed and hurried to get dressed.

When she stepped into the kitchen a short time later, she was pleased to find a cozy fire crackling in the woodstove. Martin wasn't in the kitchen. She hurried to put the teakettle on, and a few minutes later, steam began to rise out of the spout. The whistling kettle had a rich, comfortable sound to it, not a shrill sound as it did during the hotter summer months.

When the water was hot enough, she poured some into a cup, plopped a tea bag in, and stepped toward the table. There she discovered a note.

Dear Ruth,

  I've gone fishing with Abe and Gideon. I didn't want to wake you, so I had a piece of leftover apple pie Mom sent home with us last night. Now I'm about to head for Abe's place. The woodpile wasn't back when I got up, so I went over to my folks' and got enough wood to get you by for the day. I shouldn't be gone too late. Oh, and you might want to have the frying pan ready, because I aim to bring home a mess of fish.

                Love,
                Martin

Ruth sighed and sank into a chair at the table. She had hoped Martin might decide to stay home today on account of the cold weather. It upset her to know that whoever had taken their wood hadn't brought it back, but it frustrated her more that Martin thought fishing was more important than helping her unload boxes.

Ruth took a sip of tea and held the warm liquid in her mouth awhile before swallowing. *Maybe I won't unload those boxes either. I think I'll go visit Grace and the baby this morning. After that, I'll stop over at Abe's place and see how his kinner are doing.*

"Can I come, too?" Anna asked when Cleon announced during breakfast that he was going to check on his bee boxes.

Cleon shook his head and reached for his cup of coffee. "I'll be extracting honey from the hives today, and it's not safe for you to be around the bees."

"But I'd like to see where all that honey comes from," the child persisted.

"You would need to wear protective gear, and I don't have any your size."

Anna's lip jutted out, but Cleon seemed to ignore her. The child looked over at Grace. "Can we do something fun after breakfast, Mama—maybe bake some cookies?"

Grace released a weary sigh. "Not today, Anna. I have to bathe the boppli, and after that I've got some sewing to do."

"I could give the baby a bath while you sew."

"Absolutely not!" Cleon shouted before Grace could respond.

"How come?"

"You're not old enough to bathe Daniel. You might drop him or let him slip into the water, and then he could drown."

Anna's chin trembled, and tears gathered in her eyes.

Grace frowned. "You don't have to scare her like that."

"Well, it's true," he said with a grunt. "Anna's barely old enough to bathe herself, and she's sure not capable of caring for her baby brother."

"Many Amish kinner care for their younger siblings," Grace argued. "That's part of a child's training."

"She can learn on one of her dolls, not my child." Cleon pushed his chair away from the table and stood. "I've got work to do."

When the door clicked shut behind him, Grace patted Anna's hand. "We'll find something for you to do today."

Anna poked at the last bit of eggs on her plate. "Since you're so busy with the boppli, and Papa won't let me help with the bees, can I visit Aunt Martha? Maybe I can help feed the dogs."

Grace nodded. "As soon as you've finished your breakfast." She figured having Anna out of the house might be better for her too. Ever since Daniel had been born, Grace had felt irritable and depressed. Maybe it had to do with the fact that Cleon seemed so overprotective of the baby and hadn't spent much time with Anna. Grace had tried talking to him on several occasions, but he always said there wasn't a problem, despite the fact that his relationship with Anna seemed to be going downhill.

After Grace had bundled Anna into a warm jacket, she herded her to the door. "I'll watch you from the porch to be sure you make it to Grandma and Grandpa's."

"I'll be fine, Mama."

"Just the same, I'll feel better when I see that you've made it there safely." Anna shrugged and took off at a run.

Grace couldn't see the back side of her folks' place from the first house Cleon had built for them, but from their new house, Grace was able to see all the way down the driveway.

Leaning on the porch rail, she watched until Anna entered her folks' house, then she stepped back into the warmth of her kitchen. She shouldn't have to worry about her daughter's safety right here on their own property. It wasn't right that everything they did, everywhere they went, she had to be anxious about whether another attack would occur.

Grace tiptoed into the baby's room and was relieved when she found him asleep. His baby breath smelled sweet, and he looked ever so peaceful, sleeping on his side with his little thumb stuck in his mouth. She leaned over the crib and kissed Daniel's downy head. *Bless my baby, Lord. Bless Anna and Cleon too.*

She left Daniel's room and curled up on the sofa in the living room, deciding that she needed a nap. She'd only been resting a few minutes when someone called out, "Grace, are you to home?"

Grace sat up just as Ruth stepped into the room. "I didn't expect to see you today."

"Martin went fishing with Abe and Gideon, so I decided to drop by and see how you and the boppli are doing." Ruth draped her coat over the back of the rocking chair and took a seat.

"Daniel's doing well; he's sleeping right now."

"And you?"

"I'm kind of tired and feeling a bit weepy as of late."

"Do you think it's postpartum depression?"

Grace shrugged. "I suppose it could be, but what's got me feeling down more than anything is the way Cleon's been acting since the boppli was born."

Ruth's forehead wrinkled. "How's he been acting?"

"Possessive of Daniel. He hardly pays Anna any attention unless it's to scold her for something."

"Have you tried talking to him about it?"

"Jah, but he doesn't think he's doing anything wrong."

Ruth grunted. "Men sure can be stubborn."

"Surely you can't mean Martin. You two haven't been married long enough for you to see his stubborn side."

Ruth leaned slightly forward. "Last night after we got home from Martin's folks', we discovered that the pile of wood Dad had given us was gone."

"It was?"

Ruth nodded. "Martin said he thought some of his friends might have taken it as a prank and figured it would be back in our yard by morning."

"Was it?"

"No. By the time I got up, Martin had already gone fishing, but he left me a note saying he'd gotten up early and gone over to his folks' to get some wood before he left for Abe's."

Grace shifted on the sofa. "You don't suppose whoever took it was the same one who blew up the outhouse at your wedding, do you?"

Ruth shrugged. "That's what Martin thinks, but I'm not so sure. There were large tire tracks in the dirt near where the woodpile was, and that makes me think whoever took the wood was driving a truck."

"Do you think it might be another attack—done by whoever has been trying to scare us?"

"Maybe so."

"Have you spoken to Dad about this?"

"Not yet. I wanted to tell him last night, but Martin said it could wait and that we needed to see if the wood was returned."

"Are you going to tell him now?"

"I suppose I could, but it would probably be best if I waited until Martin gets home and we can discuss it more."

"I suppose you're right."

"Where are Anna and Cleon today?" Ruth asked.

"Cleon's checking his bee boxes, and Anna went down to the folks' to see Martha."

"I'm planning to go over to Abe's place to see how his kinner are doing," Ruth said. "Do you think Anna would like to join me?"

"Probably so. Anna looks for any excuse to be with Esta."

"I'd better go now and let you rest awhile before the boppli wakes up." Ruth left her seat and gave Grace a hug. "If you don't get over your depression soon, maybe you should speak with the doctor about it."

Grace nodded. "I will."

"I'll have Anna home in plenty of time for lunch," Ruth called as she retrieved her coat and headed for the door.

"Sure hope we catch some big old trout so Sue can fix 'em for supper," Abe said as he rowed his boat to the middle of the pond. "Wouldn't that be good, son?"

Gideon, who sat near the back of the boat, shrugged.

"I'm hoping to catch enough fish so Ruth can fix some for our supper too," Martin put in from his seat at the front of the boat.

"This looks like a good place to fish." Abe slipped the oars inside the boat and cast out his line. Martin did the same. Gideon just sat with his arms folded.

Abe's patience was beginning to wane. "Come on, Gideon, you've been after me for weeks to take you fishing. Now we're here—so fish."

Gideon grunted. "It's too cold."

"Then you should have stayed home and sat around the stove all day." Abe took no pleasure in snapping at his son, but he was irked that he'd taken the day off to spend time with Gideon, only to have the boy gripe about the cold and refuse to fish.

"Maybe he'll get more enthused when he sees some trout," Martin said.

"Let's hope so."

For the next several minutes, Abe and Martin visited quietly as they kept an eye on their lines. Gideon continued to sit with a scowl on his face.

Suddenly Martin shouted, "I saw a big one jump clean out of the water!"

Abe turned and saw two more fish jump. "I'd better move the boat over that way. Looks like they're just waiting to be caught."

Gideon perked up a bit and leaned over the edge of the boat. "I don't see anything. Where were they jumpin'?"

"Over there." Martin pointed to the left.

Gideon stood up and shouted, "There's one! That old fish must have jumped three feet out of the water!"

Abe grunted. "Sit down, boy; you're rocking the boat."

Gideon had only taken a few steps when suddenly the boat flipped over, dumping them all into the frigid water.

"I can't swim!" Abe shouted before taking in a mouthful of murky water.

And neither can Gideon.

Chapter 22

"Are you really going to get rid of Flo?" Anna asked Martha as the two of them sat on a bale of straw while Martha brushed the female beagle.

"I've got to, Anna. She can't have puppies, which means she won't make me any money that way. I plan to use the money I make selling her to buy another dog." Martha grimaced. By the time she had responded to that ad about the pair of cocker spaniels, they'd been sold. That meant she had to keep looking, and it wasn't likely that she'd find another pair as reasonably priced as the ones in the paper had been.

"I wish Mama couldn't have any more babies." Anna stroked Flo's floppy ears, and the dog let loose a pathetic whimper as though in tune with the child's feelings.

Martha frowned. "What makes you say a thing like that?"

"If she hadn't had Daniel, Papa would still love me."

Martha set the brush aside, and Flo crawled on her belly to the corner of the room. "I'm sure he still loves you," she said, wrapping her arms around Anna.

"He won't let me hold the boppli. Whenever I ask if I can help with somethin', he always says no."

"What kinds of things have you asked to help with?"

"I wanted to bathe Daniel so Mama could get some sewing done. Papa said I'm too little for that." Deep creases formed on Anna's forehead. "Then I asked if I could help with his bees. He said no to that too."

"Working around bees can be dangerous, Anna. You might get stung."

"That's what he said."

"Hey! What are you up to in here?" Ruth asked as she stepped into the barn.

"Aunt Martha was brushin' Flo so she looks nice when someone sees the sign out by the road and comes to look at her," Anna answered before Martha could respond.

"I saw that sign when I drove in with my horse and buggy." Ruth took a seat on another bale of straw. "Has anyone stopped to ask about the dog yet?"

Martha shook her head. "Of course, I just put the sign up last night, so I haven't lost hope." She clapped her hands and called for Flo. The dog returned to her with its tail between its legs and released a high-pitched howl.

"Maybe I should have bought Flo to give Esta instead of one of Heidi's pups," Ruth said. "That way you could have kept Winkie for breeding purposes."

"I don't think Esta would have wanted a full-grown dog that likes to howl at everything she sees." Martha picked up the brush and began brushing Flo again.

"You're probably right." Ruth reached over and squeezed Anna's arm. "Speaking of Esta, I'm heading over to see her now. Would you like to go along?"

Anna nodded eagerly. "Guess I'd better ask Mama first."

"I was already at your house and saw your mamm. She said it was fine if you ride over to see Esta with me."

Anna jumped up and raced for the door.

Ruth turned to Martha. "Would you like to come along?"

"I'd better stick around here in case someone comes to see Flo." Martha smiled. "Maybe when you bring Anna home, you can join us for lunch."

"That would be nice. Martin went fishing with Abe and Gideon, and I doubt he'll be home until late this afternoon."

"See you later, then. And be sure to say hello to Abe's kinner for me."

"I will." Ruth headed out the door.

A short time later, Martha heard a vehicle rumble up the driveway, followed by the tooting of a horn. She put Flo inside one of the empty horse stalls and went outside to see who it was. When she stepped out of the barn, she saw John Peterson getting out of his SUV.

"I was driving by and saw the sign out front advertising a female beagle. Is it one of your dogs?" he asked.

She nodded. "I bought a pair of beagles for breeding purposes several months ago, but Flo can't have any pups, so I've decided to sell her as a hunting dog."

He grinned. "Which is exactly what I'm needing. How much do you want for her?"

"I paid a thousand dollars for the pair, so if I could get—"

"I'll give you six hundred. How's that sound?"

Martha's mouth fell open. "Don't you want to look at her first?"

"Guess I probably should." John reached up to rub the bridge of his slightly crooked nose and squinted. "Unless she's sick, crippled, or just plain dumb, I'm sure she'll work out fine for me."

"She's none of those things." Martha motioned to the barn. "Follow me, and you can see for yourself."

Inside the barn, Martha took Flo out of the horse stall and led her over to John. He knelt on the concrete floor beside the dog and gave her the once-over. "She looks good to me. I'll take her."

Martha could hardly believe she had found a home for Flo so quickly. She was pleased to know the dog would be put to good use.

"Help! Help!"

Martin came up out of the water, gulped in some air, and spotted Gideon, kicking and splashing for all he was worth. "Can you swim?" he called to the boy.

"He can't, and neither can I!" Abe, who was several feet away, also struggled.

The frigid water stung Martin's skin and took his breath away. Even though he considered himself to be a good swimmer, he knew he needed to get out of the icy water as quickly as possible. Needed to get Abe and his son out too.

Since Gideon was the closest and seemed to be having the most trouble staying afloat, Martin swam over to the boy, grabbed hold of his shirt, and pulled him toward shore. He kept pulling until they were in shallow water and he knew Gideon could stand. "Climb out and wait on the shore," he instructed.

Coughing and gasping for air, Gideon did as he was told.

Martin dove back into the water and swam toward where he'd last seen Abe. Only Abe wasn't there!

Treading water, Martin looked around frantically. "Abe!" he hollered. "Where are you?"

"Don't let Papa die!" Gideon shouted from the shore.

Martin whirled around. "Don't come back in the water! Stay right there while I look for your daed."

He dove down and spotted Abe under the water near where the boat had capsized. His hand snaked out and grabbed Abe's arm, then he kicked hard, pulling them both to the surface. Abe wasn't moving, and Martin feared the man might have drowned. *Dear God,* he prayed, *don't let him be dead.*

Several grueling moments later, Martin pulled Abe onto the shore.

Gideon rushed over and dropped down beside his father. "Don't die, Papa," he sobbed. "Don't leave me like Mama did!"

Martin had learned CPR when he'd done volunteer work with the local fire department, so he quickly set to work on Abe. The cold air stung his eyes, and he struggled with each breath. His lungs burned, and he feared his strength would give out, but he wouldn't give up. Abe was his friend, and if their roles were reversed, he knew Abe would do the same for him.

Finally, Abe coughed and spit water out of his mouth.

Martin breathed a prayer of thanks. "He's going to be all right," he said to Gideon, whose eyes were wide with fear. "We need to get back to your house so we can get out of these wet clothes."

"I'm glad you came over to see me today," Esta said as she and Anna took a seat on the porch with Winkie perched between them.

Ruth smiled as she seated herself in one of the wicker chairs beside Abe's sister. "Nothing makes a little girl happier than to be with her best friend."

Sue nodded. Her blue eyes seemed to have lost the sparkle they'd had when she'd first come to help her brother and his family.

"Is everything all right?" Ruth asked, concerned. "Are you working too hard?"

Tears welled in Sue's eyes, and she blinked a couple of times. "I'm feeling kind of homesick."

"That's understandable. You've been away from your folks for several months now. I'm sure you miss them."

"I also miss Melvin."

"He's your boyfriend, right?"

"Jah. Melvin and I started courting six months before I left home. We've been writing letters, but it's not the same as seeing each other and being able to go places together."

"No, of course not." Ruth couldn't imagine being separated from Martin even for a few weeks, much less several months. "Maybe Melvin can come for a visit."

"I'd like that, but he's been busy helping his daed in their masonry business and hasn't been able to get away." Sue released a sigh. "I'd like to go home for Christmas, but I wouldn't feel right about leaving Abe in the lurch."

"Maybe some of the women in our community could take turns coming in to clean house, cook, and watch the kinner."

Sue shook her head. "I think it would be hard on everyone, especially Abe, if I went home for the holidays. It's going to be difficult for him to get through Christmas without Alma. I think he needs my support."

"I understand. I would make that sacrifice for either of my sisters."

The puppy growled as it leaped off the porch and romped in the yard with Josh, Willis, and Owen. "It was nice of you to give Winkie to Esta," Sue said. "The dog's filled a big hole in that little girl's life, and having a pet to care for is teaching her responsibility."

"I was glad to do it." Ruth turned to the girls, who sat on the steps watching the boys and Winkie play a game of tug-of-war with an old sock. "It won't be long until Christmas. Have either of you thought about what you'd like to receive for a present?"

Esta nodded eagerly. "I'm hopin' for some ice skates. Of course, we've gotta have cold, icy weather first."

"It was awfully cold last night," Ruth said. "I imagine it won't be long before your daed's pond will be frozen over."

Esta nodded. "Me and Josh found a ladybug nest on the trunk of a pine tree the other day. Mama used to say that was a sure sign of winter comin'."

Ruth smiled. She remembered how excited she used to get when she was a girl looking forward to winter games, hot chocolate with marshmallows, and gifts at Christmas.

Esta nudged Anna. "How 'bout you? What are you hopin' to get for Christmas?"

Anna shrugged. "If we get snow, a new sled would be nice."

Esta looked up at Ruth. "What are you hoping for?"

Ruth touched her stomach. The best gift she could receive would be to find out she was going to have a baby. "I'll be happy with whatever I get," she murmured.

A buggy rolled into the yard, and Sue stood, lifting Molly into her arms. "Looks like the men are back. They must have either caught lots of fish or got tired of trying, because they're here sooner than I thought they would be."

Ruth's heart gave a lurch when she noticed how wet the men's clothes were when they climbed out of the buggy. When she saw Martin put his arm around Abe's shoulders and walk him to the house, her heart nearly stopped beating.

"What happened?" she and Sue cried at the same time.

"Had a little accident with the boat," Martin replied.

"Did you fall into the water, Papa?" Esta grabbed Abe's hand as he stepped onto the porch.

"Sure did."

"But you can't swim," Sue said in a quavering voice.

"No, but Martin can. He saved us both from drowning," Gideon spoke up.

"You're all shaking." Ruth jerked open the front door. "You need to come inside and get warm."

Martin slipped his arm around Ruth's waist. "That's the last time I go fishing against my wife's better judgment. *Wasser schwimme macht mich gensheidich.*"

"Swimming in cold water gave me goose pimples too," Abe agreed.

Ruth swallowed against the lump in her throat. *Thank You, God. Thank You for saving each of these men.*

Chapter 23

I can't believe it's Christmas Eve and that we're having a white Christmas," Ruth said as she and Martin traveled down the road in his buggy toward her parents' house. She wished they were riding in an open sleigh so she could lift her face toward the sky and catch snowflakes on her tongue, the way she'd done as a child.

Martin reached for her hand. "Life's pretty good, jah?"

She smiled. "It is now. Last month when our wood was taken, and you, Abe, and Gideon got dumped into the pond, I wasn't so sure about things being good."

"But we're all okay, and your daed gave us another load of wood."

"That's true, but we never did find out who stole it."

He shrugged. "It makes no never mind to me. I'm keeping my focus on the future with you, my *schee* fraa."

She squeezed his warm fingers. "Will you still think I'm your pretty wife when I'm pregnant and *gross* around the middle?"

"I'll always think you're pretty, even when you become big around the middle."

Ruth sighed. "I hate to admit it, but I'm having a little trouble not feeling jealous whenever I see Grace with her baby. I want so much to be pregnant."

"I know, and I'm looking forward to being a daed," Martin said. "We just need to be patient. After all, we haven't been married quite two months yet. There's still plenty of time for you to conceive."

"But what if I'm barren like Martha's female beagle? You can't just sell me off, the way Martha did with Flo." She groaned. "If I'm unable to conceive, then you'll be stuck with a wife who can't give you any kinner."

He leaned over and nuzzled her neck with his cold nose. "The only reason I'll be stuck with you is because I love you. If we can't have any kinner, then we'll either live without 'em or take in foster children, the way some in our community have done."

Ruth nodded, but internally she struggled with the idea of never being a mother. Ever since she'd been a young girl playing with her dolls, she had wanted to hold a baby of her own. Surely God would answer that prayer and let her conceive.

"Are you looking forward to spending the evening with your family?" Martin asked, taking their conversation in another direction.

"Jah, of course. And tomorrow it will be nice to spend Christmas Day with your family."

"Mom and Pop really like you, Ruth. They think you're just what I need."

"And you're what I need," she replied, snuggling closer to him.

Blinding headlights from behind flashed against the buggy's front window, and Ruth whirled around. A truck bore down on them, going much too fast. But the shadowy night sky and blowing snow kept her from seeing the color of the vehicle.

"Looks like someone's in a hurry to get wherever they're going on Christmas Eve," she said. "No doubt they'll whip around us and be gone into the night."

Martin opened his mouth as if to comment, but before he could get a word out, they were bumped from behind.

Ruth grabbed the edge of her seat and hung on, while Martin gripped the reins. "What's going on? Do you suppose that vehicle hit a patch of ice?"

"I—I don't know. We haven't hit any in our buggy."

Ruth's heart hammered. "Maybe you should pull over and let him pass."

Martin pulled on the reins, and the horse slowed, but before he could guide it to the shoulder of the road, they were bumped again, harder this time. "There's no ice here. I'm guessing whoever is driving that truck must have been drinking," he mumbled. "What does that *ab im kopp* driver think he's doing? He's either got to be crazy or a real *siffer* to keep ramming our buggy like that."

"You think he could be a drunkard?" Ruth started to turn around, but the vehicle rammed them once more. Her head jerked forward, sending a spasm of pain up the back of her neck.

Twice more the truck hit the back of their buggy. The horse whinnied and reared up as Martin struggled to keep hold of the reins. The vehicle pulled out as though it was going to pass, but then it slammed into the side of the buggy, flipping it over and sending it rolling into the ditch.

"Ach!" Ruth screamed; then everything went black.

"Danki for the new ice skates," Esta said as she took a seat on the sofa beside Abe.

He smiled and patted her knee. "You'll be careful to skate only when others are around, won't you?"

She nodded. "I promise, 'cause I wouldn't want to end up in the pond like you and Gideon did when you went fishing."

"I should say not," Sue put in from the recliner, where she sat with Molly in her lap. "Besides the fact that you can't swim, that water under the ice would be freezing cold."

"The first day Martin and I were back to work after that dunking we took, he said he'd be happy to teach my kinner to swim as soon as the spring thaw comes and it's warm enough to go in the water," Abe said.

"It might be a good idea if he teaches *you* how to swim first, brother." Sue leveled Abe with one of her more serious looks. "Either that, or you'd better give up fishing, because we all need you around."

Abe thought about Alma. There was nothing she could have done to prevent the lightning strike that took her life, but there was something he could do to protect himself from drowning. "Jah," he said with a nod. "I'll see if Martin will teach me how to swim too."

"Can I go *gschwumme*?" Owen questioned. He'd been sitting on the floor near Willis, playing with the little wooden horses Abe had asked Roman to make.

"When you're old enough to learn how to swim, then you can go swimming," Abe said with a nod.

Owen's lower lip jutted out. "I ain't no boppli." He pointed to his rosy-cheeked little sister, who was almost asleep in Sue's lap. "Molly's the boppli."

"You act like a boppli whenever you're asked to do some chore," Josh countered. He and Gideon sat at a table across the room playing a game of checkers.

"Do not!" Owen shook his head forcefully. "Just 'cause you're bigger 'n me don't mean you're my boss. Only Papa can tell me what to do." He looked over at Sue. "Aunt Sue too, now that Mama's gone to heaven."

The room turned deathly silent. The children had been hiding it well as of late, but Abe knew they still missed their mother.

Sue rose from her chair. "Molly's fallen asleep, so I'm going to put her to bed. When I come downstairs, I'll make a batch of popcorn and some hot apple cider. Would anyone like to help?"

The children nodded with eager expressions, and Abe offered Sue an appreciative smile. He knew she'd wanted to go home for Christmas, but she had stayed to care for them and was doing all she could to make the holiday pleasant.

Abe leaned back in his chair as a sense of appreciation washed over him. He suddenly realized he wasn't sleeping so much during the day and was sleeping better at night. God was good, and he prayed things would go better for them in the coming year.

———◆◆———

"Why don't you let me hold that little fellow awhile?" Mom said when Grace sank to the sofa with a weary sigh. She and Cleon had walked over to her folks' house with Anna and Daniel.

Grace held out her arms gratefully. "He's been fussy all day, and nothing I've done has helped."

"Maybe he's got a touch of the colic," Mom said as she took the squalling baby and seated herself in the rocking chair across from Grace. "Have you tried giving him a bit of catnip tea?"

Anna, who had taken a seat on the floor by the fireplace next to Martha, looked up and frowned. "Catnip's for *katze*, not bopplin."

"That's true, cats do like catnip, but one of my herb books says it can also be used by itself or in combination with fennel and peppermint to help ease a baby's colic," Mom said.

"You've got to be careful when you're fooling around with herbs." Dad left his recliner and shuffled across the room to stand beside Mom. "Maybe we should try the 'colic carry.' That always worked when our girls were bopplin."

Cleon took a seat beside Grace on the sofa. "What's the 'colic carry'?"

"First, you extend your arm with your palm up." Dad bent down and took Daniel from Mom. "Then you position the boppli like this." He placed the baby chest-down and forehead resting in the palm of his big hand. "You've got to make sure the little fellow's legs are on either side of your elbow." Dad positioned the baby's legs in the manner he'd described. "Now you support the boppli with your other hand and walk around the room, keeping him in this position." He looked over at Mom and gave her a nod. "I'm sure this will help."

Cleon jumped up and rushed over to Dad. "I think I'd better take Daniel."

Dad's eyebrows pulled inward. "What's the matter, son? Are you afraid I might drop him?"

"Roman's had plenty of experience with bopplin," Mom said before Cleon could respond. "He used to carry our three around like that when they were fussy babies."

Deep grooves appeared on Cleon's forehead. "Even so—"

"Dad, maybe you should give the baby to Mom," Grace said, hoping to smooth things over between her father and Cleon. "I think if she rocks him awhile, he'll settle down."

Dad grunted and handed the baby back to Mom; then he moved over to stand in front of the fireplace. "I wonder where Ruth and Martin could be," he said, glancing at the clock on the wall above the mantel. "They should have been here by now."

Martha nodded. "I spoke with Ruth on Monday afternoon, and she said they would be here by six o'clock."

"Maybe the roads are icy because of the snow," Mom said.

"I'm hungry," Anna complained. "When are we gonna eat supper?"

"We're waiting for Aunt Ruth and Uncle Martin to get here." Mom placed the baby over her shoulder and patted his back.

"But I'm hungry now."

"You can wait." Cleon took a seat beside Grace again. "I'm sure they'll be here soon."

"Is there anything in the oven that needs tending to?" Grace asked, looking at her mother.

Mom shook her head. "The soup's staying warm on the stove, and the open-faced sandwiches Martha and I made earlier are in the refrigerator."

"Let's sing Christmas carols while we wait," Martha suggested.

Mom smiled. "Good idea. That'll make the time go quicker, and it'll help us stay focused on the meaning of Christmas."

"Can we sing 'Jingle Bells'?" Anna asked. "I like that song."

" 'Jingle Bells' is not a Christmas carol." Cleon frowned at Anna.

"Why don't we start with 'Silent Night'?" Mom said. "That was Grace's favorite Christmas song when she was a girl."

Martha was the first to lead off, and the rest of the family joined in as they sang, "Silent night! Holy night! All is calm, all is bright 'round yon virgin mother and Child. Holy Infant, so tender and mild, sleep in heavenly peace; sleep in heavenly peace."

When the song ended, Grace looked over at her baby, sleeping peacefully in Mom's arms. Maybe tonight they would all sleep in heavenly peace.

They sang several more songs until Dad held up his hand and said, "It's almost seven. Ruth and Martin should have been here by now."

"Maybe we should go look for them," Cleon suggested. "If they did hit ice, their buggy might have skidded off the road."

"You're right," Dad said. "We need to head out and see if we can spot them along the way."

The men donned their coats and stocking caps, then hurried out the door.

———————◄●●►———————

As they headed down the road in Cleon's buggy, it didn't take Roman long to realize there were some patches of ice. It had begun to snow quite heavily too, and he became even more apprehensive.

"You don't suppose they saw how hard it was snowing and decided to stay home, do you?" Cleon asked, turning in his seat to look at Roman.

"I guess they might have. Knowing Ruth, though, she would have moved heaven and earth to be with her family on Christmas Eve."

"You're probably right."

"Sure is cold out tonight," Roman said. "I can see my breath, even here in the buggy." He squinted as he studied the road ahead.

Suddenly Cleon pointed to the left. "Look, there's a buggy flipped over on its side, and it doesn't look good." He guided his horse to the shoulder of the road and jumped down. Roman did the same.

As they raced around to the front of the mangled buggy, a shiver shot up Roman's back. The mare that had been pulling the buggy lay on its side, and two people lay crumpled in the snow. "Ach! It's Ruth and Martin!"

Chapter 24

Ruth, can you hear me? Please—look at me."

Ruth tried to open her eyes, but they wouldn't cooperate. Where was she? Who was calling her name?

"Ruth. . . Ruth. . ."

Her eyelids fluttered.

"I think she's trying to wake up."

"Are you sure my daughter's going to be all right?"

"She came through the surgery well. Given some time, she should heal from all her injuries."

"Thank the Lord."

Mom, is that you? The words formed on Ruth's tongue, but she couldn't open her mouth.

"She should be fully awake soon, and then the sheriff will want to question her."

Question me about what? Why can't I open my eyes or speak to Mom?

"My son-in-law and I have already spoken to the sheriff, so I don't see what good it will do for—"

Dad, is that you? Tell me where I am and why I can't see you and Mom. Reaching from deep within, Ruth cracked one eye open, then the other. Blurry faces came into view—faces she recognized.

"Wh–where am I?" she rasped.

"You're in the hospital," Dad said.

"What happened? Why does my stomach hurt so much?"

"You were in a horrible accident." Mom's face looked pale, and her chin quivered slightly.

"Do you know how it happened, Ruth?" Dad questioned. "Did your buggy hit a patch of ice on the road?"

Ruth closed her eyes and tried to remember. She and Martin had been driving down the road, heading to Mom and Dad's on Christmas Eve. It had been snowing, and they'd been talking about wanting to have a baby. Then a truck had come barreling up behind them, and then—

"Martin! Where's Martin?"

Dad opened his mouth as if to respond, but Mom shook her head. "You need to rest, Ruth. We can talk about this when you're feeling better."

The look of sadness on Mom's face sent a jolt of panic through Ruth's body. She tried to sit up, but a woman wearing a white uniform placed a restraining hand on her shoulder.

"Lie still, dear," she said. "You've just come from surgery and you've lost a lot of blood. You don't want to rip open your stitches."

"Stitches? Where do I have stitches?"

The nurse looked over at Mom. "Perhaps it would be best if we let her sleep. She needs to remain calm."

A warm, tingling sensation shot up Ruth's arm, and she moaned. *I must be dreaming. Jah, that's all it is, just a strange dream.*

As Grace sat in the hospital waiting room with Cleon beside her, her brain felt as if it were in a fog. What had started out to be a pleasant Christmas Eve had turned into a terrible nightmare.

She glanced across the room, where her folks stood talking to Martin's parents. Mom had her arm around Flossie's shoulder, no doubt offering words of comfort. Dad was doing the same with Martin's father, Elmer.

"I just can't believe what's happened tonight," Grace said, clinging to Cleon's hand. "When the doctor came out and told us that Martin was dead and that they'd done surgery on Ruth because her intestines and uterus had been damaged, my brain wouldn't let me believe it."

"I know—it's a terrible thing. At least we can take comfort in knowing that Martin's in heaven." Cleon let go of Grace's hand and slipped his arm around her shoulders. "Ruth doesn't know the extent of her injuries, does she?"

"Not yet." Grace gulped down a sob. "When she finds out she'll never be able to have kinner, I'm sure she'll fall apart. All Ruth's ever wanted is to be a wife and mother. She loved Martin so much."

Cleon squeezed her shoulder. "Someday, when the pain of losing Martin has subsided, Ruth might find love again, and then—"

"How can you say such a thing?" Tears stung Grace's eyes, and when she blinked, they spilled onto her cheeks.

"I'm not suggesting she find another man and get married as soon as she comes from the hospital. I just wanted you to realize—"

Grace shook her head. "I can't believe Ruth has been put to the test like this. It's not fair! She's always had such a sweet, tender spirit. She doesn't deserve to have something so terrible happen to her."

"No one deserves it, Grace. Rain falls on the just, same as it does the unjust. We need to ask God to give Ruth strength and help her deal with this loss."

A *thump-thump-thump* woke Abe from his slumber. He rolled over and groaned. It sounded as though someone was knocking on the back door.

He shoved the covers aside, swung his legs over the side of the bed, and stepped into his trousers. Stumbling down the hallway, he bumped into Sue at the bottom of the stairs.

"I heard knocking and came to see who it was," she said.

"Me too." Abe pulled the back door open and was stunned to see Ivan Schrock standing on the porch. "Ivan, what are you doing here on Christmas morning?"

Ivan's solemn expression caused Abe immediate concern. "I got word from Cleon this morning. There was a horrible accident last night."

"A buggy accident?"

"Jah. It was Martin's buggy."

"Martin Gingerich?" Sue and Abe asked at the same time.

Ivan nodded. "Sorry to be tellin' you this, but Martin's dead, and Ruth's in the hospital with serious injuries."

Abe's knees nearly buckled, and he heard Sue's sharp intake of breath. Instinctively, he reached for her hand. "How did it happen? Was it caused by ice on the road?"

"We're not sure. All I know is that Cleon and Roman got worried when Ruth and Martin didn't show up at their place on Christmas Eve, so they went looking for them." Ivan drew in a quick breath. "Guess they found Martin's mangled buggy overturned on the shoulder of the road. The horse was dead, and Martin and Ruth were unconscious and bleeding pretty bad. Martin died soon after they got to the hospital, and the doctors did surgery on Ruth."

"What kind of surgery?" Sue asked.

Ivan's gaze dropped to the porch as his face flamed. "A hysterectomy. She had some damage to her intestines, and her uterus was messed up when she fell on a broken buggy wheel."

"That's baremlich!" Sue cried.

"Terrible isn't the word for it!" Abe steadied himself against the door-jamb. "Is Ruth going to be okay?"

Ivan shrugged. "I think so—in time."

Abe slowly shook his head. "I can't believe that my good friend, who saved me from drowning, is dead." Hot tears stung his eyes. "First my Alma, and now Ruth's Martin. Dear Lord, how much more can we take?"

⸺⸺⸺◆◆◆⸺⸺⸺

Ruth opened her eyes and blinked against the invading light. She'd been dreaming—a horrible, frightening dream about her and Martin riding in their buggy and a truck ramming them from behind. But it couldn't have happened. She was safe and warm in her bed at home. Everything was as it should be.

She turned toward Martin's side of the bed. He wasn't there. All she saw was a strange-looking machine with a long piece of plastic tubing that was connected to—

Ruth screamed as a sharp pain shot through her abdomen. "Where am I? What's happened to me?"

"It's all right, Ruth. You're in the hospital. We're taking good care of you."

A young woman wearing a white uniform stepped up to the side of the bed and placed a cool hand on Ruth's forehead. "The sheriff's outside. He wants to ask you a few questions."

"The sheriff?"

"That's right. He needs to talk to you about the accident."

"Accident?"

"The one you were involved in last night."

So it wasn't a dream. There really had been an accident. As the reality set in, Ruth trembled. "Wh–where's my husband?"

The woman glanced over her shoulder, then Ruth's mother stepped forward.

"Mom! I'm so glad you're here. Martin and I were in an accident. Somebody rammed the back of our buggy, and—"

"I know." Mom clasped Ruth's hand. "You were hurt badly, Ruth. When the buggy tipped over, one of the wheels broke, and you landed on it when you were thrown from the buggy. The broken wheel punctured your belly, causing some intestinal damage, as well as damage to your uterus." She paused and sniffed a couple of times. "The doctors—they had to do an emergency hysterectomy. You'll have to take antibiotics for some time to fight any possible infection."

"Wh–what are you saying?" Ruth's throat felt so dry and swollen she could barely swallow.

Mom sank into the chair beside Ruth's bed as tears dribbled down her cheeks. "The surgery to fix your bowels was a success, but I'm sorry, daughter. . . .you'll never have any babies."

"What? Oh no, that just can't be. Martin and I want a big family. We—"

Mom slowly shook her head. "Martin's gone, Ruth. He died soon after you were brought to the hospital."

Ruth stared at the ceiling. Surely Mom was wrong. Martin couldn't be dead. They'd been on their way to Mom and Dad's to celebrate Christmas Eve. It was going to be a happy time—her and Martin's first Christmas together.

"No! No! No!"

Chapter 25

As Ruth lay in her bed, staring at the cracks in the ceiling, her fingers curled into the palms of her hands and dug into her flesh. Last night she'd been released from the hospital in order to attend Martin's funeral today. Mom and Dad had brought her home to stay with them, and the doctor had given Ruth a prescription for antibiotics and instructions to get plenty of rest. He'd said she could attend her husband's funeral, but only if she used the wheelchair Dad had rented.

I don't want to go to Martin's funeral, Ruth silently wailed. *I just want to close my eyes and never wake up.*

Ruth's mind took her back to the day Sheriff Osborn had showed up at the hospital, asking her to tell him what she remembered about the accident. Her brain had been foggy, but she'd been able to remember a few things—looking over her shoulder, seeing a truck bearing down on them, being rammed over and over. She'd told the sheriff that it had been dark outside and snowing. She hadn't seen the license plate and couldn't be sure about the color of the vehicle. What she hadn't told the sheriff was that Luke had a truck he kept hidden in the woods, and she feared it may have been him who had rammed their buggy.

Tears stung the back of Ruth's eyes. *Could Luke have followed us on Christmas Eve? If so, why would he do such a horrible thing?*

"I brought you a bowl of oatmeal and some toast with your favorite strawberry jam," Mom said as she stepped into the room carrying a wooden tray in her hands.

"I'm not hungry."

"You've got to eat something. You won't get your strength back if you don't."

Ruth shook her head. "I don't care if I ever get my strength back. My husband's dead, and I can never have any children. There's nothing left for me to live for."

"Ach, don't say such a thing." Mom placed the tray on the nightstand and seated herself on the edge of Ruth's bed. "You have me, your daed, and the rest of the family to live for. We all love you, and we're grateful to God for sparing your life."

"Jah, well," Ruth said as the bitter taste of anger rose in her throat, "I wish He'd taken me instead of Martin."

Mom clutched Ruth's hand. "It wasn't your time to go, and you shouldn't be wishing it were so."

"What are you saying—that it was meant for Martin to die?"

"I can't say that God meant for it to happen, but He did allow it, and we need to accept it as His will."

Ruth swallowed hard and nearly choked on a sob. "I—I don't think I can do that. Someone rammed our buggy on purpose, and they need to pay."

" 'For we know him that hath said, Vengeance belongeth unto me, I will recompense, saith the Lord,' " Mom quoted from Hebrews.

"I know, but. . ." Ruth looked away, unable to finish her sentence.

Mom patted her hand. "Eat your breakfast. Folks will be arriving for the funeral soon, and Cleon will be up to carry you down so you can attend the services."

Ruth gave no reply. She didn't want to attend Martin's services. Hearing the bishop's words and seeing Martin's body lying in that cold wooden coffin would only confirm that her husband was dead.

Abe directed his horse and buggy behind the long procession of black buggies heading down the narrow, hilly road leading to the Amish cemetery where Martin Gingerich's body would be laid to rest. It was a raw, dreary day. The steel gray-sky looked as though it might open up and pound the earth with pelting rain, but it was too cold for that. If the clouds dropped anything, it would be more snow.

Abe observed the frozen fields on each side of the road as a bone-chilling wind lapped the sides of his buggy. He felt as if he were reliving Alma's funeral. It hadn't been quite a year since her death, but it seemed as if it were yesterday. The death of a Christian was a celebration, because he or she had left an earth full of struggles and made it to heaven. Yet for the ones left behind, there remained heartache and a silent sense of loneliness that went beyond anything Abe had ever known.

"God will see you through," Bishop King had told Abe the day they'd placed Alma's body in the grave. *"The Bible tells us in Psalm 147:3 that God 'healeth the broken in heart, and bindeth up their wounds.'"*

As Abe reflected on those words, he knew they were true. He still missed Alma, but with every new day, the pain became less. He was now able to find a sense of joy in the little things that occurred in his everyday life. His children, whom he'd previously taken for granted, had become more important to him as well. His desire to help others during their time of need seemed stronger than ever before. Most of all, Abe's personal relationship with God had taken on new meaning, for he spent more time praying and reading his Bible, which had strengthened his faith and given him purpose in life.

Abe glanced over his shoulder at his children in the backseat. Despite his sorrow over losing a good friend, he knew life must go on.

When Abe stepped down from his buggy a short time later, a blast of frigid air hit him full in the face and he shivered. *Lord, help Ruth's body to heal, ease her sorrow over losing her mate, and as she regains her strength, please give her the same sense of peace You have given me.*

Martha stood behind her sister's wheelchair, listening to the bishop's final words and watching Ruth's shoulders tremble as she fought to control her emotions. This horrible tragedy that had befallen Ruth wasn't fair. She and Martin had only been married a short time. They'd had their whole lives to look forward to until Martin's life was cut short.

Martha blinked against stinging tears and the biting December wind as she thought about her sister's injuries. Ruth had always wanted children. Martha was sure that having the hope of giving birth to babies of her own and then having it dashed away had only added to Ruth's agony over losing her mate.

How would I feel if I were in Ruth's place? Martha asked as she listened to Bishop King read a hymn. *If the man I loved had been taken from me, would I accept it as God's will or become bitter and full of self-pity?*

When Martha had gone to the hospital to see her injured sister, Ruth had said she hoped whoever was responsible for Martin's death would pay for his transgressions. She'd said she couldn't find it in her heart to forgive that person.

Martha shuddered as a group of Amish men sang a song while the pallbearers shoveled dirt into the grave. What if Ruth never got over her bitterness and self-pity? How could she find inner peace if she didn't forgive?

Grace clung to Cleon's arm as they stood behind her parents, who had positioned themselves behind Ruth's wheelchair, one on the left, one on the right. Mom's hand rested protectively on Ruth's shoulder, and Dad had his arm around Mom's waist. Knowing one of their daughters had suffered such a great loss and seeing Ruth having to witness the burial of her husband had to be hard on Mom and Dad.

I can still remember how lonely and sick with grief I felt when Wade died, Grace thought ruefully. At least she had been left with a child. Ruth would never know the joy of having children of her own.

Tears trickled down Grace's cheeks. *I had a child and gave her up because I was afraid I couldn't make it on my own.* She sniffed and reached up to swipe at the tears. All of the regrets in the world wouldn't change the past. Now she and Cleon had Anna and baby Daniel to raise.

She glanced down at her daughter, who stood like a statue between her and Cleon. They'd left the baby with Abe's sister today, which meant they would have to get Daniel as soon as the graveside service was over so Grace could feed him.

Grace's thoughts were pulled aside as the bishop asked the congregation to silently pray the Lord's Prayer, which meant the service was almost over. Martin's mother stood a few feet away with her husband and their five eldest children, all of whom were married and lived in other parts of Ohio. Flossie wept openly, and Elmer patted her back. Martin's funeral had to be hard on them too.

When the service was over and the people had started for their buggies, Ruth let out a piercing cry and slumped over in her wheelchair.

Dad and Cleon grabbed the handles of the chair and pushed it quickly toward Dad's buggy. This day had obviously been too much for Ruth.

Chapter 26

L ook who's come to visit!"
Ruth turned her head toward the door and saw Grace enter her room carrying Daniel. She knew she should say something, but she couldn't seem to find the words. She could only stare in silence at the opposite wall.

"I'm surprised to see you still in bed. It's almost ten o'clock," Grace said as she took a seat in the chair beside Ruth's bed. "It's been three weeks since you came home from the hospital. You should be getting some fresh air and a bit of exercise, don't you think?"

"I don't care about fresh air or exercise. I want to be left alone."

"Why don't you sit on the edge of your bed? You can hold Daniel while I brush your hair."

Ruth's temples throbbed, and her spine went rigid. She couldn't hold Daniel without being reminded that she could never have children of her own.

"Ruth, did you hear what I said?"

Ruth jerked her head and turned her face into the pillow. "I don't want to have my hair brushed."

Grace didn't say anything, but Ruth could hear her sister's heavy breathing. Several minutes went by, then the chair squeaked and the door clicked shut.

A few weeks ago, Ruth would have welcomed a visit from her sister. Holding baby Daniel would have been a delight. Not now. Ruth knew that whenever she looked at a baby, she would think about her loss. She remembered how desperate Martin had been to marry her, saying he was worried that something bad might happen and he wanted to protect her. It was Martin who needed protection—only there was nothing Ruth could have done to save him.

Ruth squeezed the edge of the pillow. Last night as she lay in her rumpled, damp sheets, she had stared into the darkness, imagining that she could see Martin's face. He was gone. She had to accept it as fact.

She thought about his funeral and how empty she had felt when she'd looked at his face for the very last time. She couldn't accept his death as God's will. All these months since Alma's death, Ruth had tried to reach out to Abe and his family, wanting to help heal their pain but never really understanding it until now.

Ruth had said nothing about her suspicions concerning Luke. She'd allowed her anger and resentment to fester like a bad splinter left unattended. Maybe she should have told the sheriff. Maybe she still could. She wasn't well enough to drive to town in order to speak with him, but she could use the phone shed near her father's shop.

Abe had just begun to look at some paperwork on his desk when Ivan Schrock entered the harness shop. "Are you busy?" he asked, moving toward Abe's desk.

Abe nodded. "Been even busier now that Martin's not here to help."

Ivan leaned on the corner of Abe's desk. "That's why I came by."

"To see if I'm busy?"

"To see if you could use some help."

"I suppose I could." Abe had almost forgotten that Ivan had asked about working in the harness shop a while back. Abe hadn't needed him then. Besides, Ivan knew nothing about harness making.

"If you're willing to train me, I'd like to come work for you," Ivan said with an enthusiastic nod.

Abe chewed on the end of his pencil as he mulled things over. With all of the jobs he had to finish, he knew he couldn't keep working by himself.

It would be better if he could find someone who knew the trade. But there were advantages to training someone, he supposed.

"I'll give you an honest day's work," Ivan said. "Always did for my daed; you can ask him if you like."

Abe shook his head. "No need for that."

"Then you'll consider hiring me?"

"I guess we can give it a try."

Ivan smiled. "You won't be sorry."

"When can you begin work?"

"Right now if you like."

"Jah, sure, you can begin today." Abe nodded toward the back room. "Put on a leather apron, and I'll show you what needs to be done."

Ivan rubbed his hands together. "Okay!"

The first job Abe put Ivan on was cleaning and oiling a bunch of dirty harnesses.

"How often do most folks bring in their harnesses for cleaning?" Ivan asked as Abe filled a tub with warm water and saddle soap.

"About once a year, though some folks wait much longer." Abe pointed to another metal tub, filled with pale yellow neat's-foot oil. "That's for oiling the straps so they'll be nice and soft after they dry."

"You want me to get some harnesses washed first, or should I work on oiling those up there?" Ivan asked, pointing to some straps and buckles from an old harness that hung on a giant hook.

"Those have been done already," Abe said. "Take a feel of how smooth and oily the straps feel."

Ivan reached up and ran his fingers over the leather straps. "I see what you mean. They feel soft as a cow's ear."

"You can work on cleaning those straps now, and I'll go back to my desk to get my paperwork done." Abe wandered back to his desk, and as he took a seat, his gaze came to rest on an old saddle lying on the floor across the room. It had been one of the last things Martin had worked on before his death, and there it lay, still needing to be cleaned and repaired.

Thinking about Martin made Abe wonder how Ruth was getting along. When she'd collapsed in her wheelchair at the close of Martin's graveside service, Abe had been concerned. Later when he'd attended the meal held at the Hostettlers' home, he'd been told that Ruth was resting in bed.

Might be good if I take Esta over to visit Ruth this Saturday, he decided. *Good for Ruth and good for Esta.*

"I'm deeply concerned about Ruth," Mom said as she and Martha rolled out some pie dough. "Whenever I try to coax her out of bed, she seems agitated and says she wants to be left alone."

"I know," Martha agreed. "Ruth's physical injuries are beginning to heal, but she stays in bed most of the time and doesn't want to be around anyone."

Mom nodded. "I've tried everything I can think of to get her to talk about her feelings, but she refuses to discuss Martin or the accident."

"You think we can talk her into helping us with these apple pies?"

Mom opened her mouth as if to respond, but Ruth walked into the kitchen just then.

"It's good to see you up." Mom pulled out a chair at the table. "Would you like to peel some apples for the pies Martha and I are making?"

"I'm not interested in making pies." Ruth plucked her coat off the wall peg and slipped her arms into the sleeves.

She was about to head out the door when Martha called, "Where are you headed?"

"I'm going for a walk. I need some fresh air."

"Would you like me to go along?"

"No thanks." Ruth stepped outside and closed the door behind her.

Mom looked over at Martha and frowned. "It's good to see her up and dressed, but I don't like the way she's acting. I don't think it's a good idea for her to be out walking in the cold by herself."

"I'll go with her, even if she doesn't want the company." Martha wiped her floury hands on a clean dish towel, grabbed her coat, and rushed out the door. She hurried down the stairs and spotted Ruth tromping through the snowy yard. "Ruth, wait up," she called.

Ruth kept walking.

"Where are you going?"

No reply; just the *crunch, crunch, crunch* of Ruth's footfalls in the snow.

Martha picked up speed. "It's cold out here," she said, taking hold of Ruth's arm. "You should come back inside where it's warm."

Ruth halted. "I am not cold. I don't want company."

"What if you become weak and faint, like you did the day of the funeral?"

Ruth's chin trembled, and her eyes glistened with tears.

"I know you're hurting," Martha said, carefully choosing her words, "but you can't keep your feelings bottled up forever."

"Thanks to the one who rammed our buggy, I'll never have any children." Ruth placed her hand against her belly, and Martha could see the anguish in her sister's eyes.

"When I first realized that Flo couldn't have any puppies, I was upset. But then I figured there were other things Flo could do, so—"

"Oh, please. I can't believe you're comparing me to a dog! Flo being unable to have puppies is nothing like my situation."

"I just wanted you to see that your sense of self-worth shouldn't be centered around whether or not you can have bopplin. God spared your life, and someday, when your pain has subsided, you'll realize that God has a purpose for you."

Ruth shrugged and started walking toward the phone shed near the end of their driveway.

"Are you planning to make a phone call?"

Ruth halted and whirled around. "If you must know, I'm going to phone Sheriff Osborn."

"What for?"

"I'm going to tell him who I think rammed our buggy on Christmas Eve."

"You saw who did it?"

"No, but I've figured it out." Ruth clenched and unclenched her fingers, and she began to shiver.

"Who do you think rammed your buggy?"

"Luke. He has a truck he keeps hidden in the woods. I'm sure the vehicle that hit our buggy was a truck."

Martha's heart pounded. "Luke has a truck?"

Ruth nodded. "He confessed it to me shortly before we broke up, and I promised not to tell anyone." She grunted. "I was stupid. I should have told Dad or the bishop right away. Dad thinks Luke's the one responsible for the other things that have been done to us. I'm sure he'll want to do something about it when I tell him I believe it was Luke who rammed our buggy."

"Don't you think you should talk to Luke first—find out what he has to say about it?"

"No. I want to tell the sheriff. I'm sure he. . ." Ruth's voice faltered, and she swayed unsteadily on her feet.

"Are you okay?"

"I'm fine."

Martha grabbed Ruth's arm. "Please don't tell Dad or the sheriff that you think it was Luke who rammed your buggy."

"Why not?"

"Even if it was a truck that hit the buggy, you have no proof it belonged to Luke. Please don't say anything to anyone about your suspicions until I've had a chance to speak with Luke."

"I. . .I don't know. . . ." Ruth's face had turned as pale as the snow. "Oh, I feel so light-headed." She wobbled and sank to her knees.

"I'll get Dad!" Martha raced to the woodworking shop and jerked open the door. "Ruth's fallen in the snow!"

Dad dropped the hunk of wood he'd been holding, and Cleon left the cabinets he'd been sanding. They rushed out the door. A few seconds later, Cleon lifted Ruth into his arms and carried her toward the house.

"What were you two doing out here in the cold?" Dad asked, giving Martha a stern look. "Haven't you got better sense than to go traipsing through the snow with a sister who's only been out of the hospital a few weeks?"

Martha blew out her breath. "We weren't traipsing, Dad. Ruth came down from her bedroom a while ago, and when she said she needed some fresh air, I went after her." Martha thought it best not to mention the reason for her sister's trek through the snow. If Dad had any idea Ruth thought Luke was responsible for their accident, he'd be all over the poor fellow, trying to get him to fess up.

Martha pursed her lips as she made a decision. The first chance she had, she would talk to Luke.

Chapter 27

"Is Ruth feeling better now, Papa?" Esta asked as she turned in her seat at the front of the buggy.

"I hope so, daughter. It's been three weeks since the accident, and I'm hoping she'll feel up to some company."

"I'm glad you waited until Saturday when I wasn't in school to visit Ruth," Esta said, grinning at him. "But I wish you woulda let me bring Winkie along."

Abe shook his head. "I'm not sure Ruth will be up to having that much excitement today. You know how crazy Winkie can get when he's excited to see someone."

Esta giggled. "When Bishop King came by to pick up that harness you made for him last week, Winkie got so excited, he piddled on his boot."

"That wasn't a good thing," he said, giving Esta a sidelong glance. Truth was, Bishop King had asked for the accident since he'd gotten the dog riled up when he first arrived.

"Josh was mad 'cause he couldn't come with us today."

"I explained to him and the other kinner that I thought it might be too much if we all barged in on Ruth. Maybe later, after she's had more time to recuperate from her injuries, we can all pay her a visit."

Esta's forehead wrinkled. "I heard Aunt Sue talkin' to Ruth's sister Martha the other day. They were sayin' that Ruth can't have no bopplin. Is that true, Papa?"

Abe nodded. "Ruth had some serious injuries that required surgery and left her unable to have children."

"That's a shame. I know for a fact that Ruth likes kinner and wants to be a mudder; she told me so."

"Some things aren't meant to be."

Esta sat with her lips pursed. Finally, she looked over at Abe and said, "You think you'll ever get married again, Papa?"

"What makes you ask such a question?"

She shrugged her slim shoulders. "I was just thinkin' that since you don't have no fraa anymore, and Ruth don't have no *mann*, maybe the two of you could get married. Then she could be our mamm and wouldn't feel sad 'cause she can't have no bopplin."

Abe's jaw clenched. Just the idea of his replacing Alma with another wife made him feel unfaithful to her memory. And married to Ruth Gingerich of all people! Why, the woman was a good ten years younger than him! Besides, she'd been married to his good friend and loyal worker. That just didn't seem right to Abe.

"Papa, did ya hear what I said?" Esta asked, nudging Abe's arm.

"I'm not looking for a wife right now, and it's way too soon for Ruth to even be thinking about marriage again."

"Maybe someday?"

"Esta, girl, if the good Lord desires for me to find another wife, then He'll have to drop her right in my lap."

———————

Ruth was lying on the sofa, reading a book, when Mom entered the living room with Abe and Esta Wengerd. "You've got company, daughter."

Ruth set the book aside and pulled herself to a sitting position, tucking in the quilt draped over her legs.

"It's good to see you," Abe said as he and Esta took seats in the chairs across from Ruth.

"How are you feelin', Ruth?" Esta asked in a near whisper.

Ruth shrugged.

"Abe, would you care for something to eat?" Mom asked. "I baked some gingerbread this morning, and it should be plenty cool by now."

"Danki, that'd be nice," he replied.

"How about you?" Mom smiled at Esta. "Would you like a glass of milk and a hunk of gingerbread?"

Esta nodded with an eager expression. "Sounds real good."

Mom turned to Ruth. "Would you care for some gingerbread?"

"No thanks; I'm not hungry."

"How about a cup of tea?"

"That would be fine."

"Would you like some tea, Abe?" Mom asked.

"I've never had much appreciation for tea, but a glass of milk would suit me just fine."

Mom reached out her hand toward Esta. "Would you like to help me whip up some cream in the kitchen?"

"Can I lick the bowl?"

"Jah, sure. Martha usually licks the bowls around here, but since she's gone on an errand this morning, you can take over her job."

"Can I go up to Anna's house and see if she wants some gingerbread, too?"

"If it's all right with your daed, it's fine by me."

Abe gave a quick nod. "Be sure you put your coat on."

"I will." Esta skipped out the door behind Mom, leaving Ruth alone in the room with Abe.

He leaned slightly forward in his chair. "I. . .uh, know what it's like to lose a mate, so I think I have a pretty good understanding of what you must be feeling right now."

Ruth gave no response.

"Losing Alma hurt more than words can tell." Abe stared at his clasped hands. "But God's been with me every day since Alma died, and He's given me the strength to get through it."

"Does it help to know that she died from a freak act of nature and not because someone killed her in a senseless attack?"

He lifted his gaze to meet hers. "What?"

"Whoever rammed our buggy did it on purpose," Ruth mumbled, barely able to speak around the lump lodged in her throat. "It was no accident."

"Maybe the driver of the vehicle hit a patch of ice. Could be he just lost control."

Ruth gulped down a sob that threatened to erupt. "The person who killed Martin and left me unable to have children rammed our buggy six times!"

"Does the sheriff have any idea who might be responsible? I mean, is he conducting an investigation?"

Ruth thought about her attempt to phone the sheriff. She would have tried again if Martha hadn't begged her to wait until she'd spoken with Luke herself. Well, if Martha didn't find out something soon, Ruth was going to let the sheriff know her suspicions whether Martha liked it or not!

"I don't know what the sheriff thinks," she said in answer to Abe's question. "He asked me all kinds of questions about the accident and said he would be checking things out." She sighed. "I've not heard anything since."

"I guess investigations take time."

She grunted. "If the sheriff had kept a closer eye on things like he said he was going to do, maybe the culprit would have been caught by now."

Abe drummed his fingers along the arms of his chair. "With no husband to support you, I know it's going to be hard for you financially."

"I can't stay in the house Martin and I rented," Ruth said, feeling the agony of her bitterness weighing her down. "My folks don't mind me staying here, and since Dad's willing to support me for as long as I need his help, I guess I'll manage."

"What about your hospital bills? I know you'll need help with those."

She nodded. "Some of it has already been taken care of through the community fund. Dad says there's been talk of a benefit auction to raise the rest of the money."

Abe drew in a deep breath as he pulled his fingers through the ends of his reddish-brown beard. "Martin was a good friend. I miss seeing his smiling face when I come to work each day."

Not nearly as much as I miss him every night, Ruth thought regrettably. "Have you hired anyone to take his place?" she asked.

"Jah. Ivan Schrock."

"I see."

Mom stepped into the room just then carrying a tray, which she placed on the narrow table near the sofa.

"Where's my daughter?" Abe asked.

"She and Anna are out in the kitchen having their snack at the table." Mom handed Abe a plate of gingerbread. "Those girls have been chattering ever since they got back from Grace and Cleon's."

Abe nodded and forked a piece of gingerbread into his mouth. "This is sure good."

"Danki."

Ruth swung her legs over the side of the sofa. "I'm feeling kind of tired. If you'll excuse me, I think I'll go up to bed."

Before either Mom or Abe could comment, she skirted out of the room.

———————

Martha's heart pounded as she tied her horse to the hitching rail and headed for John Peterson's woodworking shop. She had stopped by the Friesens' to speak with Luke and had been told by Luke's folks that John had asked Luke to work today. Deciding this would be a good chance to see how Flo was getting along, as well as to speak with Luke, she'd headed over to John's.

She found John sitting at his desk, talking to a customer. Luke sat on a stool in front of one of the workbenches, sanding the arm of a chair.

He looked up and smiled when she approached. "Wie geht's, Martha? What brings you over here today?"

"I'm doing okay, and one of the reasons I came by is to ask John how Flo's getting along."

"See for yourself." Luke pointed across the room to where the female beagle lay near the potbellied woodstove. "She's happy as a pig with a bucket of slop."

Martha smiled. "Glad to hear she's adjusted so well."

"From what I could tell, she took to John right away."

"That's good to hear." Martha shuffled her feet a few times, trying to think of the best way to broach the sensitive topic on her mind.

"You're lookin' kind of thoughtful. Is there something else you wanted to say?"

"Well, I was wondering. . ." She leaned closer to Luke. "Do you still have that truck you keep parked in the woods?"

His eyebrows lifted high on his forehead. "How do you know about that?"

"Ruth told me."

He grunted. "So she couldn't keep a secret, huh?"

"That doesn't matter. What matters is whether you still have a truck hidden in the woods."

His only reply was a quick nod.

"And your folks don't know about it?"

He shrugged. "Can't really say, but they've never mentioned it, so I don't think they know."

Martha shifted her weight again.

"Anything else you want to know?"

"Actually, there is. I was wondering what you did on Christmas Eve."

"Had supper with my folks."

"Were you there the whole evening?"

"All except for the short time I drove over to the Kings' place to borrow something my mamm needed."

"Did you drive there in your truck?"

"Now how would I do that when it's parked in the woods? I took one of our buggies over to the Kings'. Jah, that's what I did, all right."

"What time was that?"

"Around four, I think."

Martha felt a sense of relief. If Luke had been home all evening except to make a quick trip to the Kings' at four o'clock, there was no way he could have been driving the vehicle that rammed Martin's buggy sometime after six. She was sure Ruth was just being paranoid about this situation and would change her mind when she heard what Luke had said.

"I'd best be going," she said, turning away from him.

He tapped her on the shoulder. "What about John? I thought you came to ask him how Flo's doing?"

She nodded at the sleeping dog. "I can see for myself the answer to that."

"Oh, right."

"See you later, Luke," Martha said as she rushed out the door.

Chapter 28

"Won't you have a couple of cookies to go with your tea?" Mom asked as she took a seat on the sofa beside Ruth one morning in late February.

Ruth shook her head. "I'm still full from breakfast."

"But breakfast was a few hours ago, and you hardly ate a thing."

Ruth set her teacup on the table so hard that some splashed onto her hand. "Ouch!"

"Did you burn yourself?" Mom leaned over and took hold of Ruth's hand. "Maybe I'd better get some aloe to put on that."

"Don't bother. It'll be fine."

"It might leave a scar if you don't tend to it right away."

Ruth pulled her hand away.

"At least let me get a cold washcloth."

Ruth studied the red blotch on her hand. "It's nothing serious. I don't need a washcloth."

Mom shrugged.

They drank their tea in silence, then Mom looked over at Ruth and smiled. "It might be fun if we went to Berlin later this week. We could do some shopping and have lunch at—"

"I don't feel like shopping or going to lunch."

"But you've been cooped up in the house for so long. Some fresh air might do you good."

"I went out to the chicken coop to gather eggs yesterday. The air was cold, and I didn't like it."

Mom laid her hand on Ruth's arm. "It will get better. Give it time."

Ruth fingered the edge of her empty cup. "The weather always improves when spring comes."

"I wasn't talking about the weather. I was referring to the distress you're feeling over Martin's death. It's going to take a while, but eventually you'll work through the pain and move on with your life. I think it would be good if you talked about the way you're feeling."

Irritation welled in Ruth's chest. She didn't want to talk about her feelings. She just wanted to be left alone. "Why must you hover over me and try to make me say things I don't want to say?" she snapped.

Mom pulled back as if she'd been stung by a bee. "I'm just concerned."

Ruth gave no reply.

"Maybe I'll go over to Grace's house for a bit," Mom said, rising to her feet. "I'd like to see how the boppli's doing and find out whether Grace has been able to get his colic under control. Would you like to come along?"

Ruth shook her head.

Mom held out her hand. "I'm sure Grace would like to see you. And the boppli is growing so much these days. Why, in no time at all, he'll be crawling."

Ruth gritted her teeth. "I can hardly look at Grace's baby."

Mom's mouth hung open like a broken window hinge. "Oh Ruth, how can you say such a thing?"

"You want me to be honest, don't you? Isn't that what you said a few minutes ago—that I should talk about my feelings?"

Mom nodded slowly.

"Seeing how happy Grace is with her boppli only reminds me that I'll never have any bopplin of my own."

Mom seated herself on the sofa again. "I think I understand a little of how you feel."

"Oh?"

"I miscarried a son before Grace was born, and every time I saw my sister, Clara, holding her baby, I wept."

"But you had other children later on."

"That's true, but—"

"So your situation isn't the same as mine."

"Not exactly. When that miscarriage occurred, I didn't know whether I could ever get pregnant again. I grieved until I came to realize that I couldn't change the past any more than I could control the future. I had to go on living and look to God for my strength." Mom touched Ruth's arm. "My advice is for you to take small steps toward doing some of the things you used to enjoy."

"There's nothing I want to do."

"What about little Esta?"

"What about her?"

"Don't you want to continue your friendship with her?"

Ruth shook her head. "Esta doesn't need me now. She's got her dog, and Anna's her friend. She seems to be happy and well adjusted." She released a deep moan. "Truth is, no one needs me, and I have nothing to live for."

"Please don't say that. We all need you—me, your daed, Martha, Grace, and Grace's two precious kinner."

Ruth shook her head. "You and Dad have each other; Grace has Cleon and their little ones; Martha has her dogs. I have no one."

"You have us."

Ruth gave no response.

With a shake of her head, Mom stood. "I'm heading over to Grace's now. If you change your mind, that's where I'll be until it's time to start lunch."

Ruth leaned her head against the sofa cushions and closed her eyes. When she heard footfalls on the hardwood floor, she knew her mother had left the room.

She was tired and wanted to sleep, yet sleep wouldn't come. Some folks in their community had referred to Martin's death as an accident, but it was no accident. Ruth knew whoever had hit their buggy had done it on purpose. The bitterness she felt over this reality mounted with each passing day. She and Martin had been married less than two months, and he'd been snatched away from her in the blink of an eye. It wasn't fair. They'd made so many plans—plans to have their families over for supper, plans to build a house of their own, plans to have a baby. Someone needed to pay for Martin's death. No one should be allowed to get away with murder.

Ruth thought about how Martha had gone to see Luke a while back and how he'd told her that he hadn't been driving his truck on Christmas Eve.

"I don't believe him," she mumbled.

"Who don't you believe?"

Ruth's eyes snapped open. Sadie Esh stood just inside the living room door.

"Ach, Sadie, you scared me! I didn't hear you come in."

"Let myself in through the back door. When I didn't see anyone in the kitchen, I came out here." Sadie glanced around the room. "You seem to be alone, Ruth. Who were you talking to, anyway?"

"Myself."

Sadie lowered herself into the rocking chair. "I do that sometimes too."

Ruth sat staring at her tightly clasped hands.

"The reason I came by was to see how you're feeling and ask if you might consider coming back to work at the bakeshop. The woman who was hired to take your place when you got married had to quit, and the Clemonses haven't found anyone to replace her yet."

Ruth shook her head. "I'm not up to that."

"Maybe in a few weeks?" Sadie asked with a hopeful expression.

"I don't think so."

"Are you still feeling tired and sore from your surgery?"

Ruth shrugged. "Tired, but not sore anymore."

"What are your plans for the future?"

"I have no plans."

"Oh, but—"

"Nobody around here understands how I feel. No one seems to care that Martin was murdered."

Sadie's eyes widened. "Murdered? But I thought you were involved in an accident."

"Someone rammed our buggy from behind, and they kept doing it until the buggy flipped over." Ruth nearly choked on the sob rising in her throat. "I think whoever did the other attacks against my family is the same one who rammed our buggy. I think if Dad had let the sheriff know about things sooner, Martin would still be alive."

"Have there been any more attacks since your buggy was rammed?" Sadie asked.

Ruth shook her head. "I think whoever's at fault is lying low because the sheriff's been patrolling our area more since Christmas Eve." Tears slipped out of her eyes and dribbled down her cheeks. "Every time I see a buggy going down the road, I'm reminded of the night Martin was killed." She placed both hands against her stomach and gritted her teeth. "I don't think I'll ever forgive the one who did it either."

"I'm at my wit's end trying to help Ruth deal with her grief," Mom said when she and Grace took a seat at Grace's kitchen table. Grace had just put the baby down for a nap, and she hoped that she and Mom could visit without interruption.

"Ruth's grief is understandable." Grace handed her mother a cup of coffee. "I grieved for a time after Wade died, and even more after his folks took Anna from me."

Mom nodded, her eyes revealing obvious compassion. "That must have been hard."

"It was, but at least I knew Anna was alive and the potential of having more kinner hadn't been taken from me."

Mom leaned forward, her elbows resting on the table. "What concerns me more than Ruth's grief is her growing bitterness and refusal to talk about things."

"I don't know what we can do to help other than pray and keep suggesting things she might like to do."

"I wanted her to go shopping and out to lunch with me later this week, but she said no to that idea." Mom slowly shook her head. "Ruth doesn't want to do anything but sit around the house and pine for what she's lost."

Grace reached over and clasped her mother's hand. "It's hard being a parent, jah?"

Mom nodded as tears welled in her eyes. "But there are many rewards."

How well Grace knew that. She wouldn't trade a single moment of motherhood—not even those days when the baby was fussy and Anna whined about everything. Her heart went out to her sister.

Dear Lord, Grace prayed silently, *please give Ruth's life joy and meaning again, and help me be more appreciative of all I have.*

Chapter 29

"Why don't you go to the dog auction with Martha today?" Mom suggested when Ruth entered the kitchen one Friday morning in early March. "It should be fun."

"I'm not interested in watching a bunch of yapping dogs get auctioned off," Ruth said with a shake of her head.

"It would be good if you could find something you're interested in."

Ruth clenched her teeth as she struggled not to say something unkind. She knew Mom meant well, but she didn't understand. No one did.

"Ruth, did you hear what I said?"

Placing the jug of milk she'd taken from the refrigerator onto the table, Ruth turned to face her mother. "I heard, but I'm not going to the auction with Martha. I woke up with a koppweh."

Mom's eyebrows furrowed. "If you've got a headache, why don't you go back to bed? I'll bring you a breakfast tray."

"I don't need a breakfast tray, and I wish you'd quit treating me like a child." Ruth's hands shook as she picked up a stack of napkins and began setting the table.

"I'm sorry." Mom started across the room toward Ruth, but Martha entered the kitchen and stepped between them.

"What's going on?" she asked, looking at Ruth. "I could hear your shrill voice all the way upstairs."

Tears burned the back of Ruth's throat, and she swallowed hard, unable to answer her sister's question.

Martha turned and gave Mom a questioning look.

"I suggested that Ruth go to the dog auction with you today, but she says she's got a headache."

"I'm sorry to hear that." Martha shrugged. "You'd probably be bored watching a bunch of hyper dogs get auctioned off anyhow."

Ruth nodded and hurried over to the cupboard to get out the dishes. At least Martha hadn't suggested she go back to her room and be served breakfast in bed.

"What time will you be leaving for Walnut Creek?" Mom asked, smiling at Martha.

"In an hour or so."

"Your daed will be in from doing his chores soon, and then we can eat."

"What would you like me to do?" Martha asked.

"Why don't you make some toast while Ruth sets the table? I've got a pot of oatmeal cooking, and it should be done soon."

"Okay."

"Would you like some aspirin?" Mom asked, stepping up to Ruth.

"I'll get it."

"I bought a new bottle when I went shopping yesterday. It's in the cupboard above the sink," Mom said.

"You've had a lot of headaches lately," Martha put in. "Maybe you should see the chiropractor for a neck adjustment."

"It's not my neck causing the headaches."

"Maybe some valerian root would help," Mom said as she lifted the lid on the oatmeal and peeked inside.

Ruth dropped the silverware to the table with a clatter. "I don't need any herbs or chiropractic adjustments. I need to be left alone!" She whirled around and dashed out of the room.

As Cleon sat at the breakfast table with Grace and Anna, he made up his mind that he would try to show his stepdaughter a little more attention this morning.

"How are things going with you at school these days?" he asked, looking over at Anna.

"Okay."

"Have you learned anything new?"

Anna reached for her glass of milk and gulped some down. "I guess so."

"What have you learned?"

"Hmm. . ."

"Well?"

The child shrugged.

Cleon's patience was beginning to wane, and he gritted his teeth to keep from snapping at Anna.

Grace gently poked his arm. "Would you please pass the syrup?"

"Jah, sure." He handed Grace the bottle of syrup and turned to Anna again. "Are you looking forward to summer coming so you can spend time with your baby brother?"

Anna's forehead wrinkled. "He cries too much. I'm gonna spend all my time with Esta this summer."

"Not all your time," Grace corrected. "You'll have chores to do, remember?"

"Jah, I know."

Cleon reached for his cup of coffee. "When you're not doing chores, you should get to know Daniel better. Maybe you and your mamm can put the boppli in the stroller and wheel him down to the woodworking shop to see me and your grandpa."

Anna looked over at Grace. "I wonder why my other grandpa hasn't sent me no more letters."

"It's *any more*, not *no more*," Grace said, touching the child's arm. "And you did get a letter and some money from your grandpa Davis for Christmas."

Anna's lower lip protruded. "That was a long time ago. I wish we could see where Poppy lives since he's still not feelin' so good."

"Maybe after Daniel gets a little bigger."

"Really, Mama?" Anna's expression turned hopeful.

Grace opened her mouth as if to say something, but Cleon cut her off. "I don't think that's a good idea."

"Why not?"

"Jah, Papa, why not?" Anna looked at Cleon with questioning eyes.

"For one thing, it's going to be a while before Daniel's big enough to take a long trip." He glanced at Grace, hoping she would help him out, but she just stared at her plate of half-eaten pancakes.

"Linda Mast said she and her family went to Florida last summer, and they took their boppli along," Anna argued.

Cleon grunted. "That may be true, but the Mast baby is older than Daniel."

"So we can't go?"

"Things are really hectic around here right now," he said. "Your aunt Ruth is still hurting from the loss of Martin, and your mamm needs to be here for her."

"But she's got Grandma and Grandpa Hostettler and Aunt Martha too."

"We can talk about this later," Cleon mumbled.

"When?"

"I don't know."

"But I need to know when," Anna persisted. "I'm gonna write Poppy a letter when I get home from school. I want to tell him when I can come—"

Cleon held up his hand. "Don't tell him anything; do you understand?"

With a strangled sob, Anna pushed back her chair and dashed from the room.

"Did you have to make her cry?" Grace slowly shook her head. "I hate to send her off to school with her eyes all red and swollen."

Cleon frowned. "Why is it that every time I say something to Anna, she ends up crying and then you take her side?"

"I was not taking her side. If I'd been taking her side, I would have tried to make you realize that Daniel will be old enough to travel by summer."

"No, he won't, because I don't want him going halfway across the country. I don't think it would be good for Anna to see her grandpa right now."

"Why not?"

"You know how strained things have been between me and Anna since Daniel was born. If she saw her grandpa Davis again, she might not want to come home."

"I don't relish the idea of her seeing him again, either, but that's not the point."

"What is the point?"

"I think if you would start paying Anna more attention, things might not be so strained between you two, and she wouldn't be thinking about her grandpa Davis so much."

"Oh, so it's all my fault, is it?" Cleon's face heated up. "I was trying to make conversation with her, and you saw the kind of response I got. She barely answered any of my questions."

Grace opened her mouth to respond, but the baby's cry halted her words. "I'd better tend to Daniel." She pushed her chair away from the table and rushed out of the room.

Cleon grabbed his cup to drink the last of his coffee but discovered it had turned cold. "That figures," he mumbled. This was not the beginning of a good day.

Chapter 30

Ruth had been lying on the sofa for quite a while when she heard a knock on the front door. Her mother had gone to the woodworking shop to take Dad his lunch, and Martha was still at the dog auction. No one but her could answer the door.

Reluctantly, she sat up and plodded over to the door. When she opened it, she discovered a middle-aged English woman with short, chestnut-colored hair and dark brown eyes standing on the porch.

"May I help you?"

The woman nodded. "My name's Rosemary Cole, and I'm looking for my brother."

Ruth squinted against the invading light streaming through the open door. "I don't know anyone with the last name of Cole living nearby," she said.

"My brother's last name is Hostettler."

"Hostettler?"

"That's right. Roman Hostettler."

Ruth's mouth fell open, and she leaned against the doorjamb for support. "Are—are you my dad's sister?"

"Yes."

Ruth stared at the woman, trying to piece things together. Finally, she opened the door wider and said, "I'm Ruth—Roman's daughter. Please, come inside."

———————◆◆◆———————

Rosemary followed Ruth into the living room and took a seat on the sofa. "Is—is my brother here?"

"He's out in his woodworking shop right now," Ruth said as she seated herself in the rocking chair across from Rosemary. "Would you like me to take you there?"

"Yes. No." Rosemary gave her left earlobe a tug, a habit she and Roman had begun when they were children. "Sorry, I'm feeling kind of nervous right now. I'd like a few minutes to compose myself before I see my brother."

Ruth nodded.

"I. . .uh. . .I'm not sure what his reaction will be when he sees me. It's been a long time, and. . ." Rosemary's voice trailed off, and she stared at her trembling hands.

"Would you like something to drink? Maybe a glass of tea or cold water?"

"Yes, yes. That would be nice."

"I'll be right back."

After Ruth left the room, Rosemary leaned her head against the back of the sofa and closed her eyes. *So my brother has his own woodworking shop. He always did like fooling around with wood. He's obviously married, or he wouldn't have a daughter named Ruth. I wonder how many other children he has.*

She opened her eyes and glanced around the room. The furnishings were simple, and the place had a homey feel. Several potted plants sat in one corner of the room, a scenic calendar adorned the wall, a pair of wooden sconces with white candles bordered an antique-looking clock, and several quilted throw pillows lay on the sofa. Roman's wife obviously had good taste, even though her home wasn't fancy like most English homes.

Rosemary thought about her visit to the home where she and her brothers had grown up. She'd driven to it before coming here and found someone else living there—a young Amish couple, Michael and Karen Mast. The Masts had told Rosemary that the elderly couple who used to live there were dead. When she'd asked about her brothers, Michael had said the only one still living in the area was Roman. He'd given Rosemary the address and said it was just a few miles down the road.

Rosemary's thoughts were halted when Ruth returned with a tray of cookies and a glass of iced tea. She placed the tray on the low table in front of the sofa and returned to her seat. "Please, help yourself."

Rosemary reached for the glass and took a sip. The cool liquid felt good on her parched throat. "Are you the only one at home?" she asked.

Ruth nodded. "My mother went to the shop to take Dad his lunch, my sister Grace is at her house, and my sister Martha has gone to Walnut Creek to a dog auction."

Rosemary's interest was piqued. She loved dogs—had ever since she was a girl. But Bob wouldn't let her have a dog. He'd said they were too much trouble.

Ruth shifted in her chair. "Did my dad know you were coming?"

"No, I—" A burning lump formed in Rosemary's throat. "I stopped by the home where we grew up, but the young couple who live there said my folks had died."

Ruth's chair squeaked as she pumped her legs up and down. "Grandpa Hostettler passed away five years ago, and Grandma died a year later."

Rosemary flinched. "I should have been here. I—I didn't know."

Ruth continued to rock, wearing a troubled look on her face. Did she think Rosemary was a terrible daughter because she hadn't returned home in all these years? Rosemary had thought about it—even mentioned it to Bob a couple of times. But he'd always said no—that her family didn't care about her, which was obvious because they'd never responded to any of her letters.

I was a fool to believe him, Rosemary thought with regret. *I should have made an effort to see my family despite the things he said.*

She finished her iced tea and set her glass back on the table. "I'm ready to see my brother now."

———————•◦•———————

Martha smiled at the female beagle she'd bid on to replace Flo as a mate for Bo. The dog's name was Polly, and she'd already had one litter of pups, so Martha was sure things would work out for her to raise some beagles.

If Polly gave her a good-sized litter and Martha made enough money when she sold them, she hoped to buy a pair of cocker spaniels.

"Up you go," Martha said as she lifted Polly into the dog carrier she'd brought from home. "I'm taking you to meet Bo."

"Who's Bo?"

Martha whirled around at the sound of a male voice. "Luke! I didn't know you'd be here today."

He motioned to the ginger-colored cocker spaniel he held on a leash. "Came to buy my mamm a birthday present."

A pang of envy shot through Martha. She wished she'd been able to buy a pair of cocker spaniels, but she needed to be practical. Since she already had a male beagle, it made sense to buy him a mate.

"She's beautiful," Martha said, bending down to pet the spaniel. *"Was is dei name?"*

"Her name's Cindy, and she's a purebred with papers. I think my mamm's gonna like her, don't you?"

"Oh jah." Martha's heart skipped a beat when Luke smiled at her. How could anyone think he could be responsible for the terrible things that had been done to her family? Besides, no one had proven that Luke had been behind the break-ins or horrible attacks. He'd told her that he hadn't taken his truck out on Christmas Eve, so she was sure he wasn't the one who had rammed Ruth and Martin's buggy.

"I see you bought yourself another beagle," Luke said, motioning to the dog carrier in the back of Martha's buggy.

"I got her to replace Flo."

Luke nodded. "John's happy with her too. Said she does a real good job running down rabbits for him."

"Glad to hear it." Martha shook her head. "She sure wasn't able to give me the puppies I needed to get my business going good."

"Maybe this beagle will work out better for you."

"I hope so. The paper that came with her said she's already had one litter of pups. At least I know she's not barren."

Luke scuffed the ground with the toe of his boot. "I've been wondering—how's your sister getting along these days?"

"Which sister?"

"Ruth."

"She's still struggling with her grief over losing Martin, but we're trying to help her through it, and she's taking it one day at a time."

"That's the best way to deal with anything. Jah, just one day at a time," he said with a nod.

Martha smiled. If Luke had been the one responsible for Martin's death, he surely wouldn't be asking about Ruth or looking so sad-eyed right now. She was sure he was innocent. If only he would get baptized and join the church, maybe her dad, the bishop, and others in their community would realize Luke was one of them.

Martha glanced at the cocker spaniel again. "I would have liked to bid on a pair of spaniels to breed, but I figured it would be best to get a mate for Bo."

"Say, I've got an idea." Luke's dark eyes seemed to dance with enthusiasm. "Why don't you get yourself a male cocker and breed it with my mamm's female?"

"That's a nice thought, but it won't work."

"Why not?"

"The pups your mamm's dog might have would be hers, not mine. If she sold them, the money would be hers too."

Luke reached up to scratch the side of his head and knocked his straw hat to the ground. "Maybe Mom would be willing to split the profits with you. After all, she'd have to pay for stud service if she wanted to breed the dog on her own," he said, bending over to retrieve the hat.

"I might have to talk to your mamm about this. After I'm able to buy a male cocker, that is."

"I'm making pretty good money working for John. Maybe I could loan you what you need to buy the dog."

"I couldn't let you do that."

"Why not?"

Martha didn't feel she could tell Luke that her dad would have a fit if he got wind that Luke had loaned her money, but she couldn't accept his gracious offer either. "If I'm going to build up my business, then I want to do it on my own."

"Guess I can understand that. I pretty much feel the same way about what I'm doing."

"But you work for someone; I'm trying to build my own business."

Luke shrugged. "I've got plans for the future though. Plans I haven't told anyone about."

Martha didn't feel it would be right to press him about whatever plans he might have, so she gave the cocker spaniel another pat and said, "Guess I'd better get home. I told my mamm I'd be there around noon."

"I should go too. Gotta give this critter to my mamm before it starts thinkin' I'm its master."

Martha laughed and climbed into her buggy. "I hope to see you at the next preaching service, Luke."

"Jah, sure." He lifted a hand in a wave as he led the cocker spaniel away.

As Martha pulled out of the parking lot a few minutes later, a sense of hope welled in her soul. She was glad she had met up with Luke today.

———————◀•▶———————

Rosemary's palms turned sweaty, and her legs felt like two sticks of rubber as she followed Ruth down a dirt path toward a white building. Would Roman recognize her after all these years? Would she know him? Would he welcome her home or turn her away?

"Dad, there's someone here to see you," Ruth said as they stepped into the woodworking shop a few minutes later.

Rosemary fought the urge to sneeze as the sharp odor of stain came in contact with her nose.

A young man with dark brown hair and a square jaw looked up from the chair he was staining and smiled. Rosemary knew he wasn't her brother. The man was too young to be Roman.

"Who's with you, Ruth?" a deep voice called out. "I'm about to have lunch with your mamm."

When Rosemary peered around Ruth, she caught sight of a middle-aged Amish woman standing in front of a workbench, and when the woman moved aside, Rosemary's heart felt as if it had stopped beating. The man sitting at the workbench had to be her brother. Hair that had once been full and dark was now thinning and streaked with gray, but the slight hump in the center of his nose was still there, and so were his piercing dark eyes.

"Roman, it's me," she said, moving closer to him. "I—I've come home."

He tipped his head and stared at her. "Do I know you?"

She nodded, unable to answer his question.

"Dad, it's your sister, Rosemary," Ruth said, touching Rosemary's elbow with her hand.

Roman jerked his head. The woman beside him gasped. But neither said a word. After several awkward moments, he spoke. "Where have you been all these years?"

"I've been living in Boise, Idaho, with my husband, Bob, but he died a few months ago. So I decided to come home and see my family."

"You think you can just sashay in the door and pick up where you left off thirty-some years ago like nothing's ever happened? Is that what you think?" Roman's voice sounded harsh, and the scowl on his face spoke volumes.

"I—I would like to explain. There are things you don't know—things you need to understand."

Roman's fist came down hard on the workbench, jiggling his lunch box and sending a napkin sailing to the floor. "It's been over thirty years, Rosemary! Do you know how much can happen in that time?"

She opened her mouth to respond, but he cut her off.

"Mom and Dad are dead. I'll bet you didn't know that, did you?"

"Not until I went by their house before I came here."

"Do you have any idea how hard Mom cried after you left home? When you didn't write and let her know where you were so she could write back, she was brokenhearted."

"I did write. I—"

"Pig's foot! If you'd written, we at least would have known where you were and that you were okay." He waved his hand as if he were swatting at a fly. "Now everyone but me is gone."

"My other brothers are dead?" Rosemary's head began to pound, and she placed her fingers against her throbbing temples.

"They're not dead; they moved to Wisconsin with their wives twenty years ago. Everyone except for Walt."

"Where is he?"

"Walt and his family are living up in Geauga County now. Have been for the last couple of years. I'm the only one from our family still living in Holmes County." He compressed his lips tightly together, grabbed the mug on his workbench, and took a drink.

The woman who stood at Roman's side reached out her hand. "I'm Roman's wife, Judith, and this is Ruth, one of our three daughters," she said, nodding at Ruth.

"It's nice to meet you, Judith. I met Ruth up at your house."

Judith motioned to the young man Rosemary had seen when she'd entered the shop. "That's our son-in-law, Cleon. He's married to our oldest daughter, Grace."

Rosemary glanced over at Cleon and smiled, then she turned to face Roman. "Can we sit awhile and talk? I'd like to explain a few things."

He shook his head. "I've got nothing to say, and there isn't anything you could say that I want to hear."

"Dad, don't you think you should listen to Aunt Rosemary?" Ruth spoke up.

Roman set his cup down with such force, a splash of coffee spilled on the sandwich that lay before him. "If she'd wanted to say something to me, then she would have written or come for a visit." He picked up the sandwich, tossed it in the lunch box, and slammed the lid. "Appetite's gone now."

Cleon stepped over to the workbench and laid his hand on Roman's shoulder. "I think you'd better take a deep breath and count to twenty. You're getting all worked up, and it's not good for your health."

"Maybe we should go up to the house," Judith suggested. "I'll fix some iced tea and we can sit in the living room and talk things through."

"No way!" Roman folded his arms in an unyielding pose. "I've got work to do." He glared at Rosemary. "Besides, I've got nothing to say to the likes of you, and neither does anyone in my family."

Tears stung the back of Rosemary's eyes, blurring her vision. Coming here had been a mistake. She should have stayed in Idaho, just as her son and daughter-in-law wanted her to do.

"I'm sorry I bothered you. I should have known you would still be stubborn like you were as a child." With a strangled sob, Rosemary rushed out the door.

Chapter 31

Unable to stand the dejected look on her aunt's face, Ruth hurried out of the woodworking shop after Rosemary. She thought her father was being cruel in his unwillingness to listen to what his sister wanted to say, and it wouldn't be right to let the poor woman leave without someone saying something to her.

Aunt Rosemary was almost to her car when Ruth caught up to her. "Don't go," she panted. "You need to talk things through with my dad."

Rosemary turned toward Ruth and sniffed deeply. "You heard what he said; he has nothing to say to me."

"Dad's upset right now. Give him some time to calm down and think things through."

"Are you suggesting I try again?"

Ruth nodded. "Not right now, but maybe in a day or two."

Rosemary shook her head. "I'm not so sure—"

"Mom will talk to him, and so will I. Please, won't you come back in a few days?"

Tears glistened in Rosemary's eyes. "There's not much left for me here anymore. But I came all this way, so I suppose I should stay awhile longer."

"Life is so short, and one never knows when their loved ones will be snatched away." Ruth drew in a quick breath. "If you were to leave without making things right between you and Dad, you might regret it for the rest of your life."

"I already do. I never should have left home in the first place." Rosemary opened her car door and stepped into the driver's seat. "I've taken a room at Hannah's House, a bed-and-breakfast in Berlin, so I'll be back in a couple of days."

As Ruth watched her aunt drive out of the yard, a lump lodged in her throat. Nothing was right anymore. Misunderstanding, misery, and confusion abounded at every turn. There seemed to be no answers for any of it.

With a heavy heart, she made her way back to her father's shop. Maybe Mom had been able to talk some sense into Dad by now. Maybe when his sister returned, he would be willing to listen to what she had to say.

As Martha guided her horse and buggy up the driveway leading to her house, a gray compact car passed her on the left. A middle-aged woman with short brown hair sat in the driver's seat. Martha didn't recognize her. Maybe she was a tourist who had gotten lost and needed directions. Or maybe she'd had business at Dad's woodworking shop.

Martha directed the horse to the hitching rail near the barn and climbed down from the buggy. After she unhitched the horse and led him to the corral, she went around to the back of the buggy to remove the dog carrier.

"Did you have any success at the auction?"

Martha turned and smiled at Grace, who held baby Daniel in her arms. "Jah, I got another female beagle to take Flo's place."

"That's good. Let's hope this one isn't barren."

"She's already had one litter of pups, so I'm sure she'll be able to have more." Martha reached over and stroked the top of Daniel's head. "Are you two out for a walk?"

"Not really. Cleon was supposed to come home for lunch, but it's after one and he hasn't shown up. I thought I'd better go down to the shop and see if he's still planning to eat lunch at the house or if he wants me to bring him something there."

Martha glanced toward the woodworking shop. "If you'll wait a minute, I'll walk with you. I'd like to show Dad my new dog."

"Sure, we can wait."

Martha took the dog out of the carrier and clipped a leash to its collar. "We're ready."

Grace smiled. "She's a nice-looking dog. What'd you name her?"

"Polly. She already had the name when I got her."

"I like it," Grace said as they started walking down the path toward the shop.

"I saw Luke Friesen at the dog auction. He bought a female cocker spaniel to give his mamm for her birthday. We discussed the idea of me getting a male cocker later on and breeding the two."

"Better not mention that idea to Dad." Grace frowned. "I don't think he'd be pleased about you making plans that involve Luke."

"Dad's been irritated ever since he fired Luke." Martha grunted. "I used to think Dad liked Luke, and I can't believe he and Ruth suspect Luke might have done all those terrible things to us. Luke seems like a nice fellow. I'm sure he would never do anything criminal."

"I don't think he could either." Grace stopped walking and turned to face Martha. "It's been several months since there was an attack—not since Ruth and Martin's buggy was rammed."

"And we don't know for sure that the person responsible for the accident was the same one who broke into our house and did all of the other acts of vandalism to our property."

"That's true. Whoever hit the buggy could have been drinking. Maybe they got scared and fled the scene when they realized they had caused an accident."

Martha shook her head. "Try telling that to Ruth. She thinks the person who hit them did it on purpose, and she's convinced that Luke is the one responsible for that too."

"How could it have been Luke when he drives a horse and buggy?"

"He owns a truck and keeps it hidden in the woods."

Grace's mouth dropped open. "Really? This is the first I've heard that."

Martha clamped her hand over her mouth. She couldn't believe she'd blurted that out. Especially after Ruth had asked her not to say anything.

"Does Dad know what Ruth suspects?"

"No, but I talked to Luke soon after the accident. In fact, I came right out and asked what he was doing on Christmas Eve."

"What'd he say?"

"Said he was home all evening, except for a quick trip to the Kings' place to borrow something his mamm needed."

Deep lines etched Grace's forehead. "Then he could have done it."

Martha shook her head vigorously. "I asked Luke if he'd been driving his truck on Christmas Eve, and he said he hadn't."

"And you believe him?"

"Jah. He said he went to the Kings' around four o'clock. Since Martin and Ruth's accident happened sometime after six, he couldn't have done it."

"Well," Grace said, releasing a sigh, "we can't solve anything standing here speculating. Let's get into the shop before my arms give out." She smiled at Daniel, fast asleep in her arms. "This young man feels like he weighs a ton."

Martha chuckled. It was good to see Grace feeling better these days. For a while after Daniel was born, Grace had been sullen and mildly depressed.

They stepped onto the porch of Dad's shop, and Martha had no more than opened the door, when she heard Mom's pleading voice.

"Roman, won't you please listen to reason? This may have been your only chance to—"

"*My* only chance?" Dad bellowed. "It's that woman who had a chance. But she threw it out the window the day she left home."

"What's going on?" Grace asked, looking at Cleon, who stood off to one side with an anxious expression. "I thought you were coming up to the house for lunch."

"I was, until things got sticky in here. Figured I'd better hang around and see if I could help get your daed calmed down."

Martha felt immediate concern. "What's wrong with Dad?"

Cleon nodded toward the workbench where Dad stood beside Mom. "Better let him explain."

Martha hurried across the room. "What's going on? Why were you shouting at Mom?"

"My sister came home," he said with a groan.

Martha gasped. "The sister who's been gone more than thirty years?"

Dad gave one quick nod.

"That's wunderbaar," Grace said.

"Your daed doesn't think so." Mom shook her head. "He sent Rosemary away."

Martha glanced out the window. "That must have been her in the car I passed when I came up the driveway. Oh Dad, how could you have sent her away? Didn't you think we'd all like to meet her?"

"Ruth met her," Mom said. "Apparently Rosemary went up to the house, and then Ruth brought her down here."

"Did she say where she's been all these years?" Grace asked.

"Boise, Idaho. She said her husband died recently, so she came here to see her family."

"It's too late for that," Dad mumbled. "She never cared a whit about her family before, so why now?"

Mom frowned. "If you'd given her the chance to explain, you might have the answer to your question."

Polly whined and pulled on her leash, and Martha looked down. She'd almost forgotten her reason for coming to the shop. "I came here to tell you that I bought a female beagle today," she mumbled. "But I guess that's not so important right now."

"It is important, dear one." Mom patted Martha's arm. "But at the moment it's hard to get enthused about anything."

"Will Aunt Rosemary be back?" Grace asked. "I'd like to meet her."

Dad shook his head. "If I have my way, I'll never have to see that woman again."

———————◆◆———————

"I'm sorry about lunch being late," Sue said as Abe pulled out a chair and took a seat at the table. "Molly got into a jar of petroleum jelly and made a mess of not only herself but the sofa cushions in the living room."

Abe grimaced. Instead of things getting better for his sister, they seemed to be getting worse. Even with the four older ones in school, Sue had her hands full caring for Molly and Owen during the day.

"I'm sorry to hear about your troubles." He glanced over at Molly's high chair and saw that it was empty. "Where's my little girl now?"

"I gave her a bath after she made the mess. As I was drying her off, she fell asleep. I put her to bed and figured she could eat when she wakes up."

"That makes sense." Abe looked over at Owen and then back at Sue. "Should we bow for prayer?"

They nodded and lowered their heads. When the prayer was over, Abe helped himself to a piece of bread and slathered it with butter.

"I got a letter from home this morning," Sue said.

"Was it from the folks?"

She nodded. "It was from Dad, letting me know that Mom fell and broke her hip last week. He asked if I could come home."

Abe nearly choked on the bread he'd put in his mouth. "Ach! I'm sorry to hear about Mom."

"I hate to leave you in the lurch, but she really needs me right now, so—"

Abe held up his hand. "No problem. You're needed there more than here. I'm sure I can find someone to take your place." He grabbed his glass of water and gulped some down. "I'll start looking for a helper right away."

Chapter 32

"How did the dog auction go the other day?" Irene asked Martha as the two of them peeled apples for the pies Irene would serve to a group of tourists later in the day.

"It went well." Martha smiled. "I got another female beagle, and I'm hoping she'll give me lots of pups."

"What'd you name her?" Irene's teenage daughter, Carolyn, asked from where she stood making a fruit salad.

"She already had a name—Polly."

"I like it. Sounds real *lebhaft*," Irene put in.

"Polly seems to be pretty sprightly, all right. When I introduced Polly to Bo, she got so excited she knocked the poor critter to the ground." Martha reached for another apple. As she sliced into it, the tangy aroma wafted up to her nose and made her mouth water. Apple pie was her favorite, and she hoped there would be some left over so she could have a piece.

"Guess we know who'll be the boss in that family," Carolyn said with a chuckle.

A knock sounded at the back door.

"I wonder who that could be." Irene wiped her hands on a dish towel and went to answer the door. When Irene returned, Martha was shocked to see Gary Walker standing beside her.

"Wh–what are you doing here?" she squeaked.

"I heard about the Amish meals that are served here, so I came by to see if I could get an interview to put in one of the local papers." Gary offered Martha a slanted grin and lifted his notebook and pen.

She ground her teeth together. "I thought you had moved on."

"I did, but I missed the place so much, I decided to come back." Gary smiled at Irene, a more genuine smile than he'd given Martha. "In fact, I've decided to relocate to Holmes County, and I've been looking for a place to live. You wouldn't know of anything that's available, would you?"

Irene opened her mouth as if to respond, but Martha spoke first. "Why would you want to move to Holmes County?"

"I like it here. Besides, I've been offered a job at the newspaper in Millersburg. I'll be doing a regular column for them from now on, as well as some freelance stuff."

Martha's heart gave a lurch, and her palms grew sweaty. If Gary moved to Holmes County and he *was* the one responsible for the things that had been done to them, they could probably expect more.

Gary turned to face Irene. "Would you mind answering a few of my questions about the home-cooked meals you serve?"

"I suppose it would be all right," she replied sweetly. "In fact, some free advertising might be good for my business."

Gary pulled out a chair at the table and took a seat. "Is there anything in particular you'd like my readers to know?"

Ruth lay curled in a fetal position on her bedroom floor. The circle of sun shining through her window did nothing to diminish the loneliness encompassing her soul. When Ruth was a child, she used to lie in the sun, enjoying its warmth, finding it to be healing and comforting whenever she felt sad or lonely. Not anymore. Even the heat of the sun brought no healing or comfort. There seemed to be no reason for her to go on living.

She stared at the dust particles floating past her face. One. . .two. . .three . . . How many specks of dust were there, and where did they all come from?

Caw! Caw! Caw! The persistent chatter of a crow outside her window sounded foreboding, and she shivered. Her nose twitched as she drew in a shallow breath. When was the last time the braided throw rug on which she lay had been cleaned?

She rolled onto her back. Gazing at the cracks in the ceiling, she tried to pray, but no words would come. What was the point of praying? God never answered her prayers.

A groan escaped Ruth's lips. She needed someplace to think— somewhere to clear her head.

The floorboards squeaked as she rose to her feet, feeling as though she were in a dream. She shuffled across the room. . .one. . .two. . .three. . . four steps to the door. Her hand clasped the knob. A few more steps and she slowly descended the stairs. The house seemed so quiet. Somewhere in the distance she heard a steady *tick-tock, tick-tock.*

Dad's taken Mom to see the chiropractor. Martha's at Irene's. No one needs me. I'm all alone.

She meandered into the kitchen and leaned against the wall, stricken with grief and a longing so strong she felt as if her heart might burst. *Martin, I miss you so.*

Ruth jumped as the clang of the dinner bell beating against the side of the house rattled the kitchen window. She needed fresh air. Needed to clear her head.

She jerked open the back door and stepped onto the porch. The sun still shone, but a gust of wind whipped around her face and took her breath away.

As if her legs had a mind of their own, they led her toward the barn. She halted in front of the silo and looked up. She had climbed up there several times when she was a girl, whenever one of her sisters had dared her to do it. Ruth wasn't afraid of heights, and the silo had seemed like a good place to sit and think. She remembered how she had enjoyed the view—gazing at the lush green pasture where the horses nibbled grass, watching the clouds drift lazily overhead, counting the cars zipping past their house.

Ruth reached up and grabbed hold of the ladder, bringing one foot up behind her and then the other. Slowly, she made her way up until she reached the opening near the peak of the silo. Turning, she took a seat on the ledge, her legs resting on the top rung of the ladder. As she stared at the vastness below, her head started to spin. What was going on? She wasn't afraid of heights. Why the woozy feeling?

She closed her eyes, and an image of Martin flashed into her mind. Oh, how she missed him. It had been three months since he'd been killed, but the ache in her heart hadn't diminished. With each passing day, the bitterness toward the one who had caused the accident escalated. Forgiveness seemed an impossible feat.

Ruth's eyelids fluttered, and hot tears dribbled down her flushed cheeks. She drew in a ragged breath and struggled against the temptation to jump. *Oh God, I know it would be wrong to take my life, but I don't want to live anymore. I want the pain to end. I want to be with Martin.* She gulped, and a pang of fear twisted her insides. *Help me, Lord. Show me what to do.*

As Rosemary left her rental car and started walking toward her brother's woodworking shop, doubts filled her mind. Was she foolish for coming here again and trying to make things right between her and Roman? Would he listen to her this time? Could she make him understand the way things were? Or would he order her out of his shop again?

She sent up a silent prayer, opened the shop door, and stepped inside. Roman's son-in-law sat at a metal desk in the center of the room, but she saw no sign of Roman.

"Is my brother here?" she asked, stepping up to the desk.

Cleon shook his head. "He took Judith to see the chiropractor this morning. As far as I know, Ruth's the only one at home right now."

Rosemary stared at the floor, wondering if she should leave a message for Roman, go up to the house to visit Ruth, or head back to town.

"Ruth would probably like some company," Cleon said. "She lost her husband in a buggy accident a few months ago. She's been sad and lonely ever since."

Rosemary could relate to that. She'd been sad and lonely since Bob died, despite his deathbed confession that he'd intercepted all of the letters she'd written to her family over the years.

"Do you know when Roman will be back?" she asked. "I really would like to speak with him."

Cleon shrugged. "I'm not sure. He said something about taking Judith out to lunch and then doing some shopping before coming home. He might not be here for several hours."

Rosemary fiddled with the strap on her purse, then turned toward the door. "I guess I will stop and see Ruth. Maybe by the time we're done visiting, Roman and Judith will be home."

Cleon smiled. "In case you miss Roman, I'll be sure to tell him you were here."

"Thanks."

As Rosemary walked up the path toward her brother's house, she thought about what Cleon had said concerning Ruth. No wonder the poor girl had seemed so sad and disconnected when she'd visited with her the other day. *I should have recognized the look of pain on her face. I've seen it often enough when I've looked in the mirror. Maybe I can say something to help Ruth deal with the loss she's sustained.*

Rosemary stepped onto the porch and knocked on the door. Several seconds went by, but no one answered.

Maybe Ruth is in her room and didn't hear my knock.

Rosemary turned the knob and opened the door. "Hello! Is anyone home?"

No answer.

She stood below the stairs and cupped her hands around her mouth. "Ruth, are you up there?"

No response.

Maybe she's sleeping or went out back to check on the clothes I saw hanging on the line when I arrived.

Rosemary stepped outside and started around the house. "Hello! Is anyone here?"

No reply and no sign of Ruth. *I may as well head back to town. Maybe I'll come back tomorrow.*

She started toward her car but stopped to watch a twittering blue jay as it pecked at seeds in a nearby feeder. A downy woodpecker swooped in just then, and the blue jay took flight. She watched it soar over the treetops, past the barn, and up toward the silo.

Rosemary blinked and shielded her eyes against the glare of the sun. It looked as though someone was sitting on the ledge near the top of the ladder. It couldn't be. No one in their right mind would be foolish enough to climb up there and sit on the ledge.

She tipped her head back and stared. It was a woman dressed in Amish clothes. Could it be Ruth? Had she climbed up there to— *Oh dear God, no!*

Rosemary hurried toward the silo, a sense of urgency pressing her forward. Despite her fear of heights, she dropped her purse to the ground, grabbed the side of the ladder, and started to climb.

She'd only made it halfway up when Ruth called out, "Don't come any farther!"

Rosemary halted and looked up. "It's me, Ruth—Aunt Rosemary."

"Go away."

"I'd like to speak with you."

No response.

"Please, Ruth, come down."

"No."

"If you don't come down, I'm coming up."

When Ruth didn't move, Rosemary began climbing again. The metallic taste of fear sprang to her mouth. *Please, God, don't let her jump.*

By the time Rosemary reached the top rung, her hands shook so badly, she could barely hang on. "I'm afraid of heights," she confessed. "You need to come down so we can talk."

Ruth shook her head.

"I understand your pain. As I told you the other day, I lost my husband too."

"Was he murdered?"

"No. Bob died of a heart attack."

"Did you lose your ability to have children when he died?"

"No, but—"

"I know it would be wrong to take my own life, but I—I have nothing to live for." Ruth emitted a pathetic-sounding sob. "I want the person who rammed our buggy to pay for what he did."

"I'm aware of what it's like to feel anger and resentment," Rosemary said. "I was angry with my husband when I found out he had betrayed me."

Ruth stared straight ahead, her chin quivering and tears streaming down her cheeks. "H—how did he betray you?"

"I'd rather not discuss the details of that right now. But I do want you to know that one day while I was reading my Bible, I came across Matthew 6:14. It says, 'For if ye forgive men their trespasses, your heavenly Father will also forgive you.'" She paused and drew in a quick breath. "Ruth, the only way you'll ever have peace is to let go of your anger and forgive the one responsible for your husband's death."

Tears coursed down Ruth's cheeks. "I—I'm not sure I can, but I know taking my life isn't the answer."

Rosemary breathed a sigh of relief. "Then you'll come down the ladder with me?"

Ruth nodded.

"Thank You, God," Rosemary murmured. She knew without a shadow of doubt that she couldn't leave Holmes County. Even if she never got through to Roman, she would stay because Ruth needed her. Truth was, Rosemary needed someone too.

Chapter 33

"Wie geht's?" Abe asked as he entered Roman's woodworking shop on Friday morning and found Roman kneeling on the floor beside an old rocking chair.

"I'm doin' okay. And you?"

"I was fine until Sue told me during lunch yesterday that our mamm broke her hip. Now Sue will have to return home to help out."

Roman's forehead wrinkled. "You've got a problem with your sister helping your mamm?"

"It's not her caring for Mom that bothers me; it's the fact that she'll be moving back to Illinois and I'll be left without anyone to watch my kinner and keep up with the house."

"Sounds like you're going to need a *maad*."

Abe nodded. "I need a maid, all right, and I came by to see if you think Ruth might be interested in the job."

Roman's eyebrows shot up. "I don't think so. Ruth's been struggling with depression since Martin died."

"I think her going to work is a great idea," Cleon said from where he was sanding cabinets.

Roman looked at him with a dubious expression. "You do?"

Cleon nodded. "It's been three months since Martin died, and Ruth will barely go anywhere or take part in anything the family does. I think it would be good for her to get involved in someone else's life and do something useful. Might help take her mind off her own problems."

"Cleon's right," Abe said as a feeling of hope welled in his chest. "I speak from experience when I say that it's not good for a body to sit around and dwell on her pain. If Ruth came to work for me, she'd not only be helping us out, but it would give her something meaningful to do." He smiled. "Besides, I know for a fact that my kinner think a lot of Ruth."

Roman stood, yawned, and stretched his arms overhead. "You might be right about that." He reached around to rub a spot on his lower back. "Ruth's not only good with kinner, but she's a fine cook and knows how to keep house real well. I'm sure she would do a good job for you."

"Will you speak to her about the job?" Abe asked.

"Why don't you ask her yourself?"

Abe poked a finger under the side of his hat and scratched his head. "I figured she might respond better if you do the asking."

"I doubt that." Roman grunted. "I don't have a lot of influence on any of my daughters these days."

"I could ask her, but that might seem kind of odd," Cleon said. "I agree with Roman; you should speak to Ruth yourself, Abe."

"She's up at the house with Judith. I think they were planning to bake some cookies." Roman wiggled his eyebrows. "If you ask real nice, you might get a few."

Abe nodded. "Jah, okay. I'll head up there and see what Ruth has to say."

"Could you please check on those cookies in the oven?" Mom asked, glancing over her shoulder at Ruth. "I need to use the necessary room." She hurried from the kitchen before Ruth could respond.

With a weary sigh, Ruth opened the oven door and peered inside. The soft molasses cookies were rising nicely, but they weren't quite brown enough. She figured they needed a few more minutes.

She reached for the teakettle at the back of the stove, poured herself a cup of hot water, and added a tea bag. She was about to take a seat at the table when a knock sounded at the back door. Since Mom was still in the bathroom and Martha had gone to the barn some time ago, Ruth went to answer the door. She was pleased to find her aunt on the porch.

"I hope you're not busy," Aunt Rosemary said, "because I'd like to take you to lunch in Millersburg. Afterward, I thought it might be fun to go shopping at Walmart."

Ruth sucked in her breath. She hadn't been anywhere other than church since Martin died. The thought of going out to lunch or shopping in a big store made her feel queasy. "I—I don't know—"

"It'll be good for you to get out of the house and do something fun." Aunt Rosemary gave Ruth's arm a gentle squeeze. "I need to buy a few things, and it would be nice to have someone along to keep me company."

Ruth opened her mouth to respond, but Mom came out of the bathroom just then. "Who was at the door, Ruth?"

"It's Aunt Rosemary." Ruth stepped aside and motioned her aunt into the house.

"Oh good. I'm glad you came back. Have you been to the woodworking shop to speak with Roman?"

Rosemary shook her head. "Not today. I came by to see if Ruth would like to go shopping and out to lunch with me." She smiled at Ruth's mother. "You're welcome to join us if you like."

"That's nice of you," Mom said, "but Grace is coming over soon, and we'd planned to do some sewing." She slipped her arm around Ruth's waist. "I think you should go. It would do you a world of good to get out of the house for a while."

Ruth was on the verge of saying that she didn't feel up to going when she caught a whiff of something burning. "Ach, the cookies!" She rushed into the kitchen, flipped the oven door open, and withdrew the cookie sheet. Every one of the cookies was overly dark and crispy around the edges.

"Are they ruined?" Mom asked as she and Aunt Rosemary stepped into the room.

Ruth nodded. "I'm afraid so. It's a good thing the two batches we made earlier turned out okay." She glanced over at her aunt. "Would you like to try one of the good ones?"

Aunt Rosemary shook her head. "The offer's tempting, but I don't want to spoil my appetite for lunch. Speaking of which, have you decided whether you'll go to Millersburg with me?"

"She'll go," Mom said before Ruth could open her mouth. "And when you get back, maybe you'll have a chance to talk to that *glotzkeppich* husband of mine."

"Roman always was a stubborn one, even when he was a boy." Aunt Rosemary shook her head. "I will try to speak with him again, but I'm not holding my breath that he'll listen to anything I have to say."

"I'll be praying that he does. There's been enough misunderstanding in this family."

Ruth grimaced. She knew her mother was probably referring to the secret Grace had kept when she'd returned home after going English for a time. Ruth wasn't sure whether Dad had ever come to grips with the knowledge that Grace had kept her previous marriage to an Englisher from him for some time.

"Well, now," Aunt Rosemary said, touching Ruth's arm, "should the two of us head for town?"

Ruth glanced at the charred cookies sitting on the counter. "I've still got a couple more batches to bake."

"Never mind that," Mom said with a shake of her head. "You run along with Rosemary, and I'll finish the cookies."

Ruth figured she wasn't going to argue her way out of going, so she plucked her sweater and purse off the wall peg near the door and had just touched the doorknob when a knock sounded.

"Must be our day for company," Mom said. "Open it, Ruth, and see who's come calling."

When Ruth opened the door, she was surprised to see Abe Wengerd standing on the porch holding his straw hat. "Guder mariye," he said, shifting his weight from one foot to the other. "Mind if I come in a minute?"

"No, of course not." Ruth opened the door wider. "If you came to see Dad, he's working in his shop right now."

"Been there already. It's you I'm here to see."

"Me?" Ruth couldn't imagine what Abe would need to see her about.

"I was wondering if you'd be interested in coming to work for me."

"In the harness shop?"

"No, no," he said, looking a bit flustered. "I meant as a maad."

"But you have Sue helping you with the household chores. Isn't she able to handle things on her own?"

"She'll be leaving on Monday—going back home to help our mamm, who recently fell and broke her hip."

"I'm sorry to hear that," Mom said, stepping out of the kitchen. She nudged Ruth gently on the arm. "I think it would be a good idea for you to work as Abe's maid."

"No. I couldn't do that," Ruth said with a shake of her head.

"Why not?" The question came from Aunt Rosemary, who had stepped up behind Mom.

"Well, I. . ." Ruth's face flushed with heat, and her hands began to shake. "I'm needed here, helping you."

"Nonsense." Mom draped her arm across Ruth's shoulder. "I can get by with Martha's help, just like I did when you first got married."

Ruth flinched at the reminder. Ever since Aunt Rosemary had talked her down from the silo, she'd been trying not to think about Martin or the anger she felt toward the one who had killed him.

"I really think it would be good for you." Aunt Rosemary moved to stand beside Ruth and leaned close to her ear. "Remember the things we talked about the other day?"

Ruth knew what Rosemary was referring to—things they'd discussed after they'd climbed down from the silo, things about Ruth making an effort to start living life again.

"I've seen how well you get along with my kinner," Abe put in as if he thought Ruth needed a bit more persuasion. "And I'll pay you a decent wage."

Ruth didn't care about the money. But it would be nice to be around Abe's children. Besides, if she was gone all day, Mom wouldn't be able to hover over her.

She nodded slowly. "All right. I can begin work on Monday morning."

As Grace headed down the path toward her folks' house, she spotted Ruth and an English woman, whom she guessed might be their aunt Rosemary, coming out the back door. She would have waved, but since she had a squirming baby in her arms, she didn't think that was a good idea. By the time she got close enough to call out to them, they'd gotten into the car she'd seen parked in the driveway and pulled away.

"Was that Dad's sister with Ruth?" Grace asked her mother when she entered the house a few minutes later.

Mom nodded as she opened the oven door and removed a sheet of plump, golden brown cookies. "Rosemary came by to see if Ruth wanted to go shopping and out to lunch."

"And Ruth agreed to go?"

"She did."

"I'm surprised. She hasn't wanted to do much of anything since Martin died, not even visit with her family."

"I know." Mom set the cookie sheet on a cooling rack and nodded toward the table. "Have a seat, and I'll fix you a glass of milk to go with a couple of these soft molasses cookies."

"Sounds good to me." Grace took a seat and placed Daniel in her lap.

"There's an even bigger surprise," Mom said, handing Grace a glass. "Ruth's going to work for Abe as his maad."

"I thought Abe's sister was taking care of his house and kinner."

"She was, but she's going back to Illinois to help her mamm, who recently broke her hip."

"That's too bad." Daniel hiccupped several times, and Grace rubbed the small of his back until the hiccups subsided. "How'd you talk Ruth into working for Abe?"

"I didn't. Rosemary took care of that." Mom poured milk into Grace's glass, brought a plate of cookies to the table, and took a seat. "She seems to have some persuasion over Ruth that none of the rest of us has."

"Maybe it's a good thing she's come back to Holmes County."

"I was thinking that too." Mom held out her hands. "How about I hold the boppli while you eat those cookies?"

"Are you sure? Daniel's cutting a tooth, and he's been fussy all week."

Mom clicked her tongue. "Have you forgotten that I raised three girls of my own? I do know a thing or two about fussy bopplin."

"Guess you've got a point." Grace handed the baby to her mother. "Has Aunt Rosemary tried to speak with Dad again?"

"Not yet, but she said she might try after she and Ruth get home from Millersburg."

"I hope he'll listen. Maybe there's a good reason Aunt Rosemary never contacted any of her family."

Mom nodded. "There are always two sides to every story. Your daed ought to be smart enough to listen to his sister."

A knock sounded at the door, interrupting their conversation.

"Want me to get it?" Grace asked.

"That would be good since I've got my hands full of baby right now."

Grace pushed her chair away from the table and hurried to the back door. She found Donna Larson on the porch holding an angel food cake.

"I was at the bakeshop in town early this morning," Donna explained. "They had angel food cake on sale, so I bought two—one for me and one for your mother." She peered around Grace. "Is she at home?"

"She's in the kitchen. Would you like to come in and have some freshly baked molasses cookies and milk?"

"The cookies sound good, but I'd prefer coffee if you have any."

"Mom probably has a pot on the stove. She usually keeps some warming for my dad."

Donna followed Grace into the kitchen. "I brought you an angel food cake from the bakeshop in Berlin," she said, smiling at Mom.

"That was nice of you," Mom replied. "Why don't you join us at the table?"

"Don't mind if I do." Donna set the cake on the counter and took a seat. "That baby of yours is sure growing," she said, smiling at Grace when she handed her a cup of coffee.

Grace nodded. "He seems to grow an inch every day."

"How's Ruth getting along? Is she dealing any better with the loss of her husband?"

"I think so," Mom replied. "Abe Wengerd came by a while ago and asked if Ruth would come to work for him as his maid."

"I thought his sister was helping."

"She was, but she'll be going home to care for her mother, who was injured recently." Mom smiled. "Miracle of miracles, Ruth agreed to take Sue's place as Abe's maid."

"Where is Ruth today?" Donna asked.

Mom explained about Aunt Rosemary and how she'd been gone for thirty-some years but had come back to Holmes County. She ended the story by saying, "Rosemary's the one who convinced Ruth to agree to work for Abe. The two of them left a while ago to go shopping and out to lunch in Millersburg."

"It's good to hear Ruth's getting out. I hope working for Abe will help with the pain of her loss."

"That's what I'm hoping for too," Mom said with a nod.

Donna blew on her coffee then took a sip. "How's everything else around here? Have there been any more acts of vandalism?"

"Not since Ruth and Martin's buggy was run off the road. We're hoping things stay that way." Mom bent her head and kissed Daniel's cheek. "It's not easy to spend your days and nights worrying that something bad might be just around the corner."

Donna tapped her fingernails on the edge of the table. "If the attacks should start again and you and Roman decide you need to move someplace else, I hope you'll let Ray and me know before you put the place on the market." She smiled at Mom then at Grace. "We'd like to be given the first opportunity to buy your land."

"Roman thinks moving would be the coward's way out," Mom replied. "He said it would be like giving in to the attacker. If the attacks should start up again, we're hoping the sheriff will catch the criminal. In the meantime, we'll keep trusting the Lord to keep us safe."

Donna looked as though she was going to say something, but Martha burst into the room, interrupting their conversation. "You should see how well Bo and Polly are getting along. I think things will work out better with this dog." She skipped across the floor but halted when she spotted Donna. "Sorry. I didn't realize we had company."

"I'm not really company," Donna said with a wave of her hand. "I'm just your friendly neighbor who decided to drop by with an angel food cake because I know it's one of your mother's favorite desserts."

Martha eyed the cake sitting across the room. "Looks real tasty."

"There's soft molasses cookies, freshly baked," Mom said, motioning to the plate in the center of the table. "Pull up a chair and have a few. It'll tide you over until lunch."

Martha took a seat and plucked two cookies off the plate.

"Don't you think you should wash your hands first?" Grace asked.

"I washed them at the pump outside before I came in."

"Oh."

Martha looked over at Grace, and her eyebrows pulled together. "There's something I've been meaning to tell you, and the reason I didn't say anything sooner is because I know how shaken up everyone's been over Aunt Rosemary's sudden appearance. I didn't want to give you one more thing to worry about."

"What is it, Martha?" Mom asked. "What's happened that might make us worry?"

"When I was working at Irene's the other day, she had an unexpected visitor."

"Who was that?" Grace asked.

"Gary Walker."

Grace's mouth dropped open. "But I thought he had left Holmes County and wasn't coming back."

"He said he's been hired at the newspaper office in Millersburg and that he's decided to move here permanently."

Grace clutched the edge of the table as a sense of panic gripped her like a vise. If Gary was moving to Holmes County, then the attacks would surely begin again.

Chapter 34

As Ruth stood in front of Abe's kitchen window, watching Anna and Esta play a game of hide-and-seek, she reflected on the past. She could still remember how it used to be when she and her sisters played hide-and-seek as children. Playing childhood games used to make her happy whenever she felt sad. Now, thanks to her depression, very little made her laugh. Even her trip to Millersburg with Aunt Rosemary hadn't helped much, although she did feel comfortable in the woman's company.

Aunt Rosemary had seemed disappointed that Dad wasn't in his shop when they'd returned home that day. She'd told Ruth she would return in a few days and try again. The woman obviously wasn't one to give up easily. The fact that she'd been able to talk Ruth into taking the job as Abe's maid was a good indication of her ability to make people do things they didn't want to do. Maybe in time she would get through to Dad.

Ruth moved away from the window and over to the door. Stepping outside, she took a seat on the porch swing to better watch the children. Anna had come home with Esta after school so the girls could play, and soon after their arrival, they'd initiated the game of hide-and-seek with Esta's siblings. All but Gideon. He kept to himself most of the time and had gone to the barn as soon as he'd arrived home from school.

Ruth's eyes drifted shut as she thought about how well things had gone on her first day working for Abe. She had arrived early this morning in time to feed the children breakfast and make the older ones' lunches for

223

school. After breakfast, Abe had gone to his harness shop. Soon after that, Gideon, Josh, Esta, and Willis had headed for school. Ruth spent the rest of the morning washing clothes, baking bread, and keeping an eye on Owen and Molly.

She reflected on how warm and cuddly Molly had felt as she'd held the little golden-haired girl in her arms and rocked her to sleep after lunch. Molly had called her *Mammi* before she'd fallen asleep, and it had touched Ruth's heart to the very core. *If only I was her mammi,* she thought. *I'd give most anything to have a child of my own.*

"Here I come, ready or not!"

Ruth's eyes snapped open, and she saw Willis zip past the porch, obviously on his way to seek out the hiding places of the other children. A few minutes later, she heard giggling and figured one of the girls had probably hidden under the porch.

She yawned and was on the verge of drifting off again when a shrill scream jolted her fully awake.

With her heart pounding like a herd of stampeding horses, Ruth jumped off the swing and dashed into the yard. There lay Willis, holding his nose and whimpering. She dropped to the ground beside the boy. "What happened?"

"I was chasin' after Josh and run into the tree." Willis removed his hands, and Ruth gasped when she saw blood oozing from his nose.

She pulled out the handkerchief tucked inside the band of her choring apron and covered the boy's nose with it. "Come inside so I can get that bleeding stopped," she said, helping him to his feet.

The other children came out of their hiding places and followed Ruth and Willis into the kitchen.

"Is he gonna be all right?" Esta asked as Ruth seated Willis on a chair and placed a small bag of ice against the side of his nose.

"His *naas* doesn't appear to be broken," Ruth said. "Once we get the bleeding stopped, he should be fine."

"My nose bled like that once," Anna said, leaning over to stare at Willis's nose. "It was when I was livin' with Poppy and Grammy Davis. It happened 'cause I had a bad cold and blew too hard. Poppy soaked a piece of cotton in vinegar and put it inside my nose."

"Eww." Esta puckered her lips. "That must have stung."

"It did. But it made the bleeding stop real quick." Anna looked up at Ruth. "Are you gonna put vinegar in Willis's nose?"

"I hope the ice will do the trick." Ruth motioned to the plate of peanut butter cookies sitting on the counter. "Why don't you all help yourselves to a couple of cookies and go back outside to play?"

"What about Willis?" Owen wanted to know.

"He'll stay with me until his nose stops bleeding. Then he can have some cookies."

The children each grabbed a handful of cookies and tromped out the door.

Several minutes later, Abe stepped into the room. "What's going on?" he asked. "Josh told me Willis had a run-in with a tree."

"Jah, he did." Ruth placed her hand on Willis's shoulder. "He was looking for one of the others in a game of hide-and-seek when it happened."

Abe knelt on the floor in front of Willis and touched the boy's knee. "You gonna be all right, boy?"

Willis nodded, although a few tears trickled down his cheeks.

"The bleeding's probably stopped by now," Ruth said, removing the ice bag to take a look. "Jah, it seems to be fine." She extended the plate of cookies to Willis. "Why don't you take a couple of these and go sit on the porch? No playing or running around though."

Willis snatched up three cookies and grinned at her. "I'll sit real still; I promise."

"Good thing he's got youth on his side," Abe said when Willis had left the kitchen. "If that had happened to me, I'd probably be bleeding like a stuck pig."

Ruth smiled. It was the first genuine smile she'd been able to offer since Martin's death. "Would you like a cookie?" she asked.

He took a seat at the table. "Danki. They look good."

"I brought them from home," she said, sitting in the chair across from him. "My mamm made them on Saturday."

Abe chomped one down and smacked his lips. "They taste as good as they look. Only thing that might make 'em better would be a glass of cold milk for dunking."

"You sound like my daed. He's always got to have milk to go with his cookies." Ruth started to rise. "I'll get you a glass."

"Don't trouble yourself. I can fetch it." Abe hopped up. "Would you like one too?"

"I believe I would."

Abe was back soon with two glasses and a jug of milk.

"Danki," she said when he handed her a glass.

"How'd everything go here at the house today?" Abe asked, wiping his mouth with a napkin. "Did you have any problems?"

"Except for Willis's little accident with the tree, everything went well."

"Glad to hear it." Abe leaned his elbows on the table. "If you ever remarry, I think you'll make a fine mudder."

Ruth dropped her gaze to the table. "I thought you knew that I can't have any children." She drew in a quick breath, hoping to keep her emotions in check. She would not allow herself to break down in front of Abe, no matter how much her heart might be breaking.

Abe slapped the side of his head. "Ach, what a *dummkopp* I am. I did know about your injuries and the surgery you had; I just wasn't thinking."

Ruth lifted her gaze to meet his. "I'm sure you've had a lot on your mind, especially with Sue moving back home."

"It's still no excuse. I'm sorry I brought it up."

"Even if I could have children, I doubt I would ever remarry," Ruth said as a feeling of bitterness threatened to choke her.

"Why not?"

"I don't think I could ever love anyone the way I loved Martin."

"I know what you mean. I doubt there's anyone who could fill the place in my heart left by Alma." Abe grunted and pushed his chair aside. "Think I'll go out to the barn and see if Gideon's done all his chores."

Ruth nodded. "I'd better check on Willis. Then I'll get supper started."

"What are we having?" Abe asked as he reached the door.

"Chicken and dumplings."

"Sounds good. That's one of my favorites."

When the door closed behind Abe, Ruth put their glasses and the cookie plate in the sink. She glanced out the window and saw Abe in the yard, tossing a ball for Esta's dog to fetch.

226

A sense of despair came over her, and she nearly doubled over with the pain. *I'll never know the joy of watching my husband laugh and play with our kinner. I'll never know love again.*

Chapter 35

"Guder mariye," Grace said when Martha stepped into her kitchen. "What brings you over here on this warm spring morning?"

"Came to deliver this." Martha held out a loaf of bread. "It's cinnamon-raisin. Aunt Rosemary brought a couple of loaves by our house right after breakfast."

"Dad's sister was here again?"

Martha nodded.

"Did she talk to Dad?"

"She tried to, but he mumbled something about being late to work and hurried out the door." Martha frowned. "I don't know why he's being so stubborn. He ought to at least hear what she has to say. Don't you agree?"

"I do—but then, what I think has never mattered much where Dad's concerned. I'm not sure he's ever gotten over my keeping the secret about Anna and Wade from him and the rest of the family."

"He never mentions it," Martha said.

"Maybe not, but I'm sure it comes to mind." Grace sighed. "With Aunt Rosemary showing up, Dad has been touchier than ever." She motioned to the kitchen table. "Would you like to join me for a cup of coffee and some of that delicious-looking bread you're holding?"

"Jah, sure. That'd be nice." Martha placed the bread on the table and pulled out a chair. "It's awfully quiet in here. Anna must have left for school already."

Grace nodded as she took plates from the cupboard and set them on the table. "Cleon's at work in Dad's shop, and Daniel fell asleep right after I nursed him, so it's been quiet for nearly an hour."

"Do you ever miss working at the restaurant in Berlin?" Martha asked as she cut a slice of bread and placed it on Grace's plate.

"Not really. I enjoy being at home with my kinner more than waiting tables and trying to keep all those hungry customers happy."

"I like my job working part-time for Irene," Martha said, "but I enjoy being at home where I can work with my dogs a lot more."

"Maybe in time you'll make enough money so your business can turn into a full-time operation."

"I hope that's the case."

They finished their snack, then Martha pushed back her chair and stood. "Guess I should head home so you can get busy with whatever you had planned for the day."

"Before you go, I was wondering if you could do me a favor."

"What is it?"

"Could you stay here with Daniel while I walk down to the mailbox? Cleon's expecting a beekeeping catalog he ordered a few weeks ago."

"I don't mind staying with Daniel," Martha said, "but I'd be happy to go to the mailbox for you."

Grace shook her head. "I appreciate the offer, but if the catalog is there, I'll want to stop at the woodworking shop and give it to Cleon."

"I could do that too."

"I know you could, but I had something I wanted to say to Cleon at breakfast, and he rushed out the door before I got it said. This will give me a chance to do that as well."

Martha sat down again. "Sure, no problem. Take your time."

"If Daniel wakes before I get back, he'll probably need his windle changed. Can you handle that for me?"

"Jah, sure." Martha wrinkled her nose. "I'll just sit here and enjoy another piece of bread and pray he wakes up clean and dry."

Grace chuckled and headed out the back door. A blast of warm air greeted her, but it felt good on her face. Summer was almost here, and she preferred the hot days to the bitter cold of winter.

As Grace approached the two mailboxes at the end of her folks' driveway, her throat constricted, and her heart pounded so hard she heard it thundering in her ears. Both metal boxes had been smashed in, and a note was attached to the side of her and Cleon's mailbox. It read, "I'm Not Done with You Yet."

With a strangled sob, Grace tore the note off the box and rushed to the woodworking shop.

"I'm going to be busy cleaning house the rest of the morning," Judith said as Roman took a seat at his desk to do some paperwork. "That's why I brought your lunch out a bit early."

"No problem." Roman took the lunch box and placed it on one end of the desk. "Have a nice day."

Her forehead wrinkled as her eyebrows drew together. "Are you trying to get rid of me?"

" 'Course not. Since you've got housecleaning to do, I figured you'd want to be on your way."

Her face relaxed, and she gave his shoulder a squeeze. "From the looks of this stack of papers on your desk, I'd say you do too."

Judith was almost to the door when Cleon called out, "If you see Grace, would you tell her I'll be home for lunch around twelve thirty?"

"Jah, sure."

At that moment, Grace rushed into the shop waving a piece of paper. "He's done it again!" Her eyes were wide, her face pale.

"Who's done what?" Judith asked, taking hold of Grace's arm.

"I—I went to get our mail, and—and this is what I found tacked to the side of our smashed-in mailbox." She thrust the piece of paper into her mother's hands.

Judith pushed her glasses to the bridge of her nose. "It says, 'I'm not done with you yet.' "

Roman jumped to his feet and hurried across the room. "Let me have a look at that." He snatched the paper from Judith, and his eyelids twitched as he studied the note.

"Was it our mailbox or your folks' that got bashed in?" Cleon asked, coming to stand beside Grace.

"Both mailboxes." Her chin quivered, and her eyes filled with tears. "He's come back, Cleon. Martha told me the other day that Gary Walker is back in Holmes County. He's taken a job at the newspaper in Millersburg and plans to move here permanently." She gulped in a quick breath. "I'm sure he's the one who wrote the note and smashed our mailboxes."

"How can you be certain? There's no way you could recognize his handwriting, because whoever put this note together didn't write it by hand. It was typed in bold letters." Judith clutched Roman's arm. "Will these attacks ever stop? Will we spend the rest of our days living in fear and wondering what's coming next?"

He groaned. "I hope not—we can't stop living."

"So much for Sheriff Osborn keeping an eye on our place," Judith said bitterly. "Makes me wonder if he even cares what's happening to us."

"I'm sure he cares," Cleon put in. "But he and his deputies can't be everywhere at once."

"Donna Larson came by the other day." Judith looked at Roman. "She said if we decided to move, she and Ray would still be interested in buying our place."

Roman shook his head. "I am not selling out because someone smashed in our mailboxes."

"It's not like this is the first attack." Grace's voice sounded unsteady, and her eyes were wide with fear. "They stop and start. Just when we begin to think the attacks are over, another one happens again."

"She's right, Roman." Judith sniffed. "There must be something we can do about this."

Roman patted Judith's back, hoping to offer her comfort. " 'God is our refuge and strength, a very present help in trouble,' " he said, quoting Psalm 46:1. "We must continue to trust Him."

"It's fine to trust God and believe He will help us, but we need to do something to put an end to these attacks." Grace's voice sounded stronger, and the look of determination Roman saw on her face let him know that she meant what she said.

"What do you think we need to do?" Judith asked.

"It's me Gary is trying to punish. I'm going to find him and demand that he stop harassing us."

"No, you're not." Cleon shook his head vigorously. "I'm your husband. It's my job to look out for you. If anyone's going to talk to Gary, it will be me."

———————◦•◦———————

As Ruth moved over to the sink, she spotted Abe's empty lunch box sitting on the counter. She couldn't remember whether Abe had said he would be coming up to the house for lunch today or if he'd asked her to make his lunch and bring it out to the harness shop. Things had been so hectic during breakfast this morning, she'd barely had time to make lunches for the children and send them off to school, much less remember anything Abe might have said. Molly had poured her glass of apple juice on the floor and followed that by splattering oatmeal down the front of her clean dress. Owen had whined throughout much of breakfast because he couldn't go to school with his older brothers. Gideon and Josh had gotten into an argument about whose turn it was to muck out the horses' stalls. And Willis had accidentally poked Esta in the eye with his elbow when he reached for a piece of toast.

Ruth took a sip of water and let the cool liquid trickle down her parched throat. *Maybe I'm not up to this job. Abe might be better off if he found someone else to care for his kinner and take charge of his house.* She sighed deeply. *But I enjoy spending time with the children. It gives me something meaningful to do—a reason to get up every morning.*

She set the glass in the sink and reached for the metal lunch box, deciding to make Abe's lunch and take it out to him. It was a balmy, bright day, and the walk to the shop would be good for Molly and Owen—and for Ruth as well.

A short time later, with Abe's lunch box in her hand, she and the children headed to the harness shop.

When they stepped inside, Molly squealed when she saw her father, and Owen zipped across the room and grabbed Abe's leg. Ruth glanced to the left, and the sight of Cleon's brother standing in front of the riveting machine, wearing the same leather apron Martin used to wear, caused her to flinch.

The knowledge that Ivan was working in her husband's place and that Martin would never work in Abe's shop again was almost unbearable. Even the pungent odor of leather and neat's-foot oil reminded Ruth of Martin.

"Are you all right?" Abe asked, nudging Owen aside and stepping up to Ruth. "You look pale and kind of shaky."

"I'm fine; just a bit tired, is all." She lifted the lunch box. "I wasn't sure if you wanted to eat at the house or planned to have your lunch here, so I fixed you something and brought it out to you."

"Danki." Abe bent to pick up Molly, and then he looked back at Ruth. "Are you working too hard? Do you need a day off?"

She shook her head. "I like to keep busy. Besides, Sunday's coming, and since there won't be church this week, I can rest all day."

"I've got an idea," Abe said, nuzzling his daughter's rosy cheek.

"What's that?"

"I've been promising to take my brood on a picnic, so maybe it would be good to take this Saturday off and make good on that promise. Why don't you join me and the kinner at the pond?"

"Oh, I don't know—"

"It would help if you came along. Handling my six alone can be quite a job."

Ruth's gaze came to rest on Owen, who stared up at his father with an expectant expression. Then she looked at little Molly resting her head against Abe's broad shoulders, and her resolve weakened. It would be nice to spend the day soaking up the sun, playing with Abe's children, and watching the ducks floating on his pond. "All right," she said with a nod. "I'll pack a picnic lunch and go with you and the kinner on Saturday."

"You don't have to make the lunch," Abe was quick to say. "I'll fix some sandwiches and bring along some of those good-tasting cookies you made earlier in the week. That ought to be plenty."

"How about if I fix a jug of iced tea for us and bring some cream soda for the kinner?"

Abe nodded. "That'd be nice." He kissed Molly's cheek and handed her over to Ruth, then bent down and ruffled Owen's hair. "You be good for Ruth, ya hear?"

The boy nodded soberly and followed Ruth out the door. As she led the way to the house, a feeling she hadn't felt in many months settled over her like a welcoming breeze on a hot summer day: the feeling of anticipation.

Chapter 36

As Ruth reclined on the quilt Abe had spread on the ground near the pond, she lifted her head and stared at the cloudless sky. It was a beautiful summer day, and the sun felt good as it bathed her face with its warm, soothing rays.

Squeals of laughter from Abe's children blended with the call of a dove. It was the first time in a long while that Ruth had felt relaxed.

"Do you like being here at the pond?" Abe asked, taking a seat on the quilt beside her.

"Very much. It's peaceful here, and I feel calmer than I have in many weeks."

"Can you see the quiet?"

She smiled. "Jah. Almost."

Abe shifted on the quilt. "Are you hungry? I could get the ice chest and bring out the sandwiches I made this morning."

"I'm not quite ready to eat, but if you're hungry or you think the kinner need to eat, then please go ahead."

He shook his head. "I think they'd like to play awhile longer."

Ruth shielded her eyes from the glare of the sun and watched as Gideon, Josh, and Willis splashed around in their inner tubes. She smiled at Esta, who held Molly and Owen's hands, walking barefoot in the part of the pond that was shallow.

"It's good to see you smile," Abe said. "You have nice dimples in your cheeks."

A flush of heat climbed up the back of Ruth's neck and covered her face. "Danki."

As though sensing her embarrassment, Abe quickly changed the subject. "My kinner can't swim," he said, "so I aim to keep a close watch on them. Sure don't want to take the chance of anyone drowning."

Ruth thought about the day Martin had saved Abe's and Gideon's lives after their boat had capsized. Little had she realized that Martin would be dead less than two months later. How quickly things could change in one's life. If only there was a way to be more prepared for unexpected tragedies.

"Ach, now you're frowning." Abe nudged Ruth's arm with his elbow. "You've put those dimples into hiding again."

She released a sigh. "I was thinking about Martin and the day he saved you and Gideon from drowning."

Now it was Abe's turn to frown. "I'll always be grateful he was such a strong swimmer and cared enough to risk his life for a friend."

Ruth nodded. "Martin was a kind, caring man, and. . ." Her voice faltered, and she swallowed a couple of times.

"I know you miss him, Ruth," Abe said in a near whisper. "I miss Alma too. Fact is, hardly a day goes by when I don't think about something she said or did. Especially with Esta looking so much like her mamm and often saying something the way Alma would have said it." His sigh lifted the hair off his forehead. "But life goes on, and I take comfort in knowing Alma's resting peacefully in the arms of our heavenly Father. Martin's there, too; I'm sure of it."

"I have that assurance, but it doesn't take away the pain of knowing he was killed by that *narrisch* man who kept ramming our buggy."

Abe's forehead wrinkled as he frowned. "I agree that the person had to be crazy if they did it on purpose, but seeing the look of anger on your face lets me know you haven't forgiven the one responsible."

Ruth swallowed against the burning in her throat. Abe was right; despite Aunt Rosemary's encouragement, she hadn't been able to forgive Martin's killer. Would it help if she knew who the man was, or would that only intensify her anger?

236

"Let's not talk about this anymore," she said. "I'd like to spend my time here listening to the birds singing, soaking up the sun's warming rays, and watching your kinner frolic in the water."

"You're right. We shouldn't talk about anything negative today."

"Have you heard from your sister lately?" Ruth asked.

"As a matter of fact, I got a letter from her this morning."

"How's your mamm doing?"

"Much better. Sue says she's healing nicely."

"Will Sue return to Holmes County?"

Abe shook his head. "She's become betrothed to Melvin, so she wants to stay and prepare for their wedding, which will take place this fall."

"That makes sense." Ruth moistened her lips with the tip of her tongue. "Will you want me to continue caring for the kinner, then?"

He nodded. "As long as you're willing."

"I'm more than willing." Ruth wouldn't have admitted it to Abe, but she was glad Sue wouldn't be returning to care for his children. She had come to care a great deal for them. The thought of staying home every day with nothing to look forward to wasn't a pleasant prospect. Now that Ruth worked for Abe, she felt needed and appreciated—something she hadn't felt since Martin died.

Abe rose to his feet. "Think I'll move closer to the pond so I can keep a better eye on things. Would you like to join me?"

"No thanks. I'm comfortable right here."

After Abe walked away, Ruth stretched out on the quilt, placing her hands behind her head and gazing at the lazy clouds overhead. *I wonder what it would be like to be the mother of Abe's kinner. Of course, it would mean I'd have to be married to Abe, and that idea is too ridiculous to even think about.*

Abe glanced over his shoulder. Ruth lay on the quilt looking up at the sky as though she didn't have a care in the world. Today was the first time he'd seen her looking so relaxed since Martin's death. Truth was, Abe found himself being drawn to Ruth more every day, and that fact scared him. He couldn't allow himself the luxury of falling in love with her. Ruth was too young for him. Besides, she was newly widowed, and he was sure she wasn't ready for another man in her life. He was equally sure Ruth would never be romantically inclined toward him.

"Well, would ya look at this?"

Abe jerked his attention back to the pond. Esta held a plump little frog in her hands, and Molly and Owen stood on tiptoes trying to get a look at the critter.

"Can we take him home, Papa?" Owen asked, tipping his head in Abe's direction.

"Where would you keep him?" Abe asked the boy.

Owen shrugged. "Don't know."

"Could we put him in a jar?" Esta questioned. "I'll bet there's one in our picnic basket."

"I brought along some pickled beets. I suppose we could dump them onto a paper plate, and then you can wash the jar out in the pond and take the frog home that way." Abe squatted down on his haunches beside the children. "The frog can't live that way for long. You'll have to let it go soon or it'll die."

"Like Mama did?" Owen stared up at Abe with wide eyes.

Abe nodded as a lump formed in his throat. Why was it that they could be having a good time one minute, and the next minute something was said or done that reminded him of Alma?

Owen tugged on Abe's shirtsleeve. "Papa, can me and Molly go swimmin' in tubes, like the brieder are doin'?"

Abe shook his head. "You're not big enough for that, son."

"Guess I'm not either," Esta said.

"Not yet. When you learn to swim."

"But the brothers can't swim," she said, jutting her chin out.

"That's true, but they're staying near the shore, so if they have a problem I can wade out and grab 'em." Abe thought about the day Martin had saved him and Gideon from drowning. Martin had said he'd be happy to teach Abe and his kinner to swim, but that hadn't happened because Martin had been killed in a senseless buggy accident. No wonder Ruth hadn't come to grips with her husband's death. At least Alma hadn't been taken from Abe in such a violent way. Though her death had been hard to accept, the fact that it had been caused by an act of nature made it a bit easier to deal with.

"Papa, I'm hungry," Owen said, tugging on Abe's shirt again.

"Jah, okay. We can empty that jar of pickled beets, put your frog in the jar, and then we'll eat lunch." Abe cupped his hands around his mouth. "Come out of the water now," he called to his three older sons.

The boys paddled their way to shore, slipped the inner tubes over their heads, and trudged onto the grassy bank. Abe bent down, grabbed some towels, and handed them to the boys. Maybe by now Ruth would be hungry too.

What am I doing here? Rosemary asked herself as she left her car and headed for Roman's woodworking shop. She'd been here to see him several times already, and each time he'd given her the cold shoulder. Would it be any different today?

The last time she'd tried talking to him, he'd said he was too busy to listen to her lies and had asked her to leave.

"They aren't lies," she muttered under her breath.

Rosemary had been tempted to tell Judith or one of Roman's daughters what had happened to the letters she'd written home all those years ago, but she'd decided against it. She needed to tell Roman before she told anyone else, and she didn't want him to think his wife and daughters were playing go-between.

The front door swung open, and Rosemary bumped into Roman.

"I was on my way out," he said in a brusque tone. "Got some deliveries to make."

"Can't you spare a minute? I'd like to speak to you."

"Don't have the time." Roman brushed past her and headed for the buggy shed.

Rosemary hurried after him. "I was wondering if you could give me our brothers' addresses. I'd like to write them. And since Geauga County is only a couple hours away, I might drive up there and see Walt."

Roman halted and turned to face her. "If you didn't care enough about them to write before, you don't need their addresses now."

Rosemary clenched her fingers around the handles of her purse. "If you'd let me explain why you never got my letters—"

"I'm not interested!" Roman stalked off with a huff.

"Maybe I should forget about reconciling with my family," Rosemary muttered as she turned toward her car.

Don't give up, a voice in her head seemed to say. *This is just a testing of your faith.*

Chapter 37

As Ruth headed for Abe's harness shop with his lunch box, she mentally lectured herself. *Martin's not here; Ivan's taken his place. Life goes on; I must accept the way things are. With God's help, I'll make every day count, for I know how short life can be.*

When she stepped into the harness shop a few minutes later, the pungent odor of neat's-foot oil tickled her nose, and she sneezed.

"Gott segen eich."

She caught sight of Abe down on his haunches, oiling an old saddle. "Danki for giving me God's blessing. Now here's a blessing for you," she said, setting Abe's lunch box on his desk. "My mamm baked cinnamon-raisin bread on Saturday, so that's what your sandwich is made with today."

Abe smacked his lips. "That does sound like a blessing."

Ruth smiled. Abe was such a kind, appreciative man.

"Where are my little ones today?" he asked. "They usually tag along when you come out to my shop."

"Martha came over and got them a while ago. She took all but Gideon home with her so they could play with Anna and see Martha's new dog."

"How come Gideon didn't go along?"

"He said he had work to do in the barn."

"If he'd gotten it done first thing this morning, he would have been free to go." Abe grimaced and rose to his feet. "Seems I've got to stay after that boy all the time. I'd have him working for me here a few hours every day, but he's not dependable."

Ruth wondered if there was something she might do to make Gideon see the error of his ways, but she figured he was Abe's boy and Abe should take care of the problem.

"I'll be up at the house washing clothes if you need me for anything." She was about to walk away, but Abe tapped her on the shoulder.

"I was wondering if you'd like to go out for a meal one night next week with me and the kinner."

"But I've got all your meals planned already," she was quick to say.

"That might be so, but I figured the kinner would like an evening out at a restaurant. Since next Friday is Esta's birthday, I thought having supper out would be a nice way to celebrate."

"I hadn't realized her birthday was coming up. She never said a word about it, and neither did anyone else."

Abe smiled. "So what do you say—shall we take my brood to supper at the Farmstead Restaurant on Friday night?"

She nodded. "That sounds like fun."

<hr/>

Cleon had no sooner entered the newspaper office than he began to have second thoughts. He'd promised Grace that he would seek out Gary Walker and speak to him about the mailbox incident and the other attacks against the Hostettlers, but he wasn't sure what he should say or how it would be received. If Gary was the one responsible, he might become angry at the accusations and further harass Grace's family. On the other hand, Gary needed to know that the sheriff had been informed and had promised to keep an eye on the place. That might deter him from trying anything else.

"I understand you have a reporter working here by the name of Gary Walker," Cleon said, stepping up to the receptionist's desk.

The young woman sitting behind the desk looked up at Cleon and smiled. "That's right. He started working here last week."

Cleon shifted uncomfortably from one foot to the other. "I was wondering if I might speak with him."

"I'm sorry, but Mr. Walker isn't in right now. He left early this morning to cover a story in Sugarcreek, and I'm not sure what time he'll be back."

"Oh, I see." Cleon turned to go, feeling a sense of disappointment. He didn't know when he'd have the chance to come to Millersburg again, and he wouldn't feel right asking Roman for more time off this week.

He headed for the door and had just stepped outside when he spotted Gary Walker coming down the street. He stopped walking and waited until the man approached. "You're Gary Walker, the reporter, right?"

"That's correct."

"I'm Cleon Schrock—Grace's husband."

Gary studied Cleon a few seconds, then gave a slow nod. "You must be her second husband. She told me about you, but we haven't had the privilege of meeting until now."

"Actually, we have met. You tried to interview me in Berlin a couple of times."

Gary shrugged. "I've interviewed a lot of Amish folks."

Cleon cleared his throat and wiped his sweaty palms on the sides of his trousers. "I was wondering. . . The thing is. . ."

"If you've got something to say, Mr. Schrock, then just say it. I'm a busy man and don't have any time to spare this morning."

"As I'm sure you know, my wife's family has been attacked several times in the last several months."

Gary gave a quick nod.

"On Saturday morning, we discovered that our mailboxes had been smashed in, and there was a note attached to one of the boxes."

"What'd the note say?"

" 'I'm not done with you yet.' "

"Sounds like someone has an ax to grind with one of the Hostettlers, doesn't it?"

Cleon clenched his teeth. "Grace thinks—"

"I already know what she thinks. She believes I'm the one responsible because I told her once that she'd be sorry for breaking up with me." Gary grunted. "That woman is so paranoid. Doesn't she realize that guys say a lot of things they don't mean when they've been jilted?"

243

Cleon wasn't sure how to respond. Maybe Grace had read more into Gary's warning than there was. Maybe it hadn't been a threat but rather the wounded pride of a hotheaded teenager trying to scare his girlfriend into coming back to him.

"So you're not responsible for the vandalism to our mailboxes or any of the other things that have gone on at the Hostettlers'?"

"Nope. I'm an innocent man." Gary brushed past Cleon. "Now if you'll excuse me, I've got work to do."

Cleon watched as Gary entered the newspaper office. Maybe the man was telling the truth. But if Gary wasn't responsible for the attacks, who was?

Chapter 38

I'm glad you came out to supper with us," Esta said, smiling at Ruth as she sat at a table with Abe's family at the Farmstead Restaurant on Friday evening.

"I'm glad I did too. Happy birthday, Esta." Ruth patted the child's arm.

Esta grinned at Ruth. "Danki for the birthday present you gave me." The child looked down at the small black handbag in her lap. "Mama had one like this, only it was bigger."

Ruth smiled. "I'm glad you like it."

Esta looked at her father. "Since we've already said our silent prayer, can we go to the salad bar now? I can't wait for some pickled eggs."

Abe tweaked the girl's nose. "Sure, go ahead." He nodded at Ruth. "If you'd like to go with the older kinner, I'll wait here with Molly. Then I'll go for my salad when you get back."

"Mammi. . ."

Ruth smiled at Molly, who was sitting in the high chair the restaurant had provided, eating a cracker. She patted the little girl's chubby arm and turned to face Abe. "I don't mind waiting with Molly if you'd like to go to the salad bar first."

He shook his head. "I'll wait."

"Okay. I'll see what's there that Molly can eat and bring her something back." Ruth slid her chair away from the table and followed Abe's children to the salad bar. She was ready to take a plate when she spotted her friend

Sadie coming into the restaurant with her boyfriend, Toby. Sadie didn't appear to notice Ruth as she hurried to the ladies' room. Toby didn't see her, either, for he was busy talking to the hostess.

Ruth bent down and whispered in Esta's ear, "I'll be right back. Can you help Owen and Willis get their food?"

"Where are you going?" Esta looked up at Ruth with questioning eyes.

"Just need to use the restroom."

"Jah, sure. I'll help the boys get whatever they need."

Ruth smiled. Esta might be only nine years old, but she seemed so grown up at times.

When Ruth entered the ladies' room, she discovered Sadie at the sink, washing her hands. Sadie must have spotted Ruth in the mirror, for she turned and smiled. "I'm surprised to see you here. Did you come with your folks?"

"I came with Abe and his kinner. We're celebrating Esta's birthday."

"How nice." Sadie smiled. "How's your job going at Abe's?"

"I'm doing my best to keep up with things at the house, and it's nice to spend time with Abe's kinner." Ruth sighed. "It makes me feel useful and gives my life purpose."

"Everyone needs a purpose." Sadie nudged Ruth's arm. "Maybe you'll end up marrying Abe. Then your life will have purpose for years to come."

"What?"

"I was thinking you might marry Abe."

"That's ridiculous, Sadie. Abe's ten years older than me, and—"

"So what? My mamm's eight years younger than my daed."

"Even if there was no age difference, there's no love between me and Abe."

"Who says there has to be love? A mutual respect might be all that's needed." Sadie turned her palms up. "Look at my relationship with Toby. I love him, and he says he loves me, yet he still hasn't asked me to marry him. What good has love done me?"

Ruth mulled things over a bit. Maybe Sadie was right about love not being a necessary ingredient in marriage—especially if it meant she could be a mother.

She glanced at her reflection in the mirror and noticed that the dark circles she'd been plagued with for the last several months had diminished.

Would Abe even consider asking me to marry him? She looked away. *Surely not. He's still in love with his wife. And I love Martin.*

"Martin would want you to find happiness again," Sadie said, seeming to read Ruth's thoughts.

Ruth shrugged. "Maybe so, but I'm sure Abe would never ask me to marry him."

"How do you know?"

"I just do."

A slow smile spread across Sadie's face. "Then why don't you ask him?"

Ruth's spine went rigid. "Ach, I could never do that!"

"Why not?"

"It would be too bold." She squinted at Sadie. "I don't see you asking Toby to marry you."

Sadie's face flooded with color. "No, but I've thought about it."

Ruth folded her arms across her chest. "When you become bold enough to propose to Toby, then I'll think about asking Abe to marry me."

———◆◆◆———

Martha was bent over a small table in the section of her father's barn that had been turned into a kennel when she heard the barn door open and click shut.

"Is anyone here?"

Martha recognized her aunt's voice immediately; Rosemary had been coming over once or twice a week ever since she'd returned to Holmes County.

"I'm back here by the kennels."

"What are you up to?" Aunt Rosemary asked when she joined Martha.

Martha lifted Heidi's left front paw. "I've been clipping my dog's toenails."

Aunt Rosemary reached over and stroked Heidi behind her ear. "How's your business doing these days?"

"The female beagle I bought several weeks ago still isn't pregnant, but I haven't lost hope."

Aunt Rosemary released a sigh and leaned against the table. "Wish I could say the same regarding your dad and me."

"He still won't talk to you?"

"No."

"Dad can be real stubborn sometimes," Martha said with a shake of her head. "Have you tried talking to Mom about this? Maybe she can make him listen to reason."

"I just came from seeing her at the house—after I'd been to your dad's shop and gotten nowhere."

"Dad's still working in the shop at this hour?"

Aunt Rosemary nodded. "I saw the lights on when I drove in, so I stopped there first and found him restoring an old chair. Then I went up to the house and saw your mother. I was tempted to tell her my story but decided it would be best if your dad heard it from me, not second-hand." She sighed. "If I ever get him to listen, that is. He makes me feel so frustrated."

"I know what you mean about frustration." Martha placed Heidi back in her kennel and turned to face her aunt. "Nothing's been the same around here since someone started attacking my family, and things are getting steadily worse."

Aunt Rosemary's eyebrows shot up. "What kind of attacks? No one's mentioned anything about that to me."

"Dad thinks it's better if we don't talk about it, and Mom pretty much agrees."

"And what do you think, Martha?"

"I'd like to find out who's behind the attacks and make them stop." Martha grunted. "Of course, unless the sheriff does more than promise to keep an eye on our place, that's not likely to happen."

"You've spoken with the sheriff?"

"A couple of us have. He's been out to our place a few times to ask questions and look around too."

"And he's been patrolling the area?"

"That's what he says. But the attacks have continued, and we have no idea why we're being singled out." She shrugged. "Of course, each of us has our own idea about who could be responsible."

"You mean you have a list of suspects?"

"I guess you could say that."

"Does the sheriff know this?"

"Yes. Dad has talked to him a few times."

"Well, the man should be making every effort to do something about it."

"I agree."

"Maybe I'll pay a call to the sheriff tomorrow morning. Would you like to accompany me?"

Martha nodded. Since Aunt Rosemary wasn't Amish, maybe Sheriff Osborn would take her more seriously than he had the others.

Aunt Rosemary gave Martha a hug. "Until tomorrow, then."

"What are you doing in *my* barn, talking to *my* daughter?" Dad shouted as he stepped out of the shadows.

Martha jumped. "We were just visiting," she said before her aunt could respond.

"I wasn't talking to you, daughter. I was talking to *her*." Dad whirled toward Aunt Rosemary and scowled.

"Martha's right; we were visiting."

"Jah, well, you're not welcome here. And I'll thank you to stay away from my family."

Martha's mouth opened wide. "Dad, you can't mean that."

His forehead wrinkled as he gave one quick nod. "This woman is nothing but trouble. I don't want her influencing you."

"She's not."

"It's okay. You don't have to defend me." Aunt Rosemary gave Martha's shoulder a squeeze. "I'll be going now."

As Martha watched her aunt walk out of the barn, a sense of despair washed over her. Would Aunt Rosemary be back tomorrow so they could see the sheriff together? Or would she be on the next plane headed for home?

Chapter 39

"That man was no help at all," Rosemary mumbled as she and Martha left the sheriff's office the following day. "All we got for our troubles was the scent of smoke from his clothes." She flapped her hand in front of her face. "Sheriff Osborn must be a chain smoker."

Martha shrugged. "He did say he's been patrolling our area whenever he can. I guess that's something to feel good about."

"Didn't you get the feeling that he's not very interested in finding out who's behind the attacks on your family?"

Martha halted on the sidewalk and turned to face Rosemary. "What makes you think that?"

"He hasn't found any suspects—not even for the accident that killed your brother-in-law." Rosemary gritted her teeth. "Wouldn't you think the sheriff would have investigated that incident thoroughly?"

"He said he did the best he could with the little bit of information he was given."

"Puh!" Rosemary shook her head. "Did he try to gather evidence?"

"I don't know. He questioned Ruth about what she saw that night, and she told him she'd seen a truck but couldn't see the license plate and wasn't sure of the color of the vehicle because it was dark and snowing."

"Did he question the neighbors—someone who might have seen the vehicle?"

"No houses are in the area where they were hit. And no other cars on the road, I guess."

"Hmm. . ."

"The other problem the sheriff mentioned is the fact that except for the buggy accident, he usually hasn't heard about the attacks until several days later." Martha frowned. "Dad didn't like it when Sheriff Osborn showed up at his woodworking shop after one of the attacks and told him that he'd heard what had happened."

"I wish there was something I could do about this," Rosemary muttered. "If I could find out who's responsible for attacking your family, maybe Roman would forgive me for being gone all those years and never contacting my family."

"I'm sorry Dad's not willing to accept your apology."

"I've been here over three months already, and still he won't listen to me. It's a good thing my husband left me with adequate funds, or I wouldn't have been able to make this extended trip."

"I wish you could stay with us."

"Your dad would never allow that." Rosemary touched Martha's arm. "I don't know about you, but I'm hungry. Why don't the two of us go somewhere for lunch?"

Martha smiled. "Sounds good to me."

"Afterward, I think I'll drop by Abe Wengerd's house and see Ruth. Would you like to come along?"

"I'd better not. I'm working at Irene's tonight, and I need to be home by three."

"Maybe some other time we can go there together," Rosemary said as they approached her car. "Today I'll go alone."

———————

Ruth tiptoed out of Molly's room, relieved that she'd finally gotten the little girl down for a nap. Molly had been fussy all morning, and Ruth had rocked her almost an hour before the child had fallen asleep. Since the other children were outside playing, Ruth thought this would be a good time for her to get some sewing done. The children were growing, and the older ones would be back in school soon. That meant several hemlines needed to be adjusted.

Ruth removed a needle and thread from her sewing basket and had just taken a seat on the sofa when Sadie stepped into the living room.

"Looks like you're keeping busy."

"I am. I'm surprised to see you here though. Aren't you working at the bakeshop?"

"Today's my day off," Sadie said as she dropped into the chair opposite Ruth. "I wanted to tell you my good news."

"What news?"

"Toby and I are getting married in November."

"What?" Ruth grimaced as she jabbed her finger with the needle.

"It's true. We set the date last night, when Toby brought me home from supper at the Farmstead Restaurant."

"I can't believe he finally asked you to marry him," Ruth said, dabbing the end of her finger with a tissue.

Sadie's face flooded with color. "Actually, it was me who did the asking."

Ruth's mouth dropped open.

"Well, don't look so surprised. I told you I might."

Ruth shook her head. "No, you suggested that I ask Abe to marry me."

Sadie chuckled. "And you said you would whenever I asked Toby."

Ruth sucked in her breath. She had said something like that. But she'd never dreamed that her friend would put her to the test, or that Sadie would be bold enough to ask Toby to marry her.

Sadie left her chair and took a seat on the sofa beside Ruth. "I'd like you to be one of my *newehockers*. That is, if you're not already married by November."

Ruth's forehead wrinkled. "Why would I be married? I'm not even betrothed."

"But you might be if you ask Abe like you said you would."

"I was only kidding, Sadie. I really didn't think you would propose to Toby, or that—"

"Or what? That he would agree to marry me?" Sadie's downcast eyes let Ruth know she'd hurt her feelings.

"That's not what I meant." Ruth touched Sadie's hand. "I was going to say that I didn't think you would really expect me to propose to Abe." Her face grew warm. "I could never do that, Sadie. It wouldn't be right."

"Why not? Ruth in the Bible let Boaz know she wanted to be his wife by lying at his feet."

Ruth covered her mouth with the palm of her hand. "Ach, I could never lie at Abe's feet! What would he think of me if I did something like that?"

Sadie shook her head. "You wouldn't have to lie at his feet, silly. I'm sure if you thought about it awhile, you could come up with something else to do that would let Abe know you're interested in him and would like to be his wife." She patted Ruth's knee. "Think about it, okay?"

Ruth gave no reply.

"In the meantime, I'd like your answer about whether you'll be one of the newehockers at my wedding."

Ruth nodded slowly. "I'd be pleased to be your attendant."

"Glad to hear it." Sadie stood. "Be sure and let me know when you and Abe become betrothed." She rushed out of the room before Ruth could say a word.

Ruth reached for her Bible, which she had tucked inside the sewing basket she'd brought from home. Turning to the book of Ruth, she found chapter 3, where Ruth's mother-in-law, Naomi, told Ruth that she should mark the place where Boaz would lie and then go there and lie at his feet.

Ruth couldn't deny her attachment to Abe's family. Truth was, she often found herself wishing his children were hers. But could she ask Abe to marry her as Sadie had suggested? *Oh, that would be so bold!*

She closed her eyes. *Dear Lord, You know how much I long to be a mother. But I still love Martin, and I'm not sure I could be a good wife to Abe—if he would have me, that is.*

Ruth's prayer was interrupted when a knock sounded at the door. She went to answer it and was surprised to see her aunt standing on the front porch.

"What a nice surprise."

Aunt Rosemary smiled. "I've been meaning to come by for some time, but I've been busy getting settled into my new home."

"What new home?"

"It was too inconvenient to keep staying at the bed-and-breakfast in Berlin, so I've rented a small house owned by your neighbors, Ray and Donna Larson. They said I could rent it on a month-to-month basis since I don't know how long I'll be staying in Holmes County."

Ruth's mouth dropped open. "Is the house near here?"

"Just a mile or so down the road."

"Why, that was the house Martin and I rented when we first got married." Ruth stared at the toes of her sneakers. "After Martin died, my dad and Cleon went over to the rental and cleared out all of our things. I wasn't up to going, and I haven't been back to the house since the night Martin died."

"I'm sure it would be a painful reminder," Aunt Rosemary said.

Ruth nodded. Then, remembering her manners, she stepped aside. "Won't you come in?"

Aunt Rosemary followed Ruth into the living room and took a seat on the sofa when Ruth motioned for her to do so. "It looks like you've been doing some sewing," she said, gesturing to the pile of clothes lying on one end of the sofa.

"Yes, I have," Ruth said as she seated herself beside the clothes. "Abe's children are growing like cornstalks. I need to get their clothes ready for school since it will be starting up again in just another month."

"I've been away from the Plain life so long I'd almost forgotten that Amish children start school several weeks before most English kids do." Rosemary touched Ruth's arm. "You're looking well. Are you feeling better these days?"

"Some. Being here with Abe's kinner has made me feel needed."

"I'm glad to hear it." Rosemary motioned to the Bible Ruth had left on the sofa. "Have you found forgiveness in your heart for the one who caused the death of your husband?"

Ruth opened her mouth to respond, but her words were halted when Gideon rushed into the room.

"Ruth, come quickly! Papa's been kicked by a horse!"

Chapter 40

Ivan, get the horse!" Abe shouted from where he lay on the ground near his buggy. He had been trying to hitch the new horse he'd bought last week to his rig, and the animal had spooked and kicked him in the leg. It was broken; Abe was sure of it. Not only did the leg hurt like crazy, but it was bent at a very odd angle. Abe knew he couldn't stand up on his own. All he could do was lie there helplessly as Ivan dashed across the yard after the gelding. If the crazy animal got out on the road, they might never see him again.

"I got him, Abe!" Ivan shouted several minutes later. "Want me to put him in the corral or the barn?"

"The corral."

"You doin' okay?"

"I'll be all right. Just get the horse put away." Abe grimaced as a stab of pain shot up his leg. Where was Ruth? It seemed as though Gideon had been gone an awfully long time.

A few seconds later, he heard footsteps running across the gravel. His five oldest children were soon at his side, and so were Ruth and her aunt Rosemary.

"Papa!" Esta cried as she dropped down beside him. "Please don't die and leave us like Mama did."

"I'm not going to die," he assured the girl.

"What happened?" Ruth asked breathlessly. "Gideon said you were kicked by a horse."

Abe nodded and ground his teeth together as another ripple of pain exploded in his leg. "It was that new horse I bought last week. I was trying to get him hitched to the buggy when he got all riled and kicked me in the leg." He grimaced. "I'm sure it's broken."

Rosemary knelt beside him and studied his leg. "I'm no doctor, but it looks like a serious break to me. I think you should get to the hospital right away."

"Can you drive me there?" Abe asked.

"I don't think we should risk moving you—not with that leg looking the way it does." She pulled a cell phone from her purse. "I'm calling 911."

"Someone should ride to the hospital with Abe," Ruth said. She looked over at her aunt. "Would you mind staying with the children while I go?"

Esta grabbed Ruth's arm and hung on for all she was worth. "I don't want you to go!" Tears streamed down her ashen face.

"Aw, don't be such a boppli," Gideon grumbled. "We can stay here alone."

"No, you can't." Abe gritted his teeth. The pain in his leg was almost unbearable.

"I'll go with Abe," Ivan said as he joined the group. "Ruth can stay with the kinner."

"Are you sure you're gonna be all right?" Josh asked, bending close to Abe's ear.

"I'll be fine."

Ruth knelt on the ground beside Abe. "Would you like me to get word to my daed? He's one of your closest friends, and I'm sure he would like to know what's happened."

Abe nodded. "I'd appreciate that."

"I'll drive over to your folks' and tell him," Rosemary volunteered.

Ruth looked dubious. "Are you sure you don't mind?"

"Not at all. If your daed wants to go to the hospital, I'll drive him there."

When Abe heard sirens in the distance a while later, he breathed a sigh of relief.

"You want me to start sanding that set of cabinets for the bishop now?" Cleon asked as he stepped up to Roman's desk.

Roman glanced up from the invoices he'd been working on. "Jah, sure. Those need to get done by the end of the week."

"I'll get right on it."

"Say, I've been meaning to ask how things are going with your bees. Are they producing lots of honey?"

Cleon shrugged. "A fair amount."

"Are you wishing you could be doing that full-time instead of working for me?"

"I had hoped to generate enough honey sales to support my family, but after losing all of my bee supplies in that fire last year, it's going to take a while to build up the business again."

Roman leaned his elbows on the desk and stared at Cleon. "When you do build it back up, will you want to quit working for me?"

"I don't know. I wouldn't want to leave you in the lurch. Maybe I could continue to do both."

Roman opened his mouth to reply, but just then the shop door banged open. Rosemary rushed into the room.

"I came to tell you that your friend Abe's been taken to the hospital," she said breathlessly.

Roman's mouth went dry. "What's wrong with Abe? Is he sick?"

"One of his horses kicked him in the leg. It looked like a nasty break."

Roman leaned back in his chair and groaned. "Abe doesn't need this right now. How's he going to work and support his kinner if he's laid up with a broken leg?"

"Ivan's working for him," Cleon said. "I'm sure he can handle things in the harness shop until Abe's able to work again."

Roman looked at Rosemary. "Do you know which hospital Abe was taken to?"

"The one in Millersburg."

He pushed his chair away from the desk and stood. "I'll need to call for a ride so I can go to the hospital and see how Abe's doing."

"I can take you," Rosemary said. "Then I'll be able to check on Abe's progress and give Ruth and the children a report on my way home."

Roman contemplated her offer a few seconds. He didn't relish the idea of being alone with Rosemary, but it would be quicker than calling someone else for a ride and having to wait around until they showed up. He finally nodded and said, "Jah, okay." Then he turned to Cleon. "Can you manage okay while I'm gone?"

"No problem."

"Let's be off." Roman followed Rosemary out the door.

———————◆◆◆———————

Rosemary couldn't believe she'd been given the opportunity to be alone with her brother, but here they were, heading down the highway toward Millersburg.

She glanced over at Roman and wondered what he was thinking. His head was turned toward the window, and his shoulders were slumped. He hadn't said a word since they'd gotten in the car.

"Are you worried about your friend?" she asked.

He nodded. "Abe's been through enough this past year. He doesn't need anything more."

"From what I understand, you've been through a few things yourself over the last year."

"What do you mean?"

"The break-ins and vandalism that have occurred at your place."

"Who blabbed that information?"

"It doesn't matter who told me. What I'd like to know is why nothing's been done about it." Rosemary glanced at Roman out of the corner of her eye.

"Not much we can do except hope and pray it comes to an end." He grunted. "I figure whoever's behind the attacks is out for some kind of revenge. Once he realizes we won't be intimidated, he'll get tired of the game and leave us alone."

"I hardly think ramming Ruth and her husband's buggy is a game. I think you should have reported each attack to the sheriff right away."

"Jah, well, what would you know about it? You ran off and left your people a long time ago, so it's obvious that you don't understand our ways." His voice was laced with bitterness and a deep sense of pain. "You, who didn't even care enough about her family to let 'em know where you were or how you were doing. Don't you realize how much that hurt our mamm and daed? How does it make you feel to know they went to their graves thinking their only daughter cared nothing about them?"

Rosemary swallowed against the lump in her throat. Hearing the anger in Roman's voice and being reminded of her parents' deaths made her feel extremely guilty. She gripped the steering wheel, praying for the right words. "It's not the way you think, Roman. I didn't deliberately stay away or avoid contact with my family."

No response.

"I did write to Mama several times, but she never responded."

"Puh! If our mamm had gotten a letter from you, she would have written back."

"I thought so too, until I got no letters in return."

"You got no letters because you sent no letters."

"That's not true. I wrote home several times."

"Then what happened to your letters?"

"They were intercepted by my husband." Rosemary grimaced. "I didn't know about it until he told me the truth shortly before he died."

"Why would he want to keep you from writing home?"

"Bob was a very controlling man. He admitted to me that he'd been afraid if I kept in touch with my family, I might want to return to the Amish way of life."

Roman sat silently, as though deep in thought.

"When I wrote those letters and put them in our mailbox, I had no idea my husband followed behind me to remove and destroy them. I assumed the letters had gone out and that the reason I didn't get a response was because my family didn't want any contact with their wayward daughter."

More silence.

"I'm not making this up, Roman. I've tried to tell you on several occasions, but you've never been willing to listen."

Nothing. Not even a grunt.

"I can't undo the past. All I can do is look to the future. I want that future to include you and your family. That's why I came back—to spend time with my Amish family and try to make up some of the years I've lost."

Roman said nothing as they continued their drive, and Rosemary was certain she hadn't gotten through to him. He probably thought she'd made up the story about Bob intercepting the letters in order to worm her way into the lives of his family.

When they pulled into the hospital parking lot a short time later, Rosemary left the engine running and turned to face Roman. "Would you like me to wait and give you a ride home?"

He reached over and clasped her arm. Tears welled in his eyes, and he released a guttural groan. "I'm sorry, sister. Will you forgive me for being such a dummkopp?"

Tears filled Rosemary's eyes as she placed her hand on his. "I'll forgive you if you forgive me. If I hadn't left home in the first place, I would have been here when Mama and Papa died. I wouldn't have missed out on seeing you get married and start a family of your own. If I'd stayed in Holmes County—"

He shook his head. "Enough with the regrets. It's time to look to the future."

Chapter 41

In the weeks that followed, Ruth settled into a routine of going over to Abe's place every day to care for his children, cook his meals, and clean the house, while Ivan spent the nights there. It had been Ivan's idea to do so, saying Abe would need help during the night and that it wouldn't be proper for Ruth to stay. Ivan had taken over the harness shop, and Gideon had been helping some. But Monday would be the first day of school, so Gideon, along with Josh, Esta, and Willis, would be gone all day, leaving Ivan to run the harness shop and Ruth to care for Abe, Owen, and Molly.

Since today was Saturday and Ivan had given Gideon the day off, the boy had taken Josh and Willis fishing at the pond behind their house. Ruth had sent the boys off with a picnic lunch an hour ago. Esta was out on the porch keeping Owen entertained with a jar of bubbles. Molly was taking a nap. That left Ruth alone in the house with Abe, who was reading his Bible on the sofa in the living room.

Deciding that Abe might like some refreshments, Ruth carried a tray into the living room and placed it on the small table near the sofa. "I brought you some milk and cookies," she said, smiling down at him.

He set the Bible aside and sat up. "Danki. That was nice of you."

Ruth handed him the glass. "How's the leg feeling this afternoon?"

"Not so bad. I should be able to start working in the shop a few hours a day beginning next week." He motioned to his leg, encased in a heavy cast. "Why don't you sit here on the sofa so we can visit awhile?"

Ruth gulped. *If I take a seat on the sofa, I'll be sitting at Abe's feet. . .almost like Ruth from the Bible.*

"If you have something to do in the other room, I'll understand," Abe said. "But it would be nice to have the company. I get tired of sitting around when I should be out in the shop working."

"I have the time." Ruth lowered herself to the sofa and shifted uncomfortably when her elbow brushed the bottom of Abe's cast. "Sorry. I hope that didn't hurt."

"Nope. Didn't feel a thing." Abe took a drink of milk. "This is refreshing. Danki."

"You're welcome."

A few moments of awkward silence passed between them. Then he smiled and said, "Your help's been appreciated. You're not only good with the kinner, but you can cook and keep the house well—better than my sister did."

"She was young and inexperienced."

"You're not so old yourself," Abe said with a crooked grin.

Ruth's face heated with embarrassment.

Abe took another swallow of milk. "I'm sure you still miss Martin, but a young woman like yourself ought to think about getting married again. You'd make a good helpmate."

Ruth stared at the floor. *If Abe were to marry me, I could be his kinner's mamm. I could be his helpmate.*

She lifted her gaze to meet his. "What about you, Abe? Would you think of me as an acceptable wife for you?"

"Ach, Ruth, we're a good ten years apart. You could find a much younger man than me."

"But I wouldn't have anything to give a younger man."

"What makes you say that?"

"I couldn't give him children." She dropped her gaze again.

"Ruth, look at me."

She forced herself to face him, hoping he wouldn't see the tears threatening to escape her lashes.

"I know you would make a good mudder for my kinner, and a fine fraa for me, as well, but without love, a good marriage would be impossible."

"Are—are you saying you won't marry me?"

He nodded. "It wouldn't be fair to—"

"Papa! Papa, come quick!" Josh hollered as he burst into the room.

Abe's face blanched. "What is it, boy?"

"It's Willis! He fell in the pond when Gideon was in the woods lookin' for me, and—" Josh gulped down a sob. "And—and Gideon drug Willis out of the water, but he won't wake up."

Abe grabbed his crutches and pushed himself to his feet.

Ruth stood too, as her heart gave a lurch. "What are you planning to do?"

"I'm going to the pond."

"But it's too far to go there on crutches. You're not up to walking that far. I think it would be better if you wait here and let me go."

He shook his head and hobbled toward the door. "Josh, hitch up the pony cart. We'll use that to get us to the pond." His eyes were wide as he looked at Ruth. "Run down to the phone shed and call 911."

Ruth's heart pounded as she hurried out the door and sprinted toward the phone shed near the end of Abe's driveway. *Dear Lord,* she prayed, *please let Willis be okay.*

"Where are you going, Papa? Why's Ruth running down the driveway?" Esta asked as Abe hobbled toward the barn behind Josh.

"There's been an accident at the pond. Take Owen in the house and wait there with him and Molly until we get back."

Esta's eyes widened, and her chin trembled like a leaf caught in a breeze. "Has—has someone been hurt? Is it one of my brieder?"

"Willis fell in the pond. I've got to get to him quick. Now get up to the house, *schnell!*"

Abe didn't look back to see if Esta had done what he'd asked; he just kept moving toward the barn, praying with each step he took. *Don't take my boy, Lord. Don't take my boy.*

By the time Abe got to the barn door, Josh had one of their smaller horses hitched to the pony cart. "Here, take my crutches!"

Josh took the crutches and held them with one hand while keeping a tight hold on the horse's bridle. Abe gritted his teeth and climbed into the cart; then Josh handed him the crutches and climbed in beside him.

"Papa, I'm scared," the boy whimpered. "What if—"

"You hush now; don't even say it. Just get us to the pond as quick as you can!"

As the horse trotted across the fields, Abe continued to plead with God for the life of his son. He'd already lost one family member; he couldn't bear the thought of losing another.

The pond came into view a few minutes later, and Abe caught sight of Gideon bent over his little brother. "Get the horse next to them," he told Josh. "We'll need to put Willis in the cart."

Josh did as he was told, and Abe climbed out of the pony cart. Ignoring his crutches, he hobbled on one foot over to Gideon. "Is your bruder breathing?"

Gideon slowly shook his head. "I don't think so, Papa."

Abe dropped to the ground beside Willis. The boy lay deathly still, and Abe quickly began CPR, praying with each breath he took and each breath he released into his son's mouth.

"Papa, I'm sorry." Gideon leaned close to Abe. "I was only away from Willis a short time." He sniffed a couple of times. "He was playin' in shallow water, so I don't know what happened. I—I waded in and pulled him right out, but—"

"Stand back and give me some room!" Abe didn't look up to see Gideon's reaction. He just kept pushing on Willis's chest and sharing his breath with the boy. He was tempted to put Willis into the pony cart and take him up to the house to wait for the ambulance, but with him not responding to CPR, he figured the best thing he could do was keep trying to breathe life back into his son.

After what seemed like hours, Abe heard sirens in the distance. When the ambulance arrived, Abe's hopes were renewed. The paramedics had more training than he did, and their vehicle was full of lifesaving equipment. He hoped they could accomplish what he hadn't been able to do.

Abe moved aside as the paramedics took over.

"How long was his head under the water?" one of the men asked.

"I don't know." Abe looked at Gideon, but the boy shrugged.

As the paramedics worked on Willis, Abe continued to pray. Finally, one of the men stepped up to Abe and said, "I'm sorry, Mr. Wengerd, but your son is dead."

Chapter 42

As Abe stood near his six-year-old son's coffin, a feeling of despair settled over him like a heavy fog. It seemed like only yesterday that he'd been right here, watching his wife's casket being lowered into the grave.

Abe's nose and eyes burned with unshed tears, and he shifted uncomfortably as his crutches dug into his armpits. *Dear God, why did You allow this to happen? Wasn't it enough that You took my wife? Did You have to take one of my precious kinner too?*

Abe glanced at Gideon, who stood to his left. The boy's head was down and his shoulders shook, but he made no sound. Abe knew Gideon felt responsible for Willis's death, and well he should. The boy was supposed to watch both of his brothers, not run off in the woods to look for Josh, leaving Willis alone.

I should have seen that my kinner learned how to swim. Martin warned me that something could happen if they didn't. Since Martin wasn't here to teach us how, I should have asked someone else. Abe clenched his fingers around the crutches until they ached. *It's my fault as much as Gideon's that Willis is dead. I may as well have drowned the boy myself.*

Josh, Esta, and Owen clustered around Abe, while Ruth stood to his right, holding Molly in her arms. The little girl would grow up never knowing she'd had a brother named Willis or that she'd had a mother. Truth be told, Molly was fast becoming attached to Ruth. She'd even begun calling Ruth Mammi.

Abe noticed the sorrowful look on Ruth's face, and his heart clenched. She was no doubt reliving the pain of losing her husband. She'd grown attached to Abe's children, and he was sure that at least part of her grief was over losing Willis.

He pulled his gaze back to the coffin as the bishop read a hymn. A group of Amish men sang as the pallbearers filled in Willis's grave. With each shovelful of dirt, a stab of pain pierced Abe's soul. It wasn't fair. It wasn't right. Death was a fact of life, and he knew it must be dealt with, but he felt as if God had let him down.

All during the funeral dinner, Ruth kept a close watch on Abe's children—all except Gideon, who had gone to his room, saying he wasn't hungry and wanted to be alone.

Ruth's heart went out to the boy, as well as to Abe. She could feel the pain of his loss, as she'd come to care for young Willis, and now she felt as if she'd lost another loved one.

"Would you like me to take Molly for a while?" Ruth's mother asked as she stepped into the living room where Ruth sat rocking the child.

Ruth shook her head. "If I put her down, she'll cry. I don't want to move her until she's asleep and I'm able to put her to bed."

Mom shrugged and took a seat on the sofa. "You look exhausted. You really should rest."

"Mom's right," Grace said as she entered the room carrying Daniel. "You've been working hard ever since you came here to help Abe and his family. And since Willis's death, you've hardly slept a wink."

"The kinner need me." The chair squeaked as Ruth continued to rock Molly. How sweet she smelled. How soft and warm she felt. This dear little girl was so innocent and unaware of life's trials.

"You'll be no good to anyone if you wear yourself out," Grace argued.

Ruth patted Molly's back. "I'm resting now."

Mom and Grace exchanged glances, but neither said a word. Grace took a seat on the sofa beside Mom and handed her the baby.

"Danki," said Mom. "I was itching to hold that boppli." She nuzzled Daniel's chest with her nose. "You're sure growing; you know that, little one?"

"Do you think Abe's going to be all right?" Grace asked, turning to face Ruth. "I saw him talking with Dad during the meal, and he'd hardly eaten a thing."

Ruth sighed. "Abe's been through a lot. First losing Alma, having his sister move back home, breaking his leg, and then Willis dying. I feel sometimes like I've been put through a series of dreadful tests, but it seems I'm not alone in that regard."

Mom nodded. "You're right. Troubles come to all, but that's when we need to grab hold of God's hand and hang on tight. It's the only way we can get through the trials life brings our way." She smiled as she released a sigh. "One thing I've learned over the years is that trials can lead us to greater blessings and help us look forward to heaven."

"If Alma were still alive, she would be able to help Abe through this difficult time. It has to be so hard for him to raise his kinner alone and then be faced with something as horrible as losing one of them," Grace put in.

Ruth thought about her impromptu suggestion that Abe marry her, and she cringed. *What must he think of me for being so brazen? Should I say something—apologize for making such a bold implication?* She drew in a deep breath. Now wasn't the time. It would be better to wait until Abe wasn't grieving so much. For now, the best thing she could do was take good care of his children.

"That was one of the saddest funerals I've ever been to," Martha commented from her seat at the back of her father's buggy. "Sure don't know how Gideon's going to deal with the loss of his brother."

"Gideon?" Dad said sharply. "What about Abe? Didn't you see how much he was hurting? He barely said two words today, and I couldn't get him to eat a thing."

"Abe and his family will miss little Willis, but Ruth will be there for the kinner. And you'll be there for Abe, same as you were when Alma died." Mom reached across the seat and patted Dad's arm.

He nodded. "I'll do my best, but I can't help him if he won't talk to me."

"Give him time. He's still in shock over losing Willis."

"It was good to see so many of our English neighbors at the funeral, wasn't it?" Martha asked.

"Jah, and your aunt Rosemary too," Dad said.

Martha smiled. She was glad Dad and his sister had patched things up.

"I had thought the Larsons might be there today," Mom said. "But I guess Donna had a headache, and Ray had some kind of appointment in town."

Dad shrugged. "Not all from our Amish community were there either. That's just the way of it sometimes."

Martha thought about Luke, since he'd been one who hadn't attended the funeral. For that matter, he hadn't been at Martin's funeral or Alma's either. Was it possible that he had an aversion to funerals? Or did he think it was best to stay away since he was still going through rumschpringe and hadn't joined the church? Luke had told Martha once that his parents and the church leaders were after him to settle down and make a decision about getting baptized and joining the Amish church. Martha didn't understand why he kept putting it off. She'd joined the church soon after her sixteenth birthday and had no regrets. She couldn't help but wonder if Luke planned to leave the Amish faith. But if that were true, why hadn't he already? What was he waiting for?

"Ach! Someone's horses are out," Mom shouted as they rounded the bend near their home and found several horses trotting down the road.

"Those animals are mine!" Dad halted the horse and handed the reins to Mom.

"What are you going to do?" she asked in a shaky voice.

"I'm getting out so I can round up the horses."

"Without a rope?"

"There's one here in the back," Martha said. "Want me to help you, Dad?"

"Jah, that'd be good," he said as he climbed down from the driver's seat.

Martha grabbed the rope and stepped out too, while Mom headed their buggy up the driveway.

The next several minutes were chaotic as Martha and her father raced up and down the road, chasing the horses. Dad finally caught one and started up the driveway. "Maybe the others will follow," he called to Martha.

She waved her hands and blocked one of the mares from going the opposite way. She finally got the animal to follow the gelding Dad was leading. After that, the other four horses trotted in behind, and Martha took up the rear in case one of them tried to head back toward the road.

By the time they got to the barn, Martha was out of breath. When she heard Mom holler, her knees almost buckled.

"What's wrong, Judith?" Dad called.

Mom stood trembling on the grass. She pointed across the yard where more than a dozen chickens lay dead. "Someone's been here while we were gone, Roman. Look what they've done!"

"Go inside and wait there," Dad called to Mom. He looked over at Martha with a panicked expression. "We've got to get the horses put away first thing."

Martha glanced back at her mother. The poor woman was screaming and waving her hands. "Wh—what about Mom? Can't you see how upset she is over the chickens?"

"She'll be all right. Your mother's a strong woman." Dad cupped one hand around his mouth while hanging on to the rope with the other hand. "Judith, go into the house and wait for us there!"

Martha wasn't so sure about her mother's strength. Each attack they'd suffered seemed to make Mom more jittery than the one before.

"Martha, schnell!" Dad shouted. "We need to get the horses into the corral!"

Martha sent up a prayer on her mother's behalf and herded two horses through the corral gate while Dad got the other four.

When they were safely inside and the gate had been locked, Dad released a deep moan. "The horses didn't open that gate themselves. Someone did it on purpose."

Chapter 43

In the weeks that followed, Ruth tried to reach out to Abe, but he didn't respond. He seemed to have pulled into a shell, and the friendship they'd previously established seemed all but gone. Was it because Abe was grieving the loss of his son, or had Ruth's bold suggestion of marriage caused the distance he'd put between them? She still hadn't felt led to ask.

Then there was the situation at home. Mom had been a ball of nerves ever since they'd returned home from Willis's funeral and found their horses running free and dead chickens lying on the lawn. This time Dad had phoned Sheriff Osborn, but when one of the sheriff's deputies came out to look things over, Dad was told that there was no evidence linking anyone to the attack and that nothing could be done. Dad kept saying that they needed to keep trusting the Lord and that in time God would punish the offender.

I know it's wrong to seek revenge, but I hope whoever's responsible for killing Martin and doing such terrible things to my family is caught and brought to justice, Ruth thought as she stood at the gas stove, stirring a pot of soup for Abe's lunch.

She moved from the stove over to the window. Abe's older children had gone to school this morning, and Molly and Owen were playing in the living room, so the yard was empty and quiet. Abe, though still hobbling on crutches, had gone back to work in the harness shop. Ruth had tried to talk him out of it, knowing he couldn't do much with his leg still in a cast and him barely able to function because of his grief. But Abe said there was too much work for Ivan to do alone and that he needed to support his family.

Ruth knew from a few things she'd overheard Abe say to her father that Abe was not only missing Willis but also battling a sense of bitterness toward Gideon for not watching his brother. To Ruth, Abe had said none of those things. He seemed to be avoiding her. Whenever they were in the same room, he only spoke if she asked him a question.

Ruth sighed and glanced at the clock on the far wall. *If only I could turn the hands on that clock back to a more joyful time—when my family wasn't under attack; when Alma, Martin, and Willis were still alive; when the future looked bright and hopeful. Would I do things differently if I were given a second chance?*

Tears welled in her eyes, blurring her vision. *If only people would learn to make the most of each precious moment. No one knows when a tragedy might occur or a loved one will be snatched away.*

A loud crash, followed by a child's wail, jolted Ruth's thoughts back to the present. She dashed into the living room and discovered that the potted plant that had been sitting on a table near the window had fallen to the floor. Broken pieces of the clay pot, dirt, and chunks of green foliage lay on the floor. Molly sat in the middle of it all, sobbing her heart out. Owen stood off to one side, pointing at the plant and shaking his head.

Knowing the first order of business was to get the children out of the room so she could clean up the mess, Ruth bent over to pick up Molly. Just as she reached for the child, a painful spasm gripped her back. Her knees buckled, and she dropped to the floor.

"Ach! Owen, run out to the harness shop and get Ivan," she panted. "I don't think I can get up."

Rosemary stepped into Roman's shop and spotted him sitting at his desk with his lunch pail before him. "Looks like I got here at the right time," she said with a smile. "At least I'm not disturbing your work today."

"Nope, you're sure not. Cleon went home to have lunch with Grace, and I'm eating in peace and quiet," Roman said around a mouthful of sandwich. He nodded to the wooden stool near his desk. "I've still got plenty in my lunch box if you'd like to join me."

"Thanks for the offer, but I've already had lunch. I will sit a few minutes though." Rosemary scooted the wooden stool over to his desk and took a seat.

"Is there something on your mind," he asked, "or is this just a friendly visit?"

"A little of both."

He tipped his head and gave her a questioning look.

She moistened her lips with the tip of her tongue. "Actually, I came to say goodbye."

His eyebrows shot up. "You're going back to Idaho?"

She nodded. "Ken's found a buyer for my house, so I need to go home and finalize the sale. Then I'll have boxes to pack for my return trip here."

He looked relieved. "You'll be moving here permanently, then?"

"Yes. The little house I've been renting from the Larsons has an option to buy, and I think it will fit my needs. Once I've filled the place with my own things, it will seem more like a real home to me."

"What about your son? Is he in agreement with you moving here?"

"I have Ken's stamp of approval." Rosemary smiled. "In fact, he and his wife plan to use some of their vacation time to help me move. It will give them a chance to meet all of you."

"That would be nice. I'd like to get to know my nephew and his wife."

Roman took a drink from his thermos. "How long do you think it will be before you get moved?"

She shrugged. "I'm not sure. A couple of months, maybe."

"That's not so long."

She reached across the desk and touched his arm. "I'm sorry for all the pain I put my family through when I was gone all those years."

He shook his head. "Apologies have already been said. No need to say 'em again. What counts is the now, not the past."

"You're right, and I plan to make the most of whatever time I have left on this earth."

"Me too."

Rosemary stepped down from the stool and gave him a hug. She was pleased when he patted her back and said, "I love you, sister."

"I love you too." She blinked back tears. "Guess I'll say goodbye to Judith and the rest of the family now."

"That'd be good. I'm sure Judith will be glad to hear that you're planning to move to Holmes County permanently. She's been terribly upset since that last attack. Maybe this will give her something to smile about."

"Still no clue as to who let the horses out and killed your chickens?"

"No, and I'm beginning to think we'll never know who was behind any of the attacks."

"Would you like me to speak with the sheriff and see if he has any leads or suggestions as to what you might do to prevent further attacks?"

He grunted. "I think he's pretty much given up on finding the one responsible."

Rosemary's heart went out to her brother. She could see the look of despair on his face and wished there was something she could do to make things better. "I'll be praying," she said. "Praying that God will uphold you through this difficult time and that the culprit will be found and brought to justice."

As Abe sat at one of his workbenches, cutting strips of leather, his thoughts went to Ruth and how she had looked holding Molly this morning after breakfast. There was a look of love on Ruth's face whenever she did anything with his children. He knew without reservation that she would make a good mother. He thought about the day she'd been sitting on the sofa near his feet and had asked if he would like to marry her. Even now, he could see the desire in her eyes, but he knew it wasn't a desire to be his wife; it was a longing to be his children's mother.

He gripped the piece of leather tightly. *Ruth's a good woman, and I've allowed myself to feel something for her that I have no right to feel.*

"You're lookin' kind of thoughtful there," Ivan said, stepping up to the workbench. "Is there something you'd like to talk about?"

Abe shook his head. "No point talking about what can't be changed."

"Are you thinking of Willis?"

"Jah, that and a few other things."

Ivan opened his mouth as if to respond, but the shop door flew open just then, and Owen dashed into the room. "*Daadi, kumme*—schnell!"

Abe's heartbeat picked up speed. "Where do you want me to go quickly, son?"

Owen pointed to the door. "Ruth! *Sie is yuscht umgfalle.*"

"Ruth fell over?"

Owen nodded, and his dark eyes widened with obvious fear. "Kumme, kumme."

Abe grabbed his crutches and hobbled across the room behind Owen.

"I'd better come with you," Ivan said from behind.

Cleon hurried into the barn with the intent of getting some boxes in which to load several jars of honey he planned to deliver to some stores in Walnut Creek. He'd only taken a few steps when he heard Anna's voice.

"It's not my fault baby Daniel got borned." *Sniff.* "It's not fair that Papa don't love me no more." *Sniff. Sniff.* "If I got a new doll, I'd still love you, little faceless friend. I'd love you both, not one more than the other."

Cleon leaned against the wall, too stunned to move. Did Anna really think he didn't love her anymore? Maybe he had shown Daniel a lot of attention since he'd been born, but he was just a baby, and babies needed attention. Even so, he knew he'd been remiss in spending time with Anna, and maybe he'd been a bit short-tempered with her too. And if he were completely honest about it, he'd have to admit he'd chosen to discount Grace's warnings about Anna's feelings.

Deciding that the boxes could wait awhile, Cleon hurried toward the empty horse stall where he'd heard Anna's voice. "Anna, what are you doing?" he called.

She darted out of the stall, eyes wide and body trembling. "I didn't do nothin' wrong, Papa. I was just—"

"Anna, we need to—"

The child pushed past Cleon and dashed across the room to the ladder leading to the hayloft. She was halfway up before Cleon reached the bottom of the ladder.

"Anna, don't go any farther," he called.

She halted, turned to look at him, then whirled back around. Her foot had just touched the next rung when—*snap!*—the rung broke. Anna screamed as she fell backward.

Cleon leaped forward and caught the child in his arms. "It's okay, Anna," he said, hugging her tightly. "Papa's got you now."

Anna's tears wet the front of his shirt as she buried her face against his chest and sobbed. "I could've fallen. You saved me, Papa."

He stroked her back. "I love you, Anna."

She pulled back and looked up at him with tears clinging to her lashes. "Really, Papa?"

"Jah. You're my special little girl."

"As special as Daniel?"

He nodded. "Just as special."

"But you talk about the boppli all the time and won't let me hold him."

"I'm sorry about that, Anna," he said, his throat thick with emotion. "I've been a bit overprotective of Daniel, and I haven't been fair to you. Will you forgive me, daughter?"

She nodded and hugged him around the neck.

"Why don't you get your doll now and go into the house? I've got some boxes to get, and then I'll join you and your mamm for lunch."

"Okay."

He set Anna on the floor, and she scurried into the empty horse stall. She returned a few seconds later with her faceless doll. "See you in the house, Papa," she said as she skipped out the door.

As soon as Anna disappeared, Cleon made a beeline for the broken ladder. "This makes no sense," he mumbled. "I've had that ladder only a few months, and it shouldn't have broken like that."

A chill shot through him. What if someone had come into the barn and cut the rung on purpose? Could this have been another attack?

He grabbed the ladder and laid it on its side near the back of the barn. He would replace the rung as soon as he could, and he would keep the barn door locked from now on!

Chapter 44

"Are you comfortable enough? Is there anything else I can do for you?" Mom's wrinkled forehead and the concern in her voice let Ruth know how worried she was about her.

"I'll be fine," Ruth said as she tried to find a comfortable position on her bed. Even after several visits to the chiropractor, she was still experiencing back spasms. The doctor said she needed rest and couldn't return to work until her back was better. Much to Ruth's chagrin, Abe's neighbor, Marlene Yoder, was helping in her absence. Marlene was an older woman whose children were grown and married, so she had the time. Ruth's only concern was whether Marlene could keep up with Abe's active children, especially the two youngest ones.

I miss Abe's kinner so much. Ruth grimaced. *I find myself missing Abe too.*

"You are in pain. I can see by the look on your face that you're hurting." Mom moved closer to the bed and stared down at Ruth.

"As long as I don't move, I don't hurt." Ruth compressed her lips. "What hurts the most is not being able to care for Abe's kinner."

"You'll return to your job once your back has healed."

Ruth groaned. "I still can't believe the way it went into a spasm just because I bent over wrong."

"Dr. Bradley said it's a fairly common occurrence—especially when someone's had to deal with the kind of stress you've had." Mom's hand shook as she reached up to swipe at a wisp of hair that had worked its way loose from her bun. "I understand that, because all the attacks that have occurred around here have made me feel jittery as a June bug. They've affected my ability to sleep well too."

"I know, and now here you are taking care of me." Ruth hated to be laid up like this. Seeing how tired her mother looked today made her feel guilty for being such a bother.

"I don't mind." Mom patted Ruth's hand. "Martha's been helping when she isn't working for Irene or spending time caring for her dogs. Heidi's going to have another batch of pups now, you know."

"Jah, Martha told me."

"I still wish she'd give up the notion of raising hundlin."

"It's what she enjoys, and we can't fault her for that." Ruth sighed. "I enjoy my job working for Abe, which makes it all the harder to be stuck here in bed."

"You really miss his kinner, don't you?"

"Jah." Ruth almost said that she missed Abe too, but she caught herself in time. No point giving Mom any hope that she and Abe might marry. He'd made it clear enough the day she'd mentioned marriage that he had no interest in her.

"Well," Mom said as she moved away from the bed, "I'm going downstairs to start lunch. I'll bring up a tray for you when it's ready."

"Danki. In the meantime, would you give me my *Biwel*? I'd like to read a few chapters."

Mom picked up the Bible from the table by Ruth's bed and handed it to her. "I'll be back soon."

"Okay." Ruth turned to the book of Ruth and read the account of how the biblical Ruth had made herself known to Boaz. "It may have worked for Ruth from the Bible, but it sure didn't work for me," she mumbled when she'd finished reading it. "Whatever possessed me to do something so bold? Is the strained relationship I now have with Abe just one more test I'm being faced with?"

Knowing that Job went through numerous tests, Ruth flipped to the book of Job. " 'But he knoweth the way that I take: when he hath tried me, I shall come forth as gold,' " she read from the twenty-third chapter.

She closed her eyes. *Are the tests Abe and I have been faced with refining us, Lord? Will we someday come forth as gold?*

Her eyes popped open. *As soon as my back is better, I'm going to share that verse with Abe.*

———◦◦◦———

Abe entered the kitchen to join his two youngest children for lunch and was shocked to discover a mess. Several boxes of cereal were strewn on the floor, along with some smaller boxes of candy-coated gum. Molly and Owen sat in the middle of it, wearing blue smiles on their faces.

"Bloh," Molly said, holding up both hands, which were also colored blue.

"Jah, blue hands, blue teeth, and blue lips." Abe bit back a chuckle. It was comical to see how the children looked, but he had to wonder how they'd managed to make such a mess.

"Where's Marlene?" he asked Owen.

The boy pointed to the door leading to the living room. *"Schlofkopp."*

"Sleepyhead?" Abe repeated in English.

Owen nodded.

Abe stepped into the living room and discovered Marlene stretched out on the sofa, fast asleep.

He cleared his throat.

No response.

He moved closer to the sofa and bent close to her ear. "Marlene, wake up!"

"Was is letz do?" The poor woman jumped up as though she'd been stung by a bee.

"What's wrong here is that my two youngest kinner have been in the kitchen making a mess while you've been asleep." Abe frowned. "And I'm hungry as a mule and there's no lunch ready."

Marlene clambered off the sofa. "Ach! I had no idea it was lunchtime already. I came in here to rest my eyes a minute. Guess I must have dozed off."

"Aren't you getting enough sleep?"

"I sleep well at night, but I'm not used to running after little ones all day. To tell you the truth, I'm feeling plumb tuckered out." She sighed and pushed an errant strand of grayish-brown hair away from her face. "How soon do you think it'll be before Ruth comes back to work?"

Abe grimaced. He wasn't sure he wanted Ruth to continue working for him. He'd come to realize that not only did his offspring miss having Ruth around, but he did as well. It wasn't just the good job Ruth had done with the house and children that Abe missed either. It was her smiling face, caring attitude, and gentle ways. Even so, he wondered if it might be better if Ruth didn't come back once her back was healed. He had feelings for her, which she obviously didn't return. He figured having her around so much would only complicate things. On the other hand, if she didn't come back—

"Abe, did you hear what I asked about Ruth?"

Abe blinked. "Jah. Just don't have an answer for that right now."

Marlene shrugged and turned toward the kitchen. "I'd better tend to Molly and Owen. Then I'll get something put together for your lunch."

"Just worry about lunch," Abe said, following her into the other room. "I'll clean up the kinner."

"I'm not sure who I'm most worried about—Mom or Ruth," Grace said as she placed a sandwich on a plate and set it in front of Cleon. Since Anna was in school and the baby was asleep, Grace hoped she and Cleon would have a chance to visit without interruption.

He looked up at Grace, and his eyebrows drew together. "It won't do any good to worry. I'm sure they'll both be fine."

Grace pulled out a chair and sat down. "I'm not so certain about that."

"What do you mean?"

"First off, Ruth's back seems slow in healing, and she's getting depressed lying around all day."

"The doctor took X-rays and determined it was nothing more than a pulled muscle, right?"

She nodded.

"Then in time, she'll heal."

"I suppose, but Ruth's been through enough already. I hate to see her go through more." Grace grunted. "Now Mom's busy caring for Ruth when she can barely take care of herself." She grimaced. "Even though there haven't been any more attacks since the horse and chicken incident, Mom's been so naerfich. It's hard not to worry or blame myself because—"

"Here you go again, feeling guilty because you think Gary Walker's the one behind the attacks and you're convinced he's trying to get even with you for something that happened over six years ago." Cleon shook his head. "It could be anyone, Grace. No one but the attacker is to blame." He touched her hand. "Let's pray," he suggested, "and then we can talk while we eat if you have more to say on the subject."

She nodded. "Okay."

They bowed their heads, and Grace thanked God that things were better between Cleon and Anna. Then she petitioned the Lord to calm her mother's fears, heal Ruth's back, and protect her family from further attacks.

Chapter 45

"Ruth, where are you going?" Mom asked as Ruth plucked her black outer bonnet off the wall peg and slipped it over her white kapp. "Since Martha's gone to town to do some shopping, I thought the two of us could get a little sewing done on this rainy Saturday morning."

"Some other time, Mom. Right now, I'm going over to Abe's," Ruth replied.

Mom's eyebrows shot up. "To work?"

"Not today, but I'm hoping I'll be able to start on Monday morning."

Mom scurried across the room. "Oh Ruth, it's only been a few weeks since you hurt your back. Do you think you're ready to return to work so soon?"

Ruth opened her mouth to reply, but Mom rushed on. "Fixing meals for Abe's family is one thing, but doing housework is quite another. If you bend over wrong or pick up something too heavy, you could reinjure your back."

"I'll be careful, Mom. If there's something heavy that needs to be picked up, I'll leave it until Abe or Ivan can take care of it."

"Speaking of Ivan," Mom said, "I was talking to Irene the other day, and she mentioned that Ivan's been seeing Amanda Miller as of late."

"Is that so?"

Mom nodded. "Irene said she'd been hoping you and Ivan might hit it off and then she'd have two of my girls for daughters-in-law."

Ruth shook her head. "I would never consider marrying Ivan, even if he was interested in me in a romantic sort of way."

"You don't care for Ivan?"

"He's a nice man, but I'm not attracted to him. Besides, I couldn't allow myself to become romantically involved with any young man."

"Why not? Is it because you're still pining for Martin?"

"I do miss him, and I guess I always will, but if I were to find love again, it couldn't be with a younger man."

Mom raised her eyebrows. "I'm verhuddelt."

"It's not confusing, Mom. As I'm sure you must know, most young men want to raise a family when they get married. I can't have any children, so I wouldn't make a good wife for a young man."

Mom released a sigh. "Oh Ruth, I wish you wouldn't say things like that."

"Why not? It's true."

"If a man really loves a woman, it shouldn't matter whether or not she can give him kinner."

Ruth slipped into her sweater. "It doesn't make any difference, because I have no interest in marrying Ivan." *It's Abe I want to marry,* she added mentally. *But he doesn't want me.*

Mom pulled Ruth into her arms and gave her a hug. "Tell Abe I said hello and that we'll have him and the kinner over for supper sometime soon."

"I will. See you later, Mom."

Martha had just left the market in Berlin and was about to load her purchases into the back of her buggy when someone touched her shoulder.

She whirled around and was surprised to see Luke behind her. "Ach, you scared me!"

"Sorry." He brushed back his hair from his forehead and offered her an impish grin.

"W—were you shopping in the store?" Martha stammered. She didn't know why she always felt so flustered whenever Luke was around.

"I was, but we must have missed seeing each other." Luke reached into Martha's shopping cart and lifted the bag of dog food as if it were a feather. "Better let me help you with that."

"Danki. It was kind of heavy when I pulled it off the grocery shelf."

Luke placed the dog food into the back of her wagon, and she put the paper sacks inside.

"Have you had lunch?" he asked after she'd secured the buggy flap.

"Not yet."

"How'd you like to share a pizza with me at Outback Pizzeria?"

Martha contemplated Luke's offer. She was a little worried that someone might see her with him and tell her father, but her desire to spend time with Luke finally won out. "Jah, I would enjoy some pizza."

"Should we take separate buggies, or would you like to ride with me and then pick up your buggy after we're done?"

"Guess I'd better take my own buggy since it's got stuff in it that I don't want stolen." Truth be told, Martha was more concerned about someone seeing her riding in Luke's buggy than she was about someone stealing her purchases. If anyone she knew spotted her having lunch with Luke, they might think the two of them had arrived at the pizzeria at the same time and decided to share a table. But if she and Luke were seen riding in the same buggy, folks could get the impression that they were a courting couple.

"Okay. I'll see you at the pizzeria in a few minutes." Luke offered Martha another heart-melting smile and sprinted across the parking lot to his rig.

With a feeling of anticipation, Martha unhitched her horse and climbed into her own buggy.

When she arrived at the pizzeria, Luke was already there, sitting at a table near the back of the room. He waved, and she hurried over to join him.

"I ordered a plain cheese pizza and a couple of root beers," he said. "I didn't know what kind of meat you liked, so figured I couldn't go wrong with cheese."

She smiled as she took a seat opposite him. "Cheese is fine with me."

"So how are things going at your place?" he asked, leaning his elbows on the table and resting his chin in the palm of his hand.

"Okay. Ruth's back is doing better now. I think she'll probably return to work for Abe soon."

"I knew she was missing from church on the last Sunday we had preaching, but I didn't know there was anything wrong with her back." Luke frowned. "Is it serious?"

Martha shook her head. "I don't think so. The chiropractor said it was just a pulled muscle. After several treatments and bed rest, she's finally doing better."

"That's good to hear. My daed's back has gone out on him a time or two, and he was always in a lot of pain."

Martha took a sip of root beer. "This is good but not nearly as tasty as the homemade kind my daed makes."

Luke stared at Martha with a peculiar expression, making her squirm. "What's wrong? Have I got root beer foam on my naas?"

He grinned. "Your nose looks just fine."

She smiled in response.

"What else is new at your place? Have there been more attacks?"

"Not for several weeks. Did you hear about that last one?"

He shook his head. "What happened?"

"It was the day of Willis Wengerd's funeral. When we arrived home, we discovered that someone had let our horses out of the corral."

"Maybe the gate wasn't latched, and the horses got out themselves."

"We thought that at first, but there were dead chickens all over our front yard." She grunted. "It was obvious that someone had come onto our property while we were at the funeral."

Luke squinted his dark eyes. "Got any idea who might have done it?"

She shrugged. "Probably the same person who's done all the other horrible things at our place."

"Did you find any clues or evidence?"

"No." Martha sighed. "Bishop King came by the other day to talk to Dad about the problem. They both think that whoever's doing these things is either trying to get even with someone in the family or wants to take our property and is hoping to scare us off."

"Why would anyone want your property?"

"I don't know."

"So what's gonna be done about the situation?"

"As far as I know, nothing. Dad thinks if we just keep trusting the Lord, eventually the attacks will stop." Martha grimaced. "I have to wonder if God doesn't expect us to do something about our problems, not just sit around and wait for Him to do everything for us."

Luke studied her intently. "What do you mean?"

"I've been thinking about this for quite a spell. I've come to the conclusion that if there's another attack, it'll be time for me to take action."

"Take action?"

She nodded. "I plan to start investigating things and see if I can figure out who's behind the attacks."

Luke's eyebrows shot up. "You're kidding, right?"

"No, I'm not."

"That's not a good idea, Martha. It's not a good idea at all."

"Why not?"

Luke leveled her with a piercing look that went straight to her heart. "Playing detective could be dangerous. You shouldn't even be considering such a thing."

"Oh, but I—"

"Not only could it be dangerous, but if your daed found out what you were up to, I'm sure you'd be in trouble with him. He's not the easiest man to deal with, you know." Luke grunted. "When that man sets his mind one way, there's no convincing him otherwise. I know that better than anyone."

She took another sip of root beer. "I'll worry about my daed's reactions to me playing detective when the time comes."

———————◆•◆———————

Abe headed to the barn to get some cardboard boxes he'd stored in an empty horse stall and spotted Willis's little red wagon. He remembered how Josh had broken it the day before Willis drowned. Abe had promised Willis that he would fix the wagon as soon as his leg healed and he found the time. There was no point fixing it now. Willis was gone, and it was Gideon's fault.

Abe grunted as he bent over and grabbed the boxes. For the past several weeks, he'd only been going through the motions of living. His leg had finally healed and he could get around on it fairly well, but the pain that pricked his heart daily was worse than any physical hurt he'd ever endured. Not only did he miss Willis, but he missed Ruth. A few days ago, he'd talked to Roman and heard that Ruth's back was doing better. But she hadn't returned to work, and he wondered if she might be staying away on purpose. Since Abe had turned down Ruth's suggestion that they marry, he wondered if she'd decided that he and his brood didn't need her anymore.

I was stupid for saying no, he berated himself. *I love her, and even if she doesn't love me, at least I could have given her my name and the opportunity to be a mudder to my kinner.*

Abe started out of the stall but halted when he heard whimpering. He tipped his head and listened. It sounded as though someone was crying, and it seemed to be coming from the other side of the barn.

He placed the boxes on the floor and started in that direction. As he neared a stack of baled hay, he saw Gideon sitting on the floor, head bent and shoulders shaking.

Abe rushed forward. "Son, what's wrong? Have you been hurt?"

Gideon looked up, his eyes swimming with tears. "It's not me who's been hurt, Papa. It's you. I hurt you real bad when I let Willis die. I–I'm awful sorry. I miss my bruder too." He hiccupped on a sob. "I don't deserve to be called your son anymore. I—*hic*—should've been the one to die, not Willis."

Abe let Gideon's words sink into his brain. Losing Alma had hurt tremendously, but he'd come to grips with her death because it was an accident. But Willis's death could have been prevented if Gideon had been watching the boy as he'd been told to do. For the last several weeks, Abe had been carrying around unresolved anger and resentment toward Gideon, toward himself, and toward God for allowing Willis's death to happen. But at what cost? Was it fair to allow Gideon, who was still just a boy, to go on blaming himself for his brother's death?

Abe thought about Willis's wagon again and how the child had forgiven Josh for breaking it. "It's okay," Willis had said to his brother. "If

Jesus could forgive those who put Him on the cross, I oughta be able to forgive my own bruder."

Abe reflected on Matthew 6:14: *"For if ye forgive men their trespasses, your heavenly Father will also forgive you."* Gideon was Abe's son, not some man who had trespassed against him. How could he have shut the boy out and made him feel responsible for his brother's death?

Abe swallowed and nearly choked on the sob that tore from his throat. He had lost one son; he couldn't risk losing another. Falling to his knees beside Gideon, he pulled the boy into his arms. "I forgive you, son, but I need you to forgive me as well. I shouldn't have blamed you for Willis's death. It was an accident and might have happened even if you had been right there with him. Will you accept my apology?"

"Jah," Gideon said through his tears. "And I promise to be the best boy I can be—and never let you down again."

"I don't expect you to be perfect." Abe wiped the tears from Gideon's face. "Only God is perfect. We just need to do the best we can. I know when you ran into the woods after Josh that you didn't expect Willis to fall in the pond while you were gone."

"No, I surely didn't." Gideon sniffed deeply. "If there was any way I could bring him back, I would."

"I know." Abe rocked Gideon back and forth in his arms the way he had when the boy was a baby. "Dear God," he prayed aloud, "forgive me for the sin of unforgiveness."

———◆◆◆———

When Ruth stepped into the barn and heard Abe's voice, she halted. She had stopped at the harness shop to see him, but Ivan had told her that Abe had come to the barn to get some boxes. She'd never expected to see him kneeling on the floor, holding Gideon in his arms and praying out loud. Abe was asking God to forgive his sin of unforgiveness.

I've never really done that, Ruth thought regretfully. *Ever since Martin died, I've been struggling to forgive the one who rammed our buggy off the road. Despite my busyness and determination to do something useful with my life, my broken heart has never completely healed.*

Ruth trembled as a sense of shame welled in her soul. She knew it was a sin to harbor anger and resentment toward the person who had caused Martin's death, even though she wasn't sure who that person was and couldn't forgive him to his face.

She leaned against one of the wooden beams and closed her eyes. "Dear Lord, forgive my sin of unforgiveness and heal the hurt in my heart."

"Ruth, is that you?"

Ruth's eyes snapped open as the heat of embarrassment flooded her cheeks. She moved over to the bales of hay where Abe knelt beside his son. "Jah, it's me. I—I came over to let you know my back's doing better and that I can start working for you again on Monday." She shifted from one foot to the other, feeling suddenly shy and unsure of herself. "That is—if you still want me to come back."

Abe stood, pulling Gideon to his feet. "Son, why don't you run into the house and see if Marlene has lunch ready? I'm going to stay out here and talk to Ruth awhile."

Gideon looked at Ruth, then back at his father. "Jah, okay." He gave Abe a hug and darted out of the barn wearing a smile on his tear-stained face.

"Things are better between me and my boy," Abe said.

"I'm pleased to hear it."

He motioned to a bale of hay. "Would you like to sit down?"

She nodded and started to take a seat but tripped on her shoelace and fell into Abe's lap.

He looked stunned.

"Ach, I'm so sorry." She scooted away and lowered herself to the bale of hay, feeling another blush warm her cheeks.

"No harm done," he mumbled.

"I. . .uh. . .heard part of your conversation—the one you were having with God."

"Did you now?" Abe asked, taking a seat beside her. He wore a silly grin on his face, and she couldn't figure out why.

"The words you said made me realize that I needed to find forgiveness in my heart toward the one who killed Martin."

"I'm glad." His expression turned serious. "One can't find joy and a sense of purpose if their heart is full of anger and bitterness."

"I know. Now that I've confessed my sin to God, I feel clean inside."

"Same here."

"Abe, there's something else I wanted to share with you."

"What's that?"

"I was reading my Bible the other day, and I came upon Job 23:10. It says, 'But he knoweth the way that I take: when he hath tried me, I shall come forth as gold.'"

Abe sat several seconds, staring at his hands. Finally, he lifted his head and looked at Ruth. "I believe that verse applies to both of us."

"I think so too. That's why I felt the need to share it with you. After reading it, I was filled with a sense of hope that despite the trials and testing I've been through, God will use it for His good." She smiled. "Someday, I hope to come forth as gold."

He nodded. "It's good when we let God's Word speak to us, jah?"

"Jah."

Abe moistened his lips with the tip of his tongue. "Uh. . .Ruth. . .I have something I need to say to you."

"What's that?"

"I don't want you to come back to work for me as my maad."

"You—you don't?"

He shook his head.

"Is it because Marlene's a better maid than me?"

"She's done the best job she can, but she's not a better maid." He fingered the end of his curly red beard. "Nor would she make me a good wife."

"What?" Ruth's forehead wrinkled as she tried to digest what he had said.

The skin around Abe's dark eyes crinkled, and he reached over and took Ruth's hand. "I love you, Ruth. I'm not afraid to say it anymore. If you don't think I'm too old and will have me as your husband when you feel the time is right, I'll do my best to make you happy, even though I know you don't love me in return."

"Oh, but I do! During the time I was home resting my back, I came to the realization that I not only love your kinner, but I love you as well." Ruth gasped and covered her mouth. "I'm being too bold again."

Abe slipped his arm around her waist and drew her close to his side. "I think maybe your boldness is one of the things I've come to love about you."

Ruth's cheeks grew even warmer.

"You know," he said, leaning close to her ear, "Esta asked me once if I would ever marry again, and I told her that if the good Lord desired for me to find another wife, He'd have to drop her right in my lap." He chuckled. "Looks to me like He did just that a few minutes ago. I think maybe now is the time for me to listen."

Ruth stared down at the floor, unable to meet his gaze.

"You haven't said if you're willing to marry me."

She lifted her gaze as tears dribbled onto her cheeks. "Jah, Abe. I'd be honored."

He stood and reached out his hand. "Shall we go inside and tell the kinner our good news?"

"I think we should." Ruth slipped her hand into the crook of Abe's arm as they walked out of the barn. For the first time in many months, she felt a sense of peace, knowing that with God's help, and Abe at her side, she could deal with any test she might be faced with in the days ahead.

Ruth's Chicken Dumplings

INGREDIENTS:

2 cups chopped mixed vegetables (potatoes, carrots, celery, and onions)

1 cup chicken, chopped

Broth: water (enough to cover chicken), salt, and chicken flavoring to taste

Cook vegetables until soft. In 3-quart saucepan, add water, salt, chicken flavoring, and chicken and heat to boiling. Cook until chicken is done. Add vegetables and bring back to boil before putting in the dumpling dough.

DUMPLING DOUGH:

1½ cup flour

⅓ cup butter, softened

1 teaspoon salt

2 teaspoons baking powder

2 teaspoons sugar

Milk

Combine flour, butter, salt, baking powder, and sugar together until mixed. Add enough milk to make a stiff dough. Drop by spoonfuls into boiling chicken mixture. Cover and reduce heat for 20 minutes without lifting cover. Ready to serve.

Grace's Overnight Caramel French Toast

INGREDIENTS:

1 cup brown sugar

½ cup butter

2 tablespoons light corn syrup

12 slices bread

¼ cup sugar

1 teaspoon cinnamon, divided

6 eggs

1½ cups milk

1 teaspoon vanilla

In a saucepan over medium heat, bring brown sugar, butter, and corn syrup to a boil. Pour into greased 9x13-inch baking dish. Top with 6 slices of bread. Combine sugar and ½ teaspoon cinnamon and sprinkle half over bread. Place remaining bread on top and sprinkle with remaining cinnamon/sugar. In large bowl, beat eggs, milk, vanilla, and remaining cinnamon. Pour over bread. Refrigerate overnight. The next morning preheat oven to 350 degrees and bake for 30 to 35 minutes.

Judith's Raisin Molasses Cookies

INGREDIENTS:

2 cups raisins

1 cup shortening

½ cup white sugar

2 eggs

1½ cups molasses

4 cups flour

2 teaspoons ginger

2 teaspoons cinnamon

3 teaspoons baking powder

½ teaspoon baking soda

1 teaspoon salt

Rinse and drain raisins. Cream shortening and sugar together. Add eggs and beat well. Blend in molasses. Sift flour with spices, baking powder, soda, and salt. Blend into creamed mixture. Stir in raisins. Drop by teaspoon onto greased cookie sheet and bake for 15 to 18 minutes at 350 degrees. Makes about 6 dozen cookies.

About the Author

New York Times bestselling, award-winning author Wanda E. Brunstetter is one of the founders of the Amish fiction genre. Wanda's ancestors were part of the Anabaptist faith, and her novels are based on personal research intended to accurately portray the Amish way of life. Her books are well-read and trusted by many Amish, who credit her for giving readers a deeper understanding of the people and their customs. When Wanda visits her Amish friends, she finds herself drawn to their peaceful lifestyle, sincerity, and close family ties.

Wanda enjoys photography, ventriloquism, gardening, bird-watching, beachcombing, and spending time with her family. She and her husband, Richard, have been blessed with two grown children, six grandchildren, and two great-grandchildren.

To learn more about Wanda, visit her website at
www.wandabrunstetter.com.

Other Fiction Works by Wanda E. Brunstetter

Amish Cooking Class
The Seekers (Book 1)
The Blessing (Book 2)
The Celebration (Book 3)
Amish Cooking Class Cookbook
The Amish Cooking Class Trilogy (All 3 books in 1)

Amish Greenhouse Mystery
The Crow's Call (Book 1)
The Mockingbird's Song (Book 2)
The Robin's Greeting (Book 3)
The Amish Greenhouse Mysteries (All 3 books in 1)

Amish Hawaiian Series
The Hawaiian Discovery (Book 1)
The Hawaiian Quilt (Book 2)
Amish Hawaiian Adventures (Books 1 & 2)
The Blended Quilt (Book 3)

Amish Millionaire
The English Son (Book 1)
The Stubborn Father (Book 2)
The Betrayed Fiancée (Book 3)
The Missing Will (Book 4)
The Divided Family (Book 5)
The Selfless Act (Book 6)
Amish Millionaire (All 6 books in 1)

Brides of Lancaster County
A Merry Heart (Book 1)
Looking for a Miracle (Book 2)
Plain and Fancy (Book 3)
The Hope Chest (Book 4)
Brides of Lancaster County Collection (All 4 books in 1)

Brides of Webster County
Going Home (Book 1)
On Her Own (Book 2)
Dear to Me (Book 3)
Allison's Journey (Book 4)
Brides of Webster County Collection (All 4 books in 1)

Creektown Discoveries
The Walnut Creek Wish (Book 1)
The Sugarcreek Surprise (Book 2)
The Apple Creek Announcement (Book 3)

Daughters of Lancaster County
The Storekeeper's Daughter (Book 1)
The Quilter's Daughter (Book 2)
The Bishop's Daughter (Book 3)
The Daughters of Lancaster County (All 3 books in 1)

The Discovery – A Lancaster County Saga
Goodbye to Yesterday (Book 1)
Silence of Winter (Book 2)
The Hope of Spring (Book 3)
The Pieces of Summer (Book 4)
A Revelation in Autumn (Book 5)
A Vow for Always (Book 6)
The Discovery Saga Collection (All 6 books in 1)

The Half-Stitched Amish Quilting Club Series
The Half-Stitched Amish Quilting Club (Book 1)
The Tattered Quilt (Book 2)
The Healing Quilt (Book 3)
The Half-Stitched Amish Quilting Club Trilogy (All 3 books in 1)

The Hochstetler Twins
The Lopsided Christmas Cake (Book 1)
The Farmers' Market Mishap (Book 2)
Twice as Nice Amish Romance Collection (Books 1 & 2)

Friendship Letters
Letters of Trust (Book 1)

Stand-Alone Novels
Lydia's Charm
White Christmas Pie
Woman of Courage

Novellas and Collections
Amish Front Porch Stories
The Beloved Christmas Quilt
The Brides of the Big Valley
The Christmas Prayer
The Christmas Secret
A Heartwarming Romance Collection
Love Finds a Home
Love Finds a Way
A Time to Laugh
Twice Loved
Return to the Big Valley